Winner Takes All

A Blazing Collection

Winner Takes All

A Blazing Collection

JILL SHALVIS

ELLE KENNEDY

TARYN LEIGH TAYLOR

MILLS & BOON

WINNER TAKES ALL: A BLAZING COLLECTION © 2021 by Harlequin Books S.A.

The publisher acknowledges the copyright holders of the individual works as follows:

TIME OUT
© 2012 by Jill Shalvis
Philippine Copyright 2012
Australian Copyright 2012
New Zealand Copyright 2012

First Published 2012
Third Australian Paperback Edition 2021
ISBN 978 1 867 23447 0

BODY CHECK
© 2009 by Leeanne Kennedy
Philippine Copyright 2009
Australian Copyright 2009
New Zealand Copyright 2009

First Published 2009
Fourth Australian Paperback Edition 2021
ISBN 978 1 867 23447 0

PLAYING TO WIN
© 2015 by Taryn Leigh Taylor
Philippine Copyright 2015
Australian Copyright 2015
New Zealand Copyright 2015

First Published 2015
Second Australian Paperback Edition 2021
ISBN 978 1 867 23447 0

MIX
Paper from responsible sources
FSC® C001695
www.fsc.org

Published by
Harlequin Mills & Boon
An imprint of Harlequin Enterprises (Australia) Pty Limited (ABN 47 001 180 918), a subsidiary of HarperCollins Publishers Australia Pty Limited (ABN 36 009 913 517)
Level 13, 201 Elizabeth Street
SYDNEY NSW 2000 AUSTRALIA

Printed and bound in Australia by McPherson's Printing Group

CONTENTS

Time Out

Jill Shalvis

Dear Reader,

Who doesn't love a sports hero? There's just something about a guy who'd lay it all on the line for the win. Mark Diego is a NHL head coach, and a lifelong athlete. He's used to winning, and getting his way. Too bad no one ever told Rainey Saunders that.

Rainey and Mark haven't seen each other in years when my story opens, but their past is indelibly imprinted in their minds.

These two were a challenge for me. Mark wanted things to go his way (and since he's a man, you can guess which way that was…). And Rainey was determined to call the shots. Sparks flew from my keyboard every day during the writing of this book. My fingers are still smoking.

This is my first Harlequin Blaze novel in a while, but it won't be my last. There is still a lot more heat left in the keyboard, so stay tuned. In the meantime, I hope you enjoy *Time Out*. I sure did.

Happy reading,

Jill Shalvis

www.jillshalvis.com

www.jillshalvis.com/blog (be sure to sign up for my newsletter on the right sidebar to keep up to date!)

www.twitter.com/jillshalvis

www.facebook.com/JillShalvis

DEDICATION

Thanks to both Mary and Melinda, two dear friends, without whom this book would have had a lot of mistakes. If there's still mistakes, blame them. :)

1

As always, Rainey's brain was full, too full, but one thought kept rising to the top and wouldn't leave her alone. "Tell me again," she asked Lena. "*Why* do we like men?"

Her best friend and wingman—even though Lena was no longer technically single—laughed. "Oh, honey. We don't have enough time."

They both worked at the beleaguered North District Rec Center in Santa Rey, a small mid-California beach town. Lena handled the front desk. Rainey was the junior sports coordinator, and today she was running their biweekly car wash to raise funds for their desperate sports program. Sitting on a stool in the driveway of the rec building's parking lot, Rainey directed cars in and accepted customers' money, then sent them through to the teenagers who were doing the washing. She kept her laptop out for the slow times. In between cars she'd been working on the upcoming winter sports schedule while simultaneously discussing all things men. Rainey was nothing if not a most excellent multitasker.

And maybe the slightest bit of a control freak.

"I thought you were going to try that online dating service," Lena said.

"I did. I got lots of offers for hookups."

Lena laughed. "Well, what were you looking for?"

Coffee, a few laughs, a connection... A *real* connection, which Rainey was missing lately. Her last two boyfriends had been great but... not great enough. Lena thought she was picky. In truth, Rainey was looking for something that she'd only felt once before, a very long time ago, when she'd been sixteen and stupid. "Men suck."

"Mmm," Lena said. "If they're very good, they do. Listen, you've had a dry spell, is all. Get back in the pool, the water's warm."

"I haven't had a dry spell, I've just been busy." Okay, so she'd had a little bit of a dry spell. She'd been spending a lot of time at work, trying to keep the teens in the North District—the forgotten district—out of trouble. That alone was a full-time job. She turned to the next car. Mrs. Foster had the highest beehive in all the land, and had been Rainey's fourth grade teacher. "Thanks for supporting the rec center's car wash," Rainey said.

"You're welcome." Her beehive, bluer now than ever, still quivered. "I was going to go to South District since they're giving away ten minute back massages with each wash, but I'm glad I didn't. I overheard about your dry spell, dear. Let me get you a date with my grandson, Kyle."

Great. A pity date. "No, that's—"

"He's quite the catch, you know," Mrs. Foster said. "I'll have him call your mother for your number."

"Really, it's not necessary—"

But Mrs. Foster was already driving forward, where

her car was immediately attended to by a group of Rainey's well-behaved teens.

Okay, not all that well-behaved. Rainey had coerced them here on threat of death and dismemberment, but they desperately needed the money if they wanted a baseball and softball season.

"Score on Mrs. Foster's grandson," Lena said dryly. "Think Kyle still has buck teeth?"

"My mom won't give him my number." Probably. Okay, she totally would. Rainey had gone to school with Kyle, so her mother would think him safe enough. Plus, she'd turned thirty last week and now her mom was on a mission to get her married before it was "too late." Hot and sweaty, Rainey swiped her forehead. It might be only June, but it was ninety degrees, and she'd been sitting out here for hours. Her Anaheim Ducks ball cap shaded her face for the most part but she could feel that she'd still managed to sunburn her nose, and her sunglasses kept slipping down her damp face.

They'd fed the teens pizza about an hour ago, and the kids were using the fuel to scrub cars and squirt each other every chance they got. They were down a few bodies since Rainey had kicked four of the guys out, the same four who always gave her trouble. They'd been trying to coerce one of the younger teen girls into the woods with them.

Even long before the fires had devastated Santa Rey the previous summer, the North District had been steadily deteriorating, and that core group of four were hell-bent on deteriorating right along with the area. Working at the rec center was far more than a job for Rainey. She genuinely cared about this community and the kids, but those boys had no interest in her help. She couldn't allow them back, not after today, and given that they'd called her a raging bitch as they'd vacated the premises, the hard feelings were mutual.

"Rick promised to take me out to dinner tonight," Lena said.

Rick was a lifelong friend of Rainey's as well as her boss, and also Lena's boyfriend. "Huh," she said. "He promised me some summer league coaches." Coaches who wouldn't quit when the going got rough, like the volunteer coaches tended to do. "It's three days before the start of the season."

"He's on it," Lena said, just as the man himself walked by, all dark eyes, dark hair, and a dark smile that never failed to get him what he wanted.

He flashed it at Rainey now. "I promised," Rick said. "And I'll deliver."

"Great," Rainey said. "But *when*—"

But nothing. He'd given Lena a quick, soft smile and was already gone, back inside the building to wield his power there.

"I hate it when he does that," Rainey grumbled.

Lena sighed dreamily. "If he hadn't tasked me with a hundred things more than I have time to manage this morning, I'd totally want to have his babies."

"Honey, you're dating him. You've been dating him for a year now. Chances are decent that you *will* be having his babies."

Lena beamed, ridiculously happy. Rainey wasn't jealous. Yes, Rick was hot, but they were friends, and had been since high school. Because of it, they knew far too much about each other. For instance, Rainey knew Rick had lost his virginity behind the high school football stands with their substitute P.E. teacher. In turn,

Rick knew that Rainey had *tried* to lose her virginity with his brother—the last guy she'd felt that elusive connection with—and been soundly rejected. At the humiliating years-old memory, she slumped in her seat. "What if my dry spell is like the Sahara Desert, never-ending?"

"All you have to do is take a man at face value. Don't go into it thinking you can change them. Men aren't fixer-uppers, not like a house or a car. You buy them as is."

"Well I haven't found one yet who's not in need of a little fixing."

Lena laughed. "No kidding, Ms. Control Freak."

"Hey."

"Face it, Rainey, you always have to have a plan with a start, a middle and an end. Definitely an end. You have to know everything before you even get into it. Dating doesn't work that way."

"Well, it should." Rainey gestured the next car through, accepting the money and handing out more change. The teens were moving the cars along at a good pace, and she was proud of them. "Everyone could benefit from a well executed plan."

"A love life doesn't work that way," Lena said. "And trust me, you need a love life."

"You can get a love life in a specialty shop nowadays, complete with a couple of batteries." Rainey took a moment to organize the cash box and quickly checked her work email on the laptop. "Thirty new emails," she groaned. All timely and critical, and she'd have to deal with them before the end of the day. Goody.

"I could help you with some of that," Lena offered.

"I've got it."

"See? Control freak."

Ignoring that painful truth, Rainey deleted a few emails and opened a few others. She loved her job, and was doing what she wanted. She'd gone to business school but she'd come back here to do this, to work with kids in need, and to give back. The work was crazy in the best of times. But these days, in the wake of the tragic California coast fires that had destroyed three out of four of their athletic fields last fall, not to mention both buildings where all their equipment had been housed, were not the best of times. Worse, the lease for the building they were in was up at the end of the year and they couldn't afford renewal.

Problem was, she had a hundred kids, many of them displaced from their own burned-out homes. She wanted to give them something to do after school that didn't involve loitering, shoplifting, drugs or sex. She'd just started to close her laptop when her gaze caught on the Yahoo news page. Hitting the volume key, she stared at a sports clip showing a seedy bar fight between some NHL players from the Anaheim Ducks and Sacramento Mammoths.

The clip had been playing all week, because…well, she hadn't figured out why, other than people seemed to love a sports scandal. The video was little more than a pile of well-known professional athletes wrestling each other to the ground in some L.A. bar, fists flying, dust rising.

Rainey gestured another car through, then turned back to the screen, riveted by the million-dollar limbs and titillating show of testosterone. On the day the footage had been taken, the two teams had been in the Stanley Cup finals. The game had been decided on a controversial call in favor of the Ducks, killing the Mammoths' dreams.

That night at the bar, the Mammoth players had instigated the fight, holding their own against four Ducks until their head coach strode up out of nowhere. At thirty-four, Mark Diego was the youngest, most popular NHL head coach in the country.

And possibly even more gorgeous than his brother Rick.

On the tape, Mark's eyes narrowed in on the fight as he walked fearlessly into the fray, pulling his players out of the pile as though they weighed nothing. A fist flew near his face and he deflected it, leveling the sender of said fist a long, hard look.

The guy fell backwards trying to get away.

"That's the sexiest thing I've ever seen," Lena murmured, watching the clip over Rainey's shoulder.

Yeah. Yeah, it was. Rainey had seen Mark in action before, of course. He and Rick were close. And once upon a time, she'd been just as close, having grown up near the brothers. Back then, Mark had been tough, smart, and fiercely protective of those he cared about. He'd also had a wild streak a mile wide, and she'd seen him brawl plenty. It'd turned her on then, but it absolutely didn't now. She was grown-up, mature.

Or so she told herself in the light of day.

On the screen, hands on hips, Mark said something, something quiet but that nevertheless had the heaving mass of aggression screeching to a halt.

"Oh, yeah. Come to momma," Lena murmured. "Look at him, Rainey. Tall, dark, gorgeous. *Fearless.* I wouldn't mind him exerting his authority on me."

Rainey's belly quivered, and not because she'd inhaled three pieces of pizza with the teens an hour ago. Mark was no longer a wild teenager, but a tightly controlled, complicated man. A stranger. How he "exerted his authority" was none of her business. "Lena, you're dating his brother." Just speaking about Mark had twisted open a wound in a small corner of her heart, a corner she didn't visit very often.

"I've never gotten to see the glory that would be the Diego brothers in stereo." Lena hadn't grown up in Santa Rey. "Mark hasn't come home since I've been with Rick. Being the youngest, baddest, sexiest head coach in all the NHL must be time-consuming."

"Trust me, he's not your type."

"Because he's rich and famous? Because he's tough as hell and cool as ice?"

"Because he's missing a vital organ."

Lena gasped in horror. "He doesn't have a d—"

"A heart! He's missing a heart! Jeez, get your mind out of the gutter."

Lena laughed. "How do you know he's missing a heart?" Her eyes widened. "You have a past! Of course you have a past, you grew up here with Rick. Is it sordid? Tell me!"

Rainey sighed. "I was younger, so Mark always thought of me as a…"

"Forbidden fruit?" Lena asked hopefully.

"Pest," Rainey corrected. "Look, I don't want to talk about it."

"I do!"

Knowing Lena wouldn't leave it alone, she caved. "Fine. I had a crush on him, and thought he was crushing back. Wrong. He didn't even know how I felt about him, but before I figured that out, I managed to thoroughly humiliate myself. The end."

"Oh, I'm going to need much *more* than that."

Luckily Lena's cell phone chose that very moment to ring. God bless AT&T. Lena glanced at the ID and grimaced. "I've got to go." She pointed at Rainey. "This discussion is not over."

"Yeah, yeah. Later." Rainey waved her off. She purposely glanced away from her computer screen, but like a moth to a flame, she couldn't fight the pull, and turned back.

Mark was shoving his players ahead of him, away from the run-down L.A. bar and towards a black SUV, single-handedly taking care of the situation.

That had been three days ago. The fight had been all over the news, and the commission was thinking about suspending the players involved. Supposedly the two head coaches had stepped in and offered a solution that would involve giving back to the fans who'd supported the two teams.

She looked into Mark's implacable, uncompromising face on her laptop and the years fell away. She searched for the boy she'd once loved with all her sixteen-year-old heart, but couldn't find a hint of him.

TWO HOURS LATER, THEY'D gone through a satisfying amount of cars, fattening the rec center's empty coffers, and Rainey was ready to call it a day. She needed to help the teens clean up before the bus arrived. Many of them still had homework and other jobs to get to.

The parking lot was wet and soapy, with hoses crisscrossing the concrete, and buckets everywhere. With no more cars waiting, the teens were running around like wild banshees, feeling free to squirt and torture one another. Rainey blew her whistle to get their attention. "We're done here," she called out. "Thanks so much for all your help today. The faster we clean up, the faster we can—" She broke off as the county bus rolled up and opened its doors. Dammit. All but a handful of the kids needed to get on that bus. It was their only ride.

When the bus pulled away, Rainey stared at the messy lot and the two kids she had left.

"More pizza?" Todd asked her hopefully. He was a lanky sixteen-year-old who had either a tapeworm or a bottomless stomach.

Rainey turned and looked through the pizza boxes. Empty. She opened her bag and pulled out her forgotten lunch. "I've got a PB&J—"

"Sweet," he said, and inhaled the sandwich in three bites. His gaze was locked on Sharee, a fellow high school junior, as she began rolling hoses. Sharee was all long, long mocha-colored limbs and grace. Another fire victim from the same neighborhood as Todd, she currently lived in a small trailer with her mother. When Sharee caught Todd staring, she leveled him with a haughty glare.

Todd merely grinned.

"Go help her," Rainey told him. "She can't do it all alone."

"Sure, I'll help her," Todd said, and the next thing Rainey knew, he was stalking a screaming Sharee with a bucket full of soapy water.

Sharee grabbed a hose and wielded it at him like a gun. "Drop the bucket and no one gets hurts. And by no one, I mean you."

Todd laughed at her and waved the bucket like a red flag in front of a bull.

"Okay, okay," Rainey said, stepping between them. "It's getting late." She knew for a fact that Todd still had to go work at his family's restaurant for several more hours. Sharee, on the cusp of not passing her classes, surely had a ton of homework. The girl also had a healing bruise high on one cheekbone and a set of matching bruises on both biceps, like someone had gripped her hard and shaken her.

Her father, Rainey guessed. Everyone knew Martin was a mean drunk but no one wanted to talk about it, least of all Sharee, who lived alone with her mother except for the nights her mother allowed the man into their trailer.

"He called me a scarecrow," Sharee said, pointing at Todd. "Now his sorry ass is going to pay."

"Language," Rainey said.

"Okay, his sorry butt. His sorry *butt* is going to pay."

"I said you have legs as long as a scarecrow," Todd said from behind Rainey. "Not that you *are* a scarecrow."

Sharee growled and lifted the hose.

"Stop!" Rainey said. "If you squirt him, you're leaving yourself wide open for retaliation."

"That's right," Todd said, nodding like a bobblehead. "Retaliation."

Rainey turned to shut Todd up just as Sharee let it rip with the hose and nailed him.

Rainey gave up. They had worked their asses off and deserved to let off a little steam. She stepped aside to leave them to it, but stopped short as a big, shiny black truck pulled into the lot.

Which was when the entire contents of Todd's bucket hit her. Sucking in a shocked gasp as the cold, soapy water rained over her, Rainey whipped around and stared at the sheepish teen, who was holding the offending empty bucket. "Oh, God," he said. "I'm so sorry, but you stepped right in its path!"

"You're in *big* trouble," Sharee told him. "You got her hair wet. You know how long it must take her to get that hair right?"

Sharee was right about the hair. Rainey shoved it out of her face, readjusting the Ducks hat on her head. Her wavy brown hair frizzed whenever it rained, or if the air was humid, or if she so much as breathed wrong. She had no doubt it resembled a squirrel's tail about now. "It's okay. Just…clean up," she said, watching as the black truck rolled to a stop.

"Look at that," Todd said reverently, Rainey's hair crisis forgotten. "That's one sweet truck."

Sneakers squishing, Rainy moved toward it. She could feel water running in rivulets down her body as the driver side window powered down. "I'm sorry," she said politely, feeling like a drowned rat. "We've closed up shop. We—" She broke off. The driver was wearing a Mammoth hat and reflective Oakleys, rendering him all but unrecognizable to the general public. But *she* recognized him just fine, and her heart stopped on a dime.

The man she'd just been watching on the news.

Mark Diego.

He wore a white button-down that was striking against his dark skin and stretched across broad shoulders. The hand-painted sign behind her said: Car

Wash—$10, but he pulled a hundred-dollar bill from his pocket. She stared down at it, boggled.

"No worries on the wash," he said in a low voice as smooth as aged whiskey, the same voice that had fueled her adolescent dreams.

He didn't recognize her.

Of course he didn't. She was wearing a ball cap, sunglasses, soap suds, and was drenched to the core, not to mention dressed like a complete slob. Unlike Mark, of course, who looked like sin-on-a-stick. Expensive sin-on-a-stick.

The bastard.

"I just need a place to park," he said with the smile that she knew probably melted panties and temperamental athletes with equal aplomb. "I'm here to see Rick Diego."

"You can park right where you are," Rainey said.

He turned off the engine and got out of the truck, six feet two inches of tough, rugged, leanly muscled grace. Two other guys got out as well, and beside her, Todd nearly swallowed his tongue. "Casey Reynolds! James Vasquez! Oh man, you guys rock!"

Casey, the Mammoths' right wing, was twenty-two and the youngest player on the team. He looked, walked and talked like the California surfer he was in his spare time. He wore loose basketball shorts, a T-shirt from some surf shop in the Caicos, and a backwards Mammoths' hat.

James was the team's left wing, and at twenty-four he was nearly as wild as Casey, but instead of looking like he belonged on a surfboard, James could have passed as a linebacker in the NFL. He was wearing baggy blue jeans and a snug silk shirt that emphasized and outlined his every muscle.

If she hadn't known they were the two players who'd been in the big bar brawl, she could have guessed by Casey's nasty black eye and the bruise and cut on James's jaw. Still managing to look like million-dollar athletes, they smiled at Todd and shook his hand.

The kid looked like he might pass out.

Mark and his two players clearly had a longtime ease with each other, but just as clearly there was a hierarchy, with Mark at the top—and he hadn't taken his carefully observant eyes off Rainey.

Crap.

She turned away, but he snagged her hand and pulled her very wet self back around. She thought about tugging free.

Or kicking him.

As if he could read her mind, his lips twitched. "Easy," he murmured, and pulled off her sunglasses.

She narrowed her eyes against the sun and a wealth of unwelcome emotions as the very hint of a smile tugged at the corner of his sexy mouth.

"It's a little hard to tell with the raccoon eyes," he said. "But the bad 'tude's a dead giveaway. Rainey Saunders. Look at you."

The others were all still talking with a false sense of intimacy. Mark tapped the bill of Rainey's Ducks hat, giving a slow shake of his head, like he couldn't believe she'd be wearing anything other than the Mammoths' colors.

And suddenly she felt like that silly, love-struck teenager all over again. Having four years on her, he'd been clueless about the crush. He might never have known at all if she hadn't made a fool of herself and sneaked into his apartment to strip for him. It'd all gone straight to hell since he'd been on the receiving end of a blow job at the time. She'd compounded the error with several more that evening, which she didn't want to think about. Ever. It'd all ended with her pride and confidence completely squashed.

Worse, the night had negated the years of friendship she and Mark had shared until then, all erased in one beat of stupidity.

Okay, several beats of stupidity.

She lifted her chin, which turned out to be a mistake because water had pooled on the bill and now dripped down her face. She blinked it away and tried to look cool—not easy under the best of circumstances, and this wasn't anywhere close to best.

Mark pointed to her nose. "You have a smudge of dirt."

Oh, good. Because she'd been under the illusion she was looking perfect. "Thought you liked dirty girls." The minute she said it, she could have cut out her tongue. He'd been on *GQ* last month, artfully stretched out on some L.A. beach, draped in sand.

And four naked, gorgeous, equally sandy women.

She'd bought the damn issue, which really chapped her ass. Mark clearly knew it, and his smile broke free. She rubbed at her nose but apparently this only made things worse because his smile widened.

"Here," he said, and ran a finger over the bridge of her nose himself.

Up this close and personal, it was hard to miss just how gorgeous he was.

Or how good he smelled.

Or how expensive he looked.

All of which was hugely irritating.

"Got it," he said. "Not much I can do about the soap all over you. Let's fix this too." Then, before she could stop him, he tugged off her drenched hat, flashed an amused glance at what was surely some scary-ass hair, then replaced her hat with the one from his own head. The Mammoths, of course. He ran a hand over his own silky, dark hair, leaving it slightly tousled and perfectly sexy.

She snatched back her hat. "I like the Ducks. They're my favorite team."

At this, both of his players turned from Todd and stared at her. Rainey didn't know if it was because of what she'd just said, or because no one dared sass their fearless leader. "No offense," she said to them.

"None taken," Casey said on a grin and held out his hand, introducing himself. James did the same.

Rainey instantly liked them both, and not just because they were famous, or cute as hell—which they were—but because they were quite harmless, as compared with their head coach. He wasn't the least bit harmless. Rainey squirmed a little, probably due to the soapy water running down her body.

Or the way Mark was studying her with the same quiet intensity he used on the ice—which she knew because she watched his games. All of them.

"So how do you know Coach?" James asked her.

Rainey looked into Mark's eyes. Well, not quite his eyes, since they were still behind the reflective Oakleys that probably cost more than her grocery bill for the month. "We go way back."

Mark's almost-smile made an appearance again.

"Rainey went to school with my brother Rick." He paused, clearly waiting for her to add something to the story.

No thank you, since the only thing she could add would be "and one time I threw myself at him and he turned me down flat."

They'd seen each other since, of course, on the few occasions when he'd come back to town to visit his dad and brother. Once when she'd been twenty-one, at a local police ball that Mark had helped chair. He'd slow danced with her and the air had crackled between them. Chemistry had abounded, and she could read in his dark eyes that he'd felt it too, and she'd melted at his interest. But she hadn't been able to swallow her mortification about the fiasco on her sixteenth birthday, so she'd made an excuse and bailed on him. She'd seen him again, several times, and each accidental run-in had been the same.

The laws of physics didn't change. The sun would come up. The sun would go down. And she would always be insanely attracted to Mark Diego.

The last chance encounter had been only two years ago. They'd had yet another near miss at a town Christmas ball when they'd again slow danced. He expressed interest in every hard line of his body, some harder than others, but she'd let self-preservation rule once more.

"So are you friends?" James asked her and Mark now. "Or...?" He waggled a finger back and forth between them with a matching waggle of his brow.

Mark gave him a single look, nothing more, and James zipped his lips.

Impressive. "Neither," she told James resolutely, trying to wring out the hem of her shirt while ignoring how close Mark was standing to her, invading her personal space bubble.

"It's been a long time," he said. "You look…"

"All wet?" she asked.

His eyes heated, and something deep inside her quivered. Damn, he still had the power. He smiled, and she narrowed her eyes, daring him to go there, but his momma hadn't raised a fool.

"Different," he finally said. "You look different."

Yes, she imagined she looked quite different than the gorgeous women she'd seen hanging off his arm in magazines and blogs.

"It's good to see you," he said.

She wanted to believe that was true, but realized with some horror that she'd actually leaned into him, drawn in by that stupid magnetic charisma. But she was nothing if not a pro at hiding embarrassment. Spreading her arms, she gave him a hug, as if that'd been her intention all along. Squeezing his big, warm, hard body close, she made sure to spread as much of the suds and water from her shirt to his as she could. "It's good to see you as well," she said, her mouth against his ear, her lips brushing the lobe.

He went still at the contact, then instead of trying to pull free, merely folded her into his arms, trapping her against him. And damn if her body didn't burst to life, as if all this time it'd been just waiting for him to come back.

"Yeah, you're different," he murmured, doing as she had, pressing his mouth to her ear, giving her a shiver. "The little kitten grew up and got claws."

When she choked out a laugh, he closed his teeth over her earlobe.

She gasped, but then he soothed the ache with a quick touch of his tongue, yanking another shocked response from her. "You said you were looking for Rick," she managed to say, shoving free. "He's in his office." And then, with as much dignity as she could muster, she walked off, sneakers squishing, water dripping from her nose, and, she suspected, her shorts revealing a horrible, water-soaked wedgie.

2

AFTER CHECKING IN WITH his brother, Mark and his players got back into his truck, not heading back to the coast, but further up into the rolling hills.

Rainey Saunders, holy shit. Talk about a blast from his past. Seeing her had been like a sucker punch; her smile, her shorts. Those legs…

Once upon a time she'd been a definite sweet spot in his life. A friend of his younger brother, who always had a smile for him. He'd been fond of her, as much as any teenage guy could be fond of something other than himself. She'd hung out on the fringes of his world throughout school, and he'd thought of her as one of the pack. Until she'd changed things up by going from a cute little kid to a hot teenager.

The night she'd shown up in his college apartment had been both a shock and a loss. A shock because he'd honestly had no idea that she'd had a crush on him, at least not before she'd dropped her clothes for him without warning. Until then, she'd never let on, not once. And a loss because everything had changed afterwards. He'd never forget how she'd broken into his place and found him in the throes with a coed. By the time he'd caught up with her, she'd run off with the first guy she'd found.

And that guy had been a real asshole who'd nearly given her a birthday moment she hadn't counted on. Mark had managed to stop it, and somehow *he'd* ended up the bad guy.

Rainey had wanted Mark to notice her, to see her as a woman, and hello, mission accomplished. Hell, he could still picture her perfect body—but he'd been too old for her. Even at twenty, he'd been smart enough to know that. Too bad he hadn't been smart enough to handle the situation correctly. Nope, he'd screwed it up badly enough to affect their relationship to the point that they'd no longer been friends.

It'd taken him a shamefully long time to figure that out, though, and by then he'd been on his path and gone from the area. Leaving Santa Rey had been his dream. To go do something big, something to lift him out of the poverty of his upbringing. He'd spent the next few years climbing his way up the coaching staff ladder, working in Toronto, New York, Boston…finally landing back on the west coast with a coveted head coaching position at the Mammoths.

He'd seen Rainey several times over the years since, and on each occasion she'd definitely sparked his interest. As a bonus, they'd both been age suitable. But though she'd flirted with him, nothing had ever come of it. He had no idea what being with her would be like, but he knew one thing. It would be interesting.

The Mammoths were officially off season now and on vacation. Except for Casey and James, who were damn lucky to still be a part of the team after their stupid bar fight.

He and the Ducks' coach had agreed to teach their players a lesson in how to be a role model by making them contribute to a struggling local community. Both coaches had chosen their own home communities, areas hit hard by fires and needing to heal. The players would be volunteer laborers at charity construction sites for most of the day, then after work they'd coach summer league ball. At the end of the summer league, the two rec centers would have a big game, with all the proceeds going directly to their programs. The community would benefit, the players could get their acts together, and everyone would feel like they'd made a difference.

All that was left was to tell his idiot players that they wouldn't be summering in style, but doing good old-fashioned hard work.

"Uh, Coach? Aren't we going home?" Casey asked from the passenger seat of the truck.

"Nope." Their asses were Mark's. They just didn't realize it yet. "We're staying in town."

"Where? At the Hard Rock Café?" This from James.

"We won't be at the beach." That was the South District, and they didn't need nearly as much help as the North District did. "We're heading to the very northern part of the county."

His two players exchanged glances. Mark smiled grimly and kept driving. He had a lot to think about—recruiting and trading for next season, not to mention hundreds of emails and phone calls waiting to be returned—but his brain kept skipping back to Rainey.

She'd grown up nice. The wet T-shirt had proved that. But it'd been far more than just a physical jolt he'd gotten. One look into her fierce blue eyes and he'd felt…

Something. Not even in the finals had his heart taken such a hard leap as it had when he'd realized who she was. Or when she'd touched her mouth to his ear.

Or when he'd bitten hers and absorbed the sexy little startled gasp she'd made.

"Come on, Coach. We're sorry about the fight. We've said it a million times. But it was the big game, and we were robbed."

Just getting to the finals had been a sweet victory, considering the Mammoths were only a five-year-old franchise. It'd been a culmination of grit, determination, and hard work, and even thinking about the season had a surge of fierce pride going through him. But the bar fight—now viral on YouTube—had taken away from their amazing season, and was giving them nothing but bad press. Mark had been featured on *Sixty Minutes* and all the mornings shows, trying to put a positive spin on things. He'd been flown to New York in a helicopter to recite the *Top Ten Things That Had Gone Through His Mind After Losing The Stanley Cup*. He'd been on the *Ellen DeGeneres Show* and had plunged Ellen into the dunk tank for charity. And then there'd been the endless lower profile events filling his calendar: meet-and-greets, photo shoots and endless charity appearances.

And still all everyone wanted to talk about was the fight. It pissed him off. After working around the clock for seven months, he should be on vacation.

He'd seen the press of other players on Jay-Z's yacht in the Caribbean with a bunch of scantily-clad women. Mark wouldn't mind being on a sandy beach somewhere, a woman at his side, a drink in his hand. But no. Instead he was babysitting his two youngest players because apparently they thought with their fists instead of their brains.

That was going to change. It'd been handy having his brother as the director of the rec center. Casey and James would be working their asses off. Construction and coaching, and hopefully, if they were lucky, they'd manage to take in some positive publicity while they were at it. That would make the owners of the Mammoths happy, and Mark too.

As well as Rick.

Win-win, all around, and Mark was all about the win. Always.

James leaned forward from the backseat. "We stayed at the Santa Rey Resort last time, remember? Man, they have that great nightclub...." He sighed with fond memories.

Mark just kept driving. They weren't staying at the resort. Or the Four Seasons. Or anywhere that any of them were accustomed to. "You both agreed to do whatever it took to not be suspended, correct?"

Another long glance between the two players.

"Yeah," James said.

'You're going to work as volunteer construction crew on the fire rebuilds, then every afternoon you'll coach at the rec center."

"That sounds okay," James said. "Especially if the coach gig involves that hot little counselor they had running the car wash. What's her name... Rainey? Loved her wet T-shirt—you guys see that?"

Casey grinned. "I loved her whistle and clipboard,

and the way she barked orders like a little tyrant. Sexiest tyrant I've ever seen."

When James chuckled, Mark's fingers tightened on the steering wheel. "She's off limits." He ignored the third long look that James and Casey exchanged. But they had one thing right. Rainey *was* a tyrant, especially when she decided on something.

Or someone.

And once upon a time, she'd decided on him.

"So we're not going to the Biltmore?" James asked. "Cuz there's always plenty of hot babes there."

"James," Mark said. "What did I tell you about hot babes?"

James slumped in his seat. "That if I so much as look at one you're going to kick my ass."

"Do you doubt my ability to do so?"

James slouched even further. "No one in their right mind would doubt that, Coach."

"And anyway, you're not allowed back at the Biltmore," Casey reminded James. "That's where you got caught with that redhead by her husband. You had to jump out the window and sprained your knee and were out for three weeks."

"Oh yeah," James said on a fond sigh. "Madeline."

Mark felt a brain bleed coming on. He exited the highway, a good twenty miles from the beach and any "hot babes."

"Damn," James murmured, taking in the fire ravaged hills on either side of the narrow two-lane highway, then repeated the "damn" when Mark pulled up to a small, run-down-looking motel.

"Home sweet home for the next month," Mark told them grimly. "The Santa Rey Welcome Inn."

Casey and James just stared at the single story motel. The stucco walls were pea-green, the windows lined with wrought-iron grates. The yard was dead grass.

"They're on water restrictions," Mark said, and clapped them both on the backs. "You'll be reminded of that come shower time in the morning. There's a three-minute shower requirement here. Let's go," he said to their groans.

The Welcome Inn sign blinked on and off in flashing white lights. The door to the office was thrown open, letting out the scent of stale coffee and air freshener. Inside the office was a desk, a small couch, and a floor fan on full blast aimed at the woman behind the desk. Celia Anderson was sixty-something, and glued to the soap opera on the TV mounted on the wall—until she saw Mark. With a warm smile, she came around and squeezed him tight. "Aw, you're such a good boy," she said. "Throwing us your fancy business."

Boy? Casey mouthed to James.

"Sometimes homey is better than fancy," Mark said to Celia.

She patted his cheek gently. "Your father raised you right. I've got the three rooms you requested. Cash or credit?"

"Cash," he said, knowing how badly she needed the cash.

"I'll give you a discount."

"No," he said gently, putting his hand over hers when she went to punch a discounted rate into her computer. "Full price."

She beamed at him and handed over their room keys.

Which were actual keys. Casey looked at his like he didn't know what to do with it. They walked down the outside hallway to their rooms. Each had a single bed, dresser and chair beneath the window. All of which had seen better days but were spotlessly clean.

"Coach, I think your assistant screwed up the reservations," Casey said.

James's head bobbled his agreement. "I don't think they even have cable."

"There's been no mistake," Mark said. "Unless you guys wanted to room together?"

They looked at the narrow bed and vehemently shook their heads, both wisely deciding to drop the subject.

Mark waited until he was alone to smile. Operation: *Ego Check* was in full swing.

For all of them.

RAINEY DIDN'T FALL ASLEEP until past midnight, and dreamed badly.

Sweet Sixteen, and she stood outside Mark's bedroom door, heart pounding inside her chest so loudly she was surprised she hadn't woken the entire apartment complex.

Mark had no idea she was here. No one did. She'd stolen his key from Rick and lied to her friends that she was too tired to go out. Wearing a pretty lacy teddy beneath her sweats, carrying a borrowed pair of sexy heels in her hand, she grinned. Tonight was the night. She was finally going to tell him she loved him, that she always had. They'd live happily ever after, just like in all the good chick flicks.

Quietly she opened his bedroom door and dropped her sweats. She stepped into the heels and fluffed her hair. She was just checking her boobs to make sure they were even and perky when she heard it.

A rough moan.

Whirling around, she got the shock of her life.

Mark wasn't sleeping. He wasn't even in his bed.

He was sprawled in the beanbag chair beneath the window, long legs spread for the woman on her knees between his, head bobbing—Oh, God.

Mark's head was back, eyes closed, his perfect body taut and his hands fisted in his date's hair as she...

Rainey must have made a sound, or maybe he'd heard the crack of her heart as it split wide, because Mark sat straight up so fast he nearly choked his date. "Christ. Rainey—"

"Hey," his date complained, lifting her head with a pissed-off frown. "I'm Melody."

Rainey turned to run away and ran smack into the door—which didn't slow her down. Not that, or the sprained ankle from her stupid heels.

"Rainey!"

The pounding of bare feet told her he was coming after her. Not wanting to face him, she kicked her heels off and raced barefoot out into the night like Cinderella trying to beat the clock. Young and desperate, she'd run off looking for a way to prove herself as grown up as she imagined.

She'd been ripe for trouble, and unfortunately, she'd found it.

SITTING STRAIGHT UP in bed with a gasp, Rainey realized it was dawn, and she blinked the dream away. Fourteen years and she remembered every humiliating detail as if it'd been yesterday. Especially what had happened next. But she wasn't going there, not now. Not ever.

By that afternoon, she'd nearly forgotten all about the dream *and* Mark. She was running laps with the group of teens who'd shown up after school, counting heads to make sure none had made off with each other into the bushes, when Sharee came up to her side.

Rainey's welcoming smile faded as she locked her gaze on the new bruise on the teen's jaw. "What happened?"

Sharee switched into her default expression—sullen. "Nothing."

"Sharee—"

"Walked into a door, no big deal."

"Where was your mother?"

Sharee lifted a shoulder. "Working."

Rainey would like to get Martin alone and walk *him* into a door, but that was a stupid idea. The man scared Rainey. "You know where I live, right?"

"The Northside town houses."

"Unit fifteen," Rainey said. "Next time your mother's working nights, come have a sleepover with me."

"Why?"

"So you don't walk into any more doors. We'll watch a movie and eat crap food. It'll be more fun than any date I've had in a while."

"How often do you date?" Sharee asked.

The easy answer was not much. But that was also the embarrassing answer. "Occasionally."

Sharee nodded, then went back to running laps. Rainey ran again too, until her cell phone buzzed an incoming text from Rick.

The help I promised you for the summer league is on their way. You've got two Mammoth players and their head coach, who I believe you've met. They work for you, Rainey. You're in charge.

She'd have to kill Rick later. For now, she grabbed her clipboard and blew her whistle. "Two more laps before we scrimmage," she called out, and began stretching to cool down. She'd figured Rick would get a few local college athletes. But nope, he'd gone all the way to the top.

And all she could think was that Mark would be around for three weeks.

Twenty-one days…

She lay on her back and stared at the puffy clouds floating lazily by, trying not to delve too deeply into how she felt about this. The first cloud looked sort of like a double-stuffed Oreo. She could really go for a handful of double-stuffed Oreos about now. The next cloud came into sight, resembling—"Mark?"

She blinked up at the cloud that wasn't a cloud at all as Mark flashed her his million-dollar smile.

"Heard you need me," he said. "Bad."

AT TWENTY-ONE, MARK had been long and leanly muscled, not a spare inch on him. Rainey's gaze ran down his thirty-four-year-old body and she had to admit he was even better now. In fact, the only way to improve on that body would be to dip it into chocolate.

He offered her a hand, his grip firm as he pulled her upright. She immediately brushed the dry grass from her behind and the backs of her legs, painfully aware of the fact that once again she was a complete mess and he…he was not. He had all that perfect Latino skin, and the most amazing dark eyes that held more secrets than some developing countries. He had strong cheek-bones and a mouth that always brought sinful thoughts to her mind, especially when he flashed that rare smile of his. He'd broken his nose twice in his wild and crazy youth, not that it dared to be anything less than aristocrat straight. But even better than his arresting face was everything else—his fierce passion, his drive, his smarts. And now for the first time, she supposed she could also appreciate his coaching skills firsthand. "We're running," she said.

"Really? Because it looked like you were napping."

Clearly he was in great shape. He could probably run a marathon without breaking a sweat. The thought of what else he might be able to do without breaking a sweat made her nipples hard.

Don't go there….

Too late. She closed her eyes so she couldn't stare at him, but as it turned out, he and his hot bod were imprinted on her brain. His world was about coaching million-dollar athletes, and he'd taken it upon himself to be as fit as they were. This meant he was six feet plus of hard sinew wrapped in testosterone, built to impress any guy and pretty much render any female a puddle of longing.

Except her.

Nope, there could be no melting, not for her. She was so over him. Completely. Over. Him.

Maybe.

Oh, God, she was in trouble. Because who was she kidding? She'd never gotten over him, never, and every single guy she'd ever dated had been mentally measured up to him and found lacking.

It made no sense. Yes, she'd known him years ago. Back then she'd been insanely attracted to the way he cared deeply about those around him, his utter lack of fear of anything, and his truck. Apparently some things never changed.

He stepped closer, blocking the sun with his broad shoulders so that all she could see was him, and she forgot to breathe.

His fingertips brushed lightly over a cheek and something deep in her belly quivered. "You're getting sunburned," he said. "Where's your hat?"

The one he'd given her yesterday? She'd tried to toss it into her trash can last night. Twice.

It was sitting on her pillow at home.

But only because it would have been rude to let a gift go out with the week's trash. And that was the *only* reason she'd worn it to bed. "I'm wearing sunscreen."

He was just looking at her. His phone had vibrated no less than five times from the depths of his pockets, but he was ignoring it. She tried to imagine all he was responsible for on any given day, and couldn't.

"How have you been?" he asked.

"Good. And you? Congratulations on your season, by the way."

"Thanks. It really is good to see you, Rainey."

She laughed and spread her hands, indicating her state of dishevelment. "Yeah, well it gets better than this, I swear."

He smiled and looked past her to the girls. "Rick said to let you know the players and I are to report to you for coaching the kids. That's how both the Ducks and the Mammoths are handling the fallout from the fight. We're trying to show that players can be role models and help our local communities at the same time. At the end of summer league, we'll have a big charity fund-raising game between the two rec centers and show that it doesn't have to end in a fight."

"Hmm." The idea was fantastic, and in truth, she really needed help. There'd been a time when she'd needed *him* too, not that she'd ever managed to get him.

And Rick had just given him to her on a silver platter. Oh, the irony. "That's great."

"Will the parents have a problem with us stepping in? Don't they usually coach for summer leagues?"

"Not in this part of town, they don't. They're all working, or not interested."

He eyed the teens on the field, specifically the boys, his sharp gaze already assessing. "How about you let us handle the entire boys' program?" He turned that gaze on her, and smiled. "It's been what, a few years?"

"Two." She clamped her lips shut when that slipped out, giving away the fact that she'd kept count.

His smile widened, and she arched a brow.

"I'll hug you hello again," she warned. "And this time I'm all sweaty."

He immediately stepped into her.

"No," she gasped. "I'll ruin your expensive shirt—"

Not listening, he wrapped his arms around her. "You can't ignore me this time, Rainey, though it's going to be fun watching you try. And you know what? I think I like you all hot and sweaty." He ran a hand down her back, smiling when she shivered. Stepping away, he gestured to the boys on the field. "Bring them in," he said. "Let's see what we've got."

While she blew the whistle, he eyed the two baseball diamonds. There were weeds growing in the lanes, no bases, and the lines had long ago been washed away.

"Why are they dressed like that?" he asked.

The boys were in a variety of baggy, saggy shorts and big T-shirts. Some of the girls wore just sports bras and oversize basketball shorts. Others wore tight T-shirts, or shirts so loose they were in danger of falling off. "We don't have practice jerseys."

He pulled out his cell phone and walked a few steps away, either to make or take a call, and Rainey absolutely did not watch his ass as he moved.

Much.

When he came back, she'd divided the teens up into boys and girls, and sent the boys to the further diamond to scrimmage because they were much better at self-regulating than the girls.

She'd split the girls into two bedraggled, short teams and Sharee was at bat. She hit a hard line drive up the first base line. Pepper, their pitcher, squeaked in fear and dropped to the mound.

"Nice hit," Mark said. "But why is the pitcher lying flat on the ground like there's been a fire drill?"

"Pepper's terrified of the ball."

He shook his head. "You've got your hands full with the girls, huh?"

First base grabbed the ball but Sharee was already rounding second.

First base threw, and…second base missed the catch.

Mark groaned.

"They'll get there," Rainey said. "I've been working with them while waiting on coaches."

At her defensive tone, he took a longer look at her. "You didn't know we were coming in to help you."

"No."

He grimaced. "Rick's an idiot."

"That idiot is my friend and boss."

"So you're okay with this? Working with me, even though you've done your best to ignore me all these years?"

"You're right," she decided. "Rick *is* an idiot."

He grinned.

And oh, God, that grin. He flashed white, straight teeth and a light of pure trouble in his eyes, and she helplessly responded.

Damn hormones.

"We're grown-ups," she said. "We can handle this— you working for me. Right? We can do it for all these kids."

Mark moved into her, a small movement that set her heart pounding. She refused to take a step back because she knew it would amuse him, and she'd done enough of that for a lifetime.

"Working *for* you?" he murmured in that bedroom voice.

"I'm the athletic director, so yeah. You coaching is you working for me. You're working under me and my command." She gave him a look. "You have a problem with that?"

"No problem at all." His gaze dropped to her mouth. "Though I'd much rather have *you* under *me*."

3

RAINEY DID HER BEST to ignore all the parts of her body that were quivering and sending conflicting signals to her brain and drew a deep breath. "This is inappropriate," she finally said.

The corners of his mouth turned up slightly. "Only if someone overhears us."

She drew another deep breath. That one didn't work any better than the first, so she turned to the field, watching the girls silently for a few minutes. After three outs, the teams switched on the field.

"Uneven teams," Mark noted. "I'm going to go get a closer look at the boys."

She grabbed his hand to halt his progress. "This is rec league, Mark. It's not really about the competition."

"It's always about the competition."

"It's about having fun," she said.

His eyes met hers and held. The sun was beating down on them and Rainey resented that she was sweating and he was not.

"Winning *is* fun," he said.

Another little quiver where she had no business quivering.

Lila hit next and got a piece of the ball and screamed in surprise. Sharee sighted the ball and yelled *"mine!"*, diving for it, colliding hard with Kendra at second. Sharee managed to make the catch and the out.

Kendra rubbed her arm and glared at Sharee, who ignored her.

"Nice," Mark said. "She's got potential."

"This isn't hockey, Mark." But Rainey was talking to air because he'd walked onto the diamond like the superstar coach he was.

Sharee had her back to him, barking out orders at the other girls on the field like a drill sergeant. When she turned to face home plate, her eyes widened at the sight of Mark.

He held out his hand for the ball.

Sharee popped it into her mitt twice out of defiance, and only when Mark raised a single brow did she finally toss it to him, hard.

He caught it with seemingly no effort. "Name?"

"Sharee."

"What was that, Sharee?"

"A great pitch," she said, and popped her gum.

"After the pitch."

"A great play."

He nodded. "You're fast."

"The fastest."

He nodded again. "But you took yourself out of position and it wasn't your ball to go after. You could have let your team down."

Sharee stopped chewing her gum and frowned. She wasn't used to being told what to do, and she wasn't much fond of men. "Kendra would have missed the out," she finally said.

"Then center field would have gotten it."

Sharee eyed the center fielder, who was busy braiding her hair, and snorted.

Mark just looked at Sharee for a long beat. "Do you know who I am?"

"Yeah. Head coach of the Mammoths."

"Do you know if I'm any good?" he asked.

"You're the best," Sharee said simply but grudgingly. "At hockey."

Mark smiled. "I played hockey *and* baseball in college, before I started coaching. My players listen to me, Sharee, and they listen because I get them results. But when they don't listen, they do push-ups. Lots of them."

Sharee blinked. "You make grown guys do push-ups?"

"I teach them to play hard or not at all. You're practicing for, what, maybe an hour a day? The least you can do is play hard for that entire time. As hard as you can, always."

"Or push-ups."

"That's right."

Sharee considered this. "I don't like push-ups."

"Then I'd listen real good. One hundred percent," he said to everyone. "I am asking for one hundred percent. It's effort. You don't have to have talent for effort. You," Mark said to the girl in center field, who was no longer braiding her hair but doing her best to be invisible. "What's your name?"

She opened her mouth but the only thing that came out was a squeak.

"It's Tina," Sharee said for her. "And she never catches the ball."

"Why not?"

Everyone looked at Tina, who squeaked again.

"Because she can't," Sharee said.

"So you make all the outs?" Mark asked.

"Most of 'em."

"That's what we call a ball hog." He tossed the ball back to her. "Let's see who else besides you can play."

"But—"

Again he arched a brow and she shut her mouth.

Rainey stared, mesmerized, as he coached the uncoachable Sharee through an inning, getting everyone involved.

Even Tina and Pepper.

When it was over, Rainey sent the kids back to the rec center building so that they wouldn't miss their buses home.

"Didn't mean to step on your toes," he said.

"I'm happy for the help. Nice job with them."

"Then why are you frowning?" he asked.

Because she was dripping sweat and he looked cool as ice. Because standing next to him brought back memories and yearnings she didn't want. Pick one. She grabbed her clipboard and started across the field, but Mark caught her by the back of her shirt and pulled her to him.

And there went her body again, quivering with all sorts of misfired signals to her brain. Her nipples went hard, her thighs tingled, and most importantly, her irritation level skyrocketed.

"What's your hurry?" Mark asked, snaking an arm around her to hold her in place. The kid were all gone. She and Mark were hidden from view of the building by the dugout. Knowing no one could see her, she closed her eyes, absorbing the feeling of being this close to him. Unattainable, she reminded herself. He was completely unattainable. "I just..." Her brain wasn't running on all cylinders.

"You just..." he repeated helpfully, his lips accidentally brushing her earlobe. Or at least she assumed it was accidental. However it happened, her knees wobbled.

"I..." His hand was low on her belly, holding her in place against him. "Wait—*what are you doing?*"

"We never really got to say hello in private." He tightened his grip. "Hello, Rainey."

If his voice got any lower on the register, she'd probably orgasm on the spot.

"It's been too long," he murmured against her jaw.

Telling herself that no one could see them, she pressed back against him just a little. "I don't know about *too* long."

A soft chuckle gave her goose bumps, and then he was gone so fast she nearly fell on her ass. When she spun around, she got a good look at that gorgeous face—the square jaw, the almost arrogant cheekbones, the eyes that could be ice-cold or scorching-hot depending on his mood. And no matter what his mood was, there was always the slight suggestion that maybe... maybe he belonged on the dark side.

It was impossibly, annoyingly intriguing. *He* was

impossibly, annoyingly intriguing, and yet he called to the secret part of her that had never stopped craving him. She headed toward the building, and he easily kept pace. Between the field and the building was a full basketball court, with a ball sitting on the center line.

Mark nudged it with his foot in a way that had it leaping right into his hands. He tossed it to her, a light of challenge in his eyes. "One on one."

"Basketball's not your sport, Coach."

"And it's yours?"

"Maybe."

"Then play me," he dared.

"We're wearing the same color shirt. Someone's going to have to be skins." She had no idea why she said it, but he smiled.

"I guess that would be me."

She shrugged as if she could care less, while her inner slut said "yes please." "I guess—"

The words backed up in her throat when he reached over his head and yanked his shirt off in one economical movement, tossing it aside with no regard for the fact that it probably cost more than all her shirts added together.

Her eyes went directly to his chest. His skin was the color of the perfect mocha latte, and rippled with the strength just beneath it. She let her gaze drift down over his eight-pack, and—

"Keep looking at me like that," he said, "and we're going to have a problem."

She jerked her gaze away. "I wasn't looking at you like anything."

"Liar."

Yeah. She was a liar. She dribbled the ball, then barreled past him to race down the court. She could hear his quick feet and knew he was right behind her, but then suddenly he was at her side, reaching in with a long arm to grab the ball away.

She shoved him, her hands sliding over his heated skin. Catching herself, she snatched the ball back, then executed a very poor shot that went in by sheer luck. Grinning, she turned to face him and plowed smack into his chest.

"Foul," he said.

"What are you, a girl?"

That made him smile. "Gee, wonder where Sharee gets her attitude from?"

"Actually, she gets that from her abusive alcoholic father."

Mark lost his smile and dribbled as he studied her. "It's a good thing…what you're doing here."

Feeling oddly uncomfortable with the compliment and the way his praise washed over her, she snatched the ball and went for another shot. Competitive to the bone, Mark shouldered his way into her space, grabbed the ball and sank a basket far more gracefully than she'd done. Dammit. She took the ball back and elbowed him when he crowded her.

He grinned, a very naughty grin that did things to her insides. "Is that how you want to play?" he asked. "Dirty?"

"Playing" with him at all was a very bad idea. But as always with Mark, her best judgment went out the window. Or in this case, down the court where she took the ball. Her feet were in the air for the layup when he grabbed her and spun her away from the basket.

Oh, no. Hell, no. She struggled, and they both fell to

the ground. He landed with a rough "oomph." Lying on top of him, she looked down into his face, extremely aware of how he felt sprawled beneath her.

His eyes were heat and raw power. "Foul number two. You play panicked, Rainey. Am I making you nervous?"

"Of course not." Face hot, fingers even hotter after bracing herself on his bare chest, she scrambled off him. She walked along the side of the rec building to the storage shed to put the ball away.

Mark had picked up his shirt and followed her, pulling it on as he did. Then he backed her to the shed.

"You really don't make me nervous," she said.

"You sure about that?"

Before she could answer, he kissed her, slipping a hand beneath her shirt at the base of her spine, trailing his fingers up her back. The kiss was long and slow and deep, and her hand came up to his chest for balance.

And absolutely not to explore the tight muscles there.

By the time he broke it off, she realized she'd let one of his legs thrust between hers, and she had both hands fisted in his shirt. Clearly she was sex-deprived. That was the only way to explain how she was riding his leg, breathing like a lunatic, still gripping him for all she was worth. She stared up at him, unable to access the correct brain synapses to make her mouth work. By the time she managed to speak, he'd smirked and begun walking away.

Dammit! "I'm not nervous," she called after him. "I'm annoyed, and I won our game!"

"You cheated." He shot her a look over his shoulder. "And payback is a bitch."

AFTER LEAVING THE FIELD, Mark attempted to put both
Rainey and their kiss out of his head, which turned out
to be surprisingly difficult.

Rainey had always had a way of worming beneath
his skin and destroying his defenses, and apparently
that hadn't changed. He'd missed her in his life—her
sweet smile, her big heart, that way she'd had of making
him want to be a better person than he was.

He picked up pizza and beer, and took it to the Welcome Inn.

As per their agreement, Casey and James had been
at the construction site all day, just as their Duck coun-
terparts were doing in their chosen community a couple
hours south of them, just outside of Santa Barbara.

The two Mammoth players had been brought back
to the inn by one of the workers. Mark had purposely
stranded them in Santa Rey without a car, wanting them
to be at his mercy—and out of trouble, with no chance
of finding it. He located them in Casey's room, hunched
over the yellow pages of the phone book arguing over
food choices.

James looked up. "Did you know that there's no
room service here?"

Mark lifted the three pizzas and twelve-pack. "I'm
your room service tonight."

"Sweet." Casey looked very relieved as he tossed
aside the phone book. He stretched and winced.
"There's no whirlpool. No hot tub. No spa—"

"Nope." Mark took the sole chair in the room, turning it around to straddle it. "There's no amenities at all."

"Then why are we—"

"Because you two screwed up and are lucky to still
have jobs."

They sighed in unison.

"And," Mark went on, "because the couple who owns this place lost their home in the fire last year. Business is down, way down."

"Shock," James muttered.

"You both agreed to this. The alternative is available to you—suspension." Mark stood. "So if this isn't something you can handle, don't be here when I come to pick you up in the morning."

He turned to the door, and just as he went through it, he heard James say, "Dude, sometimes it's okay to just shut the hell up."

AFTER DROPPING OFF THE pizza and ultimatum, Mark picked up his brother and drove the two of them up the highway another couple of miles, until the neighborhood deteriorated considerably.

"He's been looking forward to this for a long time," Rick said.

"I know." Last summer's fire had ravaged the area, and half the houses were destroyed. Of those, a good percentage had been cleared away and were in various stages of being rebuilt. The house Mark and Rick had grown up in was nearly finished now. Still small, still right on top of the neighbor's, but at least it was new. They got out of the truck and headed up the paved walk. The yard was landscaped and clearly well cared for. Before they could knock, the door opened.

"So the prodigal son finally returns," Ramon Diego said, a mirror image of Rick and Mark, plus two decades and some gray.

"I told you I was coming," Mark said. "I texted you."

Ramon made an annoyed sound. "Texting is for idiots on the hamster wheel."

Rick snorted.

Mark sighed, and his father's face softened. "Ah, *hijo,* it's good to see you." He pulled Mark in for a hard hug and a slap on the back.

"You too," Mark said, returning the hug. "The house looks good."

"Thanks to you." Ramon had migrated here from Mexico with his gardener father when he was seven years old. He'd grown up and become a gardener as well, and had lived here ever since. Forty-eight years and he still spoke with an accent. "Don't even try to tell me my insurance covered all the upgrades you had put in."

"Do you like it?" Mark asked.

"Yes, but you shouldn't waste your money on me. If you have that much money to spare, give up the job and come back to your home, your roots."

Mark's "roots" had been a tiny house crowded with his dad and brother, living hand to mouth. A one-way road for Mark as he grew up. A road to trouble.

Ramon gestured to the shiny truck in the driveway. "New?"

"You know damn well it is," Mark said. "It's the truck I bought for you for your birthday, and you had it sent back to me."

"Hmm," Ramon said noncommittally, possibly the most stubborn man on the planet. Mark knew his dad was proud of him, but he'd have been even more proud if Mark had stuck around and become a gardener too. Ramon had never understood Mark not living here in Santa Rey, using it as a home base.

"You should come home more often," Ramon said.

"I told you I wouldn't be able to come during the season."

"Bah. What kind of a job keeps a son from his home and family."

"The kind that makes him big bucks," Rick said.

They moved through the small living room and into the kitchen. "If you'd use the season tickets I bought you," Mark told his dad. "You could see me whenever you wanted."

"I saw you on TV breaking up that fight. You nearly took a left hook from that Ducks player. Getting soft?" He jabbed Mark's abs, then smiled. "Okay, maybe not. Come home, *hijo,* and stay. You've got all the money you could need now, yes? Come settle down, find someone to love you."

"Dad."

"I'm getting old. I need *nietos* to spoil."

Rick rolled his eyes and muttered, "Here we go. The bid for grandkids."

"Someone to take care of you," Ramon said, and smacked Rick on the back of the head.

"I take care of myself," Mark said. *And about a hundred others.*

Ramon sighed. "I suppose it's my fault. I harp on you about walking away from your humble beginnings and culture, and I divorced your mother when you were only five. Bad example."

"I've never walked away from my beginnings, Dad. I just have a job that requires a lot of traveling. And Mom divorced you. You drove her batshit crazy." His father was an incredibly hard worker, and incredibly old world in his sensibilities. He'd driven his ambitious, wanna-be actress wife off years ago.

The living room was empty except for two beautiful potted plants. Same with the kitchen, though the cabinet doors were glass, revealing plates and cups on the shelves. "Where's the furniture? I sent money, and you've been back in this house for what, a few weeks now?"

"I liked my old furniture."

"I know, but it's all gone. You got out with the clothes on your back." Mark still shuddered to think how close he'd come to losing his dad.

"I'll get furniture eventually, as I find what suits me. Let's eat. You can tell me about your women."

There was only one at the moment, the one with the flashing eyes, a smart-ass mouth, and heart of gold. The one who still showed her every thought as it came to her. That had terrified him once upon a time.

Now it intrigued him.

His father was at the refrigerator, pulling out ingredients. "We'll have grilled quesadillas for dinner. It's a warm night. We'll sit on the patio."

"I'll take you out to dinner," Mark said.

"No, I'm not spending any more of your money. What if you get fired over this fight mess? Then you'll be broke. Save your money."

"I won't get fired, Dad. The players are working hard, making restitution."

"So you won't have to suspend them?"

"No, which is good since they've got more talent in their pinkie fingers than my entire line of offense, and I have a hot offense."

Ramon nodded his agreement to this. "The press has been relentless on you."

Rick nodded. "You were flashed on *Entertainment Tonight* with a woman from some reality show."

"That was a promo event," Mark said. "I told you, I don't need someone else to take care of right now."

"Love isn't a burden, *hijo*. You really think it'll soften you, make you that vulnerable?"

Mark sent his brother a feel-free-to-jump-in-here-and-redirect-the-converation-at-any-time look, but Rick just smirked, enjoying himself. "What happened to cooking?" Mark asked desperately.

"Your brother has someone," Ramon pointed out, not to be deterred.

Rick smiled smugly.

"You could at least have a home here in Santa Rey," his dad said. "And then maybe a family."

Mark sighed. "We're not going to agree on this issue."

"We would if you'd get over yourself. Chicken or carne quesadilla?"

No one in his world ever told Mark to get over himself. Instead they tripped over their feet to keep him happy. He supposed he should be thankful for the reminder to be humble. "Carne."

THE NEXT MORNING, both James and Casey were ready to roll right on time. They were dressed for construction work and had a coffee for Mark.

Nice to know they could still suck up with the best of them. He wondered if either of them had talked the other out of bailing, but he didn't really give a shit. As long as they were still here, willing to put in the time and maybe even learn something, he was good.

They worked until afternoon, showered, then attended the rec center's staff meeting, per Rick's request. This was held in a conference room, aka pre-school room, aka makeshift dance studio. Everyone sat at a large table, including Rainey, who didn't look directly at Mark. He knew that because *he* was looking directly at her.

Rick ran a surprisingly tight ship considering how laid-back he was. Assignments were passed out, the budget dealt with, and the sports schedule handled. When it came to that schedule and what was expected of Mark's players, Rick once again made it perfectly clear that Rainey was in charge.

Mark looked across the table and locked eyes with Rainey. He arched a brow and she flushed, but she definitely stared at his mouth before turning back to Rick attentively.

She was thinking about the kiss.

That made two of them. This was Mark's third time seeing her, and she was *still* a jolt on his system.

He realized that Rick and Rainey were speaking. Then Rainey stood up to reveal a poster that would be placed around town. It advertised the upcoming youth sports calendar and other events such as their biweekly car wash and the formal dinner and auction that would hopefully raise the desperately needed funds for a new rec building. She was looking around the room as she spoke, her eyes sharp and bright. She had an easy smile, an easy-to-listen-to voice, and who could forget that tight, toned yet curvy body.

She was in charge of her world.

Watching her, Mark felt something odd come over him. If he had to guess, he'd say it was a mix of warmth and pride and affection. He wasn't sentimental, and he sure as hell wasn't the most sensitive man on the planet. Or so he'd been told a time or a million....

But he'd missed her.

"The Mammoth players will be assisting me in this," she said, and he nodded, even though he wasn't listening so he had no idea what exactly they'd be assisting her with. He'd help her with whatever she wanted. He liked the jeans she was wearing today, which sat snug and low on her hips. Her top was a simple knit and shouldn't have been sexy at all, but somehow was. Maybe because it brought out her blue eyes. Maybe because it clung to her breasts enough to reveal she was feeling a little bit chilly—

"If it works into your schedule, that is," she said, and he realized with a jolt that she was looking right at him.

Everyone was looking right at him.

"That's fine," he said smoothly.

Casey and James both lifted their brows, but he ignored them. "We're here to serve."

James choked on the soda he was drinking.

Casey just continued staring at Mark like he'd lost his marbles.

His brother out-and-out grinned, which was his first clue.

"You just agreed to coach a girls' softball team," James whispered in his ear. "Me and Casey get the boys, but she gave you the girls."

Ah, hell.

Rainey was watching him, waiting for him to balk

and possibly leave, which was clearly what she'd been aiming for. Instead he nodded. "Great."

"Great?"

"Great," he repeated, refusing to let her beat him.

"The kids are going to love it," Rick said. "Tell him your plans, Rainey."

She was still looking a little shell-shocked that she hadn't gotten rid of him. Guess their kiss had shaken her up good.

That made two of them.

"Well, if you're really doing this…?" She stared at him, giving him another chance at a way out. But hell no. Diegos didn't take the out…ever.

"We're doing this," he said firmly. "All the way."

Color rose to her cheeks but she stayed professional. "Okay, well, the Mammoths are taking advantage of our needs in order to gain good publicity, so I figure it's only fair for us to take advantage of your celebrity status."

"Absolutely," Mark said. "How do you want to do that?"

Rainey glanced at Rick, who gave her the go-ahead to voice her thoughts. "You could let us auction off dates with you three," she said.

Mark was stunned. It was ingenious, but he should have expected no less. It was also just a little bit evil.

Seemed Rainey had grown some claws. He had no idea what it said about him that he liked it.

Casey grinned. "Sounds fun. And I'm sure the other guys would put their name on the ticket too."

"I'm in," James said agreeably, always up for something new, especially involving women. "As long as the ladies are single. No husbands with shotguns."

The meeting ended shortly after that and Rainey gathered her things, vacating quickly, the little sneak. Making his excuses, Mark followed after her. She was already halfway down the hall, moving at a fast clip. Obviously she had things to do, places to go. And people to avoid. He smiled grimly, thinking her ass looked sweet in those jeans. So did her attitude, with that whistle around her neck, the clipboard in her hands. She was running her show like…well, like he ran his. He picked up his stride until he was right behind her, and realized she was on her cell phone.

"This is all your fault, Lena," she hissed. "No. *No,* I'm most definitely *not* still crushing on him! That was a secret, by the way, and it was years ago— Yes, I've got eyes, I realize he's hot, thank you very much, but it's not all about looks. And anyway, I'm going out with Kyle Foster tonight, which is your fault too— Are you laughing? Stop laughing!" She paused, taking in what-ever was being said to her. "You know what? Calling you was a bad idea. Listening to you in the first place was a bad bad idea. I have to go." She shoved her phone into her pocket and stood there, hands on hips.

"Hey," he said.

She jerked, swore, then started walking again, away from him, moving as if she hadn't heard him. Good tactic. He could totally see why it might work on some people—she moved like smoke. He could also see why she'd want to ignore him, but they had things to discuss. Slipping his fingers around her upper arm, he pulled her back to face him.

"I'm really busy," she said.

"Girls' softball?" he asked softly. "Really?"

"Not here," she said, and opened a door. Which she shut in his face.

Oh hell no, she didn't just do that. He hauled open the door, expecting an office, but instead found a small storage room lined with shelves.

Rainey was consulting her clipboard and searching the shelves.

He shut the door behind him, closing them in, making her gasp in surprise. "What are you doing—"

"You said not out there," he reminded her.

"I meant not out there, and not *anywhere*."

He stepped toward her. Her sultry voice would have made him hard as a rock—except he already was. *"Girls' softball?"* he repeated.

She took a step back and came up against the shelving unit. "You volunteered, remember? Now if you'll excuse me."

Already toe-to-toe, he put his hands on the shelf, bracketing her between his arms. He leaned in so that they were chest to chest, thigh to thigh...and everything in between. Her sweet little intake of air made him hard.

Or maybe that was just her. "Are you punishing me for what happened fourteen years ago?" he asked. "Or for kissing you yesterday?"

"Don't flatter yourself," she said, her hands coming up to fist his shirt, though it was unclear whether she planned to shove him away or hold him to her.

"Admit it," he said. "You gave me the girls to make me suffer."

"Maybe I gave you the girls because that's what's best for them. Not everything is about you, Mark."

Direct hit.

"So we used to know each other," she said. "So what. We're nothing to each other now." But her breathing was accelerated, and then there was the pulse fluttering wildly at the base of her throat. He set his thumb to it, his other fingers spanning her throat and although he was tempted to give it a squeeze, he tilted her head up to his.

Her hands tightened on him. "I mean it," she said. "We're not doing this."

"Define this."

"We're not going to be friends."

"Deal," he said.

"We're not going to even like each other."

"Obviously."

She stared into his eyes, hers turbulent and heated. "And no more kissing—"

He swallowed her words with his mouth, delving deeply, groaning at the taste of her. He heard her answering moan, and then her arms wound tight around his neck.

And for the first time since his arrival back in Santa Rey, they were on the same page.

4

RAINEY OPENED HER MOUTH to protest and Mark's tongue slid right in, so hot, so erotic, she moaned instead. God, the man could kiss. How was it that he looked as good as he did, was *that* sexy, and could kiss like heaven on earth? Talk about an unfair distribution of goods!

Just don't react, she told herself, but she might as well have tried to stop breathing, because this was Mark, big strong, badass *Mark.* The guy from her teenage fantasies. Her grown-up fantasies too, and resistance failed her.

Utterly.

So instead of resisting, she sank into him, and with a rough groan, he pressed her against the shelving unit, trapping her between the hard, cold steel at her back and the hard, hot body at her front. "Okay, wait," she gasped.

Pulling back the tiniest fraction, he looked at her from melting chocolate eyes.

"What are we doing?" she asked.

"Guess."

See, this was the problem with a guy like Mark.

There was a good reason that his players responded to him the way they did. He didn't make any excuses—about anything—and he knew how to get his way. Oh, how he knew, she thought as her hands slid into the silky dark hair at the nape of his neck. She pressed even closer, plastering herself to him, fighting the urge to wrap her legs around his waist as a low, very male sound rumbled in his throat. Her eyes drifted shut. *He isn't for you... He'll never be for you.*

"This doesn't mean anything," she panted, not letting go. So he wasn't for her. She would take what she could get from him. But only because here, with Mark, she felt alive, so damn alive. "You still drive me insane," she said.

He let out a groaning laugh, murmured something that might have been a "right back at you" and kissed her some more.

And God help her, she kissed him back until they had to break apart or suffocate.

"God, Rainey," he whispered hotly against her lips.

"I know—"

"Maybe you should throw your clipboard at me."

"Don't tempt me." She tightened her grip on his hair until he hissed out a breath, then it was her turn to do the same when he nipped at her throat, then worked his way up, along her jaw to her ear. She heard a low, desperate moan, and realized it was her own. She tried to keep the next one in but couldn't.

Nor could she make herself let go of him. Nope, she was going to instantly combust, and he hadn't even gotten into her pants. "I still don't like you," she gasped, sliding her hand beneath his shirt to run over his smooth, sleek back.

"I can work with that." Turning her, he pinned her flat against the storage room door, working his way back to her mouth. Their tongues tangled hotly as his hands yanked her shirt from her jeans and snaked beneath, his palms hot on her belly, heading north. When her knees wobbled, he pushed a muscled thigh between hers, holding her up.

"Wait," she managed to say.

His lips were trailing down the side of her face, along her jaw, dissolving her resolve as fast as she could build it up. "Wait...or stop?"

She had no idea.

He bit gently into her lower lip and tugged lightly, making her moan.

"Stop," she decided.

"Okay but you first."

She realized she was toying with the button of his jeans, the backs of her fingers brushing against the heat of his flat abs. *Crap!* Yanking her hands away, she drew a shaky breath. "Maybe we should go back to the not talking thing. That seems to work best for us."

He ran a finger down the side of her face, tucking a lock of hair behind her ear before pressing his mouth to her temple. "Good plan." His lips shifted down to her jaw. "No talking. We'll just—"

"Oh, no," she choked out with a gasping laugh and slid out from between him and the door. "No talking and no *anything* else either." Tugging the hem of her top down, she gave him one last pointed glare for emphasis and pulled open the door before she could change her mind. She rushed out and ran smack into James and Casey.

"Whoa there, killer," Casey said, steadying her.

"How are you on the ice? We could use you on the team." He looked at the man behind her. "Isn't that right, Coach?"

Rainey felt Mark's hand skim up her spine and settle on the nape of her neck. "Absolutely."

She shivered, then laughed to hide the reaction. "I'll have my people call your people," she quipped, then made her escape to the women's bathroom.

Lena came in while Rainey was still splashing cold water on her face, desperately trying to cool down her overheated, still humming body.

"This is all your fault," Rainey told her again. "Somehow."

"Really." Lena's gaze narrowed on Rainey's neck. "And how about the hickey on your neck. Whose fault is that?"

"Oh my God, I have a *hickey?*"

Lena was grinning wide. "Nah. I was just teasing."

"Dammit!"

"So does the coach kiss as good as he looks?"

"Yes," Rainey said miserably.

Lena laughed at her. "Maybe you found him."

"Found who?"

"You know. Him. Your keeper."

Rainey shook her head. "No way, not Mark. You know he's only got endgame in hockey, not women."

"But maybe…"

"No. No maybe." Rainey left, then stuck her head back in. "No," she said again, and shut the door on Lena's knowing laugh.

HOURS LATER, RAINEY left work and headed home. Halfway there, she made a pit stop at the string of trailers that ran behind the railroad tracks dividing town. Sharee and her mother lived in one of them, towards the back.

No one answered Rainey's knock. She was just about to leave when Mona, Sharee's mother, appeared on the walk, still in her cocktail waitress uniform.

When she saw Rainey, she slowed to a stop and sighed. "You again."

"Hi, Mona."

"What now? Did Sharee get in another fight while I was at work?"

"No," Rainey said. "She walked into a door."

Mona's lips tightened.

"The last time I came out here," Rainey said quietly. "You told me that you and Martin were separated."

"We're working on things." Mona's gaze shifted away. "Look, I'm a single mom with a kid and a crap job, okay? Martin helps—he *should* help. He's an okay guy, he's just stressed, and Sharee's mouthy."

By all accounts, Martin wasn't an okay guy. He was angry and aggressive, and he made Rainey as uncomfortable as hell. "I think he hits her, Mona. If I knew it for sure, I'd report it. And then you might lose her."

Mona paled. "No."

"You tell Martin that, okay? Tell him I'll report him if he doesn't keep his hands off her."

Mona hugged herself and shook her head vehemently, and Rainey sighed. The authorities had been called out here no less than five times. But Sharee wouldn't admit to the abuse, and worse, every time she and Mona were questioned, Martin only got more "stressed."

"There are places you can go," Rainey said softly. "Places you can take Sharee and be safe."

Mona's face tightened. "We're fine."

Rainey just looked at her for a long moment, but in the end there was nothing more she could do. "Will you allow Sharee to stay at my place on the nights you're working?"

Without answering, Mona went inside.

Rainey went home. She made cookies because that's what she did when *she* was stressed—she ate cookies. Then she showered for her date with Kyle. It would be fun, she decided. And she needed fun. She would keep an open mind and stop thinking about Mark. Who knows, maybe Kyle would be The One to finally make her forget Mark altogether.

She heard the knock at precisely six o'clock. She waited for a zing of nerves. It was a first date. There should be nerves. But she felt nothing. She opened her door and went still.

Mark.

Now nerves flooded her. "What are you doing here?"

"We left a few things unfinished," he said.

"We always leave things unfinished!"

A car pulled up the street. *Kyle.* Inexplicably frantic, Rainey shoved at Mark's chest. "You have to go."

He didn't budge. "Hmm."

Hmm? What the hell did that mean? She looked around, considering shoving him into the bushes, but he leaned into her. "Don't even think about it." With his hands on her hips, he pushed her inside her town house and shut the door.

"You can't be here," she muttered. "I have a date."

He let go of her to look out the small window alongside the front door, eyes focused on Kyle as he walked up the path. "I want to meet this guy."

"What? *No*."

The doorbell rang, and Mark turned his head to look at her, his eyes two pools of dark chocolate. "You still have shitty taste in men?"

"I— None of your business!"

The bell rang again, and in sheer panic, Rainey pushed Mark behind the door and out of sight, pointing at him to stay as she pasted a smile on her face and opened the door.

Kyle was medium height and build, with wind-tousled brown hair that curled over his collar and green eyes that had a light in them that suggested he might be thinking slightly NC-17 thoughts. Rainey stared at him in shock.

He smiled. "Surprised?"

Uh, yeah. He'd grown up and out, and had definitely lost the buck teeth. Plus he had a look of edge to him, a confidence, a blatant sexuality that shocked her. Kyle Foster had grown up to be a bad boy. "It's nice to see you," she said, surprised to find it true.

"Same goes." He looked her over. "You look good enough to eat."

From behind the door came a low growl.

Rainey didn't dare glance over, but she could feel the weight of Mark's stare. "Let me just grab my purse," she said quickly.

"What smells so good?" Kyle asked, trying to see past her and inside her place.

"I made chocolate chip cookies earlier."

"I love chocolate chip cookies," Kyle said.

Was it her imagination, or did Mark growl again?

Oh, God. "Burned them," she said quickly. Liar, liar, pants on fire. She had a glorious tray of cookies on her counter, to-die-for cookies, cookies that were better than an orgasm, but if she let him in, she'd be forced to introduce him to Mark. "Sorry. If you could just give me a sec." She shut the door on his face and winced. Then she glared at Mark.

"Let him in," he said. "You can introduce us." He said this in the tone the Big Bad Wolf had probably used on Little Red Riding Hood.

She pointed at him. "Shh!" She ran into the kitchen, grabbed her purse and strode past the six-foot-plus dark and annoyingly sexy man still standing in her entryway, throwing off enough attitude to light up a third world country.

"Your top's too tight," Mark said.

"No, it's not."

"Then your bra's too thin."

She stared down at herself. He was right—Nipple City. "Well, if you'd stop crowding me."

He smiled, dark and dangerous. He had no plans to stop crowding her. "And your jeans," he said.

"What's wrong with my jeans?"

"You have a stain on the ass."

She twisted around first one way, then the other, but saw nothing. "I can't see it."

"I can. Not exactly date pants, you know?"

"Fine! Don't move." She raced up the stairs and down the hallway to her bedroom, tore off the jeans, ripping through her dresser for another clean pair.

Nada.

Dammit! She yanked open her closet and settled on a short denim skirt, which meant she had to change shoes, which also meant she had to redo her hair. Running back down the stairs, she came to a skidding halt at the bottom.

The front door was opened but Kyle was nowhere to be seen, and neither was his car. Eyes narrowed, she followed a faint sound into her kitchen, where she found Mark leaning back against her counter, Zen-calm, every muscle relaxed…eating her cookies.

"NICE SKIRT YOU'RE almost wearing," Mark said, and swallowed the last of his cookie. He brushed his fingers off, ignoring the death glare coming at him from the doorway. Rainey had changed out of the sexy jeans and into an even sexier short denim skirt, revealing perfectly toned legs that he wanted to nibble. He wanted to start at her toes and work his way up, up, up past her knees, past her thighs… to the heaven between them.

Something she most definitely wasn't ready to hear. "You're good at cookies," he said. "What else can you cook?"

She crossed her arms, which plumped up her breasts, and he revisited his thought. He wanted to nibble her all over.

Every single inch.

"Where's my date, Mark?"

He popped another cookie. "Funny thing about that."

Her eyes darkened, and she leaned against the doorway, arms still crossed as if maybe she didn't trust herself to come any further into the kitchen. He didn't know if that was because she wanted to kill him, or kiss him again.

He thought it was probably a good bet that it was the former. When he reached for yet another cookie, she let out a sound of sheer temper and stalked across the room to snatch the plate away from him. "Those are mine."

Mark was aware that he was known for always being in control, for having a long fuse and rarely losing it, for being notoriously tight with his emotions. Rarely did he find himself in a situation where he wasn't perfectly at ease and didn't know exactly what he wanted the outcome to be.

But he was right now. He had no idea what the hell he was doing here.

None.

"Your date had to leave," he said. "Unexpectedly."

"Uh-huh. What did you do to him?"

In his world, people never questioned him. And it was a good place to be, his world. Apparently she hadn't gotten the memo. "Nothing."

Earlier, in the storage closet at the rec center, he'd stalked her, pressed her against the door. She did the same to him now, but this time her grip on his shirt wasn't passion. "Tell me, Mark."

The sound of his name on her tongue did something to him, something it shouldn't. "He waxes."

"What?"

"He waxes his body hair," he said.

She blinked. Paused. "And how did you get close enough to notice that?"

"I wasn't that close, I have excellent vision. He didn't have any hair on his arms."

"He's a swimmer. So he waxes, so what?"

Yeah, genius, so what? "He had a look in his eye. He was up to no good."

She gaped at him. "Tell me, was it like staring in a mirror?"

Well, maybe a little. But Mark had taken one look at the guy and seen a player. He'd asked the asshole what his plans were. Kyle had seemed amused by the question but had answered readily enough—candlelit dinner, dancing, capped off with a canyon drive to stargaze....

Bullshit the guy wanted to stargaze. No guy wanted to stargaze. Kyle wanted to get laid. In fact, Mark would bet his million-dollar bonus that the guy had a string of condoms at the ready. "I didn't like him."

"You didn't like him," Rainey repeated. "And I should care, *why?*"

"I'm an excellent judge of character."

She made a sound of disgust. "The last time you scared one of my dates off, I told you to never interfere in my life again."

He grabbed her as she went to pass by him. "The last time I scared off your date, it was because you were about six inches away from being raped."

She jerked as if he'd hit her, reminding him of one fact—they'd never talked about that night, about what had happened when he'd finally caught up with her.

Never.

And apparently they weren't going to do it now either, because she shoved at him hard and he let her go. She turned to her kitchen window, not moving, not speaking, just staring out at the backyard, her eyes clouded with bad memories.

Feeling lower than pond scum, he sighed. "Rainey—"

"Why are you here, Mark?"

"I..." He had no idea.

She turned to face him. "I agreed to go out with Kyle tonight because I'm looking for something. Someone.

Or at least I think I am. I'm...not lonely, that's not the right word. I love my life. But I want someone in it. It's been a while for me and I'm ready. I want to be in a relationship."

His gut hurt, and he had no idea why.

Her mouth curved, though the smile didn't meet her lips. "And I'm guessing by the panic on your face that a relationship is the last thing you're looking for."

He wasn't showing panic. He never showed panic.

"Fine," she said, rolling her eyes. "I made up the panic. God forbid you show an emotion."

"You think I don't have emotions?"

"I think you're miserly with them." She gave a faint smile. "But I do sense the slightest elevation in your blood pressure."

Now he rolled *his* eyes and she let out a low laugh. "Listen, I can't be like you, Mark, that's all. I'm not tough and cool as ice in any situation. That's not me. I want someone to care about me, someone who *wants* to be with me. Now I'm all dressed up with none of that in sight at the moment, so unless you want to be witness to something as messy as an uncontrolled emotion, you need to go."

"I would," he said quietly. "But—"

"But *what?*"

"I don't want to."

At that, she dropped her head between her shoulders and let out a sound that was either another laugh or something far too close to tears for his own comfort. "Mark, you *know* what broke up our friendship."

"Yes, you kicked me out of your life."

She sighed. "I didn't kick you out of my life. You left to go coach in Ontario, and I..."

"Stopped talking to me."

"It was temporary—I was mad," she said. "You remember why."

He let out a long breath. "Something about me being an interfering asshole."

"First, you rejected me. Then—"

"You were sixteen!"

"Then," she went on stubbornly. "You followed me on a date and beat the guy up."

"It wasn't a date. He picked you up after you ran out of my place. And in the ten minutes it took me to find you, he had you pinned in his backseat and was pulling off your clothes!"

Remembered humiliation flickered in her eyes. "Okay, so I acted stupid and immature, but I was hurting."

He blew out a breath and shoved his fingers in his hair. "It wasn't your fault. What he did to you wasn't your fault."

"What he was doing was consensual."

"You didn't know what you wanted."

"I wanted a friend and you turned into a Neanderthal."

He stared at her incredulously. "Well, what the hell did you want me to do, *let* him take you? You were a virgin!"

She flushed. "I wanted you to stop interfering as if I couldn't handle my own problems. I wanted you to listen to me. I wanted sympathy."

He must have given her a what-the-fuck look because she shook her head.

"I wanted a hug, Mark. I wanted you to hold my

hand and tell me I'd find someone else, someone better. I wanted understanding."

He just continued to stare at her, dumbstruck. Not a single one of those things had ever occurred to him.

The sound that escaped her told him she was just realizing that very fact. Brushing past him, she moved to the front door and held it open. A clear invite for him to get the hell out.

"Rainey—"

"I want to be alone."

Too damn bad. He slammed the door shut, hauled her up against him, closing his arms around her in a hug.

"It doesn't count now," she said stiffly, even as her body relaxed into his and she pressed her face into his shoulder. "Dammit, do you always smell good? That just really pisses me off."

"You know what pisses me off?" he asked. "That all I want to do is this." And then he pushed her up against the door and kissed her.

5

THE SECOND MARK LEANED into her, his hard body coming into contact with her own, Rainey knew she was in trouble. Her nipples immediately tightened into two beads against her soft top. But that was before his leg slid between hers, spreading her wide, his thigh rubbing against her core.

She wanted him.

She'd always wanted him.

Not yours, she told herself even as she clung to him. He's not yours and doesn't want to be. He's unattainable, unavailable... But he was clearly as aroused as she was, and that felt good. She turned him on, and being with him like this was the closest she'd get to what she might really want from him.

He shifted his thigh, rubbed it against her, and she let out a shockingly needy whimper. His lips grazed her earlobe, his breath hot along her skin, and a rush of heat shot through her. "Mark," she choked out as his fingers slid beneath her skirt to palm her bottom. It was all she could do not to wrap her legs around his waist and beg him to get inside her now, now, now, and she mindlessly thrust her hips against his. "Please," she gasped.

"Anything." He held her against the door, his mouth sliding down her throat and over her collarbone, tugging her shirt aside to make room for himself. "Whatever you want, Rainey. Just tell me, it's yours." His hand slid beneath her top and cupped her breast, his thumb rubbing over her nipple until she quivered. "Do you want me to touch you like this? Do you want my mouth on you? What?"

"Yes." To all of it.

He tugged her shirt and her bra aside and drew her nipple into his mouth, sucking until she cried out. Lifting his head, he blew a soft breath over her wet flesh and she shivered in anticipation.

"What else, Rainey. What else do you want?"

"Everything," she gasped. "I want everything."

"Here? Now?"

"Here. Now. *Right* now."

He yanked her skirt up to her waist and her panties down to her knees. In complete contrast, his hand slid slowly up her inner thigh, taking its sweet time so that she was mindlessly rocking her hips, anticipating the touch long before his finger traced her folds. "Mmm, wet," he murmured, his mouth moving along her shoulder back to her collarbone, which he grazed with his teeth.

"Mark." She fisted her hands in his hair and pulled his mouth to hers, her entire world anchored on his finger. When it slid inside her, she thunked her head back against the door and panted. Then his thumb brushed her in a slow circle.

She cried out against his lips, arching into him,

yanking his hair. She couldn't help it. She was going up in flames. He merely pressed her hard to the door, locking her in place. Continuing the torture, he added another finger. She came hard and fast, the power of it sweeping over her like a tidal wave. And because he kept stroking, the aftershocks didn't fade away, but had her shuddering over and over....

"Christ, Rainey." He sucked her lower lip into his mouth, tangled his tongue with hers. "You are so gorgeous when you come."

All she could think about was him filling her, stretching her, making her come again. Her eyes flickered open and their gazes met. "In me," she demanded. "Now, God, now."

His eyes dilated black, filled with a staggering hunger...for her. She nearly stopped breathing. Instead she moved her hips against his, reveling in the feel of his muscles rippling beneath her touch. He'd pulled a condom from somewhere.

Thank God one of them could think.

After that, it was a blur of frenzied movements. She ripped his shirt off, he unzipped, and together they freed the essentials.

And oh God, the essentials...

It wasn't enough for him. "Everything off," he said, then lent his hands to the cause until she stood naked against the door. His gaze swept over her, hot and approving, as he lifted her up. "Wrap your legs around me— There. God, yeah, like that—" His voice was a low command, caressing her as much as his hands. "Hold on to me." Then his mouth crushed her own as he pushed her back against the door.

She threaded her hands into his hair as he thrust

deep inside of her. He made a rough sound of sheer male pleasure, his fingers digging into her soft flesh as she rocked into him. Again he thrust, slowly at first, teasing until she was begging. It was glorious torment, hot and demanding, just like the man kissing her.

They moved together, her breasts brushing his chest, tightening her nipples. She could feel his muscles bunching and flexing with each thrust, sending shock waves of pleasure straight to her core. When she came again, it was with his name on her lips as she pulsed hard around him, over and over again, taking him with her.

Still holding her, still buried deep inside, Mark sank to his knees. He looked as stunned as she felt and something deep inside her constricted. She pulled free. He grimaced but let her go without a word.

She pulled on her panties and his shirt, then leaned back against the door, knees still weak.

Mark got to his feet and handled the necessities of condom disposal and readjustment of clothing.

She had a hard time looking away from him. His pants were riding low on his hips, and he looked dangerous and primed for another round. *No,* she told herself firmly. *You may not have him again.* Not without a discussion about what this was, and what this wasn't, so that she didn't get hurt. *Her* terms, or no terms.

"I think we need some ground rules, Mark."

No shit, Mark thought, still dazed.

"Rule number one. This—" She waggled her finger back and forth between them. "Happens only when and if I instigate it. If you do it, I might mistake it for something deeper and more emotional than it is. It'll mess with my head, Mark."

His gut hurt again. The last thing he ever wanted was to hurt her.

"Look," she said, more softly. "I get that we're stuck working together for the next month. We're grown-ups, we'll handle it. Right?"

He'd never in his life done less than handle anything that came his way. And he'd also never lost his ability to speak either, but he was having trouble now, so he nodded.

"Good," she said, looking relieved that he'd agreed to her terms. *Damn, Rainey, don't give me yourself on a silver platter and ask for nothing in return....*

"You should go now," she said.

She was making things easy, giving him the exit strategy. He should be ecstatic. Instead, he stepped toward her to... Hell, he didn't know. Hold her? Yeah, he wanted to hold her until the world stopped spinning.

But she gave a sharp jerk of her head and backed away.

Right. The rules. She was in charge of physical contact. Pretending that his legs weren't still wobbling, he did as she wanted and walked out.

He'd walked away plenty of times before. It should have been a no-brainer. Hell, he should have been *running,* far and fast, with relief filling his veins. Except it wasn't easy, and he felt no relief at all.

Plus, it was damn cold outside and she was still wearing his shirt.

THE NEXT DAY AT LUNCH, Rainey and Lena sat in the small café across the street from the rec center, each inhaling a triple scoop ice cream sundae. Officially, it was a meeting about the upcoming charity auction. Unofficially, it was a discussion on their favorite topic. Men.

Specifically Mark.

"I'm surprised you didn't make me share a sundae with you," Lena said around a huge bite. "Usually you only allow yourself a single scoop."

"It's an entire sundae sort of day." Rainey ate one of the two cherries from the top. "It's got cherries on it so it's practically a fruit salad."

Lena grinned. "You know what I don't get? Why you aren't singing the 'Hallelujah Chorus.' I mean, you got lucky last night. Damn lucky by the looks of you."

Yeah, she had. It'd been everything she thought it would be, too.

And more. "I can't believe I slept with him. He chased off my date and I *still* got naked with him."

"Look, you can't blame yourself. The guy's got serious charisma. He's a walking fantasy. And you were past due." Lena paused. "Rick says you two have been past due for fourteen years."

"Rick? You talked to Rick about us?"

"Everyone's talking about you two."

"Why?"

"I don't know, Rainey, maybe because yesterday afternoon after the staff meeting you pulled Mark into the storage closet in the main hallway. And then today you come into work with that glow."

Rainey ate the other cherry and slumped in her seat.

Lena grinned. "This is going to be fun."

"No. Not fun. He's not my type."

"Right. Because he's not a fixer-upper," Lena said.

"You like the fixer-uppers so you can eventually let go of them for not being The One."

"Are you saying that Mark is perfect as is?"

"Mark is *oh-boy-howdy perfect*," Lena said.

"No, he's not. He's bossy and domineering, and *way* too alpha."

"Mmm-hmm," Lena said dreamily. "I bet he likes to be in charge. Especially in bed, right?"

Rainey felt her cheeks go hot. *They hadn't made it to a bed...*. "You're as impossible as he is."

Lena laughed and scooped up a big bite of ice cream, moaning in pleasure. "Some things just need to be appreciated for what they are, even the imperfect things. Like men. Hell, Rain. You accept the kids at the center every single day, just as is. Why not a man?"

Rainey stopped in the act of stuffing her face with a huge spoonful of ice cream and stared at Lena. Most of the time Lena's comments were sarcastic, but once in a while she said something so perfect it was shocking. "How did you get so wise?"

"Practice," Lena said. "And lots of kissing frogs before I found my prince. And you know what else? I think you found yours."

"I'm not going for Mark, Lena." It was a terrible idea. Terribly appealing...

She'd once read an article about him that said his talent in coaching came from the fact that he didn't so much inspire awe as he discouraged comfort.

She knew that to be true. Her comfort level was definitely at risk when he was around.

THAT AFTERNOON AFTER working on the construction site, Mark gathered his team on the bleachers and looked them over. Twelve teenage girls, with more attitude than his million-dollar players combined.

Casey and James had their team on the far field. Boys. Boys who could really play, by the looks of them. How the hell his in-the-doghouse players had ended up with the easier task was beyond him.

Okay, he knew what had happened.

Rainey had happened.

And he knew no matter what the girls dished out, last night had been worth every minute.

His team wore a variety of outfits from short shorts that were better suited to pole dancing to basketball shorts so big they couldn't possibly stay up while the girls were running bases. Shirts ranged from oversized T-shirts that hung past the shorts to teeny tiny tank tops or snug tees. "First up," he said. "Everyone back to the locker room to change into appropriate gear."

No one moved.

"Ladies, I just gave you a direct order. Not obeying a direct order will get you personally acquainted with push-ups."

"We're already dressed out," one of them said, and when he gave her a long look, she added, "Coach, sir."

"Just Coach," he said, and went to the large duffle bag he'd brought with him. It was the warm-up T-shirts, shorts, and practice jerseys he'd had over-nighted. He had new equipment as well; bats, batting helmets, gloves… He handed the clothing out, then waited for them to run back to the building. Instead, they all stripped and dressed right there. "Jesus," he muttered, slamming his eyes shut. "Some warning!"

"Hey, we're covered," Sharee called out. "We're all in sports bras and spandex."

"From now on," he grated out, "you change inside. Always."

"Prude," someone muttered, probably Sharee.

Prude his ass, but swallowing the irony, he risked a peek and found them all suitably dressed. "Ground rules," he said. Now he sounded as anal as Rainey. "No ripping or cutting the sleeves off, no tying the shirts up high, no bras showing, and all shirts need to be neatly tucked in. And no sagging. There will be no asses on my field."

"We're not allowed to say asses." The timid voice belonged to the same girl who called him sir. "We're not supposed to swear."

Mark slid her a look. "Pepper, right?"

She gulped. "Yes."

"Well, Pepper. No swearing is a good rule. Tuck your shirts in."

More grumbling, but there was a flurry of movement as they obeyed. So far so good. "I want to see how you hit," Mark said. "Later, I'll get someone out here to videotape you so we can analyze your swing. We'll get stats both on you and also on the teams we're going to be playing so we can strategize, not just for your season but for the big fundraising game between us and Santa Barbara."

They were all just staring at him, mouths agape. Pepper raised her hand.

"Yes, Pepper."

"We don't have a video camera. Or stats."

"You have them now," Mark said.

"We're going to play Santa Barbara?" someone asked.

"We're going to *beat* Santa Barbara," he said. "The

boys' teams too." He pulled a clipboard from his duffle bag. "Come on, move your asses—" *Shit.* "Butts. Move your butts in close so you can see."

"You need a swear jar," one of the girls said to him. "By the end of the season, you could probably take us all out to dinner."

There were some giggles at this, and he looked at the amused faces. "How about this," he said. "I'll put a buck into a swear jar every time I swear, and you ladies have to put in a quarter every time you don't give me your all. Deal?"

"Deal," they said.

Mark spent the next twenty minutes outlining what he wanted to see, and then lined them up for drills. He started with them quick-catching the pop flies he sent out. Or theoretically quick-catching, because he didn't have much "quick" on his team. Three of the twelve could catch. Well, four if you counted Pepper, who tended to catch the balls with her shins, which made him doubly glad he'd brought shin guards. He had five or six who could hit, and a bunch more who tended to keep their eyes closed.

And then there was Sharee, who'd already dropped and given him push-ups for being rude and obnoxious to her teammates.

Twice.

He put them out in the field for field practice next. "Wait for your pitch," he told the first girl up. "Take two, then hit to the right."

"Huh?"

"Sharee's pitching, right?" he asked.

"Yeah. So?"

"So she gives it her best from the beginning, but she's only got two good ones in her."

"Hey," Sharee said from the mound. "I can hear you."

"Good. Learn from it." Mark turned back to the batter. "Take the third pitch and hit to the right."

"Why the right?"

He gestured to their first baseman and right fielder, both engaged in a discussion on what their plans were for the night. "They're not even looking at you. If you get any ball at all, you'll get all the way to second."

Which was exactly what happened.

Sharee threw down her glove in disgust.

"There's no temper tantrums in the big leagues," Mark told her. Which was a lie. There were plenty of tantrums in the big leagues, all of them, and you only had to watch ESPN to see them. "Here's a strategy for you, too. Watch the signs from your catcher instead of winging it. She'll be getting a signal from me on which pitch to throw. If you listen," he added as she opened her mouth to object, "you'll be a great pitcher. I can promise you that."

"And if I don't listen?"

"Then I'll bench you and put in Pepper."

Pepper squeaked, and he smiled at her. "You have an arm and you know it. You start practicing more, and you'll be ready to pitch at the game this weekend."

"*I'm* pitching at the game," Sharee said.

"Maybe. If you listen."

"Hmph."

At the end of practice, Mark gathered the girls in and looked them over. Bedraggled and hot and sweaty. "Decent effort," he said. "I'll see you tomorrow."

They all made their way toward the building. He turned to gather his gear and found Rainey sitting on the bleachers, watching him.

6

MARK HADN'T SEEN HER since the night before when he'd left her looking dewy and sated and pissed off at the both of them.

Today she was wearing a sweat suit, beat-up sneakers, and a ball cap.

The Ducks again.

Shaking his head, he walked over to the bleachers and sat. Stretching out his legs, he leaned back on the bench behind him and stared up at the sky.

"Long day?" she asked dryly.

"Hmm."

He slid her an assessing look. She was laughing at him, which should have ticked him off, but for one thing, he was too tired. And for another, she looked pretty when she was amused, even if it was at his expense.

"Should I drop and give you twenty?" she asked in a smart-ass tone.

Rainey humor. But he'd rather she drop and give him something else entirely. No doubt that, along with everything else he was thinking about doing to her, wasn't on the agenda for the day.

A tall blond guy wearing a suit poked his head out of the building and waved at Rainey. She smiled and got up, walking over to meet him halfway, where he handed her what looked like a stack of tickets. Rainey gave him a quick hug, which was returned with enthusiasm and an expression that Mark recognized all too well.

The guy wanted a lot more than the hug.

"Keep the top one for yourself," Mark heard him tell her. "That's the seat right next to mine."

A date. She had another damn date. His eye twitched. Probably due to the new brain bleed.

Rainey came back to the bleachers. "Lena's neighbor," she said. "Jacob works at the district office and brought tickets to the ballet tonight at the San Luis Obispo Theater for everyone here who wants to go."

He held out his hand.

She stared at him. "*You* want to go to the ballet."

Okay, true, he'd rather be dragged naked through town, but hell if he'd admit it. "Yes." And if he had to go, so did James and Casey. "I'll take three, unless this is a *private* date."

She slapped three tickets into his palm, and it did not escape his notice that she took them from the bottom of the pile. "It's not a date date," she said defensively. "And he's a nice guy. A non-fixer-upper, you know?"

No. He had no idea.

"And I told you," she said. "I'm looking for someone. Someone who wants me as is."

Hell, she killed him, he thought as she averted her face and let out a long, almost defeated breath. *Not friends,* he reminded himself, even as something in his chest rolled over. "You're perfect as is, Rainey."

"Says the man who dates big-boobed blonde women from stupid reality shows."

He laughed. "That was a photo op, that's all."

"Every time?"

"Well, maybe not every time." He reached into her sweatshirt pocket and pulled out her phone, absolutely taking note that doing so caused her to suck in a breath when his fingers brushed her skin.

"What are you doing?" she asked.

"Programming myself in as your number one speed dial. In case you need another date rescue."

"I didn't need last night's rescue."

"You going to try to tell me last night didn't work out for you?"

Their gazes met, and she inhaled deeply. "Why are you doing this?"

No clue.

She looked at him for a long moment. "Are you jealous?"

Fuck, no.

Okay, yes. Yes, he was. "How can I be jealous of someone that's not a 'date date' to a *ballet?*"

She crossed her arms. "Okay, I'm sure I'm going to regret asking, but what's *your* idea of a good date?"

"Depends on the woman. With you it'd be a repeat of last night."

Color bloomed on her cheeks. "We're not going to discuss last night. Make that rule number two."

"Ah, yes. The rules of Rainey Saunders." He shook his head. "And people think *I'm* a control freak."

"Because you are."

"Hello, Mrs. Pot."

She made a sound of exasperation, and still seated, she leaned forward, stretching her fingers to her toes. Her sweatshirt rose up a little in the back, revealing a strip of smooth, creamy skin and a hint of twin dimples just above her ass, and the vague outline of a thong.

He didn't know which he wanted more, to trace that outline with his tongue or dip into the dimples. Before he could decide, she straightened, rolled her neck, and winced. "I have a kink."

"Yeah? Tell me all about it, slowly and in great detail."

She snorted. "Pervert."

Smiling, he slid over, behind her now, and put his hands on her shoulders. "You've got a rock quarry in here." He dug his fingers in, rubbing at her knots.

"I'm fine." But her head dropped forward, giving him better access. When he found a huge tension knot with his thumbs and began to work it out, she let out a soft moan that went straight through him. "Rainey."

"What?"

He pressed his face into her hair. *Go out with me instead of what's-his-name.* Before he could bare his pathetic soul, Rick came outside and saved him.

"She's home," Rick called out to Rainey. "I'm sending you over there with our famous backup." He waved Casey and James over. The guys had come from the gym, where they'd had their teams at the weights.

"Field trip," Rick said. "Rainey's in charge." He sent a grin in Mark's direction. "Need me to repeat?"

Mark flipped him off, and Rick's grin widened.

"Where are we going?" Casey asked.

"You'll see," Rick said.

Mark hated that answer.

"Shotgun." James leapt into the front seat of Rainey's car.

Casey got into the back.

Mark walked up to the passenger front door and gave James one long look.

James sighed, got out and slid into the back.

Rainey looked over her sunglasses at Mark. "Seriously?"

"No," he said, putting on his seat belt. "If I was serious, I'd have made you let me drive."

RAINEY'S CAR WAS FULL of more good-looking, great-smelling men than she had dollars in her wallet. Lena would be having an orgasm at just the thought. James and Casey were talking, keeping up a running dialogue about their day. But as she headed into the heart of the burned-out neighborhood, their chatter faded away.

From the shotgun position, Mark didn't say a word. He seemed to be in some sort of zone, with his game face on to boot. She wished she had a zone.

Or a game face.

Turning his head from where he'd been looking out the window, he met her gaze.

God, he had a set of eyes. Richly dark and deep, she got caught staring, and forced herself to look away before she drowned in him.

He slid on his cool sunglasses. She did the same. Good. With two layers between them now, she felt marginally better. "I don't know if any of you have seen the extent of the destruction," she said. "But it covers nearly 100,000 acres."

"I've been through it," Mark said. "My dad's new house isn't far from here."

Rainey glanced over at him again. "Your dad lost his house?"

"Yes. It's just been rebuilt."

"That was fast."

Mark nodded, and she understood that he'd expedited the building process. He'd pulled strings, spent his own money, done whatever he'd had to do to get his dad back into a place, and the knowledge had something quivering low in her belly.

And other parts, too, the parts that he'd had screaming for him last night. *Don't go there,* she told herself. *There's no need to go there.* Not with a man who was only here for one month at the most, a known player, and…and possessing the absolute power to embed himself deep inside her, and not just physically. He didn't want her hurt by a guy? Well the joke was on him because there was no one who could hurt her more.

When they got to the heart of the worst of the fire devastation, it was painful to see the blackened dead growth and destroyed homes where once the hills had been so green and alive.

"Damn," James said. "Damn."

"Besides doing the sports," Rainey said quietly, "I run the rec center's charity projects. We've been raising money all year to fund one of the rebuilds, the one you guys have been working on. There was a lotto drawing from the victims, and one lucky family won the place free and clear. We're going to go notify the winner."

"Mark has contacts you wouldn't believe," James said. "He can snap his fingers and make people drop money out their ass. You should have seen how much money he raised for the Mammoths' charities over our last break. Maybe he could get another house funded for you."

Rainey glanced at Mark, surprised to find him looking a little bit uncomfortable, though he met her gaze and held it. "You good at raising money?" she asked. He was good at raising holy hell, or at least he had been. Probably Mark was good at raising whatever he wanted.

Casey grinned. "Yeah, he's good. He rented out our favorite club and he had a mud wrestling pit set up right in the center of the place, then invited a bunch of supermodels."

Rainey could imagine all the wild debauchery that must have gone on in that mud pit, each player getting a model for the night.

Or two...

Just thinking about it made her eye twitch, and she carefully put a finger to the lid to hold it still. "Interesting."

"Yeah, he raked in some big bucks that night," Casey said. "Our charities were real happy."

"Does all your fundraising involve mud pits and centerfolds?"

"Models," James corrected. "Though centerfolds would have been great too. Hey, Coach, you've got a bunch of centerfolds on auto-dial, right? Maybe—"

He trailed off when Casey drew an imaginary line across his throat for the universal "shut it." "Ix-nay on the enterfolds-say." Casey jerked his head in Mark's direction. "He's trying to impress."

"No worries," Rainey said dryly. "I've already got my impression. It's burned in my brain." She pulled into a trailer park and drove down a narrow street to the end, where she parked in front of a very old, run-down trailer.

"Wow, that's the smallest trailer I've ever seen," Casey said. "Someone lives here?"

"Six someones," Rainey said. "We're here to tell them the good news, that they'll have a place by late summer." She smiled. "They're big hockey fans. Plus," she said, turning to Mark, "you've been coaching their daughter, Pepper."

The guys unfolded themselves out of her car and she looked them over, realizing that they were dripping with their usual air of privilege. "Do any of you ever look like anything less than a couple of million bucks?" she asked Mark.

James snickered, then choked on it when Mark glared at him. "I'm wearing sweats," he said calmly. "Same as you."

"Yes, but mine aren't flashy," she said. "Yours are from your corporate sponsor."

"Rainey, we're both wearing Nike."

"Yes, but yours probably cost more than I made last month."

James grinned. "Actually, you can't even buy what he's wearing. They made it just for him."

Mark let out a breath. "Should I strip?"

"No!" But as they walked through the muddy yard the size of a postage stamp to a tiny metal trailer that had seen better days in the last century, she slid him a look. "What if I'd said yes?" she whispered. "What would you have done?"

"You *didn't* say yes."

"But—"

Mark stopped and stepped into her personal space

bubble, bumping up against her as he put his mouth to her ear. "The next time we're alone," he said softly, "if you still want me to strip, all you have to do is…instigate. Or, as you so hotly did last night, demand. Careful, you're going to step on those geraniums."

She stared down at the flowers in the small pot near her feet, the only thing growing in the yard. They were beautiful, and at any other time it might have amused her that Mark Diego had known the name of the flower when she hadn't, but she was stuck on the stripping thing. She'd ask him to strip never.

Or later…

And great, now her nipples were hard. She slid him a gaze and found him watching her.

Eyes hot. Ignoring him, she moved to the door. "This trailer's just a loaner. They lost everything and have been borrowing this place from friends."

Karen Scott opened the door. She was in her mid-thirties but appeared older thanks to the pinched, worried look on her face, one that no doubt came from losing everything and having no control over an uncertain future.

"Karen," Rainey said gently. "I have a surprise for you—"

Karen took one look at Casey and James, and slapped a hand over her mouth. "Oh my God! *Oh my God!* You're—" She pointed at James. "And you! You're—"

James offered his hand. "James Vasquez."

"I know!" She bypassed his hand and threw herself at him, giving him a bear hug made all the more amusing because she was about a quarter of James's size.

Casey was treated to the next hug. "This is unbelievable! We'd heard you were in town and Pepper's told us about you, Mr. Diego, but I never in a million years thought you'd be visiting us. The kids and John are all still at work—they're not going to believe this!" She moved back, revealing the interior of the trailer, which was maybe 125 square feet total, a hovel that had been put together in the seventies, and not well. Formica and steel and rusted parts, scrubbed to a desperate cleanliness.

Karen insisted they sit and let her serve them iced tea. Mark, James and Casey sat on the small built-in, fold-out couch, their big, muscled bodies squished into each other. Rainey watched James and Casey look around with horror as they realized that *six* people lived here. Mark didn't look surprised or horrified, but there was an empathy and a new gentleness she'd never seen from him before as he watched Karen bustle around the tiny three-by-three kitchenette. She was in perpetual motion, excited about the lovely surprise visit, and finally Rainey made her sit.

"Karen," she said. "The guys aren't the surprise. At least not the main one. You remember the housing project. Your name was drawn in the lottery for a new home."

Karen went utterly still. "What?"

"You and your family should be able to move in by the end of summer."

Karen gaped at her for a solid ten seconds, before letting out an ear-splitting whoop and throwing herself at Rainey.

They both hit the floor, laughing like loons.

Later, when Karen's family came home, there were more hugs and even tears. The guys spent some time

Time Out

autographing everything the kids had and then Casey stripped off his hat and sweatshirt and gave them to an ecstatic Pepper, which prompted James to do the same for her brother.

The kids' sheer joy choked Rainey up. They'd had everything taken from them, everything, and yet they were so resilient. She turned away to give herself a minute, then found her gaze caught and held by Mark's. She had no idea how it was that he managed to catch her at her weakest every single time, but he did.

He didn't smirk, didn't even smile. Instead his eyes were steady and warm and somehow...somehow they made her feel the same.

MARK WAITED UNTIL CASEY and James had gotten into the back of Rainey's car before he took her hand and turned her to face him. "You're amazing," he said softly.

"I didn't do this."

"You do plenty. For everyone." He paused. "What do you do for yourself?"

"Tonight I'm going to the ballet."

Shit. He'd nearly forgotten about her date that wasn't a *date* date.

After refusing to let him drive, Rainey dropped him and the guys off at the rec center and promptly vanished. Mark took James and Casey back to the motel, and for the first time since they'd arrived, neither had a word of complaint about where they were staying. Compared with Pepper and her family's trailer, they had a palace, and James and Casey seemed very aware of it. The three of them ordered Thai takeout, and afterwards, Casey and James wanted to go out.

"Is there a club around here?" James asked. "We need some fun, man."

"I've got just the thing," Mark said, and drove them to the town's community theater.

James eyed the marquee and groaned. "No. No way. The last time a chick dragged me to the ballet, I fell asleep and she wouldn't put out after because she said I was snoring louder than the music. I'm not going in there and you can't make me."

"Consider it cultural education," Mark said, and gave him a shove towards the entry.

"This is about *him* getting laid," James whispered to Casey. "And how is *that* fair?"

"Dude, life's never fair."

AT THE BALLET, RAINEY sat with Jacob on one side, Lena on the other, surrounded by coworkers and friends. As the lights went down and the music began and the dancers took the stage, she could feel the tension within her slowly loosening its grip.

Mark wasn't going to show. Good, she thought. A huge relief hit her.

And the oddest, tiniest, most ridiculous bit of disappointment...

The lights dimmed even further, and Jacob slid his arm over the back of her chair, like he was stretching. But then his fingers settled on her shoulder. She waited for a zing, a thrill. But nothing happened. *Relax,* she ordered herself. He was cute. Nice. *Normal.*

His face nuzzled in her hair as he pulled her a little closer, but though she wished with all her might, she felt no zing, and definitely no thrill. When Mark so much as looked at her, her nipples hardened.

"You smell fantastic," Jacob said, and his hand nearly brushed the outside of her breast.

Her nipples didn't care.

Straightening, she pulled away with regret. "I'm sorry, can you excuse me a minute? I need to..." She waved vaguely to the exit and rose, stepping over Lena. On the other side of Lena was Rick, and on the other side of Rick sat...

Mark.

Oh, God. When had he showed up? She managed to get past the man without making eye contact, then found her way to the lobby to gulp in some air. A smattering of people were walking around looking glazed. She wondered if they were having a panic attack as well. Bypassing the bathrooms, she beelined straight for the bar. "Wine," she told the bartender, and slapped her credit card down. "Whatever you have." It didn't matter. She rarely drank wine because it tended to relax her right into a coma but she could use a coma about now. What was wrong with her that she'd been in the presence of two perfectly good guys in two days, and neither had produced a zing?

And just knowing that Mark was in the building had her so full of zing, her hair was practically smoking. The wine came and she gulped it down. "Another, please."

MARK CAME UP BEHIND Rainey. He looked at the two empty wine glasses in front of her and read a new relaxation in her body language—which was quite different from the body language she'd sported when she'd run out here—and smiled. "Better?" he asked.

Her shoulders stiffened, but she didn't look at him. "Go away."

"Can't."

"Why not?" She waved at the bartender, but he didn't see her, so she sighed. She had her hair up tonight, but a few golden-brown tendrils had escaped, brushing the nape of her neck.

She was heart-stoppingly beautiful to him, and just looking at her made him ache. He ran his finger down that nape and was rewarded by her full body shiver. Encouraged, he put his mouth to the spot just beneath her ear, smiling when she shivered again and sucked in a breath. "How's that not-a-date date with your non-fixer-upper going?" he asked.

"I think it's me." Looking morose, she propped her head on her hand. "I'm the fixer-upper."

Hating that she felt that way about herself, Mark swiveled her bar stool to face him. Her mascara was slightly smudged around her eyes, making them seem even more blue. She'd nibbled off her pretty gloss. She was wearing a little black dress, one strap slipping off her shoulder. Running a finger up her arm, he slid the strap back into place and left his hand on her. "I think you're perfect," he said softly. Beautiful, and achingly vulnerable, and…perfect.

She went still, then sighed and dropped her head to his chest, hard. "Now who's the liar?" she whispered.

With a low laugh, he tipped her head up and stared into her glossy eyes. She was half baked. "I mean it," he told her. "You don't need to change a goddamn thing."

Her gaze dropped from his eyes to his mouth, and her tongue darted out to lick her dry lips. The motion went straight through him like fire, heading south. She stood up, her hands on his chest now, but he didn't flatter himself. She needed him for balance. Her high heels, black with a little bow around the ankles that he found sexy as hell, brought her mouth a lot closer to his. Her fingers dug in a little, fisting on the jacket of his suit.

He placed a hand on the small of her back, holding her to him, right there where he liked her best, when she murmured his name and sighed. "I'm going to instigate now."

His heart kicked. "Instigate away."

Just as their lips touched, a low, disbelieving male voice spoke behind them. *"Rainey?"*

They turned in unison to face Jacob, who was holding Rainey's shawl in his hands. Mouth grim, eyes hooded, he handed her the shawl, gave Mark an eat-shit-and-die look, and walked out of the theater.

7

THE BARTENDER BROUGHT Rainey a third glass of wine. She looked at it longingly but pushed it away. "All I want to know," she said to Mark, "is why. Why are you so hell-bent on sabotaging my dating life?"

Mark couldn't explain it to her. Hell, he couldn't explain it to himself. But apparently it was a rhetorical question because she began a conversation with her wineglass, something about men, stupidity, and the need for a vacation in the South Pacific. While she rambled on, Mark texted James.

Lobby. Now.

Mark then stole Rainey's keys from her purse, and when he saw James appear, he shifted out of earshot of Rainey. "When the ballet's over, take Rainey's car back to the motel."

"Do we have to wait until it's over?"

Mark handed him Rainey's keys. "Yes. I'll retrieve her car for her later."

James looked past Mark to see Rainey sitting at the bar. "What's the matter? Is she sick?"

"Indisposed."

James knew better than to try to get information from Mark when Mark didn't want to give it, but it didn't stop a sly smile from touching his lips. "I take it you're not going to be indisposed too."

Mark just looked at James, who sighed and left.

Mark turned back to Rainey, still seated at the bar, still talking to herself.

Nope, not to herself.

There was a guy seated beside her now, smiling a little too hard. "Hey, gorgeous," he said, leaning in so that his shoulder touched Rainey's bare one, making Mark grind his teeth. "How about I buy you another drink?" the slimeball asked.

"No, thank you," Rainey said. "I'm with someone."

"I don't see him."

"Right here." Mark stepped in between them, sliding an arm along Rainey's shoulders. "Let's go."

She stared up at him. "Not with you, you... you date wrecker."

The situation didn't get any better when he felt a tap on his shoulder. He turned and came face to face with Slimeball, who said, "I think the lady is making herself pretty clear."

"This doesn't involve you," Mark told him.

"She was just about to agree to come home with me."

"No she wasn't," Rainey said, shaking her head. At the movement, she put her fingers on her temples, as if she'd made herself dizzy. "Whoa."

Slimeball opened his mouth, but Mark gave a single shake of his head.

The guy was a couple of inches shorter than Mark and at least twenty pounds heavier. He was bulky muscle, the kind that would be slow in a fight, but Mark was pretty sure it wouldn't come to that. He waited, loose-limbed and ready...and sure enough, after a moment, the guy backed away.

"I'm taking you home, Rainey," Mark said. "Now."

"I've never been spoils of war before."

Shaking his head, Mark slipped an arm around her waist and guided her outside. The night was a cool one, and as they stepped into it, Rainey shivered in spite of her shawl. Shrugging out of his jacket, Mark wrapped it around her shoulders. "Pretty dress," he said.

"Don't."

"Don't tell you how beautiful you look?"

"I'm trying to stay mad at you." She wobbled, and he pulled her in tighter, breathing in her soft scent, which was some intoxicating combination of coconut and Rainey herself.

But she backed away. "Don't use those hands on me," she said, pointing at him. "Because they're magic hands." She pressed her own palms to her chest as if it ached. "They make me melt, and I refuse to melt over you, Mark Diego."

"Because...?"

"Because..." She pointed at him again. "Because you are very very very verrrrrrryyyyyy bad for me."

He didn't have much to say to that. It happened to be a true statement. Even if he wanted to give her what she was looking for, how could he? The hockey season took up most of his year, during which time he traveled nonstop and was entrenched in the day-to-day running of an NHL team. If he wasn't at a game, he was think-

ing about the next one, or the last one, or he was dealing with his players, or planning game strategies, or
meeting with the owners or the other coaches… It was
endless. Endless and—

And it was bullshit.

The truth was he could make the time. If he wanted.
If a woman wanted…

Granted, a woman would have to want him pretty
damn bad to put up with the admittedly crazy schedule,
but others managed it. People all around him managed
it.

And Jesus, was he really thinking this? Maybe *he'd*
had the wine instead of Rainey. But ever since he'd
left Santa Rey all those years ago, he'd felt like he was
missing a part of himself.

Someone had once asked him if the NHL had disillusioned him at all, and he'd said no. He'd meant it. He
hadn't been disillusioned by fame and fortune in the
slightest. But he did have to admit, having a place to
step back from that world, a place where he was just a
regular guy, was nice. Real nice.

And wouldn't his dad love hearing that.

"You should have left me alone tonight," Rainey
said, standing there in the parking lot.

Looking down in her flushed face, he slowly nodded.
"I should have."

From the depths of her purse, her cell phone vibrated. It took her a minute to find it and then she
squinted at the readout. "Crap. It's my mom. Shh, don't
tell her I'm drunk."

He laughed softly as she stood there in the parking
lot and opened the phone.

"Hey, Mom, sorry I missed your call earlier, I was on

a date date. Or a not-so-date-date." She sighed. "Never mind." She paused. "No, I have no idea what I was thinking going out with a guy who has tickets to the ballet. You're right. And no, I'm not alone. I'm with Mark Diego— No, he's not still cute. He's…" Rainey looked Mark over from head to toe and back again, and her eyes darkened. "Never mind that either! What? No, I'm not going to bring him to dinner this week! Why? Because…because he's busy. Very busy."

Mark leaned in close. "Hi, Mrs. Saunders."

Rainey covered the phone with her hand and glared up at him. *"What are you doing?"*

He had no idea. "Does she still make that amazing lasagna—"

"Yes, not that you're going to taste it. Now *shh!* No, not you, Mom." She put her hand over Mark's face, pushing him away. "Uh oh, Mom, bad connection." She faked the sound of static. "Love you. Bye!"

Mark remembered Rainey's parents fondly. Her father was a trucker and traveled a lot. Her mother taught English at the high school. She was sweet and fun, and there was no doubt where Rainey had gotten her spirit from. "Your mom likes me."

"Yeah, but she likes everyone." She walked through the parking lot, then stopped short so unexpectedly he nearly plowed into the back of her. "I can't remember where I parked." Her phone rang again. "Oh for god's sake, Mom," she muttered, then frowned at the read-out. "Okay, not my mom. Hello?" Her body suddenly tensed, and she peered into the dark night. "Who is this?"

Mark shifted in closer, a hand at the small of her back as he eyed the lot around them.

"No," she said. "I didn't say that. And I certainly didn't threaten you then, but I am now. Keep your hands off Sharee, Martin, and don't ever call me again." She shoved the phone back into her purse.

"Who was that?"

"Sharee's father. Says I'm interfering where my interfering ass doesn't belong. I'm to shut up and be quiet—which I believe is a double negative." She looked around them and shivered. "And I still can't remember where I parked, dammit."

"Over here." He led her to his truck and got her into the passenger seat, leaning down to buckle her seat belt before locking her in. "Did he threaten you?" he asked when he was behind the wheel.

"No, I threatened him. And I'm really not supposed to do that."

"Your secret's safe with me," Mark said. "Tell me exactly what he said to you."

She sighed and sank into his leather seats, looking so fucking adorable, he felt his throat tighten. "It should piss me off when you get all possessive and protective," she said. "But it's oddly and disturbingly cute."

He stared at her. *"Cute?"*

"Yeah." She was quiet as he pulled out of the lot, and he wondered if she'd fallen asleep.

"Did you know I hadn't had sex in a year?" she asked, then sighed. "I really missed the orgasms."

Since he was dizzy with the subject change it took him a moment to formulate a response. "Orgasms are good."

"Better than lasagna."

"Damn A straight." He had them halfway home before she spoke again.

"Mark?"

"Yeah?"

She turned her head to look at him, her face hidden by the night. "My car isn't a truck."

"No?"

"And my car doesn't go this fast, and certainly not this smooth."

"Huh," he said.

"Wait." She sat straight up, restrained by the seat belt. "Are you kidnapping me?"

He slid her a look. "And if I was?"

"I don't know. I'm not tied up or anything."

"Did you want to be?"

"No, of course not." But her eyes glazed over and not from fear, making him both hard and amused at the same time.

RAINEY WAS STILL NICE and buzzed but she knew that she was mad at Mark. Somehow that made him all the more dark and sexy. She eyed his tie. He was so sexy in that tie. "I've been thinking...."

"Always dangerous."

"Maybe the other night wasn't as good as I remembered it."

"It was."

"I don't know...." She shrugged, and the jacket he'd wrapped around her slipped off her shoulders. "I might need a review."

He slid her a look that nearly had her going up in flames. He turned back to the road and took a deep breath. And then another when she leaned across the console and loosened his tie, slowly pulling it from around his neck, during which time her other hand

braced on his thigh, high enough to maybe accidentally even brush against his zipper.

"Christ, Rainey." His voice was strained in a new
way, an extremely arousing way, egging her on. The
next thing she knew, the truck swerved. She gripped
the dash, laughing breathlessly as he whipped them to
the side of the road and let her do as she wanted, which
was crawl into his lap. His eyes dilated to solid black,
his hands cupping her behind as she kissed him.

And kissed him...

She kissed him until she knew with certainty—it
had been as good as she remembered.

Better.

RAINEY WOKE UP WITH A start and stared into two dark
melted pools of... "Mmm," she said. "Chocolate."

"Wake up, Sleeping Beauty." Warm fingers ran over
her forehead, brushing the hair from her face. "You're
home."

She sat straight up in the passenger seat of his truck
and stared around her. They were parked at her place.
"I fell asleep?"

"Little bit." He was crouched at her side between her
and the opened door.

She looked into his face and sighed. After a very
sexy make out session, he'd gently put her back on
her side of the truck and that was all she remembered
before falling asleep. She knew that much of Mark's job
involved taking care of people: his players, his management team, the press...everything. It all fell under his
jurisdiction. And here he was, taking care of her.

That burned. She took care of herself. And to that

end, she unhooked her seat belt and turned to him. "Excuse me."

He obliged her by rising to his full height and offering her a hand. Which she only took so as not to be rude. And because she was just a little bit wobbly. And maybe because God, he looked so good. He was wearing a suit— Wait. Nope. *She* was wearing his jacket… and his tie. He was in just black slacks and a dark gray shirt shoved up to his elbows, revealing forearms that she knew from firsthand experience were warm and corded with strength.

The corners of his mouth tipped into an almost smile, a light of wicked naughtiness playing in his eyes. Suddenly suspicious, she ran her hands down her body, checking. Yep, she was still in her little black dress, bra and panties in place, though the latter seemed to have a telltale dampness…

His soft laugh brought her gaze back up to his.

"Relax." His voice was low and husky, the corners of his mouth twitching up into a smile. He set a hand at the base of her back and used his other to glide a fingertip slowly from her temple to her chin, the touch setting off a trail of sparks. "If we'd gotten naked again, you'd have woken up for it."

Her nipples tightened. "That's…cocky."

"That's fact," he assured her, and kissed her, slow and sensual.

"What was that?" she whispered when he pulled back.

"If you don't know, I'm doing something wrong."

Actually, he couldn't do it *less* wrong.

Mark propelled her up the path to her town house.

At the door, she stopped to fumble through her purse for her keys. "Where are they?"

"I gave them to James."

"You stole my keys? When?"

"When you were flirting with Dumbass at the bar."

"I wasn't flirting!"

He ran a hand along the top of the doorway, feeling the ledge.

She allowed herself to admire the flex of his shoulders and back muscles beneath his shirt. Not finding a key, Mark squatted low to peek beneath the mat while she peeked too—at his terrific ass.

"Where's your spare key?" he asked.

"How do you know I have one?"

"All women do."

She tore her gaze off his butt. "Excuse me. *All* women?"

He turned and eyed the potted plant besides the door before lifting the heavy ten gallon container with ease, smiling at the spare key lying there.

Dammit.

He calmly opened the door and nudged her in, turning on lights and looking curiously around. The town house was small, and given that she had a great job with crappy pay, it was also sparsely furnished. Most everything was reclaimed from various places, but she'd gathered them all herself, and it was home. "Thanks for the ride," she said.

He turned to her and slowly backed her to the door, resting his forearms along either side of her head. "That's not how you promised to thank me."

"Um—"

Shifting closer, he ran his hands down her body. "Don't tell me you've forgotten."

"Well..." A hint. She needed a hint.

"You talk in your sleep." He remained so close she was breathing his air, and he hers. "It was very enlightening," he said.

Oh, God. What had she said? Given the naughty dreams she'd had about him all week, it could have been anything.

He laughed softly, but then he moved away from her and into her kitchen. She managed to walk on trembly limbs to her couch and sink into it, listening to him help himself to her cupboards.

A minute later he came out with a full glass of water and a few aspirin, both of which he handed to her. "Drink the whole glass, just in case you have a morning hangover coming your way. 'Night, Rainey."

She stared in shock at his very fine ass as it walked to the front door. "You're...leaving?"

She saw his broad shoulders rise as he took a deep breath, and when he turned to face her, she realized he wasn't nearly as calm and relaxed as she'd thought. "Yes," he said.

"But—"

"Rainey, if I come an inch closer, I'm going to pick you up and rip that sexy dress off you, and then the bra and panties you were worried about earlier, leaving you in nothing but my tie and those heels, which, by the way, have been driving me crazy all night."

She felt her heart kick into gear.

"And then," he said. "I'm going to take you to your bedroom and do what you so sweetly begged me to do in your sleep."

"Wh-what did I ask you to do?" she whispered.

"Tie you up to your headboard and ravish you."

Oh, God. "I—I asked you to do that?"

"You asked me to do it until you screamed my name."

"I've never..." She broke off and squirmed a little on the couch. Her skin felt too tight, and her heart was thudding against her ribs. "Some of that would be... new." Some, as in all.

He looked at her for a long beat, then moved back to her. Slowly he crouched at her side and tugged playfully on the tie. "Go to bed, Rainey. Alone. Drink the water and I'll see you tomorrow."

Right. She nodded and closed her eyes.

She heard him move away, but the door didn't open. So she opened her eyes and found him standing in front of it, his hand on the doorknob, head bowed against the wood.

"What are you doing?" she asked.

"Trying to make myself leave." He lifted his head. "Because tomorrow you're going to remember that you don't like me, and I'm going to want to kick my own ass for not sticking around while you do."

In her tired state, that somehow made sense. Sad, sad sense. "You're right. Tomorrow I'll probably go back to being an uptight, bitchy control freak."

He smiled. "You're not bitchy."

"Just an uptight control freak?"

"Well, maybe a little."

She laughed. *Laughed.* And suddenly, she didn't want him to leave. She really really didn't. What she *did* want was him. Again. She wasn't sure exactly why she was still so attracted to him, but she had a nice buzz going and decided it was okay not to think about it right now. So she stood up.

"What are you doing?"

"Instigating again." She climbed up on the coffee table. She wasn't sure why she did it exactly, except maybe because he was tall and sure and confident, and she needed to be those things too. Plus it just seemed like a striptease should be done from a tabletop. Reaching behind her, she unzipped her dress.

"Rainey."

His voice was hoarse, and very very serious, and ooh, she liked it.

She liked it a lot.

"You need to stop," he said, sounding very alpha.

She liked that too. She wondered if he'd boss her around when they got into bed.

She kind of hoped so.

She let the little straps slip off her shoulders, holding the material to her breasts. She thought she was being sexy as hell, so his telling her to stop confused her. "Why?"

"I'm not having drunk sex with you."

"I'm not drunk." She let the dress slowly slip from her breasts, revealing her pretty black lace push-up bra.

Mark appeared to stop breathing. "Rainey—"

"Whoops." She let go of her dress. "Look at that...." She'd planned the dress sliding gracefully down her body to pool at her feet, but that's not what happened. It caught on her hips. She tried a little shimmy but her heels were much higher than her usual sneakers. Which meant that her ankle gave and she tumbled gracelessly to the floor.

"Jesus."

She heard Mark drop to his knees at her side, felt his hands run over her body. She could also feel that her dress had bunched at both the top and the bottom, ending up around her waist like a wadded belt. Probably she wasn't looking as sexy as she'd hoped.

"Rainey."

There was both a warning and a sexy growl to his voice, so she lay there, eyes closed, playing possum with those big, warm hands on her.

You just executed the most pathetic striptease ever, you idiot.

"Rainey."

She scrunched her eyes tighter, wondering what the chances were that he'd believe she'd died and would just go away.

"Dead women don't have hard nipples," he said, sounding amused. "Or wet panties."

With a gasp at his crudeness—and her body's traitorous reaction—she sat straight up and cracked her head on his chin.

He fell to his ass at her side and laughed, and when he straightened up, she shoved him. Staggering to her feet, she took stock. Now her dress was around her ankles. Perfect. Nice work on bringing the sexy. Turning away from him, she weeble-wobbled across the living room, dragging the dress behind her, limping on her left ankle.

From behind her, Mark made a sound that told her either he liked the view or he'd swallowed his tongue. She tried not to picture what she looked like as she went to her bedroom and slammed the door on his choked laugh.

Bastard.

Her ankle was really burning now. She probably needed ice, but since that meant walking back out there, she'd do without. Somehow—she wasn't sure how exactly—this was all Mark's fault. In fact, she was positive of it.

Crawling onto her bed, she proceeded to cover her head with her pillow, where she planned to stay forever and pretend the entire evening had been a bad dream.

8

RAINEY CAME AWAKE SLOWLY and lay very still, trying to figure out why she felt like she wasn't alone. What had she done last night? The ballet. Jacob. The wine. Mark… The entire evening came crashing back to her, and eyes still closed, she groaned miserably. "Oh, no."

"Oh, yes," said an amused male voice. Mark, of course.

Her eyes flew open. It was morning, which she knew because the sun was slanting in the windows across her face, making her eyeballs hurt. Mark was lying on top of her covers, head propped up on his hand, casual as he pleased. He wore only his slacks, unbuttoned, and was sprawled out for her viewing pleasure, all lean, hard planes and—

No. *Stop looking at him.* "What are you doing here?"

He leaned over her, and utterly without thinking, she ran her hands up his back with a little purr of sheer pleasure.

Mark went still, staring down at her in rare surprise while his arm kept moving, grabbing a mug of steaming coffee from her nightstand. "I just wanted to make sure you were alive before I left," he said.

She forced her hands off him and tried to pretend she hadn't opened her legs to let him slip between them. She took the proffered coffee and drank away her embarrassment. "Thanks," she finally murmured, setting the mug down. Then casually lifted the covers to peek beneath.

She was still in her black lacy bra and panties. And his tie…

No heels.

Her left ankle was propped on a pillow with an ice pack. Ah, yes. Her oh-so-sexy striptease.

Mark had taken care of her. While she processed this, he rolled off the bed. She stared at his bare chest and felt the urge to lick him from his Adam's Apple to those perfect abs. And beyond too, down that faint silky happy trail to his—

"I'm pretty sure it's just a sprain, but you need to wrap it." He nodded to a still plastic-wrapped Ace bandage next to the coffee on the nightstand. "Figured you'd want to shower first."

Mouth dry, she nodded and very carefully sat up. He watched her as he reached for his shirt hanging off the back of her chair and shrugged into it. He tucked his shirt in, adjusting himself in the process before fastening his pants.

She swallowed hard at the intimate moment. "Thanks," she said. "For bringing me home."

He had a faint smile on his face as he studied her expression. "Anytime."

"I'm sorry if I was…a handful."

A small smile touched his lips. "Like I said. Any-time."

With a deep breath, she got out of the bed. She figured he'd turn away and give her a moment of privacy, but he didn't. He might not sleep with buzzed women, but he had no problem looking. He looked plenty as the sheet fell away.

"Pretty," he said, and came close when she winced at the weight on her ankle. Lifting her up, he carried her into the bathroom.

"I think I can manage from here," she said.

"Are you sure? I'm good in the shower."

Since he was good at everything, that wasn't a stretch. But she was definitely not at her best. "I'm sure."

With a slow nod, he left her alone.

Stripping off her bra and panties, she limped to the shower, turned it on, then proceeded to smack her ankle getting in. "Ouch, ouch, ouch, ouch. *Dammit.*"

And then suddenly Mark was back, whipping aside the shower curtain, expression concerned. "You okay?"

Was she? She had no idea. She was standing there, naked, wet. *Naked.* Lots of things were crowding for space in her brain, and oddly enough, not a one of them was embarrassment. "I'm instigating again," she whispered, and tugged him into the shower, clothes and all.

Without missing a beat, as if crazy naked women dragged him into their showers every day, his arms banded around her. His hair, dark brown and silky and drenched, fell over his forehead and nearly into his equally dark eyes. He clearly hadn't shaved and his jaw was rough with at least a day's growth. His shirt was so wet as to be sheer, delineating every cut of every muscle on him. And there were a lot of muscles. He looked lethally gorgeous, and was lethally dangerous to her mental health as well, especially since all she could think about was ripping off his clothes to have her merry way with him. "Mark?"

"Yeah?"

"I'm naked."

One big, warm hand slid down to her butt and squeezed. The urge to lift her legs around his waist was so shockingly strong, she had to fight to remain still. "I'm naked," she said again. "And you're not."

"That could be fixed," he said, volleying the ball into her court, leaving the decision entirely up to her. He waited with the latent, powerful patience of a predator who had its prey cornered.

"You turned me down last night," she pointed out, smoothing a palm down his chest, taking in every well-defined muscle before sliding her hands under his shirt. "I'm not sure I could take a second rejection."

"Are you still under the influence?"

"No. Was that your only barrier?"

His eyes were two fathomless pools of heat. "For now."

"Then please," she whispered, lending her hands to the cause, tugging up his shirt. "Please fix your not-naked status."

With quick, smooth grace, he stripped out of his clothes, discarding them in a wet heap on the floor. God, he was so damn gorgeous. And that's when she knew. Even though she'd made the rules to keep herself from drowning in him, she was in over her head and going down for the count.

MARK STOOD THERE WITH Rainey in his arms, the water running down them, the air steamy and foggy, unable to believe how good she felt against him. She was looking at his body, and getting off on it—a fact he greatly appreciated because he enjoyed looking at her, too. So much he was currently hard enough to pound nails. "Are you going to instigate again?"

"I'm thinking about it," she said, water streaming over her in rivulets. "But for the record, this isn't about liking each other."

He traced the line of her spine down to her ass, slipping his fingers in between her legs, nearly detonating at the wet, creamy heat he found. "Because you don't. Like me," he clarified.

"Right."

He ignored the odd pang at that, and tipping her face up to his, he kissed her, kissed her long and deep and wet, until she was clutching at him, making soft little whimpers for more, and he'd damn well lay money down that she liked him now. He had no business caring one way or the other, but suddenly he wanted her to. Very much. "We can work on the like thing," he said. "We could start small."

"Yes, well, there's nothing *small* about you."

Laughing softly, he went on a little tour, kissing his way down her throat, over her collarbone, to a breast. Her nipples were tight, already hard when he ran his tongue over a puckered tip. "How about this, Rainey? Do you like this?"

She let out a barely there moan but didn't answer.

"Tell me." Sucking her into his mouth, he teased and kissed, absorbing her sexy whimper, but when she still didn't speak, he stopped and looked at her.

Her head was back, eyes closed, water streaming over her, so beautiful she took his breath.

Unhappy that he'd stopped, she lifted her head.

"Say it," he said.

"I liked that," she whispered.

"Good. How about this?" He gently clamped his teeth on her nipples and gave a light tug.

This ripped a throaty gasp from her and she tightened her fingers in his hair. "Mark—"

"Yes or no, Rainey?"

"Yes!"

"Okay, good, that's real good. Now let's see what else you like."

"I don't think—"

"No, we're addressing the problem, as you so smartly suggested." Dropping to his knees, he worked his way down her torso, kissing each rib, dipping his tongue into her belly button, making her squirm. "How about this," he asked. "Do you like this?"

When she said nothing, he once again stopped.

"I liked that!" she gasped, her hips rocking helplessly. "Please, don't stop."

Gripping her hips, he held her still and moved lower, pressing his mouth to her belly, then lower still, hovering right over her mound.

Above him, she stopped breathing.

With a smile, he reached up and extricated one of her hands from his hair, placing it against the tile wall at her side so she'd be better balanced.

"Mark—"

"And this? Do you like when I do this, Rainey?" He kissed her thigh, her knee.

"Y-yes," she whispered shakily. "I like that."

He gently kissed that same spot again, running his palm up her belly to graze a breast. "I'm glad." Carefully, he gripped her foot with the slightly swollen ankle and lifted it to the tub's ledge, which opened her up to him and gave him a heart-stopping view.

"Mark—"

Unable to resist, he leaned in and kissed first one inner thigh, and then the other.

And then in between.

"Yes," she gasped before he'd even asked, making him smile against her as his heart squeezed with a myriad of emotions so strong it shocked him. Affection, warmth, amusement and heat. There was so much heat, he could come from just listening to the sounds she made. He kissed a slow trail over her center, lingering in the spots that made her cry out. She took her other hand out of his hair and slapped it against the opposite wall so that both hands were straight out, bracing her, and still he felt her legs quiver.

"Oh, God—" Apparently unable to say more, she broke off, panting for breath.

Loving the taste of her, he parted her with his fingers, using his tongue, his teeth, to take her even higher, then closed his mouth over her and sucked, slipping first one finger and then another into her.

"Mark!"

Yeah, she liked that. And he loved the sound of his name on her lips. He wanted more. He wanted it all, which he realized just as she came, panting and shuddering for him, whispering his name over and over as she did.

RAINEY WOULD HAVE surely fallen to the floor of the shower if Mark hadn't caught her. She'd warned herself to hold back but that had proved difficult if not impossible. Still trembly and breathless, she found herself pressed between the cool hard tiles at her back and a hot, hard Mark at her front, the shower still pulsing hot water over them.

Before she could regroup, he cupped a breast, letting his thumb rub over her nipple as he slid a powerful thigh between hers, pressing in just enough to graze her heated, pulsing flesh, wrenching a moan from her.

"Rainey, look at me."

Her eyes flew open and she blinked away the water. "I like that," she heard herself murmur. *Way to hold back...* She leaned out of the shower and fumbled into her top vanity drawer for the sole condom she had there. A sample from somewhere. God bless samples.

His smile nearly made her come again. "Goal oriented," he said. "I like that." Dipping his dark, wet head, he pressed openmouthed kisses over her shoulder, nipping softly.

She slid her fingers into his hair and brought his head up, touching her tongue to his bottom lip, feeling the groan that rumbled from his chest to hers. Good. He was as gone as she was. It was her last thought as he took control of the kiss, cupping the back of her head in his big palm as his lower body ground into hers, sending shock waves of desire flooding through her.

She gasped when he pulled away, murmuring a protest at the loss of the contact, and then gasped again when he swiped everything off the wide tub edge at the opposite end from the shower head. Her shampoo, conditioner and face wash hit the shower floor, then before she could blink he sat and pulled her on his lap. His long, inky black lashes were stuck together with little droplets of water, his eyes lit with a staggering hunger as he spread her thighs over his, opening her to him. The very tip of him sank into her, stretching her, making her gasp.

He went still, his face strained, his entire body tense as he struggled to give her time to adjust. It took only a heartbeat for her to need more, and she rocked her hips against him to let him know.

"Slow down," he rasped, voice rough. "I don't want to hurt you—"

"More."

With a low groan, he gave her another couple of inches and it was good, so good she sank all the way on him until he filled her up. The sensation was so incredible she cried out, but at the sound he went utterly still.

"Rainey, I'm sorry—"

"No, *I like!*"

He choked out a laugh at that, but she couldn't put a sentence together. She couldn't think past the deep quivering inside her that was spreading to every corner of her being. Instead, she rocked her hips again, mindless, trying to show him with her body how very okay she was.

Evidently he got the message because he began to move with her in slow, delicious thrusts, his big hands on her hips, controlling her movements.

He broke away from her mouth and locked his gaze with hers. His face was close, so close she saw something flicker in his eyes, something so intense it stole her breath. She couldn't name the emotion, she only knew it matched what was going on inside her, and it was something new. "Mark, I need—"

"I know."

And he gave it to her, slow and sure, his thumb gliding over the spot where they joined, teasing, stroking... He drove her to the very brink, then held her suspended there, mindless, beyond desperate for her release before he finally allowed it. She came hard, which he clearly liked because he immediately followed her over, her name on his lips.

A long moment passed, or maybe a year, before he stirred against her, brushing his mouth across hers. "Next time, we do that in your bed," he murmured, still deep inside her.

Her body agreed with a shiver that made him drop his head to her shoulder and groan. They remained there, entwined, until the hot water suddenly gave way to cold, leaving Rainey gasping in shock and Mark laughing his ass off.

STILL GRINNING, MARK flicked off the water and eyed Rainey, who sat on the closed commode, chest still rising and falling as she tried to get her breath back.

He wasn't having much luck either. It was crazy. He ran five miles a day and could keep up with his world-class athletes just about any day of the week, and yet being with her had knocked his socks off.

And rocked his axis.

Grabbing a towel, he wrapped her in it, smiling when she just stared up at him. He liked the soft sated stupor in her eyes.

She shook her head. "I'm turning into a sex addict."

She rose to her feet and gingerly put weight on her ankle. "At least now we know."

"Know what?"

"That there's some crazy chemical thing going on here. It happens, I guess."

Yeah, it did happen. It happened a lot. But that wasn't all that what was happening here, and he was smart enough to know it. So was she. "Rainey—"

She turned towards him and kissed him, hard. Deep. And deliciously hot and wet. But when he groaned and reached for her, she shoved free. "Sorry. My fault. You've *got* to put clothes on." Pushing her wet hair from her face, she limped into her bedroom. With an impressive but frustrating talent, she managed to pull on clothes while keeping herself fully covered with the towel. "If I could stop kissing you, this wouldn't happen," she said. "When we kiss, I lose my inhibitions."

"Yeah?" he asked, intrigued. "All of them?"

"No, not all of them. But most."

A dare if he'd ever heard one. "Which ones don't you lose?"

She snatched her purse off the dresser, the tips of her ears bright red. "You know what? We are not discussing this."

"Can't be up-against-the-door sex," he said, enjoying teasing her. "Or shower sex. We've done both of those. Maybe you don't like to do it from behind. Or I know, you have an aversion to dirty talk. Are there dirty talk parameters we should discuss?"

"You made me dirty talk while we were having sex," she reminded him.

"You didn't use any dirty words. Maybe you have

some words that are okay, some that aren't. For instance, my penis. Would you want me to call it a dick, or a cock? Or how about your sweet spot? There are lots of names for that, like p—"

"Seriously?" She planted her hands on her hips. "Out of all of our issues, *this* is the one you want to discuss?"

"It's a good one."

She shook her head. "I'm leaving."

"This is your place."

"Right. God, you drive me nuts." She looked at her clock. "But I actually have to go to work." She moved out of the bedroom to the front door.

In nothing but the towel around his hips, he followed her. "Rainey."

"What?"

He maneuvered her to the door and kissed her. "Bye."

With a moan, she yanked him back and kissed him, running her hands over him as if she couldn't get enough before suddenly shoving him away. "Dammit, I said to put some clothes on!" She stormed out the front door, only to come to a skidding halt on her porch. "Crap!"

Her car wasn't there.

She sighed and turned back to him. "I need a ride to work."

When he smiled, she slapped her hands over her eyes. "Oh my God."

"What?"

"I'm adding smiling to the list. No smiling!"

"Why?" Pulling her back inside, he trapped her

against the door. "Do my smiles make you lose your inhibitions too? *All* of them?"

"Maybe."

"Okay, now you're just teasing me." He flicked his tongue over her earlobe and absorbed her soft moan.

"Argh!" Yanking free, she stormed back to the bedroom to grab his wet clothes, which she tossed into her dryer and turned it on. "You have to drive me to work. And you have to do it without making me want you. Got it?"

"I'll try. But I'm pretty irresistible when I put my mind to it."

9

MARK SPENT THE NEXT three days wielding a hammer alongside his players at the construction sites during the day, practicing with the teen girls in the late afternoons, and handling Mammoth business at night. He also had dinner with his dad, who'd gotten wind of Mark's interest in Rainey. *Thanks, Rick.* Ramon had told Mark that Rainey was a perfect fit for him, but they both knew what he really meant was *she'd keep you with one foot in Santa Rey, where you belong.*

Mark had his usual hundred balls in the air at all times, but in spite of doing the opposite of what his dad wanted, he couldn't stop thinking about Rainey.

He'd tried calling and had gotten her voice mail—twice—and a new and entirely foreign feeling had come over him.

She was avoiding him.

Four days after the ballet, he walked into the rec center and ran smack into her. She looked up from her clipboard, an apology on her lips, which tightened at the sight of him. "You."

Yeah. She'd been avoiding him. She was wearing

cargo shorts that emphasized the toned, tanned legs he'd loved having wrapped around him, a UCSB T-shirt and her favorite accessory—her whistle. And suddenly he wanted to see her wearing that whistle in his bed.

Just the whistle.

"You're early for practice," she said.

"Yeah, a little bit. Thought I could help out somehow." Or see you...

"Great." She slapped her clipboard to his chest. "Can you figure out which supplies we need to order?"

"What?"

"Check the list against the stock in the storage closet," she directed, and pointed to the same supply closet where only a week ago he'd kissed the both of them senseless. But before he could remind her of that, she was gone.

"Nice technique," Rick said as he came down the hallway. "Is that how you landed that Victoria's Secret model you dated last month?"

"Shut up." Mark looked down at the clipboard. "She wants me to be the supply boy."

"Huh. Probably she doesn't realize how important you are."

Mark sighed. "You're an ass."

"Are you sure that's me?"

Mark ignored this and opened the door to the closet, eyeing the shelf he'd pinned Rainey against. Clearly, he was losing his mind. It was obvious she didn't need him or even particularly like him. She didn't take his calls. She didn't seek him out.

And she wasn't just playing with him either, or being coy. That's not how she operated. What you saw was what you got with Rainey. She was the real deal.

And she didn't want him.

He wasn't sure how the shoe had gotten on the other foot, but it had and he needed to accept it and move on. Except…he couldn't seem to do that, which made no sense. He'd never been more on top of his world. His career was solid, his bank account was solid.

Maybe this vague unease was just from being back in Santa Rey, back with his father and brother, the two people in his life who didn't buy into his press. Yeah, that had to be it, being with family, with people who knew bullshit when they saw it and called him on it with no qualms. Here there was no snapping his fingers and getting his every need taken care of. Here no one looked at him to solve their every problem and deferred to him as if he were their god.

Here, he was the supply boy.

He supposed his dad was right about one thing— Santa Rey was home, since he hadn't bothered to get attached to anyplace else he'd been.

He thought briefly of his past girlfriends, or more accurately, lovers. He'd been with some incredibly beautiful women and yet he'd never gotten too attached for the sole reason that he hadn't wanted the additional responsibility.

It was possible he'd made a mistake there, that in trying to protect himself, he'd made it so he couldn't engage.

No, that wasn't it. He'd engaged with Rainey just fine. He'd engaged everything he had—body and heart and soul.

And maybe that was it. All this time he'd been just fine on his own with the occasional woman for fun and diversion and stress release. But Rainey was shock-ingly different.

Why her? What was it about her that had so lowered his defenses? Because she was a nightmare waiting to happen to his life. She wasn't arm candy—not that she wasn't beautiful, because she was. She simply wasn't the type of woman to be content with the few crumbs he'd be able to give her, a mere side dish to the crazi-ness of his life.

In fact, she had her own crazy life.

And what if *she* got attached? What then?

Except.

Except…she sure as hell didn't appear to be too at-tached.

He blew out another sigh and spent the next ten min-utes comparing the list of needed supplies to what was on the shelves. There was no comparison, really. The center was short of everything, and he grabbed his phone. If he was doing this, then he was doing it right. He snapped a picture of the list and emailed it to the one person who could help him, then followed with a phone call.

Tony Ramirez answered with, "Yo, what can I get you?"

Tony was the Mammoths' supply manager. He stocked everything the players and staff needed, spe-cifically the locker room, medical room and kitchen. It was a big job, and not an easy one. During the season, the team's needs varied on a day-to-day basis, from Ace bandages to the latest Xbox game to a turkey club sandwich on sourdough from the deli down the street, to a new Mammoths jersey on a moment's notice…

which meant that Tony was pretty much a world-class concierge service.

"Need some supplies," Mark said. "I'm in Santa Rey."

"Good for you, I'm in Cabo."

"Shit," Mark said. "Never mind."

"No, I've got my laptop. I can work my magic from anywhere, no worries. What do you need? Is it for Operation: Make The Mammoths Look Good Again, or for that chick that James and Casey tell me you're trying to impress?"

Mark pictured himself happily strangling his players.

"They make 'em pretty there in Santa Rey, huh?"

They did. They also made them feisty and sharp as hell, not to mention loyal and caring, and warm. So goddamn warm that Mark could still feel Rainey wrapped around him, the gentle heat of her breath on his throat as she pressed her face there, moaning his name. He could still feel the way she'd moved against him, driving him crazy. The way she'd shattered in his arms, clutching at him as if he was everything.

And then in the next moment she'd decided it didn't mean anything. Which he was fine with. Fucking fine. "The rec center here is in desperate need of some supplies. I just sent you the list."

"Didn't I just send you a bunch of baseball and softball equipment?"

"Yeah. This list is more for the rec center itself. Office supplies. But also, the kids I'm coaching are short on stuff I didn't anticipate. Running shoes, cleats, and…girlie stuff."

"Girlie stuff?"

"Sports bras."

"*Sports bras.* Are you shitting me?"

"You order jockstraps and compression shorts all the time."

"Yes," Tony said. "Because I know how to fit a dick into a cup. I have no knowledge of breasts—well, other than personal knowledge." He laughed to himself. "Where the hell am I supposed to get sports bras?"

"Hell, I don't know. The bra store? You said you were magic."

"Aw, man, you're going to owe me. The next blonde reality star that throws herself at you, you have to give to me. Make that the next *two* blondes."

"Yeah, yeah," Mark said. "Also get water bottles, enough for each kid and staff member because there's never enough water on the fields. Use the aluminum Mammoth ones if you want. And I want an iPad for stats, and—"

"An iPad?"

Turning, Mark came face to face with Rainey, who was standing in the doorway.

"We're barely budgeted for sports," she said dryly. "Pretty sure we're not budgeted for miracles."

Mark hung up on Tony. "Just trying to help."

"Or micromanaging," she suggested.

He smiled. "Again, hello, Mrs. Pot."

She sighed and shut the door, closing them in the closet. "It's very generous of you to do this," she said, staying firmly out of reach. A real feat in the small space.

"Yes, it is." Because she smelled amazing, he shifted closer without even thinking about it. "Feel free to thank me in any way you see fit."

Her mouth quirked, but she remained cool, calm and collected, in charge of her world.

It was a huge turn-on. Hell, everything about her was. Especially those shorts. Pressing her back against the door, he flattened his hands on either side of her head. "You've been avoiding me."

"I've been busy, is all." Her breasts brushed his chest and they both sucked in a breath.

Slowly he tipped his head down and watched as her nipples puckered and poked against the material of her shirt. "You're instigating again."

"My nipples have a mind of their own!"

Crowding her, he closed his teeth over her earlobe and tugged, not all that lightly.

She moaned and grabbed the fabric of his shirt. "No fair. I can't control my body's response to you."

Even better. He nipped his way down her jaw to her throat, nearly smiling when she tilted her head to make room for him. "God. Mark, stop." But even as she said it, she tightened her grip so he couldn't get away, tugging on a few chest hairs as she did. "Please," she said softly.

"I'll please anything you want, Rainey."

"Please don't do this. Don't make me want you."

Well, hell. He was a lot of things, but he wasn't a complete asshole. At least not when it came to her. He pulled back and met her gaze. "There are two of us in this, Rainey. Two of us wanting each other." With one last long look at her, he left the closet and made his way to practice, where he found the girls in various poses on the stands.

At least they were dressed in the gear he'd given them. Pepper was on the top row reading a book. Cindy was sprawled across three benches, staring at the sky, twirling a strand of her hair, yammering on her cell phone. Kendra was at the bottom eating a candy bar and sucking a soda. The others were scattered in between, talking, laughing, doing each other's hair and texting.

Only Sharee was on the field, stretching.

Mark shot her a small smile, then walked up to the stands. "What's this?"

Every single one of the girls kept doing whatever they were doing. He mentally counted to three and asked again, using the voice that routinely terrified his world-class athletes in a blink.

The girls still didn't budge. With a sigh, he blew his whistle. With a variety of eye rolls, the teens made their way down to the grass in front of him.

"When you're dressed out," he said, "I expect to see you here running your drills. Not texting, not talking on the phone, not eating candy. You do all of that on your own time. This is *my* time."

Grumbling, they turned away to start their drills. "And what did I say about sagging?" he asked Kendra, whose shorts were so low he had no idea how she kept them up. "No shorts down past your ass—" Dammit. He pulled out a buck and handed it to Pepper, the keeper of the swear jar. "Or you won't play. Now start stretching, following the routine I showed you, or you'll be running laps."

They headed to join Sharee on the field. Mark watched them go, aware of Rainey coming up to his side. He waited for her to blast him about...hell, he didn't know what. Maybe breathing incorrectly.

Instead, she gave him an interminable look. "You do

realize that they're teenage girls, not grown men," she finally said.

"I have minimum requirements, regardless of the age or sex of the athlete. They're not difficult to meet."

"What are they?"

"Honesty, loyalty and one-hundred-percent participation."

She looked at him for a long moment. "Those are all good requirements," she said, and began walking back to the building.

Nice ass, he thought, and walked in the opposite direction, onto the field, handing Pepper another dollar.

"What's this for?" she asked.

"I thought a bad word."

RAINEY MADE HER WAY to her office, then stared out the window at the field. She had a million things to do and yet she was riveted in place, watching Mark coach the girls just as she'd occasionally watched him on TV. Hell, who was she kidding, she'd watched him more than occasionally. He had a way of standing at his team bench looking deceptively calm except for all that unfailing intensity and dogged aggression.

He was coaching the girls the same way he did his guys—hard and ruthless, and somehow also shockingly patient. And while not exactly kind, he had a way of being incredibly fair.

The girls, who'd given her and every other coach they'd had such endless grief, did everything in their power to please him.

"Rainey?"

She turned from the window to her office door and found Cliff from Accounting smiling at her. He was lanky lean, with dark spiky hair and smiling eyes. He was shy as hell, but also one of the nicest guys she'd ever met. "Did I forget to sign my expense account again?" she asked.

Cliff laughed. They didn't have expense accounts. Hell, they were lucky to have salaries. "No." He looked behind them as if to make sure they were alone. "I was wondering if you wanted to go out sometime."

Some of her surprise must have shown on her face because he smiled with endearing self-consciousness and lifted a shoulder. "I know. We've worked together forever so why now, right? But—"

"Lena," Rainey guessed. "Lena put you up to this."

"She mentioned you were open to dating right now, but honestly I've always wanted to ask you out."

Aw. Dammit. And she *was* open to dating. Supposedly. And if it hadn't been for a certain alpha, obnoxious, annoying man outside on the field voluntarily helping her with the teens, the same alpha, obnoxious, annoying man she kept accidentally having sex with, she'd probably have said yes. "Cliff, I—"

"Just think about it," he said quickly, already backing away. "Don't give me your answer now. I'll call you sometime, okay?"

And then he was gone.

Rainey looked out the window again. Yep, Mark was still out there, batting pop flies to the girls for catching practice. He'd given them directions on how to improve and they were doing their best to follow.

And failing, a lot.

Never giving up, Mark kept at them, not afraid to get right in there to show them exactly what he wanted. He moved with easy grace and intensity, and she flashed back to a few days prior, when he'd moved inside of her with that same grace and intensity.

The memory made her legs wobble. She pressed her forehead to the window. The girls were trying to do what Mark wanted, tossing him back the balls as soon as he hit them.

Sharee was the fastest and the best, even with the healing bruise on her face and sullen attitude. She'd missed a practice, then showed up today without a word of explanation. Rainey had tried to press the girl for details on what was going on at home, asking if she needed any help, interference, *anything,* but Sharee was an island.

Which might have something to do with the phone call Rainey had taken yesterday from the girl's father, the second extremely obnoxious "mind your own fucking business" phone call. Martin needed a new tune to sing.

Sharee rocketed a ball to Mark at the same time as Pepper. Mark caught Sharee's, and took Pepper's ball in the crotch.

Though she couldn't hear the collective gasp that went up from the entire team, Rainey sensed it as Mark bent at the waist. Whirling, she ran out of her office, hitting the field, pushing her way through the circle of girls around Mark. She put a hand on his shoulder. "Are you all right?"

He didn't answer, just sucked in another breath.

"Mark?"

Still bent over, hands on his thighs, he held up a finger indicating he needed a minute.

"What can I do?" she asked.

"Stop talking."

It was late enough to call practice, so Rainey excused the girls. As they shuffled by, they offered a chorus of "Sorry, Coach" and "get better, Coach."

When she was alone with Mark, Rainey asked, "Do you need a doctor? Ice for the swelling?"

With a slight groan, he finally straightened and sent her a dark glare.

"What?" she asked. "That's what you do for an injury. You ice it, right? It eases the pain and swelling."

"This is not the kind of pain and swelling I need you to manage for me," he grated out.

"Are you sure?"

He drew another deep breath and gained some of his color back as he walked stiffly past her. "I'm fine."

"I'm just trying to help. Offer a little TLC."

"Tell you what," he said. "If you really want to get your hands on my cock again, then—" He broke off at her surprised gasp. "Oh, sorry, we never did decide what you deemed an acceptable term for that particular body part, did we?"

She lifted her chin. "Clearly, you're feeling better."

At that, a hint of amusement came into his eyes. "Yeah. But any time you want to kiss it and make it all better, you know where I'm staying."

A FEW NIGHTS LATER, the Mammoths were scheduled for an exhibition game for a huge local charity event at home in Sacramento against the San Jose Sharks.

Rick drove Lena and Rainey to the game. Rainey didn't know what she'd expected, but it wasn't to sit with the players' girlfriends and wives, with a crystal-clear view of the ice and an even better one of the Mammoths' bench.

Mark was there with his players, of course, wearing his hat low, mouth grim as the tight game stayed tied all the way to the end, when his team pulled a goal out of nowhere in overtime.

Rainey was pretty sure she never took her eyes off Mark, not even when Casey was body checked into the end boards or when James took a flip pass to the head. Afterwards, Rick took her and Lena to the team room. There was a huge spread of food, reporters and players. Everyone was eating, relaxing, speaking to the media... having a good time.

Mark was in his big office off to the side, a large wall of glass revealing him standing at a huge desk, on his phone and laptop at the same time.

"Post game crap," Rick said, handing her a drink. "The Mammoths are working on their media coverage."

She nodded and continued to watch Mark in his element until he lifted his head and leveled his gaze unerringly on her.

She caught his surprise in the slight widening of his eyes before he left his office and came to her.

"You didn't know I was here," she said when he stood directly in front of her.

"Rick is a sneaky bastard."

"We had great seats," she said. "Usually I sit way up in the nose bleed section—" She broke off, but it was too late. Her secret was out. She met his gaze, his eyes full of laughter.

"You come to the games," he said.

She sighed. "Sometimes. But mostly I watch them on TV."

"To see me?"

"Well let's not go overboard."

"Admit it."

She sighed again. "Sometimes I really hate you."

His grin widened, and two players across the way gawked at him. So did the members of his coaching staff. In fact, everyone near them stared.

Apparently he didn't grin like that very often here at work.

"You don't hate me," he said, not paying the people around them any attention whatsoever. "You like me. And you know something else?" He leaned in. "You want me again, bad."

His mouth on her ear made her shiver but he was laughing, the bastard, his body shaking with it. She gave him a shove and stalked off to the food table. She needed meaningless calories, and lots of them.

Because yeah, she wanted him.

Bad.

She ate with Lena and Rick, then watched the team gather together and shove a present in Mark's hands.

"Just a little something from us, Coach," Casey said with far too much innocence. "To protect you when you're coaching the girls."

Mark gave him a long look and opened the box.

As his players hooted and hollered, he pulled out a jockstrap.

Mark's laughing eyes met Rainey's and heat bolted through her.

He'd rather have a box of condoms.

He didn't say it out loud, he didn't have to, but she felt her face heat. Because she wished he'd gotten a box of condoms too....

Two days later, Mark gathered the teenagers in the rec center parking lot. They'd had two home games so far, and had won one, lost the other. Today they were heading to their first away game against a neighboring rec league in Meadow Hills, twenty-five miles east of Santa Rey.

The guys took one bus, the girls another. Mark boarded after his last player, then stopped short at the sight of Rainey, sitting next to the driver.

"I try to go to as many of the away games as I can," she told him. "Especially the first one, in case a coach can't handle it."

He raised a brow. "Pretty sure I can handle it." He turned to take a seat but she pointed to the iPad in his hands. "What's that for?"

"I have stats I want to go over with the girls before the game." He pulled up a file for her. "See?"

She stared down at the numbers. "These stats aren't for our team."

"No, they're for the team we're playing today."

"How did you get them? We don't keep stats in our league. It's a noncompetitive league."

The word *noncompetitive* wasn't in Mark's vocabulary. "I had someone to go out and watch their games this week."

"You had…" She stared up at him for a full minute. "Okay, maybe you didn't get the memo. This is a *rec* league, and for *fun*."

"There's nothing wrong with being prepared."

"Mark." She appeared to pick her words carefully, and he let her, mostly because he was still standing over her and had a nice view right down her shirt.

"You can't coach these girls with the same fierce intensity you coach your players," she finally said.

He liked her pink lace bra. And he was pretty sure he could see the very faint outline of her nipples—

"Are you listening to me?" she asked.

"No," he said. "I stopped listening to you after you said noncompetitive."

She rolled her eyes. "You're a control freak."

Yeah, and it took one to know one. He was just about to say so when there was a tussle in the back of the bus between Sharee and Kendra. He strode down the aisle, eyes narrowed, but by the time he got to them, everyone was quiet and angelic. The bus began to move, forcing him to sit where he was—right in the middle of the team.

From her comfy seat up front all by herself, no kids near her, Rainey gave him a smirk.

The sexy tyrant...

"You need to switch over to thongs," Tina said to Cindy. "No VPL. Guys like that."

"VPL?" Cindy asked.

"Visible panty lines."

Mark shuddered and turned his head, only to catch another conversation.

"Ethan is such a jerk," Kendra was saying to Sharee on his other side, their earlier fight apparently forgotten. "He goes crazy when guys talk to me, and whenever I go out with anyone, he shows up."

To Mark, the guy sounded like a punk ass stalker. Except...

Except he'd essentially done the same to Rainey. Twice.

"What do you think, Coach?"

He blinked at Sharee.

"Should Kendra dump Ethan's sorry possessive butt?" she asked him.

"Yes," he said without hesitation. "Boys are like drugs, just say no."

Sharee rolled her eyes. "More like boys are like candy—yummy and good to eat."

Mark groaned. He was so far out of his comfort zone. "Aren't you fifteen?" he asked Kendra.

"Sixteen."

His mind spun, placing Ethan as one of the guys banned from the rec center. They'd been causing trouble in town, vandalizing, partying it up. From what he understood, most of the girls were scared of them. "*No dating Ethan.*"

"You're not my dad."

"No, but I'm your coach. I control your field time."

Kendra narrowed her eyes. "That sounds like blackmail."

"Call it whatever you want. Date someone who's not an idiot."

Mark desperately tried to tune out all the chattering going on around him.

It didn't happen.

"Aiden is way hotter than Trevor," Tina said behind him.

"Definitely," Cindy agreed. "Aiden has facial hair. It means he's…mature."

"Mature how?" Tina wanted to know.

"Well, you know what they say about big feet, right? They say it about facial hair too. If he's got facial hair, he's got a big—"

Mark jammed his iPod earphones in his ears and

cranked his music, feeling like he was a hundred-year-old man. Jesus. These girls lived in a shockingly grown-up world for their age. They were already jaded, sarcastic, and in some cases, like Sharee, in daily danger.

He and Rick had grown up poor, but they'd been lucky to have Ramon's hardworking, caring influence. Some of these girls didn't have that, or any positive role model other than what they found at the rec center or at school in the way of coaches and teachers. That made it difficult, if not impossible, for a good guy to gain their trust.

He needed to try harder. He shut off the iPod and opened his eyes, then nearly jumped out of his skin when he saw Pepper staring at him.

She'd slid into the seat next to him. "Hi," she said.

"Hi. You okay?"

"Yeah." She looked down at her clasped hands. "But my, um…friend has a problem."

"Yeah?"

"Yeah. The guy she likes finally asked her out and they went, only now he's pretending she doesn't exist. So I'm wondering what could have happened. Do you know? Why he'd suddenly act so weird toward me—I mean my *friend*?"

Mark stared down at her bowed head. *Shit*. Yeah, he knew exactly why a guy would do that. Probably she hadn't put out, the bastard. He felt his heart squeeze with affection and worry. "The ass doesn't deserve you. Forget him."

Pepper held out her hand. Mark sighed and reached into his pocket for a dollar.

"Ryan likes you, Pepper," Sharee said. "Why don't you go for him?"

"Or stay single," Mark said desperately.

"She's not going to lose her virginity staying single," Sharee said.

Dear mother of God. "Abstinence is perfectly acceptable," he said firmly.

They all looked at him.

"Were *you* abstinent during your high school years?" Sharee wanted to know.

Fuck. He shoved his hands through his hair, and when he opened his eyes again, Pepper was once again holding out her hand. He'd said the word out loud. He fished in his pocket for another buck, but Pepper shook her head.

"The F-bomb is a five-dollar offense," she said.

He shoved a ten in her hand. "Keep the change. I'm going to need the credit."

10

AFTER WATCHING MARK coach the girls to a hard-earned win, Rainey went home and made brownies. Then she drove to the Welcome Inn Motel.

She wasn't quite sure what her goal was.

Okay, that was a big, fat lie. She knew *exactly* what her goal was. She was just conflicted about it. She'd watched Mark on that bus with those girls, completely out of his element and still completely one hundred percent committed.

It'd made him so damn attractive. *Too* attractive. Sitting in her car outside the motel, she called Lena. "Tell me to turn around and go home."

"Where are you?"

"Never mind that. Just tell me."

Lena cackled, the evil witch. "You're at Mark's," she guessed.

"Yes," Rainey said miserably.

"You're wearing good underwear, right? Something slinky?"

"Lena." She thunked her head against the steering

wheel. "I'm just here to deliver brownies as a thank-you."

"Uh-huh. And I'm the Easter Bunny. You should know that I put a condom in your purse the other day. Just in case. Side pocket. Magnum-sized. Ribbed for your pleasure."

"Oh my God."

"'Night, hon. Don't do anything I wouldn't do."

"There's *nothing* you wouldn't do!"

"Well, then you're in for a great night, aren't you?" Lena laughed and disconnected.

Rainey stared at the pristine black truck in the parking lot, sticking out among the beat-up cars and trucks around it. They weren't friends. They weren't having any sort of a relationship—hot sex aside—and yet...

And yet...

Somehow it felt like both of those things were happening in spite of themselves. She wasn't here to give him brownies. She and every single one of her hormones knew that. But she was already dangerously close to not being able to keep this casual. She wasn't good at going with the flow and letting things happen. Not when she knew in her heart that she could feel much more than simple lust for him.

That she already felt more.

And what if she gave in to it, what then? She'd have to deal with the consequences when he left—and he would—and she didn't have a game plan for that.

But then there was the fact that no matter what she threw at him, he managed it. Handled it. Even fixed it. She thought about earlier, how he'd managed to coach the girls to a strong win. How they listened to him. They *talked* to him.

A part of her wanted him for that alone. The rest of her wanted him because he was sharp and fearless and intelligent.

No, you want him because he oozes testosterone and pheromones.

Oh, yeah. That, too.

Blowing out a breath, she got out of her car and walked into the lobby, telling herself she was just going to give him the brownies and go.

Casey and James were in the lobby, reading trade magazines and newspapers, drinking beer, watching soap operas with the woman behind the front desk.

"Hey, Rainey, I smell chocolate," Casey said, pouncing on her brownies like he was starving, making her join them.

James showed her the calluses on his hands from all the hammering he'd been doing. Casey had a nice gash across his forehead after he'd apparently walked into a two-by-four on the job. The talk slipped to coaching the teens and Casey grinned. "Man, as many women as Coach always has throwing themselves at him, it's been fun watching him have to work at getting the chicks to like him."

Rainey's bite of brownie stuck like glue in her mouth at the thought of how many women loved Mark.

"You're an idiot," Casey told James.

"No, it's okay," Rainey assured him. "I'm perfectly aware of his reputation."

"I didn't mean it like that," James said earnestly. "It's not like he's a male ho or anything, I swear. It's just that…I don't know…he's sort of bigger than life, and women are curious, you know? Most of the time, he doesn't even pay any attention to them leaving their phone numbers and panties on his hotel room door."

Rainey stood up, not needing to hear more. "So... where is he?"

"In his room making calls and doing some work," Casey said. "But he's grumpy."

"Huh," Rainey said. *Join the club.* "Think brownies'll help?"

They all looked at her like she was crazy, and she sighed. "Right. He can get anything he wants. Why would brownies help?"

"Um, Rainey?" Casey smiled gently. "We meant that no, the brownies won't help, but *you* will."

Two minutes later Rainey knocked on Mark's door, heart hammering in her throat. This was ridiculous, using brownies as a ruse to see him. So ridiculous. She turned to go, which of course was the exact moment the door opened. Walking away, she closed her eyes.

"Rainey." Even in that not-close-to-happy voice, the sound of her name on his lips made her nipples hard. Slowly she turned to face him. He wore a pair of Levi's and nothing else, half-buttoned and almost indecently low on his hips, revealing the perfect cut of his chest and abs.

And dammit, even his bare feet were beautiful.

He was holding a cell phone to his ear and his iPad in his hand. At her thorough inspection of his body, he arched a brow and tossed the iPad to the small desk. Still holding her gaze, he said into the phone, "I have to go, something just came up."

Without waiting for a reply, he disconnected and tossed the phone to the desk as well.

It immediately began vibrating, but Mark ignored it, eyes locked on her.

Fighting the twin urges to squirm and/or jump him, Rainey forced herself to stand there, cool and calm as could be. Because suddenly she accepted what she'd come here for.

Him.

She'd come here for him, any way that she could get him. "You busy?"

He didn't bother to answer that one, just leaned against the doorjamb.

Her eyes traveled the breadth of his shoulders down his bare torso, along the eight pack to the narrow silky trail of barely-there hair that vanished into the opened button fly of his jeans, and she felt her entire body respond. Was he wearing underwear? Because she couldn't see any... The thought of him commando under those jeans gave her a serious hot flash. Her brain tried to signal a warning that she was in over her head but she told herself she'd worry about the aftermath later.

Much later. "I brought brownies," she said. "I'm-sorry-for-being-an-ass brownies."

"My favorite," he said. He stepped back and gestured her in ahead of him, kicking the door closed.

She set the brownies on the desk next to his phone and iPad, then slid her hands to his biceps and turned him, pressing him back against the door.

His eyes went from unreadable to scorching as he permitted her to maneuver him. "You have plans," he murmured.

"Turns out that I do."

"Does it involve instigating? Or that TLC you promised me?"

"What if it does? What do I get in return?"

His smile was slow and sure and so sexy her bones melted. "Babe, you can have whatever your heart desires."

If only that were true, she thought, and stepped into him anyway, plastering herself to that body she dreamed about every night as she covered his mouth with hers.

The kiss ignited like a rocket flash. Not that this surprised her. Everything pertaining to Mark seemed to burn hot and fast. Frustration, lust...

His mouth was rough, hot and hungry on hers as he pulled her closer, taking control. She heard herself moan, kissing him with helpless desperation. If dessert was her usual drug of choice, it'd just been replaced because she couldn't seem to get enough of him.

Apparently feeling the same way, he gripped her hips, then slid his hands up to cup and mold her breasts. "I don't know exactly what your plan is," he murmured silkily. "But if it isn't me stripping you naked and then licking every square inch of you, you need to stop me now." His mouth got busy on her throat as his talented hands slid beneath her shirt, gliding up her belly, heading north.

All she managed was another moan, squirming a little, trying to encourage his hands to hurry. Obliging, he pushed up her shirt, tugged down her bra and ghosted the tips of his fingers over her nipples, leaving her body humming, throbbing for more.

His lips left hers for the barest breath. "Rainey."

"Yes." God, yes.

"Yes what?"

"Ohmigod, you and the dirty talk!"

He nipped her jaw. "Tell me," he murmured, voice husky. "Tell me you want me to strip you and lick you all over."

He wanted to hear the words from her, she got that. And in her daily life, she always had plenty of words, but he scrambled her brain. Plus, talking dirty felt...well, dirty. She nearly laughed, but Mark wasn't laughing. He was waiting for an answer with that same simmering intensity he gave to all aspects of his life, emitting a raw sensuality that made her feel sexy, so damn sexy. And he was like a drug, an addiction. A seductive addition... "Yes, I want that," she said. "What you said."

She'd have sworn his lips twitched, the smug bastard. "The stripping?" he asked.

"Yes, and the other." *Please to the other!*

"I can't remember what that was," he said.

Liar. He was such a liar. "I want the licking too," she whispered, and pressed her face to his chest.

He slid one arm around her waist, and lifted his other hand to run it down her hair, the gesture possessive and protective at the same time. "Anything else?"

"You really want me to say it?"

"Yes."

"Gah," she managed, and burrowed in even tighter, realizing she was nuzzling his chest, her nose pressed against a flat male nipple. He sucked in a breath through his teeth, nothing more than a low hiss that was the sexiest sound she'd ever heard. She opened her mouth on him, tempted to bite him, but as if he guessed her intent, he wrapped his hand in her hair and tugged lightly until she looked up at him.

"After all we've done together," he said in amused disbelief. "How can you still be embarrassed?"

"I don't know!" She squeezed her eyes shut. "Can't we *just* do it?"

He reversed their positions, pressing her against the door now, and she promptly lost her train of thought because she could feel his every inch.

Every. Single. One.

He kissed her, sweeping his tongue over hers in a slow, languid stroke that melted her bones. She ran her hands up his sides and down again, sliding them into the back of his loose, low-slung jeans, and…

Oh, yeah. Commando.

She tried to get closer, and it still wasn't close enough. She'd have climbed inside him if she could, and she let out a low sound of frustration and need and desperation. His lips left hers for a bare second to whisper her name soothingly before hungrily devouring her again, until her entire body was trembling. Breathless, she tore her mouth free. "Mark, I can't… I can't stand up."

Almost before the words were out of her mouth, he lifted her and carried her to the bed. Then he stripped out of his jeans, shoving them down his thighs and off, his eyes never leaving hers.

At the sight of him, she gulped.

"Did you change your mind about the stripping or licking or…" His mouth curved, though his eyes remained serious. "Other stuff?"

"No."

He put a knee on the bed, then crawled up her body,

looking bigger and badder than she remembered, and with a momentary bout of nerves, she scooted backwards.

He immediately stopped stalking her. There in the middle of the bed on his knees, gloriously naked, gloriously hard, he went still. "You have all the power, Rainey. You know that, right?"

She didn't feel like that at all. This had started out as a way to have him, knowing that it wasn't real. For keeps. Even if she had *any* of the power, he was way too in control for her tastes. To even the playing field, she pulled off her shirt, then felt better when his eyes glazed over. She wriggled out of her jeans and panties, soaking up his appreciative groan. He was kneeling between her legs when he took one of her feet in his big hand and kissed her ankle, her calf, and then the inside of her knee.

At the soft sigh that escaped her, he looked at her from those smoking eyes. "Good?"

"So good. Don't stop."

"I won't." He set her foot flat on the bed, her knee bent, affording himself a front row center view of ground zero. "Mmm." The sound rumbled from his chest, and he slid his hands beneath her bottom and tugged her to him. Then he put his mouth on her, sending her flying with shocking ease.

When she'd stopped shuddering, he pushed up on his forearms. "I like that expression you're wearing."

"The one that says I no longer have a thought in my brain?"

"You have a thought. You want me inside you."

"More than my next breath." She hesitated, then admitted the rest of that truth. "There's a condom in my purse."

His smile was slow and sure and sexy as hell. "Brownies *and* a condom."

It took him less than ten seconds to locate it. And then he positioned himself above her and filled her in one smooth stroke, making her gasp and clutch at him. Her eyes closed involuntarily at the sensation of him pressing deep, so deep that she cried out from the sheer perfection of it, and then again when he stroked his thumb over her. "I'm—I need—"

"I know. I've got you." And he did. He brought her to another shattering climax, staying with her through it, then when she could open her eyes, she found his, black and scorching on hers. Still hard within her, he leaned over her, thrusting deep, sending her spiraling again, and this time he followed her.

RAINEY LAY THERE STARING at the ceiling, sucking air, trying to get her breath back. Mark appeared to be in the same state. After a minute, he rolled to his side and pulled her in close, fitting her against him so that she could feel the after-shock when it ran through his body. It caused the same tremor within her, so strong it was almost another orgasm—from nothing more than knowing she'd given him pleasure.

With a low, very male sound of satisfaction, he ran his fingers over her heated skin. Thriving on the touch, she had to fight the urge to crawl under the covers with him to fall asleep in his arms.

Definitely, she needed to go.

Sitting up, she slid off the bed and began to search for her clothing, not missing the irony—she'd told him

to stop interfering with her life, and yet she'd been the
one to bring them to this point. The naked point. Which
was about as deep into the interference of one's life as
it got. At his soft chuckle, she looked up.

Mark was still sprawled across the bed, arms up
behind his head, feet crossed, casual as could be,
seeped in the supreme confidence of someone who
didn't have to worry about whether or not he looked
good naked.

Because he did.

So good.

So.

Damn.

Good.

"Why are you laughing?" she asked, wearing only
her bra and one sock. "And where are my panties?"

He sat up, the muscles of his abs crunching and
making her mouth go dry. In one fluid motion, he was
off the bed and handing her the panties.

She reached for them, but with a wicked smile, he
held them high above her head.

"Give me," she said.

"Don't you mean *please* give me?"

"You want me to beg?"

That smile spread slightly. "Nah. I just heard you
beg plenty."

"I did not beg."

But she had. She so had.

Still grinning, still naked, he pulled her against him
and pressed his mouth to her shoulder.

"My panties, Mark."

Eyes warm, he handed them to her, and then suddenly it was like her brain disconnected from her mouth

because she heard herself say, "Do I really have all the power?"

"After what we just did, you can doubt that?"

"I want the power to do something with this thing between you and me. Something more than just sex."

He went still, and her heart stopped. "Or not," she said. Feeling *very* exposed, she backed away. She shoved her legs into her panties and pulled them up. Then her jeans.

"Rainey—"

"No, you know what? That was leftover pheromones talking. Ignore it. Ignore me." Oh, God. "I gotta go."

He let out a long breath, then reached for her. "I thought you had me figured for a bad bet."

"You are. A really bad bet, at least for me, because you operate day-to-day."

And she operated long term. They both knew that. "I'm not a keeper, Rainey."

There was something in his voice, something terrifyingly regretful and terrifyingly firm.

Did he not realize that to her, he was the ultimate keeper? Sharply intelligent, funny as hell, hardworking, caring... But she wouldn't argue this, because as he'd pointed out, she'd already done her begging tonight. She went back to dressing, getting out of here her only plan. He'd told her that she had the power, but that was all wrong. *He* had the power, the power to stomp on her heart until it stopped functioning.

She turned to look for her shoes and bumped into his chest, which was a little like walking into a brick wall. "Excuse me," she said.

"I want to make sure you understand."

"I do."

"I don't think so," he said. "This isn't just sex for me, Rainey." He took her arms in his big hands to keep her from escaping and her belly quivered.

Stupid belly.

"I just don't have anything to offer more than what we have right now," he said quietly.

"Which is what, that day-to-day thing?"

"Yeah."

Okay, she got that. Loud and clear. Sex was great. More than sex…not so much.

"Where does that leave us?" he asked, his eyes serious.

"In the same place we've always been," she managed to say.

"So then… why exactly are we dressing?" His eyes were dark and focused on her breasts. "Because from here," he said softly, "going back to bed looks like a great idea."

"Because…" Hell. This was getting complicated. This had been all her doing, she should be fine. She wanted to be fine. But her feelings for him had deepened, and she was afraid. He was going to hurt her without even trying. "Excuse me a minute?" Vanishing into the bathroom, she locked herself in and whipped out her cell phone. "Lena," she whispered when her best friend picked up. "I need your help."

"What's the matter?"

Rainey sank to the closed toilet lid and dropped her head to her knees. "I'm with Mark."

"Nice."

"No, I mean I'm with him with him."

"Like I said, nice."

"Listen!" Rainey lowered her voice with effort. "He fooled me!"

"Huh?"

"You said I should go for a guy who *isn't* a fixer-upper, right? And I figured I was safe with Mark because he *is* a fixer-upper, the ultimate fixer-upper, actually. But I was wrong. He's not a fixer-upper at all. I like him just how he is. And now I'm screwed."

Lena laughed.

"I don't mean that in a good way! Okay, well it was good, but you know what I mean!"

"Ah, honey. You're afraid."

Yeah. She was. So deeply afraid she'd fallen in love—madly, irrevocably in love.

"Look, I realize I'm speaking Greek when I tell you this," Lena said. "But just enjoy the ride on this one." She paused. "Pun intended."

"But the plan was for this to be light!"

"Honey, you don't always have to have a plan."

Rainey sighed and hung up. God, what to do? Could she really just go with the flow and let this thing play out?

Yes, said her body.

No, said her brain. Hell, no. Because when he left, and he was going to, she'd be devastated. With a sound of frustration, she shoved her phone into her pocket, drew a deep breath, and stood up. Gathering her courage, she opened the door.

Standing there in the doorway, hands up over his head and latched onto the jamb, was six feet plus of pure testosterone wrapped in tough, rugged sinew.

They stared at each other for a long beat.

"She tell you to dump me?" he asked quietly.

"She told me to enjoy the ride."

His smile was slow and sure and sexy. Damn. She pointed at him. "None of that or my clothes will fall off again. Move. I need space to think."

He moved. He moved into her, sliding his arms around her and melting her damn knees.

11

A PART OF MARK HAD BEEN braced for Rainey to grab her purse and walk out of his motel room.

And out of his life.

He'd fully expected it. Hell, he deserved it. But she let him pull her in, even pressed her face to his throat and inhaled deeply, and relief flooded him. Knee-knocking, gut-squeezing relief. "Rainey—"

"I don't want to talk about it. You're not sticking around, we've never made each other any promises. There was no plan, so there's no reason for me to try to back you into one now." Her cell phone vibrated. "It's Lena," she muttered. "Probably apologizing for being a bad wingman." She opened her phone. "It's too late to help me now, I—" She broke off and came to immediate attention, straightening up. "Sharee?"

Mark watched the furrow across Rainey's brow. Her hair was wild, probably thanks to his fingers. Her make-up had smeared beneath her eyes a little and she had a whisker burn down her throat. Lifting his hand, he ran a thumb over the mark.

"Sharee?" Rainey said. "Honey, what's wrong?"

Mark shifted in closer and put a hand on her shoulder. She looked up at him, her eyes dark with concern, and surprised him even further when she leaned into him as she listened. "I'm coming right now," she said. "Stay in a lit area—Hello? *Sharee?*" She stared at her phone. "Dammit, her battery died. I've got to go."

Mark was already grabbing a shirt and keys. "I'll drive."

RAINEY'S NERVES WERE in her throat as she picked up her purse. She'd never heard Sharee upset before. Pissed-off, yes. Pure bravado, often. Upset and scared, no. "She's at the high school," Rainey told Mark. "She got dropped there after shopping with friends. Her mom was supposed to get her but isn't there yet and Sharee said those boys are there, the ones I kicked out of the rec center last week. They're harassing her because she's the one who told me who they were."

Mark opened the door for her, then followed her out. "Oh, you don't have to—"

"I'm driving," he repeated in that quiet but firm voice she'd heard him use in interviews, on the teens, and on his players. It was a voice that brooked no argument while at the same time instilled confidence and a belief that everything was going to be okay.

She wanted to believe it. They moved through the lobby. The guys were still there and waved at them.

"The walk of shame," Rainey murmured.

Mark's hand slid warmly to the back of her neck. "They won't say anything."

"Are you kidding? Look at me."

He pulled her around to look at her, and his eyes softened. "You look like you just—"

"Rolled around in bed? Had an orgasm?"

An affectionate smile crossed his face. "Or three."

She smacked him lightly in the abs—which didn't give—and he grabbed her hand, holding her at his side as they continued to walk.

True to Mark's word, Casey and James didn't say a thing, but that was because Mark was giving them a long look over her head, which she managed to just catch. She waited until they were outside heading to his truck. "What did you threaten them with?"

He slid her a glance. "You were standing right there. I didn't say anything."

"Uh-huh."

He smiled. "Push-ups. Laps. Sitting their ass on the bench. Pick one."

"They're grown-ups. You'd do that?"

"I don't care how old they are, their asses are mine."

She shook her head and laughed. "You sound like a dictator."

"I am."

"And you like it? All that power?"

He just shot her a look.

Yeah. He liked it.

They stepped out into the cool night. Rainey reached into her purse for her keys while Mark caught sight of her car and went utterly still.

Someone had spray-painted *Bitch* across the trunk.

"Huh," she said. "That's new." And unwelcome. And more than a little unnerving.

"The boys?" Mark asked, hands on hips, grim. Pissed off.

"I don't know."

Mark pulled out his phone.

"What are you doing?"

"Calling the police. We need to make a report."

"Later. We need to get Sharee first."

Not looking happy, he took her hand again and led her to his truck. As they drove, the moon slanted into the windshield at an angle, giving her only peeks at the man beside her. He took two calls and made one, though she missed out on eavesdropping because she was busy demon-dialing Sharee, who wasn't answering.

Mark slipped his phone away and continued driving with single-minded purpose, fast, but steady. In his zone. He pulled into the high school parking lot, where they found Sharee huddled on the front steps. Rainey ran out and hugged her. "You okay?"

Sharee allowed the contact for a brief moment before pulling back. "Yeah." She looked around uneasily. "I think they left."

Mark was alert, his eyes missing nothing as he scanned the lot, his posture both at ease and utterly ready for anything. "Let's get out of here."

Twenty minutes later, they pulled up to the trailer that Sharee shared with her mom.

It was dark.

Rainey turned to face the girl in the backseat. "Sharee—"

"I'll be fine," she said, getting out of the truck. "Thanks for the ride."

Mark got out with her and looked at Rainey. "Stay here."

Before she could say a word, he'd engaged the locks and walked Sharee to the door. He waited there, keeping both Rainey and Sharee in sight until lights were on in the trailer. Then he came back to his truck and drove Rainey to the motel, where they met a police officer and filed a report about her car.

Then Mark followed her home and saw her to the door just as he had Sharee.

But the smoking hot kiss he laid on her was hers alone.

THE NEXT DAY MARK POKED his head into Rainey's office and surprised her. "Hungry?" he asked.

It was late afternoon and she'd worked through lunch. She was starving. "Maybe," she said. "Why?"

"Thought we'd go get dinner."

A date? She wasn't sure what that meant, not that it mattered. "I can't. I have plans."

Nothing about his body language changed. He was too good for that. But she sensed that her statement hadn't made him happy. "Plans?" he asked.

"I'm going to my parents' house."

"Are you taking a date with you?"

No. She'd decided she couldn't be dating while she was doing...whatever this was that she was doing with him. It wouldn't be fair to anyone else. She barely had the mental capacity to handle Mark, much less another man as well.

And...

And the truth was, she didn't have the emotional capacity either. Mark was currently using up all she had. "Would that bother you?"

"Hell yes."

Odd how that made her all soft and warm inside. "I'm not taking a date to my parents," she said quietly. "My plans to date are temporarily on hold."

He closed her office door behind him, then came around her desk and hauled her up to her toes, kissing her until she couldn't remember her own name. "Good," he said, and was gone.

RAINEY'S PARENTS LIVED in a small, modest home in an area that had been spared the fires but not the economic downturn. Here, the houses were tired, the yards were tired, *everything* was tired. In addition, thanks to the drought, they were under strict water restrictions. The grass hadn't survived but there were potted wild flowers on the porch, which made Rainey smile.

So did the fact that her mother stood in the front door, waiting with a warm hug. "Honey, it's so good to see you!"

"Mom, you just saw me a week ago."

"I know." Elizabeth Saunders was blonde with gray streaks, medium build like Rainey, with the softness that having two kids and then thirty years of happiness gave a woman. "You look different, honey." Her mom studied Rainey's face. "What is it?"

"Nothing." Lots of sex… "New face lotion."

"Well it's done something fantastic to your skin. You need to use it more often."

Rainey nodded. Keep having orgasms. Got it.

Her mom cupped Rainey's face, staring into it. "It really suits you."

Oh, for the love of—"What's for dinner?"

"Lasagna. And a *surprise*."

Rainey hoped it involved chocolate. She moved into the kitchen to check things out. Her younger sister Danica was there, stirring something on the stove. Danica was married to her high school sweetheart.

"your surprise arrived." She appeared in the kitchen doorway. "I ran into him today at the gas station," she whispered.

"I thought my surprise was chocolate," Rainey said, a very bad feeling coming over her.

"Nope. Better than chocolate." Her mother smiled, then turned and revealed...

Mark Diego.

MARK NEVER GAVE MUCH thought to his next meal. During the season, he ate at the Mammoths facilities, the same as his team. When he was on the road, there was room service and restaurants. Even off season, he usually went that route.

But one thing he rarely had—a home-cooked meal.

Rainey's mom had made lasagna and cheese bread, which was delicious, but his favorite part was after-wards, when Danica brought out the photo albums and showed him the old family pictures, including one of a two-year-old diaper-clad Rainey waddling away from the camera, diaper slipping low, thighs thick and chunky.

"Seriously?" Rainey asked.

"Oh, you don't like that one?" Danica flipped the pages to reveal a pre-teen Rainey in braces, looking... well, as annoyed as she was right now. Heart softening, Mark reached for her hand but she stood up.

And gave his feet a little nudge. Actually, it was more like a kick. "Mark has to go now," she said. "He's got a thing."

"A what?" Danica asked.

"A thing. Somewhere to be."

"I don't have a thing," Mark said, remaining seated, ignoring Rainey's dirty look.

"Okay," she said. "Then I have a thing."

Mark snagged her wrist. He was extremely aware that she thought that he was in this just for the sex, but she was wrong. He was in for more. He just wasn't sure what that more was. All he knew was that sitting in the slightly shabby living room surrounded by Rainey and her family made him feel more relaxed and calm than he could remember being in far too long.

Danica smiled at him and continued to flip through the photo album. "Uh-oh," she said. "Don't look now but here's Rainey's first boyfriend. You were what, like eighteen? Slow bloomer. Probably because you still had a crush on this one." She gestured to Mark, then grinned at him. "We all had a crush on you," she told him. "But I think Rainey's lasted a little longer than most."

Rainey tugged free of Mark's hold and headed to the door.

"Ah, don't get all butt-hurt and embarrassed," Danica called after her. "I'm sure Mark already knew—everyone knew."

The front door slammed.

Mark made his thank-yous and goodbyes, and got outside in time to see Rainey drive off. Given that she drove a POS and he didn't, he had no trouble keeping up with her. Especially since she stopped at a convenience store. He watched her go in and then come out five minutes later with a brown bag. He followed her to her town house and parked next to her.

"So," he said conversationally, following her up the

path to her door, gesturing to the brown bag. "Alcohol or sugar?"

"Sugar. I don't need an escort."

"There's some guy out there writing BITCH on your car, I'm walking you up."

She unlocked her door, stepped in, and tried to close it on him.

"I'm also coming in," he said.

"Fine, but we are *not* talking."

"Not talking is right up my alley." He moved through her place, checking out the rooms. Satisfied, he found her standing in the dark living room, staring out the window into the night. "Rainey."

She dropped her head to the window. "Don't."

He wasn't exactly sure what she was saying *don't* to, but had a feeling it was *don't* come close, *don't* talk, *don't* touch, *don't* so much as breathe. He was bound to disappoint her since he was going to insist on all of the above, and coming up behind her, he risked his neck by stroking a hand down her hair. "You okay?"

She made a soft sound, like a sigh. "She's right, you know. I've screwed up my love life, over and over again, because of how I felt for you. I think I compared every guy to you." She shook her head and let out a low laugh. "It was real nice of you to pretend you didn't know how I felt back then."

Catching her arm, he pulled her around to face him, unhappy to see the look in her eyes, the one that said she felt a little defeated, a little down, and definitely wary. "I wasn't pretending. I was really that slow, especially that night when you came to my apartment."

"Well of course you were slow that night. You were deep in the throes of getting…pleasured."

He let out a breath. "That's actually not the part of that whole nightmare of a night that I was referring to."

She crossed her arms. "Well, there's no other part of that night that I want to discuss. Ever." She looked away. "Certainly not why you felt the need to come after me if you didn't want me."

He stared at her bowed head and felt an unaccustomed squeeze in the region of his heart. "You were sixteen."

"I want to go back to the no-talking thing."

"I cared about you, Rainey. But you were off limits to me, with or without the girl in my bedroom that night. I didn't allow myself to look at you that way, and with good reason."

"I wasn't a child."

"You were a *felony*."

She seemed to stop breathing, which he took as a good sign. She was listening. "As for what happened after, I'm not sorry about that. He was drunk and being aggressive with you, and I don't care what you think of me now, surely you know I'd never walk away from that."

She said nothing.

"Never, Rainey. As far as I knew, you were innocent—"

She made a soft moan of protest, and he paused, taking in her profile, which wasn't giving much away. "And I'm not sorry I kicked his ass either."

At that, she looked up. "You did?"

He hesitated, knowing she wasn't going to thank him for this part. "After I made sure you got home, I went after him. I threatened to kill him if he ever went near you again."

Her eyes narrowed, and he raised a brow, daring her to protest. Finally, she blew out a breath, and even gave him a little smile. "Thanks." Pushing away from him, she headed for the kitchen.

Catching her by the waist, he turned her around and had to duck to look into her eyes. "And I didn't desert our friendship, I went to Ontario for a job. When I left, you weren't speaking to me."

"I'm not speaking to you now either."

He pulled her up against him. "I liked you," he said quietly. "A lot. You were fearless and a little wild, and a whole lot determined."

She snorted.

"I liked you," he repeated quietly, firmly. "But let's be honest. I liked all women back then. I wasn't much for commitment or a relationship beyond what I could get in the hours between dinner and breakfast. It was day-to-day for me."

"By all accounts, that hasn't changed much."

"Fair enough," he said. "I still tend towards the day-to-day. It suits my lifestyle." He hadn't given a lot of thought to having a deep, serious relationship in a while. He'd been there, done that, and it was more trouble than it was worth. He didn't play with women, he didn't lead them on. He enjoyed them. Made sure they enjoyed him. And then when things got sticky or uncomfortable, or too much to handle, he moved on.

Day to day…

"With my job, having a deep, meaningful, heavy relationship just hasn't been on my radar."

She nodded.

"None of that doesn't mean that I don't like the

woman you've become," he said. "Because I do. Very much."

"Even though I'm different?"

"Especially because you're different."

Her eyes lifted to his, revealing a vulnerability that cut him to the core. "Doesn't hurt that you're smart and smoking hot," he said.

"I'm a sure thing, Mark," she said on a low, embarrassed laugh. "You don't need to—"

"And fiercely protective about those you care about," he murmured. "And strong. So damn strong. I think that's what I like the best. Watching you run your world and make a difference while you're at it."

She shook her head. "If it's my turn to say I like you now, you're going to be disappointed. I got over liking you."

He grinned. "Aw, Rainey. You like me. You like me a whole hell of a lot."

"We really need to work on your self-confidence." But she blew out a breath and relaxed into him a little. "You've read your press, right? You know they call you a hard-ass." She lifted her hand and touched his face. "But they're wrong." She pressed her face to his throat and inhaled him in, like maybe he was her air and she needed more. And when her hands slid around his waist, beneath his shirt, and up his back, he knew he was a goner.

12

RAINEY WAS LOST IN MARK'S kiss when her phone vibrated.

Mark groaned.

"I'm sorry," she gasped. "I have to look." She pulled out her phone and eyed the text from a number she didn't recognize.

Are you up for a walk on the beach and dessert? Cliff

One of Mark's big hands cupped the back of hers and his thumb hit *delete*.

"Hey. Maybe I wanted dessert."

"I've got your dessert," he said, moving her backwards until the couch hit the backs of her knees and she dropped into it.

Following her down, he took both her hands in one of his and slowly drew them up over her head, pinning them there as he pressed his lower body into hers before hooking one of her legs around his waist, opening her up to him.

She moaned and he breathed out her name as he

cupped her breast, his thumb gliding over her nipple, causing her to arch up into him like a puppet on a string.

His mouth nipped at her ear, her jaw, then finally, oh God, finally, her mouth, and when he started to pull away, she whimpered.

"Shh," he murmured, and then her clothes were gone, and their hands were fighting to rip off his. He tackled the buttons on his shirt, shrugging out of it, revealing a torso and chest she wanted to rub her face against like a cat in heat. His short hair was mussed, his mouth wet, his eyes at half mast, a sexy heat to them that said her pleasure was his. She pushed him and then followed him to the floor, straddling him.

"And you say *I* have to be in charge," he murmured, chuckling low in his throat as his hands went to her butt. "You have a serious queen bee issue—Jesus!" he gasped when she slid down his body and licked him like a lollipop. She couldn't fit him all in her mouth but she gave it the old college try, and given the rough, raw sounds coming from him and the erotic way he writhed beneath her, she was doing more than okay. After a few minutes, he gasped, "Rainey, stop. I'm going to—"

She didn't stop. Swearing, he hauled her up his chest and rolled them again, pinning her beneath two hundred pounds of very determined Latino sex god. "You don't listen very well."

"Maybe I just wanted you to wrestle control away from me again."

He laughed roughly, then sank his teeth into her lower lip and tugged. "Rainey?"

"Yeah?"

"We're done playing."

"About time."

He produced a condom, then slowly entwined their fingers and drew her hands above her head, then he kissed her long and deep and hot. When they eventually tore apart to breathe, he stared down into her face. "Still mad I deleted Cliff's text?"

"Cliff who?"

With a smug smirk, he kissed her again, then slid into her. Pleasure flooded her, so intense it arched her back and had her crying out, clutching at him. The teasing and fun vanished in a blink, replaced by something so intense she could hardly breathe. Mark's eyes were dark and sultry, and she reared up to press her mouth to his. He took control of the kiss, making her melt into him all the more as he buried himself in her over and over, deeper, harder, faster, the entire time holding her gaze with his, letting her see everything she did to him.

It took her right over the edge. She was still quivering when he grabbed her hips and thrust one last time, holding himself tight against her as he came hard.

When she could think again, she realized he'd lain down beside her and was holding her close, running a hand over her heated, damp skin, waiting while she caught her breath. His wasn't all that steady either. It was her last thought before she drifted off to sleep, comforted by the sound of his heart beating wildly against her ear.

RAINEY WOKE UP ENTANGLED in a set of strong, warm arms. Dawn had come and gone. The sun crept in the window, highlighting the form of the man lying next to her.

His eyes were closed, his decadently inky black

lashes brushing against his cheeks. His dark hair was tousled, his jaw shadowed by a night's beard growth.

They hadn't slept much. Damn testosterone. In spite of herself, the need for him had called to her, over and over again.

It'd been an amazing night. She could replay every touch, every moan he'd wrenched from her, each moment of ecstasy.

And there'd been lots.

The sheet rode low on his hips and she soaked him up, the broad shoulders and wide chest tapering to that stomach she still, after licking every inch of him last night, wanted to press her mouth to. His chest was rising and falling steadily, but as if he sensed her perusal, he drew in a deep breath. The arm he had curled around her tightened, drawing her in closer. "Mmmm." The sound rumbled up from his chest as a hand slid into her hair. He had an obsession with her hair, she'd noticed, he loved touching it, burying his face in it.

His other hand slid down her back and gripped her butt, squeezing. She arched into the touch and felt herself practically purr with contentment.

And hence the danger. The sleeping portion of the night had given her a sense of intimacy—a *fake* intimacy. It'd brought contentment, warmth, affection. She didn't want to feel those things for him, but just like when she'd been a love-struck teenager, it'd happened. Only this time she'd known better.

This could be fixed, she hurried to assure herself. She just needed a time-out. *Now.*

He stirred when she slipped out of bed, opening his eyes. "Rainey." His voice was low and rough from sleep, and he was lying in her sheets like he belonged there, long sinewy limbs at rest, eyes warm and getting warmer, heating all her parts equally.

"You need to stop giving me orgasms," she said.

"Aw, you don't mean that. Come here, I'll show you."

She actually took a step toward him before stopping short. "Oh my God. I think I'm actually addicted to you—"

This sentence ended with her letting out a startled scream because suddenly she was airborne. Mark had risen from the bed and tossed her to the mattress. He followed her down, crawling up her body. They were both naked, and at the contact, she arched up and moaned.

His smile was pure trouble.

"Oh, no," she said, scooting backwards. "I'm going to work."

He grabbed her ankles and tugged.

She landed flat on her back, legs spread wide, held open by him. "I'm not playing," she said, having to try real hard not to be turned on. "We're having another car wash today, and I have a staff meeting about the formal dinner and auction next Saturday. Busy day," she said, breathless from just the way he was looking at her. "And besides, you wanted a day to day, right? Well it's a new day and I have plans. Gotta go."

"I think I'm missing something," he said, slipping his hand into her hair, tugging lightly until she looked into his eyes. "What's the real problem here?"

"The problem is that I have thirty minutes to get into work! Let go." She attempted to leave the bed, but he merely tightened his grip, pulling her to him until their faces were so close that she could feel his warm breath on her lips. She could see the heat in his eyes, and also a curiosity. Probably the man had never been kicked out of a woman's bed before. "It's nothing personal," she said.

"Bullshit."

She sighed. "Okay, you're right. It's personal. It's just that…remember when I said I had to instigate or I'd get screwed up?"

"Yeah."

"Well, it happened anyway. I'm screwed up."

"What are you screwed up about?"

The fact that I've fallen in love with you… She fought to get free and rolled off the bed. "I have to go, Mark. Don't make this harder than it is."

"I'm not making this anything," he said, sitting up, watching her from inscrutable eyes. "That's all you. If things veer off the path of your plan in any way, you panic, like now. Things happen, Rainey. You know that."

"Hey, *you're* the one with the plan," she said. "The plan that can't go more than a day in advance. I'm not even sure why, except that it leaves you open in case something better comes along."

"Is that what you think?" He caught her before she could grab her clothes—damn he was fast—and pulled her back to his chest. "Rainey, there's no one else. Not while we're…"

"Having all the sex?" She crossed her arms, doing her best to ignore that her butt was pressed into his groin. But then he stirred. Hardened. "Are you kidding me? *Now?*"

With a sigh, he let her go. "I can't help it. You're naked. And hot. I'm hard-wired to react."

They both looked at his erection. A little part of her
wanted to push him back down to the bed and jump him.

Okay, a big part of her.

"I'm seriously late," she said. "We can finish this
tonight."

"Can't. I'm flying to New York after the car wash,
doing some press. I'll be gone three or four days."

"Oh," she said, hopefully hiding her disappointment.

"I'll see you when I get back," he murmured, watching her body with avid attention as she gathered some
clothes.

"Can you make plans that far out?"

"Ha ha." He pulled out his phone and opened his calendar file, flipping through the days with his thumb.
"Shit. Five days. I'll be back Saturday, just in time for
the auction and the big games on Sunday."

"That's almost a whole week," she said. "I might find
another non-fixer upper by then. Gotta leave my options
open." She went into the bathroom, carefully avoiding
the mirror and her rosy oversexed complexion as she
got into the shower. When she went back into the bedroom to dress, she didn't look at Mark's oversexed self
either, still naked and sprawled out on her bed, working on his phone. She grabbed her purse and turned to
the door, only to be forced back around by Mark's firm
hands on her arms.

"Lunch," he said. "Today."

"Can't."

"Can't? Or won't?"

"Can't. I have a meeting. And won't. I need a little
space, Mark."

He stared at her as if it hadn't occurred to him that
she wouldn't want him.

"Tell me you've been turned down before," she said.

"Sure. In fifth grade Serena Gutierrez said she'd go out with me, but then I found out she'd also said yes to five other guys. She broke my heart."

Hands on hips, she narrowed her eyes. "Something past puberty."

"I was dumped right before my high school prom and had to go stag."

"Yes, and you ended up with three dates once you got there," she reminded him. "Three girls who were also solo."

"Oh yeah," he said with a fond smile.

Whirling, she headed down the hallway to the front door.

"Okay, okay," he said on a laugh, following her. "I've been dumped plenty. I work twenty-four/seven, and I travel all the time. I don't have a lot left to give to a relationship. Women don't tend to like that."

"Hence the day-to-day thing?"

"Don't fix what isn't broke," he said.

Right. She nodded, throat tight. "Good idea." Too bad it was too late. She was already broke. "Goodbye, Mark," she said softly, and walked out the door.

MARK STARED AT THE CLOSED door and felt cold to the bone. That hadn't felt like an "I'll see you in five days" goodbye. That had felt like a *goodbye* goodbye.

Which meant he'd messed up. It'd been a while since he'd done that, and even longer since he'd faced a problem that he had no idea how to fix.

Needing to try, he yanked the door open and stepped onto the porch, just in time to see Rainey's taillights vanish down the road.

"Damn," he muttered, and shoved his fingers through his hair. He was the biggest dumbass on the planet.

A female gasp interrupted his musings, and had him turning to face a woman standing on the next porch over. She was in her forties, looking completely shell-shocked as she stared at him.

"You're...*naked*."

Shit. Yes, he was. Bare-assed naked, giving her the full Monty. With as much dignity as he could, he turned to go back inside, but the door had shut behind him.

And locked.

Mark once again faced the woman, who let out a low, inarticulate sound at the sight of him. "I'm going to need to borrow your phone," he said.

13

MARK WAS SITTING OUT front of Rainey's town house with the neighbor's towel around his hips when Rick drove up and honked.

"Shut up," Mark muttered as he walked to the car.

"Watch the towel, man, these are leather seats."

Mark flipped him off.

"Aw," Rick said with a tsk. "Rough day already?"

"I don't want to talk about it. Ever."

"I bet." Rick drove off with lots of grinning and the occasional snicker, which Mark ignored.

They went to the motel so Mark could get clothes, and then to the construction site, where he spent the next few hours compartmentalizing. Swinging a hammer, wielding his phone for Mammoth business, and…thinking about Rainey dumping his sorry ass.

Don't go there….

Late afternoon he left the construction site and headed to the rec center for the car wash. Casey and James helped staff members set up but there was a lot of chaos, and for that Mark was glad because it gave him something to do other than think too hard. His softball team straggled in one by one, dropped off by parents or riding in with friends who had a license, and for a minute, Mark's spirits rose. The girls would annoy him in no time flat, taking his attention away from himself.

They weren't in their uniforms today. Nope, they'd come dressed as they pleased, which was hardly dressed at all. Bikinis, low-riding shorts, tight yoga pants…the combination made his head spin. "Okay, no," he said. "Go add layers. *Lots* of them."

When he turned around, Rick was standing there, holding two sodas. "You do realize that they're not your million-dollar guys, being paid to be bossed by you, right?"

"You brought me here to clean up their act and make players out of them."

"No, I brought you here so your players could clean up their act."

Oh, yeah. Right. "Well, we'll kill two birds with one stone."

Rick shook his head and offered him one of the sodas. "You look like hell, man. So how did you end up the one dumped? And has that ever even happened before?"

"What part of I don't want to talk about it don't you get?" He let out a breath when Rainey came out of the building wearing denim shorts and a tee, and…

Mark's ball cap.

She was finally wearing *his* ball cap. Ignoring the pain in his chest, he looked her over as indifferently as he could manage. A ponytail stuck out the back of the hat, her beat-up sneakers were sans socks, and she looked every bit as young as his softball team. Across the parking lot, their gazes met. Hers was wary, uncertain, vulnerable, and… hell.

Sad.

He imagined his was more of the same, minus the vulnerable part. He didn't do vulnerable.

"Want my advice?" Rick asked.

"No."

His brother clapped a hand on Mark's shoulder. "Gonna give it to you anyway. Whatever it is, whatever stupid ass thing you've done, suck it up and apologize. Even if you weren't wrong. Works every time, and as a bonus, you get make-up sex."

"*That's* your advice?" Mark asked. "To grovel?"

"You got anything better?"

"No."

Rick laughed and walked off, heading for Lena, who greeted him with a sweet smile and a kiss.

Rainey was still looking at Mark. Raising her chin slightly, she headed right for him, and his heart, abused all damn morning, kicked hard. For the first time in his entire life, he actually had to fight a flight response but he forced himself to hold his ground as more cars pulled in.

Guys. Teenage guys. The ones James and Casey were working with. They piled out of their cars with greetings for Rainey and his girls, who were coming back outside, only slightly more covered than they'd been when they arrived.

"Mark."

Sharee hadn't changed out of her short shorts and she was sauntering up to Todd, who had his eyes locked on her body.

"*Mark,*" Rainey repeated.

Zach was a marine, out on his second tour of duty at the moment. Rainey's seven-year-old niece sat on the counter sucking a Popsicle. Hope's mouth was purple, as were her lips and hands. Actually, just about everything was purple except for her dancing blue eyes. "Rainey!" she squealed in delight.

Rainey leaned in for a kiss and got a sloppy, wet smack right on the lips. "Yum. Grape."

Hope grinned.

Danica looked behind Rainey towards the doorway. "Where's your date?"

"I don't have one."

"Mom said you did."

"Nope."

"She said you were dating Mark Diego."

"Mom's crazy."

"Yeah. So?"

Rainey shook her head. "So I'm not dating Mark." *I'm just doing him.*

"Then can *I* date him?" Danica wanted to know.

"You're married."

Danica grinned. "Yes, but I'm not dead."

Rainey sighed. "He's not all that."

"Liar."

"Okay, he's all that with frosting on top." Bastard. Rainey plopped down in a kitchen chair, accepting the grape Popsicle that Hope pulled out of the freezer and handed her.

Danica waited until her daughter had gone looking for grandma. "So you're *not* doing Mark?" she whispered.

"Okay, that's not what you asked me."

"Honey," their mom called from the living room,

"What the hell are they wearing?"

"Who?"

"The girls. Look at them, do you call that a swim-suit?" he asked. "Because I call it floss."

She made a choked reply, and he turned to look at her. She was laughing at him. This morning she'd walked away from him and now she was laughing at him. "How is this funny?" he demanded.

"You're micromanaging. Listen, Coach, all you have to do this afternoon is stand around and look pretty."

"What?" he asked incredulously, but then he was distracted by Todd, who was running a finger over Sharee's shoulder. What the hell?

Rainey moved in front of Mark and waited until he tore his attention away from the teens. "It's a car wash, Mark. A summer car wash for the teenagers' sports program. We do this biweekly. They're having fun, as they should."

He tried to look over her head but she merely went up on her tiptoes and held eye contact. "You going to tell me what happened this morning?"

"We…" He refused to say they broke up. One, they hadn't had that kind of a relationship, and two, even if they had, he sure as hell didn't want to admit it was over. "Had a difference of opinion."

She blinked, then took a step back. "I meant about you getting locked out on my porch naked."

Shit. "I don't know what you're talking about."

"Nice," she said, nodding. "And I can see how you manage to fool people with that voice. It's absolutely authoritative." She pulled out her phone, brought up a picture, and showed it to him.

It was him. Bare ass. On her porch.

"It's a little blurry," she said, staring at it. "Because Stacy—my neighbor—was extremely nervous. She was also impressed. It was chilly this morning."

His jaw set. "She sent this to you?"

"Yes. She was worried about the naked guy trying to break into my place." Mercifully she put her phone away. "Now, about that 'difference of opinion'."

Oh, hell. He braced himself. "You walked away from me."

"Yes, because I had to go to work." She paused again, her eyes on his. "And...you thought I walked away from you." She waited a beat. "You actually thought I'd—" Now she shook her head. "It was an argument, Mark. And I'm guessing by your reaction that you don't have many of them. Of course not." She smacked her own forehead. "Because in your world, you're the dictator. Well, Mark, welcome to the *real* world. Where I get to be right some of the time, and that means you have to be wrong occasionally."

"Wrong," he repeated slowly.

"Yeah, wrong," she said on a mirthless laugh. "Even the word sounds foreign coming off your tongue." She was hands on hips, pissed off. "So is that what usually happens? You just write off anyone who disagrees with you?"

Actually, very few people ever disagreed with him. He was paid the big bucks to be in charge, in control, and to make small decisions, and he was good at those things. He didn't have much of a margin of error, and frankly, he'd surrounded himself with people who knew this and were either always in line with his way of thinking, or they kept their opinions to themselves.

"Wow, you are so spoiled." Her smile had vanished,

and now she just looked disappointed in him. That was new too.

New and entirely uncomfortable. "Rainey—"

"Tell me this. You came here this morning thinking what, that we were totally over?" She stared at him, obviously catching the answer in his eyes. "I see," she said slowly. "How convenient that must have been for you."

"It didn't feel convenient," he said. "It felt like a knife in my chest."

She absorbed that silently, without any hint of how she felt about it. Fair enough, he supposed, since he'd kept his feelings from her often enough.

THEY MADE FIVE thousand dollars at the car wash, Mark made sure of it. He called in favors and made nonnegotiable requests of everyone he could think of, and the cars poured in.

When it was over, Rick pulled him aside. "I take back every shitty thing I said about you."

Mark slid him a look.

"Well, for today anyway." Rick grinned, hauling him in for a guy hug. Mark shoved free and wrote the rec center a check, matching the funds as he'd promised to do. "How's it going finding a new building?"

"It's not." Rick's smile faded. "But we still have until the end of the year. Hopefully something will work out or we're out of a lot of jobs, not to mention what will happen if the kids end up with no programs to keep them busy."

Mark nodded.

"How about you and Rainey?"

"What about us?" Mark asked.

"You forget what I said about groveling?"

"I'm not groveling, Rick."

"Right, because that would be too big a step for you. You try the supply closet? That seems to work well for you two."

"Hey, we were *talking* in that closet."

"Uh-huh. Listen, I love you, man," Rick said. "Love you like a brother..."

Mark rolled his eyes.

"But you can't screw with Rainey like you do your other women."

"I don't screw with women."

"No, you screw 'em and leave 'em. We all watch *Entertainment Tonight,* you know."

"It was a photo shoot!"

"Rainey's a sweetheart," Rick said. "She's strong and tough and fiercely protective, and she takes care of those she cares about, but sometimes she forgets to take care of herself."

"I know that."

"And did you also know that in her world, being with you, sleeping with you, is a relationship? She's invested."

"We've discussed it," Mark said tightly. "We're taking it day-to-day."

Rick's eyebrows went up, then he shook his head. "Day to day? Are you kidding me? You let a woman like Rainey hang on your whim?"

Mark pulled out his phone but for once it wasn't ringing. That was great.

"You're an even bigger idiot than I thought," Rick said.

"Thanks."

"Hey, I'm trying to help here. Figured since I'm the only one of us in a successful relationship, I should spread the wealth of knowledge."

"You had nothing to do with your *relationship*. Lena set her sights on you, and you just happened to be smart enough to let her."

"Which begs the question," Rick said. "Why aren't you just as smart?"

ON THE WAY TO THE AIRPORT, Mark made a drive-by past Rainey's place. She wasn't in, which just about killed him. He took the red-eye to New York and hit the ground running the next day. In his hotel room that night, he stared at the ceiling. He'd told himself he'd been too busy to think of Rainey, but that was a lie, and one thing he never did was lie to himself.

He'd thought of her.

And as stupid as it seemed given that he'd just seen her the day before, all wet and soapy and having a great time at the car wash, he missed her. It wasn't a physical ache. Okay, it was. But hell, she'd looked damn good in those shorts and tee, better than any of the teenagers and their newfound sexuality.

Rainey had looked comfortable in her skin. Happy with herself and what she'd chosen to do with her life. Sure of herself.

It had been the sexiest thing he'd ever seen, and yeah, now he was lying in bed with a hard-on the size of Montana, but he missed more than her body.

He'd be back in Santa Rey in a few days, he told himself. Just in time for the black-tie dinner and auction, and then the big games against Santa Barbara the next day. Every penny that was donated was going to the rec center, and Mark had made sure that there would be a lot of pennies. The Mammoths had donated the money for the event, the supplies, the ads, and the ballroom at the Four Seasons—everything, and all the players had agreed to get auctioned off.

The money should be huge, and then there were the games the next day. After that, Mark and the guys could leave town knowing they'd done their best to give back to a community that had badly needed the help.

And Rainey...Rainey would go back to dating. Hell, maybe she was out on a date right now. Which would be no one's fault but his own.

Rick had been right. Mark was an idiot. If he'd played his cards better, he could have postponed the trip and right this minute be gliding into Rainey's sweet, hot, tight heat, listening to those sexy little sounds she made when she got close, the ones that made him want to come just thinking about it.

Shoving up from his bed, he hit the shower, standing there at two-thirty in the morning beneath the hot water, his only company his regrets and his soapy fist.

RAINEY WALKED INTO the auction, her stomach in knots. She'd come with Lena and Rick, the three of them dressed to the hilt. She was wearing a little black dress and heels that bolstered her courage.

The ballroom glittered with the rich and famous. Santa Rey was four hours north of Hollywood and Malibu, and thanks to Mark offering up all the Mammoth players for auction, celebrities had flocked to the event. Casey was up on the block first, and was bought by a blonde television starlet. James went up next. Lena started to bid on him but Rick yanked her back into her seat. James ended up going to some cute young twenty-something, happily spending her daddy's money.

And so it went, with Rainey dazzled by the money pouring in.

After the last player was auctioned off, the entire team of Mammoth players dragged Mark up onto the stage. She knew he'd just come back into town and had to be exhausted, but he looked incredible in a tux. He didn't look thrilled about being auctioned off, but resigned to his fate, he stood there as the bidding started. And the crowd wasn't shy either. Rainey's heart started pounding, and her palms went sweaty as she lifted her bid paddle.

One hundred dollars. She'd just bid one hundred dollars on a man she was more than a little pissed at. Three women were in the bidding with her. One hundred twenty five. One hundred fifty. One hundred seventy-five… Unable to sit calmly, Rainey stood up and shouted her next bid. "*Two* hundred." It was all she had left on her Visa. Maybe if she didn't eat for the next month she could go to three hundred.

The next bidder was from Los Angeles. A woman producer, someone whispered. She bid a thousand dollars and Rainey sagged back in her seat. Probably for the best. It'd been silly to even think about bidding on him.

She felt a tap on her shoulder. Turning, she found James, crouched down low so he couldn't be seen. "Here," he said, and shoved something into her hand.

She looked down and her eyes almost fell out of her head. It was a wad of hundreds. "James—"

"It's from the guys. You can't turn it down, you'll insult them. Plus, we all voted. We need you to win him, Rainey, *bad*. He's been a complete ass this week, even from three thousand miles away. Only you can soften him up. Please win him and do whatever it is you do to make him nice again."

She looked across the ballroom at the players, who were all watching her hopefully. "How much is here?" she asked.

"Five grand."

"Five *grand*?"

James smiled. "Just hedging our bets. Plus, it's a write-off. Don't second-guess it, beautiful. It's lunch money for some of these guys."

"Mark Diego, going for thirty-five hundred," the auctioneer said. "Once, twice—"

"Five thousand!" Rainey shouted.

The players cheered and hooted and hollered.

Lena leapt up and hugged her tight.

Rick was looking pleased.

James just grinned from ear to ear.

And from the stage, Mark's gaze narrowed on Rainey, unreadable as ever.

WHEN THE AUCTION ENDED, Rainey headed out to her car and found a certain big shot NHL coach leaning against the hood, watching her walk toward him with dark, speculative eyes.

Up close and personal, he took her breath. Like his expensive players, he was looking GQ Corporate Hot tonight in that very sexy tux, black shirt, black on black tie, and those badass eyes glinting with pure trouble. It was a cool evening, and yet she felt herself begin to perspire.

She'd purchased him. Good Lord. She'd fought for

him tooth and nail and she'd won, and all she wanted to do was tear off that suit with her teeth.

And then lick him head to toe.

Not good. She'd already licked him from head to toe and knew that he tasted better than any of her favorite foods. She knew that he felt the same about her.

And she knew something else too. She knew by the way that her heart was pounding, pounding, pounding, threatening to burst out of her ribs, that this was no simple thing that she'd be getting over anytime soon.

The closer she got, the more her stomach jangled. It was crazy, her reaction was crazy. He was just a guy, a bossy, demanding, alpha guy she'd once known....

And yet somewhere along the way, maybe when he'd so readily and willingly stepped up to the plate to help, becoming a true role model for the team, she'd realized how much more he was. Watching him step outside his comfort zone only intensified the experience.

You could do the same, a little voice said. Take a real risk for once. Step outside the box, veer from the plan...

Don't let your fear hang you up. Take a risk on him.

His eyes never wavered from hers, and she hoped like hell she wasn't broadcasting her thoughts because she really wasn't ready for him to know them. "Hey."

His smile went a little tight, but he gave her a soft "hey" and backed her to her car, pressing up against her, slipping his hands in her hair to tip her face up to his. "I missed you," he said.

Her heart squeezed. "Are you sure? Because before you left, I thought maybe I was driving you a little nuts."

"Definitely, you're driving me nuts."

She thought about getting annoyed at his present

tense except he pressed his mouth to her temple, then took a tour along to her ear. Taking the lobe lightly in his teeth, he tugged.

She clutched at him, the bones in her knees vanishing. "Mark."

"I have something I want to show you."

"I know," she said, feeling his erection press into her belly.

He snorted. "Not that. Come on, let's go."

Easier said than done. The parking lot was mobbed by everyone trying to leave the auction.

"Excuse me, Mark Diego!"

They both turned and faced two guys in their early twenties, carrying cameras that flashed brightly in their faces.

Rainey grimaced and covered her eyes.

Mark didn't so much as flinch, but grabbed Rainey's hand and kept them moving.

"Sorry about the Stanley Cup, man," one of them said, keeping pace. "Is this your girlfriend? What's your name, sweetheart?"

Rainey opened her mouth but Mark spoke up. "No comment," he said, and walked her toward his truck so fast she could barely keep up, damn her four-inch heels. Mark opened the passenger side door for her, then stood practically on top of her as she attempted to get in. But his truck was high and her little black dress was short. And snug. "Back up," she said. "I need some room for this."

"Babe, I'm the only thing blocking the money shot."

Rainey realized he was right. Without his protection, the photographers could get a picture of her crotch.

"It's either me or them," he said. "And somehow I think you'd rather it be me than the entire free world."

"Fine. But don't look."

"I won't," he said as she slid in, and he totally looked.

"Hey!"

She caught his quick, bad boy grin before he shut the truck door, locking her inside.

MARK DROVE RAINEY UP the highway a few miles, into the burned-out area of the county, nerves eating at his gut. He was more nervous now than he'd been at the finals. When he turned off the paved road and onto what was little more than a field of dirt, he stopped the truck and got out, walking around for Rainey.

She eyed the large trailer in front of them. "What's this?"

Saying nothing, he unlocked the trailer and led her inside and hit the light switch.

Rainey looked around at the office equipment and architectural plans spread across one of the desks. "Mark?"

"Look out there." Heart pounding, he pointed to the window as he flicked another switch and the land on the other side of the trailer lit up. "That's where it'll go."

She moved to the window and stood highlighted there in her little black dress and heels, the elegance of her outfit clashing with her hair, which was trailing out of the twist she'd had it in, brushing her shoulders and neck. "Where what will go?" she asked, pressing her nose to the glass.

"The new parks and rec center."

She turned and looked at him, eyes shocked. "What?"

"Yeah, I bought and donated this land to the rec center. By this same time next year you'll be in your new office."

She stared at him for a long beat. "Did you do this so I'd sleep with you again?"

"Is that even a possibility?"

She just stared at him some more, taking a page out of his own play book with a damn good game face.

"No," she said, her eyes on his mouth. "I'm not going to sleep with you again."

He went icy cold and couldn't breathe. "No?"

"No. Sleeping with you is what went wrong. Sleeping with you makes me want more than you can give."

He let out a breath and nodded. He understood but it felt like he'd just taken a full body hit.

"But," she said, taking a step closer to him, "the not sleeping part—that works for me." She was breathing a little hard and her nipples were pebbled against that mouthwatering black dress.

He wanted to strip her out of it and leave her in just the hot heels, but she was throwing more than a little 'tude, and the shoes might be detrimental to his health. Nope, it all had to go, everything, leaving her gloriously naked. Then his gaze locked on the pulse frantically beating at the base of her neck and he knew he wasn't alone. Reaching out, he cupped her throat, his thumb brushing over the spot. She was flushed, and the low cut of her dress was affording him a view that made his mouth water.

"Does it work for you?" she asked.

"Hell, yes."

14

THE WORDS WEREN'T OUT of Mark's mouth before Rainey
pretty much flung herself at him. She couldn't help it,
there wasn't a woman in all the land who could have
helped it.

He caught her. Of course he caught her. He always
caught whatever was thrown at him, but he was also
protective and warm and caring, and had the biggest
heart of anyone she'd ever known. She backed him to
the waist-high window she'd just been staring out and
kissed him, long and deep, and when his hands came
up to hold her, a rough groan vibrating from his chest,
she tore her mouth free to kiss his throat while she
pushed his jacket off his broad shoulders. He tossed it
aside while she worked open the buttons on his shirt.
Clearly relishing her touch, he held himself still, his
hands tight on her arms, as if it was costing him to give
her the reins.

But when she licked his nipple, he appeared to lose
his tenuous grip. He whipped her around so that she
was against the window now, the wood sill pressing
into the small of her back. His eyes were dark, scorch-

ing, and as his hands skimmed up her thighs, bringing the material of her dress with them, she shivered, a flash of excitement going through her.

"Hold this," he commanded, peeling her hands from his shoulders, forcing her to hold her dress bunched at her waist.

"I'm in the window!"

"No one's here. You're so beautiful, Rainey."

Her stomach quivered, and she was glad she'd worn her sexiest black silky thong. "It's the dress."

"Mmmm." His eyes ran up the shimmery material she was holding at her waist, at her panties, and darkened. "Love the dress."

"And the heels. It's the heels, too."

He ran a hand over the delicate ankle strap and hummed another agreement. "Definitely love the heels."

"And—"

"Rainey."

"Yeah?"

He smiled that wicked smile again and kissed her, then cupped her face and said against her mouth, "It's you. It's all you. I'm going to take you here."

"Here?"

"Here." That said, he dropped to his knees and put a big hand on each of her thighs, pushing her legs apart.

"Um, the window—"

He kissed her hipbone.

"I—" God, she couldn't remember what she'd wanted to say.

He skimmed his fingers up her legs, playing with the tiny strings on her hips.

"Oh," she breathed, when his mouth brushed from

one hip to the other, low on her belly, just above the material of her thong.

"So pretty." He stroked over the wet silk.

"But this was supposed to be *your* pleasure—ohmigod," she gasped when he nipped her skin, catching the silk in his teeth and very slowly tugging. "Mark—"

"Hmm?"

She started to drop the hem of her dress but he covered her hands with his, indicating he wanted her to keep it out of his way.

Then he let his fingers take over the task of pulling the thong down to midthigh, groaning at the sight he'd unveiled for himself. "Trust me, Rainey. This *is* my pleasure."

Acutely aware of the glass at her back, she tried to squeeze her legs together but he was on his knees between them. "Someone could come."

"Yes, and that someone's going to be you."

Oh, God. He sent her a wicked smile. His hands, still on her hips, spread wide, allowing his thumbs to meet, glancing over her center.

Her head hit the glass. She was already panting. "But…"

Another slow, purposeful stroke of his thumb had her moaning.

He was right. She was going to come. Her hands went into his hair. "Mark— We've been here too long already. Someone might show up to investigate the lights."

"Tell you what," he said silkily, pushing her onto the ledge so that it was more like a narrowed seat. "You keep a watch and let me know if you see anyone."

"Okay." Except the back of her head was against the glass. And her eyes were closed.

And...*oh*. He was gliding his fingers over her while his mouth—

God, his mouth. Beneath his tongue and hands she writhed, unable to stay still.

"I'm going to make you come with my fingers, Rainey. And then I'm going to make you come with my mouth. And then I'm going to bury myself in your body. I won't be able to stroke you hard and deep though. I'll barely move, so that if someone drove by, they wouldn't be able to tell what we're doing. But you'll know. I'm going to make love to you until neither of us can remember our names. All while you sit right here and look beautiful and elegant and untouchable to anyone who happens by."

He slid a finger into her and she nearly jerked off the ledge.

"Hold still, Rainey. We don't want to have to stop."

"No." She tightened her grip on his hair. "Please don't stop."

He kissed first one inner thigh and then the other, and she could feel his hot breath against her. She wanted to rock up into him but she managed to stay still.

"Good girl," he whispered against her, his thumb purposely brushing over her in a steady rhythm now, her rhythm.

Holding still was the hardest thing she'd ever done. Her toes were curling, her belly quivering, and when he increased the pace of his fingers, her eyes crossed behind her closed lids. She didn't even realize her hips were rocking helplessly until he set a hand on them.

"If you stop," she said. "I'll hurt you."

He laughed softly, then pulled her thong off entirely, gently pushing her thighs open even more. When he added another finger, she bit her lower lip to keep her cry in.

"No, I want to hear you," he whispered against her skin, and stroked his tongue over ground zero.

She cried out again and sank her fingers into his hair for balance.

"Yeah, like that," he said huskily. "Do you know what it does to me to hear those sexy sounds?"

She was beside herself, utterly incapable of answering him, lost in the sensations he was sending rocketing through her. "It makes me crazy," he told her. "Crazy for you."

Crazy worked.

She felt crazy, too.

"Come for me, Rainey. I want to taste you when you're coming."

She pretty much lost it then. First to his fingers, then to his mouth, and then he sank into her silken wet heat. As he'd promised, he barely moved within her, and yet took her to a place she'd never been.

It was the hottest, most erotic experience of her life.

THE NIGHT WAS DARK AND chilly, but inside his truck on the way back into town, with the heater on low and Rainey next to him, all snuggled into his suit jacket, rumpled and sexy as hell, the oddest feeling came over Mark.

Comfort.

Bliss.

Contentment.

Reaching out, he took her hand and brought it to his mouth, then settled it on his thigh as he glanced at her. She was out cold, breathing deep and slow, dreaming....

Of him?

Her mouth curved slightly, and his did the same. He hoped she was dreaming of him.

His dreams were certainly filled with her often enough. Of course his dreams didn't necessarily make him smile sweetly the way she did. More like they made him groan and wake up hard as a rock. He hadn't jacked off so much since middle school.

But it was more than that. He couldn't believe how much she'd come to mean to him. So damn much...

He pulled up to her place and stroked a strand of hair from her face. She let out a low purr of pleasure and stretched. "How come I always fall asleep in your truck?" she murmured.

"It's a mystery." But it wasn't. Even he knew why. Because no matter how much sexual tension there was between them, there was still an ease, a very natural one.

He walked with her up the path to her town house. At the door, she cupped his face in her hands, and stroked his jaw gently. "I love what you did," she told him. "Buying that land, getting plans drawn for the rec center. You're helping so many people, Mark. You're changing lives." Her thumb ran over his bottom lip, making it tingle before she leaned in and brushed her mouth over his in a sweet, far too short kiss. "You've changed my life, too."

He started to deny this but she stopped him. "You did," she said very softly. "You don't even realize how much. I've always let Mr. Wrong work for me because it gave me something to do—fix him. Which was merely a way to avoid the truth that I myself was the real fixer-upper."

"Rainey, no. You're perfect."

"No, I'm not." She ran her fingers over his lips, gently shushing him. "I'm flawed, and far from perfect. I pick men that aren't right for me and then try to scare them off."

"You're not that scary."

"Give me some time," she quipped.

"I still won't find you scary."

"That's because you'll be gone," she reminded him. "Back to your whirlwind life."

"I get to Santa Rey occasionally."

She smiled but there was something different in her gaze now, something sad. "Good night, Mark."

"Rainey." He couldn't explain his sudden panic, but it was like he'd missed something. "Why do I feel like you really mean goodbye?"

"It used to be," she said with a terrifying quietness, "that I'd take any scrap bit of affection from you I could get. That was the sixteen-year-old in me, the pathetic, loser sixteen-year-old who didn't respect or love herself. I realize that it didn't start out all that different this time either. I mean, I played a good game, but we both know my crush is still in painful existence." She shook her head. "The bad news is that it's grown even past that." Again, she leaned in and brushed her lips to his, clinging for a minute. He could feel her tremor and tried to tighten his grip on her, but she wriggled loose, closing her eyes when he pressed his mouth to her forehead. "Tonight was amazing. I'll never forget it. Or you."

"Rainey—"

"I love you, Mark," she whispered, and then slid out of his embrace and inside, leaving him standing there wondering what the fuck had just happened.

THE NEXT DAY DAWNED BRIGHT and sunny. Perfect game weather. The Santa Barbara rec center teams had arrived by bus. The girls played first. Rainey sat with Lena, watching from the sidelines as Mark coached the teens in a tight game. The stands were filled. The entire town had turned out, it seemed, and a good number of people had come from Santa Barbara too. The mood of the crowd was fun and boisterous.

In between plays, Rainey told Lena the whole story of the night before, leaving out a whole bunch of what had happened in the trailer, much to Lena's annoyance.

"A real friend would give details," Lena said. "Like size, stamina…"

"Hey. Can we focus on the real problem here?"

"Yeah, I'm not seeing the *real* problem," Lena said. "Mark's rescued you from crappy dates, pretty much single-handedly saved your job, and he's been there whenever you've needed him, for whatever you've needed. What a complete ass, huh?"

"Look, I know he's been there." Always, no matter what she needed. "But he doesn't want a relationship. Nothing changes that fact."

Casey, James and Rick had been sitting with the boys but they came over and joined the two of them for a few minutes. "So what are we talking about?" Rick asked.

"Nothing," Rainey said.

"How perfect Mark is for her," Lena said.

"Aw," Casey said, disappointed. "That's not news."

"If they're so perfect for each other, then why does he look like shit?" James asked. "I don't think he's slept."

"Mark never looks like hell," Lena said reverently. "Unless you mean *hot* as hell."

"Sitting right here," Rick said to Lena.

Lena smiled and kissed him. "The hotness runs in the family."

Rainey hadn't slept either. She looked at Mark standing just outside the dugout, but if he was tired, hurting, unhappy, he gave no sign of it as he coached the girls through a three-run inning. At the break, he left the dugout and walked to the stands, ignoring everyone to stop in front of Rainey. He wore a pair of beat-up Nikes and a pair of threadbare jeans, soft and loose on his hips, still managing to define the best body she'd ever had the pleasure of tasting. His T-shirt was sweat-dampened and sticking to the hard muscles of his arms and chest. It'd been given to him by the girls, and was bedazzled and fabric painted with a big *COACH* on the front.

He should have looked ridiculous. Instead, with his expensive sunglasses and all the testosterone he wore like aftershave, he looked…

Perfect.

"Hey," he said, sliding off his glasses, his gaze intense as it ran over her.

She became incredibly aware that the entire Santa Rey side of the stands had gone silent, trying to catch their conversation. "Hey."

"I want to talk to you after the game," he said. "You busy?"

She did her best to look cool in front of their avid audience and shook her head. "Nope. Not busy."

"Good." He strode back to the game, and she might or might not have been staring at his very fine ass when Lena nudged her in the side with her elbow.

"Do you think 'talk' is a euphemism for—"

Rainey stood up. "Going to the snack bar."

IT WAS A TIME-OUT AND Mark stood in the dugout talking to the girls.

Or rather, the girls were talking to him.

"We can tell you're having a bad day, Coach," Pepper said. "Did you get dumped?"

"This is a time-out," he said. "We are going to discuss the game."

"Aw. You did." Pepper put her hand on his shoulder. "What'd you do? Because Rainey's a really great person, you know? Probably if you just said you were sorry, she'd take you back."

Mark shook his head. Never once in his entire professional career had he had a time-out like this one. In his world, his players lived and breathed for his words and never questioned him. "We're in the dugout," he said. "In the middle of a very important game." The press was there, which had been Mark's intention all along. But he found he could care less about the press. It was about these girls. "We're talking about the game."

"That's not as much fun," Kendra said. "I bet if you tell us what you screwed up, we could tell you how to fix it."

"How do you know he screwed up?" Cindy asked.

"Please," Sharee said. "Rainey wouldn't have

screwed up. She never screws anything up. She's on top of things, always."

Mark scrubbed his hands over his face. How the hell had this gotten so out of control? He couldn't even wrangle in a handful of teenage girls.

Oh, who the hell was he kidding. He'd lost control weeks ago, his first day back in Santa Rey. They wanted to know what he'd screwed up, and he had no way to tell them that he'd screwed up a damn long time ago.

She loved him. She saw right through him and still loved his sorry ass. The words had slipped out of her mouth so easily, so naturally, words he'd never dreamed he'd hear directed at him from a woman like her. A woman he could trust in, believe in, a woman with whom he could be himself. She was so amazing, so much more than he deserved, and she was meant to be his.

He also knew that things didn't always work out the way they should.

Pepper put her hand on Mark's. "My dad says it's okay to make mistakes," she said very quietly.

Mark's dad had often told him the same thing. In fact, Ramon was right this minute out there in the stands cheering his son on, which he'd do no matter what mistakes Mark made.

"Everyone makes them," the girl said. "But only the very brave fix their mistakes."

Mark lifted his head and looked her into her old-soul eyes. "You're right." He'd pulled Rainey in even as he'd pushed her away. He was good at that, the push/pull. Standing, he locked eyes with Rainey. She stood off to the side between the bleachers and the snack bar. Close enough to have heard the entire conversation.

The ump whistled that the time out was over. Sharee went off to bat, and the other girls plopped back down on the bench of the dugout.

Mark didn't move, didn't break eye contact with Rainey. He had no idea how long they could have kept that up, communicating their longing without a word, when the sharp crack of Sharee connecting with the ball surprised them both.

SHAREE'S HIT WENT STRAIGHT up the line and Rainey watched as the girl took off running. The teen still had an attitude the size of the diamond, but she had it under control these days. There were fewer blowups and hardly a single bad word out of her all week.

Of course that might have been because Todd was in the stands watching her, cheering her on.

Sharee glanced at the teen and blushed.

Todd, already in uniform for his game, grinned.

Watching them caused both a pang in Rainey's heart and a smile on her face.

But that faded fast as she caught sight of the man in dirty jeans and wrinkled shirt walking toward the field from the parking lot. He staggered a bit, but his eyes stayed focused on the diamond.

Martin, Sharee's father.

Drunk.

Just what Sharee needed, for her father to humiliate her today.

Rainey moved towards him, wanting to run the other way, but she couldn't let him ruin the game for Sharee. "Martin, wait."

"Gettoutta my way."

He smelled like a brewery and looked like he'd slept in one. "Did you come to see the game?" she asked.

"I came to see my daughter," he slurred, blinking slowly like an owl. "She stole money from my wallet. She's going to pay for that."

Rainey's gut tightened. "I have your money in my office," she said, gesturing in the opposite direction of the field. No way was she letting him out there to embarrass Sharee.

Not that Rainey was going to take him to her office either. Hell, no. He was a mean drunk, and her unease had turned to fear. She led him around the side of the building, heading back toward the parking lot, her phone in her hand to call Rick for help if necessary, when suddenly she was slammed up against the brick building, hard enough that she saw stars. But that wasn't her biggest problem. That would be the forearm across her throat, blocking her airway.

Her fear turned to terror.

"You told her to call the police on me," Martin hissed, his fingers biting into Rainey's arms. "Didn't you, bitch?"

Bitch... It *hadn't* been those kids who'd painted her car. It'd been Martin. Rainey blinked the spots from her eyes and looked around.

There was no one in sight. They were all watching the game. She wasn't quite in view of the parking lot, and was out of view of the stands. In succeeding to get him away from the field, she'd screwed herself. "Martin, I can't...breathe."

"Because of you, Sharee called the police on me

the other night. I went to jail, and lost my job when I couldn't make bail."

"You shouldn't...hit her."

Martin gave Rainey another shove against the brick wall, and her head snapped against it, hard. More stars. She'd have slid to the ground if he hadn't been holding her up. He pressed harder against her throat and her vision shrank to a pinpoint. "Stay away from my kid," he gritted out. "Stay away from me. You hear me?"

She heard him, barely, over the rush of blood pounding through her ears. Unable to draw a breath, she clawed at his hands.

"Answer me, bitch!"

She answered in the only way she could. With a knee to his crotch.

His scream was high-pitched, and thankfully very loud as he let go and they both hit the ground.

Martin bellowed in pain again.

Someone hear him, she thought. *Please, someone hear...*

Pounding footsteps sounded, and cool hands reached for her. "Jesus. *Rainey.*"

Mark.

"I've got you," he said firmly, pulling her against him, his voice raw with emotion. "I've got you, Rainey."

There were others with him, the whole field by the sounds of it, but she could only sigh in relief as the spots claimed her.

15

RAINEY BLINKED AND FOUND herself staring up at a white ceiling. She was in the hospital.

"You're okay." Mark's voice, then his face, appeared in front of her, looking more fierce and intense than she'd ever seen him.

"You have a concussion," he said. "And your windpipe is strained." As was his voice. "You're going to hurt like hell, but you're okay."

She nodded and held his gaze. It was blazing with bare emotion. She tried to say his name, but nothing came out.

"Don't," he murmured. He leaned over her, one arm braced at her far hip, the other stroking her hair back from her face. "Talking will just hurt." Turning, he reached for a cup with a straw and helped her drink. "You're supposed to just lie there quiet until morning," he said.

She felt surrounded by him, in a really warm way. She swallowed and winced. "Martin—"

"In jail," he said tightly, and dropped his head, eyes closed for a beat. Then he met her gaze. "You did great,

Rainey. You took a really bad situation and handled it. Do you have any idea how amazing you are?"

"Did you win?"

He stared at her in shock for a beat, before an exhausted but warm smile crossed his face. "Yeah. I won." He pressed his forehead to hers. "But not the game. We declared a tie. God, Rainey. I thought I'd lost you. I just found you and I thought you were gone."

She remembered how he'd looked earlier, in his sunglasses, hat low over his game face, letting nothing ruffle him.

Nothing.

In fact, she'd never seen anything ruffle the man... except her.

She got to him. And there was a good reason for that. He loved her, too.

And if she hadn't already been head over heels, she'd have fallen for him right then and there, even as she watched the pain and hurt flash in his eyes, neither of which he tried to hold back from her. "Sixty-five seconds," he said. "You weren't breathing for sixty-five seconds after we found you. I lived and died during each one of them." He let out a breath. "Never again."

Her heart stopped. Never again...?

"Never again do I want to be without you."

Her heart had barely kicked back on when Mark cupped her face and peered deeply into her eyes. "I want to be with you tonight," he said.

"Here in the hospital?"

"Here. And tomorrow night. The next night, too."

She swallowed hard. "What happened to day-to-day?"

"It went to hell," he said. "Do you have any idea how

addicting you are? The minute I'm away from you I'm already thinking about the next time I'm going to see you. Touch you. Taste you."

"That sounds like sex."

"It's always been more than sex, Rainey. Always. You said you love me." He gently set his finger on her lips when she would have spoken. "That threw me. You throw me. You were unexpected, and you've changed my endgame. And then you—" His eyes burned hot emotion. She was surprised when he wrapped his arms around her and buried his face between her breasts, breathing deeply. "You could have died before I could tell you." His grip on her tightened. It wasn't something he'd ever done before, taking comfort from her instead of offering it. Eyes burning, she wrapped her arms around him and pulled him in even closer.

"I can't remember my life before this summer," he said, lifting his face. "Before you came back into my world. I don't want to be without you, Rainey. I've known that for a while, before what happened to you today, but I guess I thought knowing it made me weak."

And he wasn't a man who had any patience with weaknesses, especially his own. She laid her cheek on top of his silky hair. "And now?"

He let her see everything he was feeling. "I don't give a shit whether it makes me weak or not. You're the only thing I care about. I love you, Rainey. I think I always have. You make me feel."

"What do I make you feel?"

"Everything. You make me feel everything."

* * * * *

Body Check
Elle Kennedy

ABOUT THE AUTHOR

Elle Kennedy grew up in the suburbs of Toronto, Ontario, and holds a B.A. in English from York University. From an early age she knew she wanted to be a writer, and actively began pursuing that dream when she was only a teenager. When she's not writing, she's reading. And when she's not reading, she's making music with her drummer boyfriend, oil painting, or indulging her love for board games. Elle loves to hear from her readers. Visit her at her Web site, www.ellekennedy.com, or stop by her blog, sizzlingpens.blogspot.com, to chat with Elle and her fellow Harlequin writers.

Dear Reader,

I am absolutely thrilled about writing for Harlequin Blaze. *Body Check* is a story that's been in my head for quite a while. It's a dream come true to be able to share it with you!

Growing up in Canada, I suppose it's not surprising that I ended up writing about our nation's most beloved sport. After all, there's nothing sexier than a hockey player. And, of course, no romance would be complete without a scandal or two!

I had a blast writing *Body Check,* from its initial conception to the research phase (where I pestered my hockey-playing buddies with questions ike "What *really* goes on in the locker room?") to those final, finishing touches.

I hope you enjoy Hayden and Brody's story, and I'd also love to hear from you! Drop me a line at www.ellekennedy.com or swing over to The Sizzling Pens at sizzlingpens.blogspot.com to see what some of my fellow Harlequin authors and I are blogging about!

Happy reading!

Elle Kennedy

DEDICATION

I could not have written this book without my fantastic critique partners, Lori Borrill and Jennifer Lewis, two incredible authors in their own right, and the best support system a girl could have.

I'd also like to dedicate this book to...

My family and friends, for not letting me give up.

Tyler, Amanda and Brad, for all their help with this story.

My fabulous editor Laura Barth. And senior editor Brenda Chin for taking a chance on me and my hockey-playing hero!

1

"I REALLY NEED to get laid," Hayden Houston said with a sigh. She reached for the glass on the smooth mahogany tabletop and took a sip of red wine. The slightly bitter liquid eased her thirst but did nothing to soothe her frustration.

The pictures staring at her from the walls of the Ice House Bar didn't help, either. Action shots of hockey players mid slap shot, framed rookie cards, team photos of the Chicago Warriors—it seemed as if the sport haunted her everywhere she went. Sure, she was a team owner's daughter, but occasionally it would be nice to focus on something other than hockey. Like sex, perhaps.

Across from her, Darcy White grinned. "We haven't seen each other in two years and that's all you've got to say? Come on, Professor, no anecdotes about life in Berkeley? No insightful lectures about Impressionist art?"

"I save the insightful lectures for my students. And as for anecdotes, none of them involve sex so let's not waste time with those."

She ran her hand through her hair and discovered that all the bounce she'd tried to inject into it before heading to the Ice House Bar had deflated. Volume-enhancing mousse? Yeah, right. Apparently nothing could make her stick-straight brown hair look anything other than stick-straight.

"Okay, I'll bite," Darcy said. "Why do you have sex on the brain?"

"Because I'm not getting any."

Darcy sipped her strawberry daiquiri, a drink she'd confessed she hated but drank anyway, claiming men found it sexy. "Aren't you seeing someone back in California? Dan? Drake?"

"Doug," Hayden corrected.

"How long have you been together?"

"Two months."

"And you still haven't done the mattress mambo?"

"Nope."

"You're kidding, right? He's not down with getting it on?" Darcy paused, looking thoughtful. "Or should I say, he's not *up* with it?"

"Oh, he's up. He just wants, and I quote, 'to get to know each other fully before we cross the intimacy bridge.'"

Her friend hooted. "The intimacy bridge? Girl, he sounds like a total loser. Dump him. Now. Before he brings up the intimacy bridge again."

"We're actually on a break right now," Hayden admitted. "Before I left I told him I needed some space."

"Space? Uh-uh. I think what you need is a new boyfriend."

God, that was the last thing she wanted. Toss her line in the dating pool and start fishing again? No, thank you. After three failed relationships in five years, Hayden had decided to quit falling for bad boys and focus on the good ones. And Doug Lloyd was definitely a good one. He taught a Renaissance course at Berkeley, he was intelligent and witty, and he valued love and commitment as much as she did. Having grown up with a single father, Hayden longed for a partner she could build a home and grow old with.

Her mom had died in a car accident when Hayden was a baby, and her dad had given up on finding love again, opting instead to spend more than twenty years focusing on his hockey-coaching career. He'd finally remarried three years ago, but she suspected loneliness, rather than love, had driven him to do so. Why else would he have proposed to a woman after four months of dating? A woman who was twenty-nine years his junior. A woman he was in the process of divorcing, no less.

Well, she had no intention of following her dad's example. She wasn't going to spend decades alone and then jump into marriage with someone totally unsuitable.

Doug held the same mind-set. He was a traditionalist through and through, a believer that marriage should be valued and not rushed into. Besides, he had a rock-hard body that made her mouth water. He'd even let her touch it…once. They'd been kissing on the couch in the living room of her San Francisco town house and she'd slid her hands underneath his button-down shirt. Running her fingers over his rippled chest, she'd murmured, "Let's move this into the bedroom."

That's when he'd dropped the no-intimacy bomb on her. He'd assured her he was unbelievably attracted to her, but that, like marriage, he didn't believe sex should be rushed. He wanted the first time to be special.

And no amount of chest rubbing could persuade him to let go of his chivalrous intentions.

And therein lay the problem. Doug was simply too *nice*. At first she'd thought his views on making love were really very sweet. But two months, coupled with *eight* months of celibacy prior to meeting Doug, added up to extreme sexual frustration on her part.

She loved that Doug was a gentleman but, darn it, sometimes a girl just needed a *man*.

"Seriously, this Damian guy seems like a wimp," Darcy said, jerking her from her thoughts.

"Doug."

"Whatever." Darcy waved a dismissive hand and tossed her

long red hair over her shoulder. "Screw intimacy. If Dustin won't have sex with you, find someone who will."

"Believe me, I'm tempted."

More than tempted, actually. The next couple months were bound to be pure hell. She'd come home after final exams to support her father through his messy divorce, to be the good daughter, but that didn't mean she had to like the situation.

Her stepmother was determined to squeeze Hayden's dad for every dime he had. And, boy, did he have a lot of dimes. Though he'd spent most of his life coaching, Presley had always dreamed of owning a team, a goal he'd finally reached seven years ago. Thanks to the substantial insurance settlement he'd received after her mom's accident, and his wise investment in a pharmaceutical company that had made him millions, he'd been able to purchase the Chicago Warriors franchise. Over the years he'd continued investing and building his fortune, but his main priority was the team. It was all he ever thought about, and that's what made coming home so difficult.

Her childhood had been chaotic, to say the least. Traveling with her dad across the country for away games, living in Florida for two years when he'd coached the Aces to a championship victory, five years in Texas, three in Oregon. It had been tough, but Hayden's close relationship with her dad had made the constant upheaval bearable. Her father had always shown an interest in her life. He'd listened while she babbled about her favorite artists, and taken her to countless museums over the years.

Now that she was an adult and he was busy with the team, he no longer seemed to care about making time to connect with her outside of the hockey arena. She knew other team owners didn't get as involved as her father did, but his background as a coach seemed to influence his new position; he had his hand in every aspect of the Warriors, from drafting players to marketing, and he thrived on it, no matter how time-consuming the work was.

That's why three years ago she'd decided to accept the full-time position Berkeley had offered her, even though it meant relocating to the West Coast. She'd figured the old absence-makes-the-heart-grow-fonder cliché might kick in and make her father realize there was more to life than hockey. It hadn't.

So she'd come back to see him through the divorce in hopes that they could reconnect.

"Have you become a nymphomaniac since you left town?" Darcy was asking. "You never mentioned it in your e-mails."

Hayden forced herself to focus on her best friend and not dwell on her issues with her dad. "I haven't become a nymphomaniac. I'm just stressed-out and I need to unwind. Do you blame me?"

"Not really. The evil stepmother is throwing poison apples all over the place, huh?"

"You saw the morning paper, too?"

"Oh, yeah. Pretty crappy."

Hayden raked her fingers through her hair. "Crappy? It's a disaster."

"Any truth to it?" Darcy asked carefully.

"Of course not! Dad would never do the things she's accusing him of." She tried to control the frustration in her tone. "Let's not talk about this. Tonight I just want to forget about my dad and Sheila and the whole messy business."

"All right. Wanna talk about sex again?"

Hayden grinned. "No. I'd rather *have* sex instead."

"Then do it. There are tons of men in this place. Pick one and go home with him."

"You mean a one-night stand?" she asked warily.

"Hell, yeah."

"I don't know. It seems kind of sleazy, hopping into bed with someone and never seeing them again."

"How is that sleazy? I do it all the time."

Hayden burst out laughing. "Of course you do. You're commitment-phobic."

Darcy went through men like socks, and some of the details she shared in her e-mails made Hayden gape. *She* certainly couldn't remember ever experiencing seven orgasms in one night, or indulging in a ménage à trois with two firefighters she'd met—figure this one out—at an illegal bonfire in Chicago's Lincoln Park.

Darcy raised her eyebrows, blue eyes flashing with challenge. "Well, let me ask you this—what sounds more fun, having a few screaming orgasms with a man you may or may not see again, or hiking across the intimacy bridge with Don?"

"Doug."

Darcy shrugged. "I think we both know my way is better than the highway. Or should I say the bridge?" She fluttered her hand as if waving a white flag. "Sorry, I promise to refrain from any further bridge comments for the rest of the evening."

Hayden didn't answer. Instead, she mulled over Darcy's suggestion. She'd never had a one-night stand in her life. For her, sex came with other things, relationship things, like going to dinner, spending a cozy night in, saying *I love you* for the first time.

But why did sex always have to be about love? Couldn't it just be purely for pleasure? No dinner, no I-love-you's, no expectations?

"I don't know," she said slowly. "Falling into bed with a man when last week I was still with Doug?"

"You asked for space for a reason," Darcy said. "Might as well take advantage of it."

"By going to bed with someone else." She sipped her wine, thoughtful and hesitant at the same time.

"Why not?" Darcy said. "Look, you've spent years searching for a guy to build a life with—maybe you should try looking for one who jump-starts your libido instead. The way I see it, it's time for you to have some fun, Hayden. I think you need fun."

She sighed. "I think so, too."

Darcy's grin widened. "You're seriously considering it, aren't you?"

"If I see a guy I like, I just might."

Her own words surprised her, but they made sense. What was so wrong with hooking up with a stranger in a bar? People did wild things like that all the time, and maybe right now she needed to be a little wild.

Darcy twirled the straw around in her daiquiri glass, looking pensive. "What's your pseudonym going to be?"

"My pseudonym?" she echoed.

"Yeah. If you're going to do this right, you need total anonymity. Be someone else for the night. Like Yolanda."

"No way," she objected with a laugh. "I'd rather just be myself."

"Fine." Darcy's shoulders drooped.

"We're getting ahead of ourselves, Darce. Shouldn't I pick the guy first?"

Darcy's enthusiasm returned. "Good point. Let's spin the man wheel and see who it lands on."

Stifling a laugh, Hayden followed her friend's lead and swept her eyes around the crowded bar. Everywhere she looked, she saw men. Tall ones, short ones, cute ones, bald ones. None of them sparked her interest.

And then she saw him.

Standing at the counter with his back turned to them was

the lucky winner of the man wheel. All she could see was a head of dark brown hair, a broad back clad in a navy-blue sweater and long legs encased in denim. Oh, and the butt. Hard not to notice that tight little butt.

"Excellent selection," Darcy teased, following her gaze.

"I can't see his face," she complained, trying not to crane her neck.

"Patience, grasshopper."

Holding her breath, Hayden watched the man drop a few bills on the sleek mahogany counter and accept a tall glass of beer from the bartender. When he turned around, she sucked in an impressed gasp. The guy had the face of a Greek god, chiseled, rugged, with intense blue eyes that caused her heart to pound and sensual lips that made her mouth tingle. And he was huge. With his back turned he hadn't seemed this big, but now, face-to-face, she realized he stood well over six feet and had the kind of chest a woman wanted to rest her head on. She could see the muscular planes of his chest even through his sweater.

"Wow," she muttered, more to herself than Darcy.

A shiver of anticipation danced through her as she imagined spending the night with him.

Beer in hand, the man strode toward one of the pool tables at the far end of the bar, and headed for the cue rack. Setting his glass on the small ledge along the wall, he grabbed a cue and proceeded to rack the balls on the green felt table. A second later, a tall, lanky college-age kid approached and they exchanged a few words. The kid snatched up a cue and joined Mr. Delicious at the table.

Hayden turned back to Darcy and saw her friend rolling her eyes. "What?" she said, feeling a bit defensive.

"What are you waiting for?" Darcy prompted.

She glanced at the dark-haired sex god again. "I should go over there?"

"If you're serious about doing the nasty tonight, then, yeah, go over there."

"And do what?"

"Shoot some pool. Talk. Flirt. You know, look under the hood before you commit to buying the car."

"He's not a car, Darce."

"Yeah, but if he was, he'd be something dangerously hot, like a Hummer."

Hayden burst out laughing. If there was one thing to be said about Darcy, it was that she truly was one of a kind.

"Come on, go over there," Darcy repeated.

She swallowed. "Now?"

"No, next week."

Her mouth grew even drier, prompting her to down the rest of her wine.

"You're seriously nervous about this, aren't you?" Darcy said, blue eyes widening in wonder. "When did you become so shy? You give lectures to classes of hundreds. He's just one man, Hayden."

Her eyes drifted back in the guy's direction. She noticed how his back muscles bunched together as he rested his elbows on the pool table, how his taut backside looked practically edible in those faded jeans.

He's just one man, she said to herself, shaking off her nerves. Right. Just one tall, sexy, oozing-with-raw-masculinity man.

This would be a piece of cake.

BRODY CROFT CIRCLED the pool table, his eyes sharp as a hawk's as he examined his options. With a quick nod, he pointed and said, "Thirteen, side pocket."

His young companion, wearing a bright red Hawaiian T-shirt that made Brody's eyes hurt, raised his eyebrows. "Really? Tough shot, man."

"I can handle it."

And handle it he did. The ball slid cleanly into the pocket, making the kid beside him groan.

"Nice, man. Nice."

"Thanks." He moved to line up his next shot when he noticed his opponent staring at him. "Something wrong?"

"No, uh, nothing's wrong. Are—are you Brody Croft?" the guy blurted out, looking embarrassed.

Brody smothered a laugh. He'd wondered how long it would take the kid to ask. Not that he was conceited enough to think everyone on the planet knew who he was, but seeing as this bar was owned by Alexi Nicklaus and Jeff Wolinski, two fellow Warriors, most of the patrons were bound to be hockey fans.

"At your service," he said easily, extending his hand.

The kid gripped it tightly, as if he were sinking in a pit of quicksand and Brody's hand was the lifeline keeping him alive. "This is so awesome! I'm Mike, by the way."

The look of pure adoration on Mike's face brought a knot of discomfort to Brody's gut. He always enjoyed meeting fans, but sometimes the hero worship went a little too far.

"What do you say we keep playing?" he suggested, gesturing to the pool table.

"Yeah. I mean, sure! Let's play!" Mike's eyes practically popped out of his angular face. "I can't wait to tell the guys I played a round of pool with Brody Croft."

Since he couldn't come up with a response that didn't include something asinine, like "thank you," Brody chalked up the end of his cue. The next shot would be more difficult than the first, but again, nothing he couldn't manage. He'd worked in a bar like this one back when he'd played for the farm team and was barely bringing in enough cash to feed his goldfish, let alone himself. He used to hang out after work shooting pool with the other waiters, eventually developing a fondness for the game. With the way his schedule was now, he rarely had time to play anymore.

But with rumors about a possible league investigation swirling, thanks to allegations made in a recent interview with the team owner's soon-to-be ex-wife, Brody might end up with more free time than he wanted. Mrs. Houston apparently had proof that her husband had bribed at least two players to bring forth a loss and that he'd placed substantial— *illegal*—bets on those fixed games.

While there was probably no truth to any of it, Brody was growing concerned with the rumors.

A few years ago a similar scandal had plagued the Colorado Kodiaks. Only three players had been involved, but many innocent players suffered—other teams were reluctant to pick them up due to their association with the tarnished franchise.

Hell would freeze over before he'd accept a payout, and he had no intention of being lumped in with any of the players who might have. His contract was due to expire at the end of the season. He'd be a free agent then, which meant he needed to remain squeaky clean if he wanted to sign with a new team or remain with the Warriors.

He tried to remind himself that this morning's paper was filled with nothing but rumors. If something materialized from Sheila Houston's claims, he'd worry about it then. Right now, he needed to focus on playing his best so the Warriors could win the first play-offs round and move on to the next.

Resting the cue between his thumb and forefinger, Brody positioned the shot, took one last look and pulled the cue back.

From the corner of his eye, a woman's curvy figure drew his attention, distracting him just as he pushed the cue forward. The brief diversion caused his fingers to slip, and the white ball sailed across the felt, avoided every other ball on the table and slid directly into the far pocket. Scratch.

Damn.

Scowling, he lifted his head just as the source of his distraction drew near.

"You could do it over," Mike said quickly, fumbling for the white ball and placing it back on the table. "It's called a mulligan or something."

"That's golf," Brody muttered, his gaze glued to the approaching brunette.

A few years ago an interviewer for *Sports Illustrated* had asked him to describe the type of women he was attracted to. "Leggy blondes" had been his swift response, which was pretty much the exact opposite of the woman who'd now stopped two feet in front of him. And yet his mouth went dry at the sight of her, his body quickly responding to every little detail. The silky chocolate-brown hair falling over her shoulders, the vibrant green eyes the same shade as a lush rain forest, the petite body with more curves than his brain could register.

His breath hitched as their eyes met. The whisper of an uncertain smile that tugged at her full lips sent a jolt to his groin. Jeez. He couldn't remember the last time a single smile from a woman had evoked such an intense response.

"I thought I'd play the winner." Her soft, husky voice promptly delivered another shock wave to Brody's crotch.

Stunned to find he was two seconds away from a full-blown erection, he tried to remind his body that he wasn't a teenager any longer, but a twenty-nine-year-old man who knew how to control himself. Hell, he could control the puck while fending off elbows and cross-checks from opposing attackers; getting a hold of his hormones should be a piece of cake.

"Here, just take my place now," Mike burst out, quickly pushing his cue into her hands. His gaze dropped to the cleavage spilling over the scooped neckline of the brunette's yellow tank top, and then the kid turned to Brody and winked. "Have fun, man."

Brody wrinkled his brow, wondering if Mike thought he was graciously passing this curvy bombshell over to him or something, but before he could say anything, Mike disappeared in the crowd.

Brody swallowed, then focused his eyes on the sexy little woman who'd managed to get him hard with one smile.

She didn't look like the type you'd find in a sports bar, even one as upscale as this. Sure, her body was out of this world, but something about her screamed innocence. The freckles splattering the bridge of her nose maybe, or perhaps the way she kept biting on the corner of her bottom lip like a bunny nibbling on a piece of lettuce.

Before he could stop it, the image of those plump red lips nibbling on one particular part of his anatomy slid to the forefront of his brain like a well-placed slap shot to the net. His cock pushed against the fly of his jeans.

So much for controlling his hormones.

"I'm guessing it's my turn," she said. Tilting her head, she offered another endearing smile. "Seeing as you just blew your shot."

He cleared his throat. "Uh, yeah."

Snap out of it, man.

Right, he needed to regroup here. He played hockey, yeah, but he wasn't a player anymore. His love-'em-and-leave-'em ways were in the past. He was sick to death of women fawning all over him because of his career. Nowadays all he had to do was walk into a place—club, bar, the public library—and a warm, willing female was by his side, ready to jump his bones. And he couldn't even count the number of times he'd heard, "Do you like it rough off the ice, baby?"

Well, screw it. He'd been down the casual road, had his fun, scored off the ice as often as he scored on it, but now it was time to take a new path. One where the woman in his bed actually gave a damn about *him,* and not the hockey star she couldn't wait to gush to her friends about.

The sexual fog in his brain cleared, leaving him alert and composed, and completely aware of the flush on the brunette's cheeks and the hint of attraction in her eyes. If this woman was looking to score with Mr. Hockey, she had another think coming.

"I'm Hayden," his new opponent said, uncertainty floating through her forest-green eyes.

"Brody Croft," he returned coolly, waiting for the flicker of recognition to cross her features.

It didn't happen. No flash of familiarity, no widening of the eyes. Her expression didn't change in the slightest.

"It's nice to meet you. Brody." Her voice lingered on his name, as if she were testing it out for size. She must have decided she liked the fit, because she gave a small nod and turned her attention to the table. After a quick examination, she pointed to the ball he'd failed to sink and called the shot.

Okay, was he supposed to believe she genuinely didn't know who he was? That she'd walked into a sports bar and randomly chosen to hit on the only hockey player in attendance?

"So…did you catch the game last night?" he said with a casual slant of the head.

She gave him a blank stare. "What game?"

"Game one of the play-offs, Warriors and Vipers. Seriously good hockey, in my opinion."

Her brows drew together in a frown. "Oh. I'm not really a fan, to be honest."

"You don't like the Warriors?"

"I don't like hockey." She made a self-deprecating face.

"Actually, I can't say I enjoy any sport, really. Maybe the gymnastics in the summer Olympics?"

He couldn't help but grin. "Are you asking or telling?"

She smiled back. "Telling. And I guess it's very telling that I only watch a sports event once every four years, huh?"

He found himself liking the dry note to her throaty voice when she admitted her disinterest in sports. Her honesty was rare. Most—fine, *all*—of the women he encountered claimed to love his sport of choice, and if they didn't truly love it, they pretended to, as if sharing that common interest made them soul mates.

"But I love this game," Hayden added, raising her cue. "It counts as a sport, right?"

"It does in my book."

She nodded, then focused on the balls littering the table. She leaned forward to take her shot.

He got a nice eyeful of her cleavage, a tantalizing swell of creamy-white skin spilling over the neckline of her snug yellow top. When he lowered his eyes, he couldn't help but admire her full breasts, hugged firmly by a thin bra he could only see the outline of.

She took the shot, and he raised his brows, impressed, as the ball cleanly disappeared into the pocket. She was good.

All right, more than good, he had to relent as she proceeded to circle the table and sink ball after ball.

"Where'd you learn to play like that?" he asked, finally finding his voice.

She met his eyes briefly before sinking the last solid on the table. "My dad." She smiled again. Those pouty lips just screamed for his mouth to do wicked things to them. "He bought me my own table when I was nine, set it up right next to his. We used to play side by side in the basement every night before I went to bed."

"Does he still play?"

Her eyes clouded. "No. He's too busy with work to relax around a pool table anymore." She straightened her back and glanced at the table. "Eight ball, corner pocket."

At this point, Brody didn't even care about the game Hayden was certain to win. The sweet scent of her perfume, a fruity sensual aroma, floated in the air and made him mindless with need. Man, he couldn't remember the last time he'd been so drawn to a woman.

After sinking the eight ball, she moved toward him, each step she took heightening his desire. She ran her fingers through her dark hair, and a new aroma filled his nostrils. Strawberries. Coconut.

He was suddenly very, very hungry.

"Good game," she said, shooting him another smile. Impish, this time.

His mouth twisted wryly. "I didn't even get to play."

"I'm sorry." She paused. "Do you like to play?"

Was she referring to pool? Or a different game? Maybe the kind you played in bed. Naked.

"Pool, I mean," she added quickly.

"Sure, I like pool. Among other things." *Let's see how she handles that.*

A cute rosy flush spread over her cheeks. "Me, too. I mean, I like other things."

His curiosity sparked as he stared at the enigma in front of him. He got the distinct impression that she was flirting with him. Or trying to, at least. Yet her unmistakable blush and the slight trembling of her hands betrayed the confident air she tried to convey.

Did she do this often? Flirt with strange men in bars? Looking at her again, now that he was able to see through the fog of initial attraction, it didn't seem like the case. She was dressed rather conservatively. Sure, the top was low-cut, but it covered her midriff, and her jeans didn't ride low on her hips like those of most of the other women in this place. And sexy as she was, she didn't seem to be aware of her own appeal.

"That's good. Other things can be a lot of fun," he answered, unable to stop the husky pitch of his voice.

Their gazes connected. Brody could swear the air crackled and hissed with sexual tension. Or maybe he just imagined it. He couldn't deny the hum of awareness thudding in his groin like the bass line of a sultry jazz tune, but maybe he was alone in the feeling. It was difficult to get a read on Hayden.

"So…Brody." His name rolled off her lips in a way that had his body growing stiff. That didn't say much, considering that every part of him was already hard and prickling with anticipation.

He wanted her in his bed.

Whoa—where had that come from?

Five minutes ago he was telling himself it was time to quit falling into bed with women who didn't give a damn about him and look for something more meaningful. So why the hell was he anticipating a roll in the hay with a woman he'd just met?

Because she's different.

The observation came out of nowhere, bringing with it a baffling swirl of emotion. Yes, this woman had somehow managed to elicit primal, greedy lust in him. Yes, her body was designed to drive a man wild. But something about her seriously intrigued him. Those damn cute freckles, the shy smiles, the look in her eyes that clearly said, "I want to go to bed with you but I'm apprehensive about it." It was the combination of sensuality and bashfulness, excitement and wariness, that attracted him to her.

He opened his mouth to say something, anything, but promptly closed it when Hayden reached out to touch his arm.

Looking up at him with those bottomless green eyes, she said, "Look, I know this is going to sound…forward. And don't think I do this often—I've never done this actually, but…" She took a breath. "Would you like to come back to my hotel?"

Ah, her hotel. An out-of-towner. That explained why she hadn't recognized him. And yet he got the feeling that even if she did know what he did for a living, she wouldn't care.

He liked that.

"Well?" she said, fixing him with an expectant stare.

He couldn't stop the teasing twinge in his voice. "And what will we do in your hotel room?"

A hint of a smile. "We could have a nightcap."

"A nightcap," he repeated.

"Or we could talk. Watch television. Order room service."

The little vixen was teasing him, he realized. And, damn, but he liked this side of her, too.

"Maybe raid the minifridge?"

"Definitely."

Their eyes met and locked, the heat of desire and promise of sex filling the space between them. Finally he shoved his pool cue in the rack and strode back to her. Screw it. He'd told himself no more sleazy bar pickups, but damn it, this didn't feel sleazy. It felt *right*.

Barely able to disguise the urgency in his tone, he curled his fingers over her hot, silky skin and said, "Let's go."

2

DEAR GOD, he'd said yes.

She'd invited a gorgeous stranger back to her hotel room for a *nightcap* (translation: sex) and he'd actually said *yes*.

Hayden resisted the urge to fan her hot face with her hands. Instead, trying to remain cool and collected, she said, "I'll meet you outside, okay? I just need to tell my friend I'm leaving."

His smoldering blue eyes studied her for a moment, making her grow hotter. With a quick nod, he exited the bar. Tearing her attention away from his criminally sexy backside, she spun on her heel and hurried back to Darcy, dodging people along the way. When she reached the table, Darcy greeted her with a delighted grin. "You bad girl, you," she teased, wagging her finger.

Sliding into the chair, Hayden swallowed hard and willed her heartbeat to slow. "Jesus. I can't believe I'm doing this."

"I take it he said yes?"

Hayden ignored the question. "I just propositioned a complete stranger. Granted, he's a very sexy stranger, but hell! I'm not sure I can do this."

"Of course you can."

"But I don't even know him. What if he hacks me to pieces and hides my dismembered body parts in the air-conditioning system of the hotel or something?"

"You have your cell phone?"

Body Check

She nodded.

"If you see any sign of trouble, call the cops. Or call me and I'll call the cops." Darcy shrugged. "But I wouldn't worry. He doesn't seem like the serial-killer type."

Hayden blew out a breath. "That's what they said about Ted Bundy."

"You can back out, you know. You don't have to sleep with this guy. But you want to, don't you?"

Did she want to? Oh, yeah. As the image of Brody's chiseled face and scrumptious body flashed through her brain, some of her nervousness dissolved. He was hands down the most gorgeous man she'd ever met. And she got the feeling he knew his way around a bedroom. The raw sex appeal pouring out of him told her she might be in for a very stimulating night.

"I want to." Newfound confidence washed over her. "And I probably shouldn't keep him waiting."

Darcy winked. "Have fun."

"Are you going to be okay here alone?"

"Of course." Darcy gestured to her fruity pink drink. "This daiquiri will attract the fellows like flies to honey. For the purpose of this analogy, I'll be the honey."

Hayden laughed. "Whatever you say."

With a quick wave, she threaded through the crowd toward the door. When she stepped into the cool night air, she spotted Brody standing near one of the potted plants in the entrance, his hands slung in the pockets of his jeans. A shiver tickled her belly as she took in his profile. He really was spectacular. Her gaze lowered to his lips. She wondered what they would feel like pressed against her own. Would they be soft? Hard? Both?

"Hey," she said, her voice wavering.

She took a step forward just as he turned to face her. His expression, appreciative, anticipatory, sizzled her nerves. "Your car or mine?" he asked in a rough voice that made her toes curl.

"I don't have a car. My friend drove here." A squeak, her voice had come out in a damn squeak.

"My car's over there." He nodded, then began walking toward the parking lot. He didn't check to see if she was following. As if he just assumed she was.

This was her chance to walk away. She could hurry into the bar and pretend she'd never asked this man to come back to her hotel. She could phone up Doug, have a heart-to-heart, maybe entice him into engaging in some phone sex…. Ha! Fat chance.

She hurried to keep up with Brody's purposeful strides.

"Nice car," she remarked when they reached the shiny black BMW SUV.

"Thanks." He pulled a set of keys from his front pocket and pressed a button. The car's security system beeped as the doors unlocked, and he reached for the passenger door and opened it for her. Hayden settled against the leather seat and waited for Brody to get in.

After he'd buckled his seat belt and started the engine, he turned to her and asked, "Where to?"

"The Ritz-Carlton."

He raised his eyebrows but didn't say anything, just pulled out of the parking lot and made a left turn. "So where are you from, Hayden?"

"I was born in Chicago, but I've been living in San Francisco for the past three years."

"And what do you do out there?"

"I'm a junior professor at Berkeley. I teach art history, and I'm also working toward a Ph.D."

Before she could ask him what he did for a living, he said, "Sounds exciting."

She got the feeling he wasn't talking about her career

anymore. Her suspicions were confirmed when his gaze swept over face and dropped to her cleavage. Under his brief—but appreciative—scrutiny, her nipples tightened against her lace bra.

She played with the sleeve of the green wool sweater she'd brought instead of a coat, focusing on the scenery along South Michigan Avenue, afraid to look at him again. If he got her this aroused from one hooded glance, what on earth would he do to her in bed?

Gosh, she couldn't wait to find out.

The rest of the car ride was silent. They reached the hotel, and Brody pulled into the lot and killed the engine. Still, neither of them spoke. As she unbuckled her seat belt, her pulse began to race. This was it. An hour ago she'd been complaining to Darcy about the lack of sex in her life, and now here she was, walking into the lobby of the Ritz with the sexiest man she'd ever encountered.

Her heart thumped against her rib cage as they rode the elevator up to the penthouse. Shooting her a quizzical look, he said, "You must make good money at Berkeley."

She simply nodded, her expression vague. She didn't want to tell him that the lavish penthouse actually belonged to her father. Her dad had lived here up until three years ago, before he'd married Sheila. He kept the place so Hayden would have somewhere to stay when she came to visit. But she didn't want to tell Brody, mostly because that would lead to questions like *what does your father do?* Which would then lead to questions about her dad's hockey team and that was one topic of conversation she tried to avoid.

With the exception of Doug, most of the men she'd dated over the years had gone a little crazy when they found out her father owned the Warriors. Once, she'd dated a man who'd badgered her constantly to get him season tickets—which had driven her to promptly break up with him.

She understood the sports obsession that came with most males, but just once it would be nice if *she* were the source of a man's infatuation.

The elevator doors opened right into the living room. Decorated in shades of black and gold, the room boasted four enormous leather couches in the center, all positioned in the direction of a fifty-six-inch plasma television mounted on the far wall. The suite had three large bedrooms, as well as a private covered balcony with a ten-person hot tub. In the corner of the main suite was a wet bar, which Hayden made a beeline for the second they stepped inside.

She wasn't a big drinker, but her nerves were shaky, making her hands tremble and her heartbeat erratic, and she hoped the alcohol might calm her down.

"What can I get you?" she called over her shoulder. "There's beer, scotch, whiskey, bourbon—"

"You." With a soft laugh, Brody eliminated the distance between them.

Oh, God, he was huge. She had to fully tilt her head up to look at him. At five feet three inches, she felt like a dwarf next to him. Her heart jammed in her throat as he stepped even closer. She could feel his body heat, his warm breath tickling her ear as he leaned down and whispered, "That was the nightcap you were referring to, wasn't it?"

His low, husky voice heated her veins. When she met his eyes, she saw the unmistakable desire glittering in their cobalt-blue depths. "Well?" he prompted.

"Yes." The word squeaked out of her mouth.

He settled his big hands on her waist, yet didn't press his body against hers. Despite the pounding of her heart, anticipation began to build in her belly, slowly crept up to her breasts like a vine and made them grow heavy, achy. She wanted him closer, wanted to feel his firm chest on her breasts, his hardness between her thighs.

Brody lifted one hand and brushed his thumb against her lower lip. "If you want to change your mind, now's the time."

He waited for her answer, watching her closely. Her throat grew dry, while another part of her grew wet.

Did she want to change her mind? Maybe she should call her own bluff now, before things got out of hand. But as she studied his handsome face, she realized she didn't want him to leave. So what if this wouldn't result in I-love-you's and cosigning a mortgage for a house? Tonight wasn't about that. Tonight she was stressed and tired and sexually frustrated. And just once she wanted to be with a man without thinking about the future.

"I haven't changed my mind," she murmured.

"Good."

He skimmed his hand over her hip, moving it to her back, grazing her tailbone. Then he stared at her lips, as if pondering, debating.

His slow perusal lasted too long for her throbbing body. She wanted him to kiss her. Now. She let out a tiny groan to voice her anguish.

Amusement danced across his features. "What? What do you want, Hayden?"

"Your mouth." The words flew out before she could stop them, shocking her. Since when was she this forward?

"All right." He dipped his head and planted a soft kiss on her neck, lightly biting the tender flesh with his teeth.

She whimpered and he responded with a chuckle, his warm breath moistening her skin. He trailed his tongue up to her earlobe, flicked over it, licked it, then blew a stream of air over it, making her shiver.

Fire began simmering in her blood, heating all the parts that already ached for him. She reached up and touched his dark hair, relishing the silky texture. She'd never known a simple kiss could have such a slow buildup. Most of the men in her past had thrust their tongues into her mouth and quickly followed suit by thrusting themselves into her.

But Brody, he took his time.

He tortured her.

"Your skin tastes like…" He kissed her jaw, then nipped at it. "Strawberries. And honey."

All she could do was shiver in response.

"Take off your clothes," he said roughly.

She swallowed. "Now?"

"Now would be a good time, yes."

She reached for the hem of her sweater, trying to fight the insecurity spiraling through her. She'd never stripped for a man before. Was she supposed to put on a show? Dance? Well, forget that. No matter how much she wanted him right now, she wasn't going to pretend to be the sexy seductress she wasn't.

She pulled her sweater and tank top over her head, pleased to hear Brody's breath hitch at the sight of her lacy wisp of a bra. When she reached for the front clasp, he shook his head. "No. Not yet. First the jeans."

Well. Commanding, wasn't he?

Obligingly, she wiggled out of her jeans and let them drop to the floor. Her black panties matched her bra, and they, too, left little to the imagination.

Brody's eyes widened with approval. She was starting to get the hang of this stripping thing. Hooking her thumbs under the spaghetti-thin straps that constituted a waistband, she pulled her panties down her thighs, slowly, bending over a little so he could get a peek at her cleavage.

Naked from the waist down, she held his gaze. "Like what you see?"

His serious expression never faltered. "Very much. Now the bra."

In one slow, fluid movement, she unclasped her bra and tossed it aside. Strangely enough, she no longer felt insecure.

"I like—" he stepped closer and brushed his thumb over the swell of one breast "—these. A lot."

She wondered if he realized he still hadn't kissed her lips. Though the way his eyes burned every inch of skin she'd just exposed to him, she felt thoroughly kissed.

"Your turn. Get rid of your clothes."

He grinned. "Why don't you do it for me?"

The thought of undressing him was so appealing that her nipples hardened. He didn't miss the reaction, and his grin widened.

"Gets you going, doesn't it, the thought of peeling these clothes off my body?" he taunted.

"Yes," she blew out.

"Then do it."

With a shaky breath, she grasped his sweater, bunching the material between her fingers before lifting it up his chest and over his head. That first sight of his bare chest stole the breath from her lungs. Every inch of him was hard. His defined pectorals, the rippling abs and trim hips. He had a two-inch scar under his collarbone, and another under his chin that she hadn't noticed before, but the scars only added to his appeal, making him appear dangerous.

A badass tribal tattoo covered one firm bicep, while the other boasted a lethal-looking dragon in mid-flight. It reminded her of her own tattoo, the one she'd gotten for the sole purpose of pissing off her father after he'd grounded her for missing curfew when she was seventeen. Even now the spontaneity of her actions—getting a *tattoo!*—surprised her.

Darcy always teased that she had a secret wild side, and maybe she did, but it rarely made any appearances.

Tonight, though, her wild side had definitely come out to play.

"Like what you see?" Brody mimicked, the heat in his eyes telling her he was enjoying the attention.

She licked her lips. "Yes." Then she reached for his fly, unbuttoned it and pulled the zipper down. She bent over to slide his jeans off, admiring his long legs and muscular thighs and the erection that pushed against the black boxer briefs he wore, a thick ridge that made her mouth water.

Dear God, this was insanity.

Stumbling to her feet, she tugged at his waistband and helped him out of the briefs. Leaving him as naked as she was.

She shyly appraised his body, which was toned, muscled and unbelievably *male*. She eyed his impressive erection, then trembled at the thought of that hard, pulsing cock buried deep inside her.

Suddenly she could no longer bear it.

"For God's sake, kiss me," she blurted out.

"Yes, ma'am." His eyes gleaming, Brody pressed his body against hers and finally bent down to capture her mouth.

Oh, sweet Jesus.

He felt and tasted like heaven. With skilled ease, he explored her mouth, swirling and thrusting his tongue into every crevice, hot and greedy. When he sucked on her bottom lip, she let out a deep moan then pulled back and stared at him in awe.

Brody seemed to know exactly what to do, turning her on in a way she'd never anticipated. He fondled her breasts for an excruciatingly long time before finally dipping his head and sampling one mound with his tongue.

He sucked the nipple hard, flicked his tongue over it,

nibbled on it until she cried out with pleasure that bordered on pain, and just when she thought it couldn't possibly feel better than that, he turned his attention to her other breast.

Arousal drummed through her body, until her thighs grew slick from her own wetness, and she found herself choking out, "We need a bed. Now."

DAMN, HE HADN'T expected her to be like this. Deliciously demanding and so gorgeous. Something about Hayden sent lust and curiosity spinning through him, the need to both claim her and unravel the mystery of her.

And there was definitely plenty to learn about this freckle-faced professor who had initiated a one-night stand when it was obviously not in her nature.

He sucked on her nipple once more before pulling his head away and straightening his back. His mouth went dry as sawdust as he stared at the evidence of his handiwork on those high, full breasts. His stubble had chafed the hell out of her creamy white skin, leaving splotches of red, and the tips of her dusky pink nipples glistened with the moisture, making him want to feast on her again.

His eyes dropped to the wispy line of dark hair between her thighs. He knew it was called a landing strip and goddamn but he couldn't wait to land his tongue down there. The sparse amount of hair offered a mouthwatering view of her swollen clit.

His already hot and hard body grew hotter and harder.

"Where's the bedroom?" he groaned.

Hayden's mouth quirked. Without answering, she turned on her heel toward the unlit hallway.

Brody took two steps, then stopped when he noticed the tattoo on her lower back. Oh, man. In the shadowy corridor he could just make out the shape of a bird. A hawk, or an eagle. Dark, dangerous, incredibly sexy and completely surprising. He'd known this woman was different. Her tattoo was so tantalizing he marched up to her and gripped her slender waist with both hands.

The top of her head barely reached his chin. How had this saucy little woman reduced him to a state of foolish hunger?

As his hands trailed down her hips, she twisted her head slightly to send him a look that said she was curious about his next move.

His next move consisted of dropping to his knees and outlining the tattoo with his tongue.

Hayden shuddered, but he kept one hand on her waist, keeping her steady. "Why an eagle?" he murmured, kissing her lower back.

"I like eagles."

A very simple answer from a very complicated woman. He stroked her ass with his hand, then lowered his head and bit into the soft flesh.

"Bedroom," she gasped.

"Screw it," he muttered.

Still holding her secure with one hand, he slid the other around to her front and ran one finger over her clit. She hissed out a breath, then jerked forward, pressing her palms to the wall and raising that firm ass so that he got a very naughty view of her glistening sex.

He moved closer as if being pulled by a magnet. As his pulse drummed in his ears, he licked her damp folds from behind and used his finger to stroke her clit.

Hayden shuddered again. "That feels…" she moaned "…amazing."

"What about this? How does this feel?"

He shoved his tongue directly into her opening.

Her breath hitched.

He chuckled at her reaction, then thrust his tongue right back inside her enticing sex before she could catch her breath.

Hayden's soft moans filled the wide hallway. Her breathing grew ragged, her clit swollen beneath his thumb, her sex wet with arousal. He kissed her once more, then moved his mouth away and replaced it with two fingers.

"Are you trying to make me come?" she choked out.

"That was the plan, yeah."

He explored her silky heat, fingering her deftly, enjoying her soft whimpers of pleasure while at the same time trying to ignore his erection, which was threatening to explode.

Any second now his control would shatter, he knew it would, but he held on to that one tiny thread of restraint, feeling it slowly unravel and fray inside him. Hayden's cry of abandon made him move faster, increase his pressure over her clit and add another finger into the mix. And then she came. Loudly. Without inhibition. She pushed her ass into his hand as her inner muscles tightened and contracted over his fingers.

"Oh, God…Brody…" Her voice dissolved into a contented sigh.

A moment later she slid down to the carpeted floor, her bare back pressing into his chest as he continued to trace lazy figure-eights over her clit.

She shifted so they were face-to-face, her green eyes burning with need, her face flushed from her climax. She looked so good that he leaned forward to push his tongue through her pliant lips, intent on exploring every recess of her hot, wet mouth, desperate to taste every part of this woman.

Without breaking the kiss, he rolled her gently onto her back and covered her body with his.

"I need to be inside you," he choked out.

It was a primal urge, an overwhelming desire to possess

and one he never knew he had, but sure enough it was there, making his entire body tense with need, waiting to be released.

Tearing his mouth from hers, he stood up and left her in the hall. He returned a moment later with the condoms that had been tucked in his wallet. Only three condoms, he realized as he glanced down at his hand. Maybe he was being overly optimistic, but as he looked at Hayden, he suspected he might need to make a trip to the drugstore. She hadn't bothered getting up and she looked ridiculously sexy lying there on the floor beneath him. Sexy and trashy and so damn appealing his cock twitched with impatience.

The air was thick with tension, the hallway quiet save for their heavy breathing. Before he could tear open the condom packet, she sat up and murmured, "Not yet."

Then she wrapped her lips around him.

"Jesus," he mumbled, nearly keeling over backward.

The feel of her eager mouth surrounding him brought on an unexpected shudder. She took him deeper into her mouth, cupping his balls, stroking his ass and licking every hard inch of him.

A few moments of exquisite torture were all he could bear. Hard as it was to pull back from the best blow job of his life, he gently moved her head, so close to exploding he wasn't sure how he managed to hold back.

He lowered himself onto her again and Hayden sighed as one palm closed over her breast. "It's been so long…"

"How long?" he asked.

"Too long."

He lightly pinched her nipple before bending down to kiss it. "I'll take it slow then." He sucked the nipple deep in his mouth, rolled the other one between his thumb and forefinger.

She forced his head up and kissed him. "No." She took his hand and dragged it between her legs. "I want fast."

He swallowed when he touched her sex, still moist from her climax.

He grew even harder, wanting so badly to put the damn condom on and slide into her slick heat. But the gentleman in him argued to go slow, to taste every inch of her body and bring her over the edge again before he took his own release. Once more he tried to slow the pace, stroking her with his thumb.

His gentlemanly intentions got him nowhere.

"I'm ready," she said between gritted teeth. "I don't need slow. I need you to fuck me, Brody."

His cock jerked at the wicked request.

Oh, man. He'd never have pegged this woman as a dirty talker. But, damn, how he liked it.

Without another word, he rolled the condom onto his shaft, positioned himself between her thighs and drove deep inside her. They released simultaneous groans.

Burying his face in the curve of her neck, Brody inhaled the sweet feminine scent of her and withdrew, slowly, torturously, only to thrust into her to the hilt before she could blink.

"You're so tight," he muttered in her ear. "So wet."

"Told you I was ready," she said between gasps of pleasure.

He slammed into her, over and over again, groaning each time she lifted her hips to take him deeper. It was too fast for him, and yet it felt like everything was moving in slow motion. The way she dug her fingers into his buttocks and pulled him toward her, squeezing his cock with her tight wetness. The rising pleasure in his body, the impatient throb in his groin that forced him to move even faster.

She exploded again, quivering, shuddering, making little mewling sounds that had his entire body burning with excitement.

He continued plunging into her until finally he couldn't take it anymore. He came a second later, kissing her harshly as his climax rocked into him with the force of a hurricane. Shards of pleasure ripped through him, hot, intense, insistent. Uncontrollable. He fought for air, wondering how it was possible that the little woman beneath him had managed to bring him to the most incredible release of his life.

They lay there for a moment, breathing ragged, bodies slick, his cock still buried inside her.

Hayden ran her hands along his sweat-soaked back, then murmured, "Not bad."

Even in his state of orgasmic numbness Brody managed a mock frown. "Not bad? That's all you can say?"

"Fine, it was tremendously good."

"That's better."

With a small grin, she disentangled herself from his embrace and got to her feet. Her gaze ruefully drifted in the direction of the bedroom they'd never managed to reach. "Five more steps and we could've been on my big, comfortable bed."

He propped himself up on his elbows, the soft carpet itching the hell out of his back. "Don't you worry, Hayden," he said with a rakish glint in his eye. "The night is still young."

3

"How MANY?" Darcy demanded the next day.

Hayden moved her cell phone to her other ear and maneuvered her rental car through afternoon traffic. Chicago's downtown core was surprisingly busy; tonight's Warriors game had probably compelled more than a few people to leave work early. Hayden, on the other hand, didn't have a choice in the matter. Whether she wanted to or not, she was about to spend the evening sitting next to her dad in the owner's box, watching a sport she not only found dismally boring, but one she'd resented for years.

God, she couldn't even count how many games she'd been dragged to over the years. Hundreds? Thousands? Regardless of the final tally, she was no closer to liking hockey now, at twenty-six, than she had been at age six, when her father took her to her first game. To her, hockey meant constant uprooting. Traveling, moving, sitting behind the bench with a coloring book because her dad hadn't felt right hiring a nanny.

A shrink would probably tell her that she was projecting, taking out her frustration with her father on an innocent little sport, but she couldn't help it. No matter how hard she'd tried over the years, she couldn't bring herself to appreciate or enjoy the damn game.

"I don't kiss and tell," she said into her cell, stopping at a red light. An El train whizzed overhead, momentarily making her deaf to anything but the thundering of the train as it tore down the tracks.

"Like hell you don't," Darcy was saying when the noise died down. "How many, Hayden?"

Suppressing a tiny smile, she finally caved in. "Five."

"Five!" Darcy went silent for a moment. Then she offered an awe-laced obscenity. "You're telling me the hunk gave you *five orgasms* last night?"

"He sure did." The memory alone brought a spark of heat to her still-exhausted body. Muscles she hadn't even known she had were still aching, thanks to the man who could definitely give the Energizer Bunny a run for its money.

"I'm stunned. You realize that? I'm utterly stunned."

The light ahead turned green and Hayden drove through the intersection. A group of teenagers wearing blue and silver Warriors jerseys caught her attention, and she groaned at the sight of them. She was so not in the mood to watch a night of rowdy hockey with her father.

"So how was the big goodbye and 'thanks for the five O's'?" Darcy asked.

"Strange." She made a left turn and drove down Lakeshore Drive toward the Lincoln Center, the brand-new arena recently built for the Warriors. "Before he left, he asked for my number."

"Did you give it to him?"

"No." She sighed. "But then he offered me *his* number, so I took it."

"It was supposed to be a one-night stand!"

"Yeah…but…he looked so dismayed. I made it pretty clear that it was a one-night thing. You'd think he'd be thrilled about that. No strings, no expectations. But he was disappointed."

"You can't see him again. What if things get serious? You'll be going back to the West Coast in a couple months."

Darcy sounded surprisingly upset. Well, maybe it wasn't that surprising, seeing as Darcy found the idea of falling in love more petrifying than the Ebola virus. The phobia had taken form a few years ago, after Darcy's father broke up his marriage of twenty years by falling in love with another woman. Since then Darcy had convinced herself the same would happen to her. Hayden had tried to assure her friend that not all men left their wives, but her words always fell on deaf ears.

"Nothing will get serious," Hayden said with a laugh. "First of all, I probably won't see Brody again. And second, I won't allow myself to develop a relationship with any man until I figure out where things stand with Doug."

Darcy groaned. "Him? Why do you continue to keep him in the picture? Turn your break into a breakup, before he mentions the intimacy bridge and—"

"Goodbye, Darce."

She hung up, not in the mood to hear Darcy make fun of Doug again. Fine, so he was conservative, and maybe his comparison of sex to a bridge was bizarre, but Doug was a decent man. And she wasn't ready to write him off completely.

Uh, you slept with another man, her conscience reminded.

Her cheeks grew hot at the memory of sleeping with Brody. And somehow the words *sleeping with Brody* seemed unsuitable, as if they described a bland, mundane event like tea with a grandparent. What she and Brody had done last night was neither bland nor mundane. It had been crazy. Intense. Mind-numbingly wild and deliciously dirty. Hands down, the best sex of her life.

Was she a complete fool for sending him away this morning?

Probably.

Fine, more like absolutely.

But what else should she have done? She'd woken up to find Brody's smoky-blue eyes admiring her and before she

could even utter a good-morning he'd slipped his hand between her legs. Stroked, rubbed, and brought her to orgasm
in less than a minute. As a result, she'd forgotten her name,
her surroundings and the reason she'd brought him home in
the first place.

Fortunately, the amnesia had been temporary. Her memory
had swiftly returned when she'd checked her cell phone
messages and saw that both her father and Doug had called.

Brody had made it clear he wanted to see her again, and
sure, that would be nice…okay, it would be freaking incredible. But sex wasn't going to solve her problems. Her
issues with Doug would still be there, lurking in the wings like
a jealous understudy, as would the stress of her father's recent
struggles. And if Brody wanted more than sex, if he wanted
a relationship (as unlikely as that was) what would she do
then? Throw a third complication into her already complicated
personal life?

No, ending it before it began was the logical solution. Best
to leave it as a one-night stand.

She reached the arena ten minutes later and parked in the
area reserved for VIPs, right next to her father's shiny red
Mercedes convertible. She knew it was her dad's, because of
the license plate reading "TM-OWNR." *Real subtle, Dad.*

Why had she even bothered coming home? When her
father had asked if she could take some time off to be with
him during this whole divorce mess, she'd seen it as a sign
that he valued her support, wanted her around. But in the
week she'd been home she'd only seen her dad once, for a
quick lunch in his office. The phone had kept ringing, so
they'd barely spoken, and it was unlikely they'd get any time
to talk tonight. She knew how focused her dad was when he
watched hockey.

With a sigh, she got out of the car and braced herself for a night of watching sweaty men skating after a black disk, and listening to her father rave about how "it doesn't get better than this."

Gee, she couldn't wait.

"WATCH OUT FOR Valdek tonight," Sam Becker warned when Brody approached the long wooden bench on one side of the Warriors locker room. He paused in front of his locker.

"Valdek's back?" Brody groaned. "What happened to his three-game suspension?"

Becker adjusted his shin pads then pulled on his navy-blue pants and started lacing up. For thirty-six, he was still in prime condition. When Brody first met the legendary forward he'd been in awe, even more impressed when he'd seen Becker deke out three guys to score a shorthanded goal, proving to everyone in the league why he still belonged there.

And what had impressed him the most was Becker's complete lack of arrogance. Despite winning two championship cups and having a career that rivaled Gretzky's, Sam Becker was as down-to-earth as they came. He was the man everyone went to when they had a problem, whether personal or professional, and over the years, he'd become Brody's closest friend.

"Suspension's over," Becker answered. "And he's out for blood. He hasn't forgotten who got him suspended, kiddo."

Brody ignored the nickname, which Becker refused to ease up on, and snorted. "Right, because it's my fault he sliced my chin open with his skate."

A few more players drifted into the room. The Warriors goalie, Alexi Nicklaus, gave a salute in lieu of greeting. Next to him, Derek Jones, this season's rookie yet already one of the best defensemen in the league, wandered over and said, "Valdek's back."

"So I've heard." Brody peeled his black T-shirt over his head and tossed it on the bench.

Jones suddenly hooted, causing him to glance down at his chest. What he found was a reminder of the most exciting sexual experience of his life. Over his left nipple was the purple hickey Hayden's full lips had branded into his skin, after he'd swooped her off the hallway floor and carried her into the bedroom—where he'd proceeded to make love to her all night long.

This morning he'd woken up to the sight of Hayden's dark hair fanned across the stark white pillow, one bare breast pressing into his chest and a slender leg hooked over his lower body. He'd cuddled after sex plenty of times in the past, but he couldn't remember ever awakening to find himself in the exact post-sex position. Normally he gently rolled his companion over, needing space and distance in order to fall asleep. Last night he hadn't needed it. In fact, he even remembered waking up in the middle of the night and pulling Hayden's warm, naked body closer.

Figure that one out.

"Remind me to keep you away from my daughter," Becker said with a sigh.

Next to him, Jones guffawed. "So who's the lucky lady? Or did you even get her name?"

Brody's back stiffened defensively, but then he wondered why it bothered him that his teammates still viewed him as a playboy. Sure, he *had* been a playboy, once upon a time. When he'd first gone pro, he couldn't help letting it all go to his head. For a kid who'd grown up dirt-poor in Michigan, the sudden onslaught of wealth and attention was like a drug. Exciting. Addictive. Suddenly everyone wanted to be his friend, his confidante, his lover. At twenty-one, he'd welcomed every perk that came with the job—particularly the endless stream of women lining up to warm his bed.

But it'd gotten old once he'd realized that ninety percent of those eager females cared most about his uniform. He didn't mind being in the limelight, but he was no longer interested in going to bed with women who thought of him only as the star forward of the Warriors.

Unfortunately, his teammates couldn't seem to accept that he'd left his playboy days in the dust. It was probably a label thing; the guys on the team liked labels. They all had 'em— Derek Jones was the Prankster, Becker was the Elder, Craig Wyatt was Mr. Serious. And Brody was the Playboy. Apparently admitting otherwise screwed up the team dynamic or something.

Ah, well. Let them believe what they wanted. He might not be a Casanova anymore but he could still kick their butts any day of the week.

"Yes, I got her name," he said, rolling his eyes.

Just not her number.

He kept that irksome detail to himself. He still wasn't sure why it bugged him, Hayden's refusal to give him her phone number. And for the life of him, he also couldn't make sense of that bomb of a speech she'd dropped on him earlier.

I'd rather we didn't see each other again. I had a great time, but I never had any intention of this going beyond one night. I hope you understand.

Every man's dream words. He couldn't remember how many times he'd tried to find a way to let a woman down gently when she asked for something more the morning after. Hayden had pretty much summed up the attitude he'd had about sex his entire life. One night, no expectations, nothing more. In the old days he would've sent her a fruit basket with a thank-you card for her casual dismissal.

But these days he wanted more than that. That's why he'd gone back to Hayden's hotel room, because something about the woman made him think she was the one who could give him the *more* he desired. A sexy professor who hated sports and set his body on fire. Almost made him want to call up that *Sports Illustrated* interviewer and get a retraction printed: *Brody Croft is no longer attracted to leggy blondes.*

"Hope you didn't tire yourself out," Becker said. "We can't afford to screw up tonight, not in the play-offs."

"Hey, d'you guys get a look at the paper this morning?" Jones asked suddenly. "There was another article about the bribery accusations Houston's wife made." He frowned, an expression that didn't suit his chubby, *Leave It to Beaver* face. At twenty-one, the kid hadn't mastered his supertough hockey glare yet. "Like any of us would take money to purposely put a loss on our record. Damn, I want to toilet paper that chick's house for all the trouble she's causing."

Brody laughed. "When are you going to grow out of these pranks? Grown men don't toilet paper people's homes."

"C'mon, you like my pranks," Derek protested. "You were laughing your ass off when I replaced Alexi's pads with those pink Hello Kitty ones."

From across the room, their goalie Alexi Nicklaus gave Jones the finger.

"Simmer down, children," Becker said with a grin. He turned to Brody, his eyes suddenly growing serious. "What do you think about the articles?"

Brody just shrugged. "Until I see the proof Mrs. Houston allegedly has, I refuse to believe anybody on this team threw a game."

Jones nodded his agreement. "Pres is a good dude. He'd never fix games." He paused, then chuckled. "Actually, I'm more intrigued by the other allegation. You know, the one from an unnamed source claiming that Mrs. H is hitting the sheets with a Warriors player?"

Huh? Brody hadn't read the paper yet, and the idea that the

owner's wife was sleeping with one of his teammates was both
startling and absurd. And worrisome. Definitely worrisome.
He didn't like how this scandal seemed to be snowballing.
Bribery, adultery, illegal gambling. Shit.

Jones turned to Brody. "Come on, admit it. It was you."

Uh, right. The thought of hopping into the sack with Sheila
Houston was about as appealing as trading in his hockey
skates for figure skates and joining the Stars on Ice. He'd only
needed a handful of encounters with the woman to figure out
she had nothing but air between her pretty little ears.

"Nah. My bet's on Topas." Brody grinned at the dark-
haired right wing across the room. Zelig Topas, who'd won
Olympic silver playing on the Russian team at the last Games,
was also one of the few openly gay players in the league.

"Funny," Topas returned, rolling his eyes.

The chatter died down as Craig Wyatt, the captain of the
Warriors, strode into the room, his Nordic features solemn as
always. Wyatt stood at a massive height of six-seven, and that
was in his street shoes. With his bulky torso and blond buzz
cut it was no wonder Wyatt was one of the most feared players
in the league and a force to contend with.

Without asking what all the laughter was about, Wyatt
dove right into his usual pregame pep talk, which was about
as peppy as a eulogy. There was a reason Wyatt was nick-
named Mr. Serious. Brody had only seen the guy smile
once, and even then it was one of those awkward half smiles
you pasted on when someone was telling you a really un-
funny joke.

Needless to say, Brody had never clicked with his somber
captain. He tended to gravitate toward laid-back guys like
Becker and Jones.

Promptly tuning out the captain's voice, he proceeded to
rehash this morning's conversation with Hayden, musing over

her insistence that they leave things at one night. He understood wanting to end with a bang but…

Nope, wasn't going to happen.

Hayden might've neglected to hand out her number, but she'd left her calling card by inviting him to her hotel suite. After tonight's game Brody planned on strolling right back to the Ritz and continuing what he and Hayden had started last night. Just one night?

Not if he could help it.

"THERE'S NOTHING BETTER than this," Presley Houston boomed as he handed his daughter a bottle of Evian and joined her by the glass window overlooking the rink below.

They had the owner's box to themselves tonight, which came as a great relief. When she was surrounded by her father's colleagues, Hayden always felt as if she were one of those whales or dolphins at Sea World. Frolicking, swimming, doing tricks—all the while trying to figure out a way to break through the glass, escape the stifling tank and return to the wild where she belonged.

"Do you get to any games out in California?" Presley asked, picking an imaginary fleck of lint from the front of his gray Armani jacket.

"No, Dad."

"Why the hell not?"

Uh, because I hate hockey and always have?

"I don't have the time. I was teaching four classes last semester."

Her father reached out and ruffled her hair, something he'd done ever since she was a little girl. She found the gesture comforting. It reminded her of the years they'd been close. Before the Warriors. Before Sheila. Back when it was just the two of them.

Her heart ached as her dad tucked a strand of hair behind her ear and shot her one of his charming smiles. And her father undeniably had charm. Despite the loud booming voice, the restless energy he seemed to radiate, the focused and often shrewd glint in his eyes, he had a way of making everyone around him feel like he was their best friend. It was probably why his players seemed to idolize him, and definitely why *she* had idolized him growing up. She'd never thought her dad was perfect. He'd dragged her around the country for his career. But he'd also been there when it counted, helping with her homework, letting her take art classes during the off-season, giving her that painful birds-and-bees talk kids always got from their parents.

It brought a knot of pain to her gut that her father didn't seem to notice the distance between them. Not that she expected them to be bosom buddies—she was an adult now, and leading her own life. Nevertheless, it would be nice to at least maintain some kind of friendship with her dad. But he lived and breathed the Warriors now, completely oblivious to the fact that he'd pushed his only daughter onto the back burner of his life these past seven years.

She noticed that gray threads of hair were beginning to appear at his temples. She'd seen him six months ago over Christmas, but somehow he seemed older. There were even wrinkles around his mouth that hadn't been there before. The divorce proceedings were evidently taking a toll on him.

"Sweetheart, I know this might not be the best time to bring this up," her father began suddenly, averting his eyes. He focused on the spectacle of the game occurring below, as if he could channel the energy of the players and find the nerve to continue. Finally he did. "One of the reasons I asked you to come home…well, see…Diane wants you to give a deposition."

Her head jerked up. "What? Why?"

"You were one of the witnesses the day Sheila signed the prenuptial agreement." Her dad's voice was gentler than she'd heard in years. "Do you remember?"

Uh, did he actually think she'd forget? The day they'd signed the prenup happened to be the first meeting between Hayden and her only-two-years-older stepmother. The shock that her fifty-seven-year-old father was getting remarried after years of being alone hadn't been as great as learning that he was marrying a woman so many years his junior. Hayden had prided herself on being open-minded, but her mind always seemed to slam shut the second her father was involved. Although Sheila claimed otherwise, Hayden wasn't convinced that her stepmother hadn't married Presley for his money, prenup or not.

Her suspicions had been confirmed when three months into the marriage, Sheila convinced her father to buy a multimillion-dollar mansion (because living in a penthouse was *so* passé), a small yacht (because the sea air would do them good) and a brand-new wardrobe (because the wife of a sports team owner needed to look sharp). Hayden didn't even want to know how much money her dad had spent on Sheila that first year. Even if she worked until she was ninety, she'd probably never earn that much. Sheila, of course, had quit her waitressing job the day after the wedding, and as far as Hayden knew, her stepmother now spent her days shopping away Presley's money.

"Do I really have to get involved in this, Dad?" she asked, sighing.

"It's just one deposition, sweetheart. All you have to do is go on record and state that Sheila was in her right mind when she signed those papers." Presley made a rude sound. "She's claiming coercion was involved."

"Oh, Dad. Why did you marry that woman?"

Her father didn't answer, and she didn't blame him. He'd always been a proud man, and admitting his failures came as naturally to him as the ability to give birth.

"This won't go to court, will it?" Her stomach turned at the thought.

"I doubt it." He ruffled her hair again. "Diane is confident we'll be able to reach a settlement. Sheila can't go on like this forever. Sooner or later she'll give up."

Not likely.

She kept her suspicions to herself, not wanting to upset her father any further. She could tell by the frustration in his eyes that the situation was making him feel powerless. And she knew how much he hated feeling powerless.

Hayden gave his arm a reassuring squeeze. "Of course she will." She gestured to the window. "By the way, the team's looking really great, Dad."

She had no clue about whether the team looked good or not, but her words brought a smile to her father's lips and that was all that mattered.

"They are, aren't they? Wyatt and Becker are really coming together this season. Coach Gray said it was tough going, trying to make them get along."

"They don't like each other?" she said, not bothering to ask who Wyatt and Becker were.

Her dad shrugged, then took a swig from the glass of bourbon in his hand. "You know how it is, sweetheart. Alpha males, I'm-the-best, no-I'm-the-best. The league is nothing more than an association of egos."

"Dad…" She searched for the right words. "That stuff in the paper yesterday, about the illegal betting…it's not true, is it?"

"Of course not." He scowled. "It's lies, Hayden. All a bunch of lies."

"You sure I shouldn't be worried?"

He pulled her close, squeezing her shoulder. "There is absolutely nothing for you to worry about. I promise."

"Good."

A deafening buzz followed by a cheesy dance beat interrupted their conversation. In a second Presley was on his feet, clapping and giving a thumbs-up to the camera that seemed to float past the window.

"Did we win?" she asked, feeling stupid for asking and even stupider for not knowing.

Her father chuckled. "Not yet. There's five minutes left to the third." He returned to his seat. "When the game's done how about I take you for a quick tour of the arena? We've done a lot of renovations since you were last here. Sound good?"

"Sounds great," she lied.

BRODY STEPPED out of the shower and drifted back to the main locker area. He pressed his hand to his side and winced at the jolt of pain that followed. A glance down confirmed what he already knew—that massive check from Valdek at the beginning of the second period had resulted in a large bruise that was slowly turning purple. Asshole.

"You took a shitty penalty," Wyatt was grumbling to Jones when Brody reached the bench.

The captain's normally calm voice contained a hint of antagonism and his dark eyes flashed with disapproval, also uncharacteristic. Brody wondered what was up Wyatt's ass, but he preferred to stay out of quarrels between his teammates. Hockey players were wired to begin with, so minor disagreements often ended badly.

Derek rolled his eyes. "What are you complaining about? We won the freaking game."

"It could've been a shutout," Wyatt snapped. "You gave up a goal to Franks with that penalty. We might be up by two games, but we need to win two more to make it to the second round. There's no room for mistakes." Still glowering, Mr. Serious strode out of the locker room, slamming the door behind him.

Jones tossed a what-the-hell's-up-with-him? look in Brody's direction, but he just shrugged, still determined to stay out of it.

Dressing quickly, he shoved his sweaty uniform into the locker, suddenly eager to get out of there.

On his way to the door he checked his watch, which read nine forty-five. Too late to pay a visit to Hayden's penthouse suite? Probably. Maybe inappropriate, too, but, hell, he'd never been one for propriety. Hayden had been on his mind all day and he was determined to see her again.

"Later, boys," he called over his shoulder.

The door closed behind him and he stepped into the brightly lit hallway, promptly colliding with a warm wall of curves.

"I'm sor—" The apology died in his throat as he laid eyes on the woman he'd bodychecked.

Not just any woman, either, but the one he'd been thinking about—and getting hard over—all day.

A startled squeak flew out of her mouth. "You."

His surprise quickly transformed into a rush of satisfaction and pleasure. "Me," he confirmed.

Looking her up and down, Brody was taken aback by the prim white blouse she wore and the knee-length paisley skirt that swirled over her legs. A huge change from the bright yellow top and faded jeans she'd worn last night. In this getup she looked more like the conservative professor and less like the passionate vixen who'd cried out his name so many times last night. The shift was disconcerting.

"What are…you're…" Hayden's eyes darted to the sign on the door beside them. "You play for the Warriors?"

"Sure do." He lifted one brow. "And I thought you said you weren't a hockey fan."

"I'm not. I…" Her voice trailed off.

What was she doing in this section of the arena? he suddenly wondered. Only folks associated with the franchise were allowed back here.

"Sorry to keep you waiting, sweetheart," boomed a male voice. "Shall we continue the tour—" Presley Houston broke out in a wide smile when he noticed Brody. "You played well out there tonight, Croft."

"Thanks, Pres." He looked from Hayden to Presley, wondering if he was missing something. Then a hot spurt of jealousy erupted in his gut as he realized that Presley had called Hayden *sweetheart*. Oh, man. Had he screwed around with Houston's mistress?

A dose of anger joined the jealousy swirling through him. He eyed the woman he'd spent the night with, wanting to strangle her for hopping into bed with him when she was obviously very much *taken*, but Presley's next words quickly killed the urge and brought with them another shock.

"I see you've met my daughter, Hayden."

4

WHAT WAS HE *doing* here? And why hadn't he told her he played for the Warriors?

Hayden blinked a few times. Maybe she was imagining his sleek, long body and devastatingly handsome face and the hair that curled under his ears as if he'd just stepped out of a steamy shower—

He's not a hallucination. Deal with it.

All right, so her one-night stand was undeniably here, flesh and blood, and sexier than ever.

He also happened to be one of her dad's players. Was there a section in the league rule book about a player sleeping with the team owner's daughter? She didn't think so, but with all the rumors currently circulating about her father and the franchise, Hayden didn't feel inclined to cause any more trouble for her dad.

Apparently Brody felt the same way.

"It's nice to meet you, Hayden." His voice revealed nothing, especially not the fact that they were already very much…acquainted, for lack of a better word.

She shook his hand, almost shivering at the feel of his warm, calloused fingers. "Charmed," she said lightly.

Charmed? Had she actually just said that?

Brody's eyes twinkled, confirming that the idiotic reply had indeed come out of her mouth.

"Hayden is visiting us from San Francisco," Presley explained. "She teaches art at Berkeley."

"Art history, Dad," she corrected.

Presley waved a dismissive hand. "Same difference."

"So what position do you play?" Hayden asked, her voice casual, neutral, as if she were addressing a complete stranger.

"Brody's a left winger," Presley answered for him. "And a rising star."

"Oh. Sounds exciting," she said mildly.

Presley cut in once more. "It is. Right, Brody?"

Before Brody could answer, someone else snagged her dad's attention. "There's Stan. Excuse me for a moment." He quickly marched away.

Hayden's mouth curved mischievously. "Don't mind him. He often takes over conversations only to leave you standing in his dust." Her smile faded. "But you probably already knew that, seeing as you play for his team."

"Does that bother you?" Brody said carefully.

"Of course not," she lied. "Why would it?"

"You tell me."

She stared at him for a moment, then sighed. "Look, I'd appreciate it if you didn't tell my father about what...happened between us last night."

"Ah, so you remember." Amusement danced in his eyes. "I was starting to think you'd put it out of your mind completely."

Sure. Like that was even possible. She'd thought about nothing but this man and his talented tongue all day.

"I haven't forgotten." Her voice lowered. "But that doesn't mean I want to do it again."

"I think you do."

The arrogance in his tone both annoyed her and thrilled her. Jeez, how *hadn't* she figured out he was a hockey player last night? The man practically had *pro athlete* branded into his forehead. He was cocky, confident, larger than life. Something told her he was the kind of man who knew exactly what he wanted and did everything in his power to get it.

And what he wanted at the moment, disconcerting as it was, seemed to be *her*.

"Brody—"

"Don't bother denying it, I rocked your world last night and you can't wait for me to do it again."

She snorted. "There's nothing like a man with a healthy ego."

"I like it when you snort. It's cute."

"Don't call me cute."

"Why not?"

"Because I hate it. Babies and bunny rabbits are cute. I'm a grown woman. And stop looking at me like that."

"Like what?" he said, blinking innocently.

"Like you're imagining me naked."

"I can't help it. I *am* imagining you naked."

His eyes darkened to a sensual glitter, and liquid heat promptly pooled between her thighs. She tried not to squeeze her legs together. She didn't want him seeing the effect he had on her.

"Have a drink with me tonight," he said suddenly.

The word *no* slipped out more quickly than she'd intended. Brody's features creased with what looked like frustration. He stepped closer, causing her to dart a glance in her father's direction. Presley was standing at the end of the hall, engaged in deep conversation with Stan Gray, the Warriors' head coach. While her dad seemed oblivious to the sparks shooting between her and Brody, Hayden still felt uncomfortable having this discussion in view of her father.

It didn't help that Brody looked so darn edible in gray wool pants that hugged his muscular legs and a ribbed black sweater that stretched across his chest. And his wet hair… She forced herself to stop staring at those damp strands, knowing that if she allowed herself to imagine him in the shower, naked, she might just come on the spot.

"One drink," he insisted, with a charming grin. "You know, for old time's sake."

She couldn't help but laugh. "We've known each other for all of twenty-four hours."

"Yes, but it was a very wild twenty-four hours, wouldn't you say?" He moved closer and lowered his head, his lips inches from her ear, his warm breath fanning across her neck. "How many times did you come again, Hayden? Three? Four?"

"Five," she squeezed out, and then quickly looked around to make sure nobody had heard her.

Her entire body started to throb from the memory. Nipples hardened. Sex grew moist. That she could experience such arousal in a hallway full of people—one of them her father—made her blush with embarrassment.

"Five." He nodded briskly. "I haven't lost my touch."

She resisted the urge to groan. He was too damn sexual, too sure of himself, which gave him a definite advantage, because at the moment she wasn't sure of anything.

Except the fact that she wanted to tear off her clothes and hop right back into bed with Brody Croft.

But, nope, she wouldn't do it. Sleeping with Brody again had Bad Idea written all over it. It had all been much simpler last night, when he'd just been an exciting, sensual stranger. But now…now he was real. Even worse, he was a hockey player. She'd grown up around enough hockey players to know how they lived—the constant traveling, the media, the eager females lining up to jump into bed with them.

And along with being involved in a sport she hated, Brody was so…arrogant, flirtatious, bold. Yesterday it had added to the allure of sex with a stranger. Today it was a reminder of why she'd decided bad boys no longer played a part in her life.

Been there, done that. Her last boyfriend had been as arrogant, flirty and bold as Brody Croft, and that relationship had ended a fiery death when Adam dumped her on her birthday because the whole "fidelity thing" cramped his style. His words, not hers.

She wasn't quite sure why she had such terrible judgment when it came to men. It shouldn't be so hard finding someone to build a life with, should it? A home, a solid marriage, great sex, excitement *and* stability, a man who'd make their relationship a priority—was that too much to ask for?

"Why are you so determined to see me again?" she found herself blurting, then lowered her voice when her father glanced in their direction. "I told you this morning I wanted to leave things at one night."

"What about what I want?"

She bit back an annoyed curse, deciding to go for the honest approach. "My life is complicated right now," she admitted. "I came home to support my father, not get involved with someone."

"You were pretty involved with me last night," he said, winking. He uncrossed his arms and let them drop to his sides. "And you can't deny you liked it, Hayden."

"Of course I liked it," she hissed.

"Then what's the problem?"

"The problem is, I wanted one night. Seeing you again wasn't part of the plan."

"Plan, or fantasy?" he drawled, a knowing glimmer in his eyes. "That's it, isn't it? You fantasized about indulging in one night of wicked sex with a stranger and now that you have it's time to move on. I'm not judging you, just pointing out that the fantasy doesn't have to end yet."

The word *fantasy* sounded intoxicating the way he said it. Before she could stop herself, she wondered what other fantasies they could play out together. Role play? Bondage? Her cheeks grew warm at the latter notion. It turned her on, the idea of tying Brody up...straddling him while he lay immobile on the bed...

No. No, she was *so* not going there. She seriously needed to quit letting this guy jump-start her sex drive.

"The way I see it, you've got two options," he said. "The easy way or the hard way."

"I can't wait to hear all about it."

"Sarcasm doesn't become you." His cheek dimpled despite his words. "Now, the easy way involves the two of us heading over to the Lakeshore Lounge for a drink."

"No."

He held up his hand. "You haven't heard the rest." A devilish look flickered across his face. "If you choose to pass on the easy option, that's when things get a little...*hard.*"

Heat spilled over her cheeks. Her eyes dropped to his groin, almost expecting to see the long ridge of arousal pressing against the denim of his jeans. Fine, no almost about it. He had an erection, all right, and the second she noticed it her nipples grew even harder.

"See, if you deny me this one harmless drink," he continued, "I'll be hurt. Maybe even a tad offended. Also, your father seems to be nearing the end of his conversation—yup, he's shaking Stan's hand. Which means he'll head back over here just in time to hear you say no, and then he'll ask you what you're saying no to, and I'm sure neither one of us wants to open *that* can of worms."

She turned her head and, sure enough, her father was walking toward them. Great. Although she knew her dad could handle the knowledge that his twenty-six-year-old daughter wasn't a virgin, she didn't want him privy to her sex life. Especially a sex life that involved one of his players.

Her dad might be totally gaga over his team, but he'd often warned her about the turbulent nature of hockey players. The latest warning had come during her last visit to Chicago, when she'd been hit on by an opposing player after a Warriors game. She'd declined the dinner invitation, but it hadn't stopped Presley from launching into a speech about how he didn't want his daughter dating brutes.

If he knew she'd gotten involved with Brody, it would just add to his stress.

"So how about that drink, Hayden?"

Her pulse quickened when she realized if she agreed to Brody's request, chances were they wouldn't get around to the drink anyway. The second he had her alone he'd be slipping his hands underneath her shirt, palming her breasts, sucking on her neck the way he'd done last night, as he'd slid inside her and—

"One drink," she blurted, then chastised herself for yet again letting her hormones override her common sense. What was *wrong* with her?

With a soft chuckle, Brody rested his hands on his trim hips, the poster boy for cool. "I knew you'd see it my way." He grinned.

THE LAKESHORE LOUNGE WAS one of those rare bars in the city that offered an intimate atmosphere rather than an intrusive one. Plush, comfortable chairs looked more suited to an IKEA showroom; tables were situated far enough apart that patrons could enjoy their drinks in privacy, and a pale yellow glow took the place of bright lighting, providing an almost sensual ambience. It was also one of the only establishments that still adhered to a strict dress code—blazers required.

It was a damn good thing he was Brody Croft. Even better

that Ward Dalton, the owner of the lounge, claimed to be his number-one fan and turned a blind eye to Brody's casual attire.

Dalton led them across the black marble floor to a secluded table in the corner of the room, practically hidden from view by two enormous stone pots containing leafy indoor palms. A waiter clad in black pants and a white button-down appeared soon after, taking their drink orders before unobtrusively moving away.

Brody didn't miss the baffled look on Hayden's gorgeous face. "Something wrong?" he asked.

"No. I'm just…surprised," she said. "When you said we were going for a drink, I thought…" Her cheeks turned an appealing shade of pink. "Forget it."

"You thought I'd drive you right back to your hotel suite and pick up where we left off?"

"Pretty much."

"Sorry to disappoint you."

She bristled at the teasing lilt of his voice. "I'm not disappointed. In fact, I'm glad. Like I said before, I'm not interested in getting involved."

He didn't like the finality of her tone. For the life of him, he couldn't figure out why Hayden didn't want a repeat performance of last night. They'd been so good together.

He also couldn't decide whether or not she'd known who he was all along. Her father was Presley Houston, for chrissake. She didn't need to *like* hockey to know who the players were, especially the players on her own father's team. And yet the shock on her face when she'd bumped into him outside the locker room hadn't seemed contrived. He'd seen authentic surprise on her beautiful face. Not to mention a flicker of dismay.

No, she couldn't have known. It wouldn't bother her this much if she had.

He appreciated that she liked the man and not the hockey

player, but that only raised another question—what held her back from getting involved with him? Was it the fact that he played pro hockey, or was it something else? *Someone* else, perhaps?

His jaw tightened at the thought. "What exactly is stopping you from pursuing this?" he asked in a low voice. "It's more than Presley's current problems, isn't it?"

The way she stared down at the silk cocktail napkin on the table as if it were the most fascinating item on the planet deepened Brody's suspicions.

He narrowed his eyes, unable to keep the accusation out of his tone. "Is there a husband waiting for you in California?"

Her gaze flew up to meet his. "Of course not."

Some of the suspicion thawed, but not entirely. "A fiancé?"

She shook her head.

"A boyfriend?"

The blush on her cheeks deepened. "No. I mean, yes. Well, kind of. I *was* seeing someone in San Francisco but we're currently on a break."

"The kind of break where you can sleep with other people?"

Whoa, he had no idea why he'd become antagonistic, or why his shoulders were suddenly stiffer than Robocop's.

What was up with this sudden possessiveness? They'd only had one night together, after all. Staking claims at this point was ridiculous.

"As I keep telling you, my life is complicated," she said pointedly. "I'm in the process of making some serious decisions, figuring out what my future looks like."

He opened his mouth to reply only to be interrupted by the waiter, who returned with their drinks. The waiter set down Brody's gin and tonic and Hayden's glass of white wine, then left the table without delay, as if sensing something important was brewing between them.

"And this boyfriend," Brody said thoughtfully. "Do you see him in your future?"

"I don't know."

Her tentative answer and confused frown were all he needed. He wasn't an ass; if Hayden had expressed deep love for the other man in her life, Brody would've backed off. He had no interest in fighting for a woman who belonged to someone else. But the fact that she hadn't answered a definite yes to his question told Brody this was fair game.

And nothing got him going more than a healthy bout of competition.

He lifted his gin and tonic to his lips and took a sip, eyeing her from the rim of his glass. Despite her prim shirt that buttoned up to the neck, she looked unbelievably hot. He could see the outline of her bra, and the memory of what lay beneath it sent a jolt of electricity to his groin.

"We're not doing it again," she said between gritted teeth, obviously sensing the train of thought his mind had taken.

He laughed. "Sounds like you're trying to convince yourself of that."

Frustration creased her dainty features. "We had sex, Brody. That's all." She took a drink of wine. "It was amazing, sure, but it was only sex. It's not like the damn earth moved."

"Are you sure about that?"

He pushed his chair closer, so that they were no longer across from each other, but side by side. He saw her hands shake at his nearness, her cheeks flush again, her lips part. It didn't take a rocket scientist to see she was aroused, and, damn, but he liked knowing his mere proximity could get this woman going.

"It was more than sex, Hayden." He dipped his head and brushed his lips over her ear. She shivered. "It was a sexual hurricane. Intense. Consuming." He flicked his tongue against her earlobe. "I've never been that hard in my life. And you've never been wetter."

"Brody…" She swallowed.

He traced the shell of her ear with his tongue, then moved his head back and lowered his hand to her thigh. He felt her leg shaking under his touch. "I'm right, aren't I?"

"Fine," she blurted out. "You're right! Happy?"

"Not quite." With a faint smile, he slid his hand under the soft material of her skirt and cupped her mound. Running his knuckles against the damp spot on her panties, he gave a brisk nod and murmured, "Now I'm happy."

Hayden's focus darted around like a Ping-Pong ball, as if she expected their waiter to pop up in front of them any second. But the table was well secluded, and nobody could approach it without entering Brody's line of sight. He took advantage of the privacy, cupping Hayden's ass and gently shifting her so that her body was more accessible. He dragged his hand between her legs again, pushing aside the crotch of her panties and stroking her damp flesh.

The soft sounds of people chatting at neighboring tables excited the hell out of him. He was no stranger to sex in public, but he couldn't say he'd ever pleasured a woman in an upscale bar where any minute he could get caught.

A sharp breath hissed out of her mouth as he rubbed her clit in a circular motion. "What are you doing?" she whispered.

"I think you know exactly what I'm doing."

He continued to boldly rub her clit, then danced his fingertips down her slick folds and prodded her opening with the tip of his index finger. The wetness already pooling there made his cock twitch. He wanted nothing more than to shuck his jeans and thrust into that wet paradise. Right here. Right now. But he wasn't *that* bold.

"Brody…you've got…to stop," she murmured, but her body said otherwise.

Her thighs clenched together, her inner muscles squeezed his finger and a soft moan slipped out of her throat.

"You'll come if I keep doing this, won't you, Hayden?"

He looked from her flushed face to the neighboring table, several feet away and barely visible through the palm fronds separating the two tables. He hoped to hell the couple seated at that table hadn't heard Hayden's moan. He didn't want this to end just yet.

"Brody, anyone can walk by."

"Then you'd better be quick."

He pushed his finger into her core, smiling when she bit her lip. The look on her face drove him wild. Flushed, tortured, excited. He was feeling pretty excited himself, but he managed to get a handle on his own rising desire. He'd pressured her to spend the evening with him because he had something to prove, and what he wanted to prove wasn't that he was dying for a second go, but that *she* was dying for it.

Applying pressure to her clit with his thumb, he worked another finger inside her, pushing in and out of her in a deliberate lazy rhythm. His mouth ached with the need to suck on one of her small pink nipples, but he tightened his lips before he gave in to the urge and tore her shirt open. Instead, he focused on the heat between her thighs, the nub that swelled each time he brushed his thumb over it and the inner walls that clamped over his fingers with each gentle thrust.

Keeping one eye on Hayden's blissful face and the other on his surroundings, he continued to slide his fingers in and out, until finally she let out a barely audible groan and squeezed her legs together. He felt her pulsing against his fingers and resisted a groan of his own as a soundless orgasm consumed her eyes as well as her body.

She came silently, trembling, biting her lip. And then she released a sigh. Her hands, which at some point she'd curled into fists, shook on the tabletop, making her wineglass topple and spill over the side of the table.

He quickly withdrew his hand as Hayden jumped at the startling sound of the glass rolling and shattering on the marble floor. Her sudden movement caused her knee to hit one of the table legs, making the table shake and the ice cubes in his drink collide into the side of the glass with a jingling sound.

From the corner of his eye Brody saw the waiter hurrying over, and yet he couldn't fight a tiny chuckle. Turning to meet Hayden's dazed eyes, he laughed again, swiftly fixed her skirt and said, "Still want to tell me the earth didn't move?"

5

ABOUT TWELVE HOURS after experiencing her very first public orgasm, Hayden strode into Lingerie Dreams, the classy downtown boutique owned by her best friend.

She was in desperate need of Darcy right now. Darcy and her one-night-stand mentality would definitely help her get her thoughts back on the right track and *off* the track that sent her hurtling straight into Brody Croft's bed.

Funny thing was, he hadn't pushed her after their interlude at the lounge last night. He'd paid for their drinks, walked her out to her rental car and left her with a parting speech she couldn't stop thinking about.

The next move's yours, Hayden. You want me, come and get me.

And then he'd left. He'd hopped into his shiny SUV, driven off and left her sitting in her car, more turned-on than she'd ever been in her entire life. Though she'd been ready to go home with him, he'd made it clear it wouldn't happen that night, not when he'd had to twist her arm to get her there.

Oh, no, he wanted *her* to initiate their next encounter. Something she was seriously tempted to do. Which was why she needed Darcy to talk her out of it.

The bell over the door chimed as she walked into the boutique. She sidestepped a mannequin wearing a black lace teddy and a table piled high with thongs, and approached the cash counter.

"Something terrible has happened," Darcy groaned the second she saw her.

"Tell me about it," Hayden mumbled.

But the look of dismay on Darcy's face made Hayden push the memory of last night aside for the moment. She caught a whiff of sweet floral scent, looked around and finally spotted a bouquet of red and yellow roses peeking out of the metal wastebasket next to the counter.

"Courtesy of Jason," Darcy sighed, following her gaze.

"Who's Jason?"

"Didn't I mention him?" She shrugged. "I hooked up with him last week after yoga class. He's a personal trainer."

Like she could actually keep track of all the men Darcy hooked up with. Hayden didn't know how her friend did it, wandering aimlessly from guy to guy.

"And he sent you flowers? That's sweet."

Darcy looked at her as if she'd grown horns. "Are you insane?" she said. "Don't you remember how I feel about flowers?"

Without waiting for an answer, Darcy leapt to her feet and checked to make sure the store was void of customers. Then she marched over to the front door, locked it and flipped the Open sign over so that it read Closed.

With her kitten heels clicking against the tiled floor, Darcy gestured for Hayden to follow her, drifting over to the fitting-room area. Along with four dressing rooms, the large space offered two plush red velvet chairs.

Hayden sank into one of the chairs and reached for the bowl of heart-shaped mints Darcy left out for her customers. Popping a mint into her mouth, she studied her friend, who still looked upset.

"Wow, this flower thing is really bugging you."

Darcy flopped down and crossed her arms over her chest,

her face turning as red as the hair on her head. "Of course it bugs me. It's not normal."

"No, *you're* not normal. Men give women flowers all the time. It's not poor Jason's fault he picked you as the recipient."

"We went out for smoothies after yoga and fooled around in his car when he dropped me off at home." Darcy made a frustrated sound. "How in bloody hell does that warrant flowers?"

"What did the card say?" Hayden asked curiously.

"'I hope to see you again soon.'"

She was about to comment on Jason's thoughtfulness again but stopped herself. She knew how Darcy felt about relationships. The first sign of commitment had her fleeing for the exit and looking for the next one-night stand. But it really was too bad. This Jason fellow sounded as nice as Doug.

Shoot, she'd promised herself she wouldn't think about Doug today.

She still hadn't returned his phone call, and when she'd woken up this morning there had been another message from him on her cell. How could she call him back, though? She'd only been gone a week and already she'd jumped into bed with another man. She wondered how nice Doug would be when she told him about *that*.

"I'm going to have to find a new gym," Darcy grumbled, her blue eyes darkening with irritation. She started fidgeting. Crossed her legs, then uncrossed them, clasped her hands together, then drummed them against the arms of the chair.

Hayden could tell her friend was about to explode. Any minute now…no, any second now…

"What is the *matter* with the penis species?" Darcy burst out. "They claim that *we're* the needy ones, calling us clingy and high-maintenance, accusing us of being obsessed with love and marriage. When really, really, it's what *they* want. They're the mushy ones, sending flowers as if a smoothie and a backseat blow job qualify as a monumental event that needs to be celebrated…" Darcy's voice trailed and she heaved a sigh.

"I'm obviously going to have to set him straight," Darcy declared, reaching for a mint and shoving it into her mouth. She still looked aggravated, but her anger seemed to have dissolved.

"At least thank him for the flowers," Hayden said gently.

"I already called and did that. But I think I need to make another call and make sure Jason knows what happened between us won't go any further. Like the way you set your hunk straight."

"Right. About that…you're not going to believe this." She quickly filled her friend in on her visit to the arena and how she'd run into Brody outside the locker room.

"He's a hockey player? I bet you were just thrilled to find that out." Darcy grinned. "So, you told him to get lost, right?"

"Um…"

Darcy's jaw dropped. "Hayden Lorraine Houston! You slept with him again, didn't you?"

"Not exactly. I did go out for a drink with him, though."

"And?"

Hayden told her about the under-the-table orgasm. When her friend shook her head, she added, "I couldn't help it! He just started…you know…and it was really good…" Her voice drifted.

"You have no self-control." Darcy shot her a weary look and asked, "Are you going to call him?"

"I don't know. God knows I want to. But calling him defeats the purpose of a one-night stand." She groaned. "I just wanted some stress-busting sex. And now I'm even more stressed-out."

"So tell him to take a hike. You've got enough on your plate without an arrogant hockey player demanding overtime sex."

Hayden laughed. "He is pretty determined." She remembered the passion flaring in his eyes when he'd brought her to climax yesterday. "He's driving me crazy, Darce."

"Good crazy or bad crazy?"

"Both." A shaky breath exited her throat. "When I'm with him all I can think about is ripping off his clothes, and when I'm not with him all I can think about is ripping off his clothes."

"I don't see the bad part here."

She bit her bottom lip. "He's a hockey player. You know how I feel about that." She blew out a frustrated breath. "I don't want to be with anyone involved in sports. God, I hated it when Dad used to coach. No real place to call home, no friends. Hell, my friendship with you is the only one that lasted, and half of it took place via e-mail."

Reaching for another mint, she popped it into her mouth and bit it in half, taking out her frustration on the candy. "I don't want to date a guy who spends half the year flying to other states so he can skate around an ice rink. And besides, I'm dealing with too much other stuff at the moment. The franchise is taking some heat, Dad's dumping all his Sheila problems on me, and Doug has already called twice wanting to talk about *us*. I can't launch myself into another relationship right now." She set her jaw, practically daring Darcy to challenge her.

Which, of course, she did. "You know what I think?" Darcy said. "You're making too big a deal out of this."

"Oh, really?"

Darcy leaned back in her chair and pushed a strand of bright red hair behind her ear. "You're only in town for a couple of months, Hayden. What's the problem with having some fun in the sack while you're here?"

"What happened to your one-night-stand speech?"

"Apparently it isn't working out for you." Darcy shrugged. "But you seem to believe it's black and white, one-night stand or relationship. You're forgetting about the gray area between the two extremes."

"Gray area?"

"It's called a fling."

"A fling." She said the word slowly, trying it on for size. She'd never been a casual-fling girl, but then again, she hadn't thought she was a one-night girl, either. Maybe a fling with Brody wouldn't be so disastrous. It wasn't like he wanted to marry her or anything; he just wanted to burn up the sheets for a while longer, continue the fantasy…

But if she agreed to let their one night lead into a fling, who's to say the fling wouldn't then lead to something more?

"I don't know," she said. "Brody is a distraction I can't deal with at the moment." She paused, her mouth twisting ruefully. "But my body seems to have a mind of its own whenever he's around."

"So take control of your body," Darcy suggested.

"And how do I do that?"

"I don't know, next time you get the urge to jump Brody Croft's bones, try an alternative. Watch some porn or something."

A laugh tickled Hayden's throat. "That's your answer? Watch porn?"

Darcy grinned. "Sure. At least you won't be thinking about Mr. Hockey when you're busy getting turned-on by other men."

"Right, because the men in porn are so wildly attractive," Hayden said with a snort. "What's the name of that guy who used to be really popular, the chubby one with the facial hair? Ron Jeremy?"

"It's not the seventies, hon. Male porn stars have come a long way. Trust me, just take a long bubble bath, put in a DVD and go nuts. You won't think about Brody even once."

"This is possibly the most ridiculous conversation we've

ever had." Hayden rolled her eyes. "If I watch anything tonight, it'll be the van Gogh special on the Biography Channel."

Darcy released an exaggerated sigh. "A man who cut off his own ear is not sexy, Hayden."

"Neither is porn." She glanced at her watch, eyes widening. "Shoot. I've gotta go. I'm supposed to give a deposition today about Sheila's state of mind when she signed the prenup."

"Sounds like a blast. Unfortunately I left my party shoes at home so I can't come with you."

They got up and wandered over to the door. Darcy unlocked it and held it open, her attention straying back to the flowers poking out of the wastebasket. "At least your guy only wants sex," Darcy said, looking envious.

"Brody is not my guy," Hayden responded, hoping if she said the words out loud she might convince her traitorous body of it. "Are we still on for dinner tonight? I'm down as long as I get home in time to watch that biography."

"And I'm down as long as it's Mexican. I'm feeling spicy." Darcy waved as Hayden left. "Enjoy the deposition," she called out after her.

"Enjoy the flowers," Hayden called back.

She turned just in time to see her best friend flipping her the bird.

"THANK YOU, Hayden," announced Diane Krueger, Presley's divorce attorney. "We're finished here."

Hayden smoothed out the front of her knee-length black skirt and pushed back the plush chair, getting to her feet. Next to her, her father stood as well. On the other side of the large oval conference table of the Krueger and Bates deposition room, Sheila Houston and her lawyer were huddled together, whispering to each other.

Hayden couldn't help but stare at her stepmother, still as

startled by Sheila's appearance as she'd been when the woman had first strode into the law office. The last time Hayden had come to town, Sheila had looked as if she'd stepped from the pages of a fashion magazine. Long blond hair brushed to a shine, creamy features flawless and perfectly made up, expensive clothes hugging her tall, slender body.

This time Sheila looked…haggard. Much older than her twenty-eight years and far more miserable than Hayden had expected her to be. Her hair hung limply over her shoulders, her normally dazzling blue eyes were distressed, and she'd lost at least fifteen pounds, which made her willowy shape look far too fragile.

Though she hated feeling even an ounce of sympathy for the woman who was making her father's life hell, Hayden had to wonder if Sheila was taking this divorce process a lot harder than Presley had let on. Either that, or she was devastated by the thought of losing that yacht she'd forced Presley to buy.

"Thanks for doing this, sweetheart," her father said quietly as they exited the conference room. "It means so much that you're going to bat for your old man."

For the third time in the past hour, Hayden noticed her dad's slightly glazed, bloodshot eyes and wondered if he'd had something to drink before coming here. His breath smelled like toothpaste and cigars, but she got a wary feeling when she looked at him.

No, she was being silly. He was probably just tired.

"I'm happy to help," she answered with a reassuring smile.

He touched her arm. "Do you need a ride back to the suite?"

"No, I've got my rental."

"All right." He nodded. "And don't forget about the party on Sunday night. Gallagher Club, eight o'clock."

Shoot, she'd already forgotten. There was a huge shindig at the prestigious gentlemen's club of which her dad was a member. And apparently her appearance was necessary, though she had no clue why.

Her father must have noticed her reluctance because he frowned slightly. "I'd like you to be there, Hayden. A lot of my friends want to see you. When you were here over the holidays you declined all of their invitations."

Because I wanted to see you, she almost blurted. But she held her tongue. She knew her father liked showing her off to his wealthy friends and boasting about her academic credentials—something he didn't seem to care about when they were alone.

She swallowed back the slight sting of bitterness. Considering they'd just spent an hour with the woman determined to bleed him dry, Hayden figured she ought to cut her dad some slack.

"I'll be there," she promised.

"Good."

They said their goodbyes, and she watched her father hurry out of the elegant lobby onto the street as if he were being chased by a serial killer. Not a stretch, seeing as the law firm was called Krueger and Bates. Hayden wondered if she was the only one who'd made the connection.

"Hayden, wait."

She stopped at the massive glass entrance doors, suppressing an inward groan at the sound of her stepmother's throaty voice.

Hayden turned slowly.

"I just..." Sheila looked surprisingly nervous as she plowed ahead. "I wanted to tell you there are no hard feelings. I know you're trying to protect your father."

Hayden's eyebrows said hello to her hairline. No hard feelings? Sheila was in the process of sucking the money out of Presley's bank accounts like a greedy leech and she wanted to make sure there were no hard feelings?

Hayden could only stare.

Sheila hurried on. "I know you've never liked me, and I don't blame you. It's always hard to watch a parent remarry, and I'm sure it doesn't help that I'm only two years older than you." She offered a timid smile.

"We really shouldn't be talking," Hayden said finally, her voice cool. "It's probably a conflict of interest."

"I know." Sheila ran one hand through her hair, her features sad. "But I just wanted you to know that I still care about your father. I care about him a lot."

To Hayden's absolute shock, a couple of tears trickled out of the corners of Sheila's eyes. Even more shocking, the tears didn't look like the crocodile variety.

"If you care, then why are you trying to take everything he owns?" she couldn't help but ask.

A flash of petulant anger crossed Sheila's face. Ah, *here* was the Sheila she knew. Hayden had seen that look plenty of times before, usually when Sheila was trying to convince Presley to buy something outrageous and not getting her way.

"I'm entitled to something," Sheila said defensively, "after everything that man put me through."

Right, because Sheila's life was *so* unpleasant. Living in a mansion, wearing haute couture, not paying a dime for anything…

"I know you think I'm the bad guy here, but you need to know that everything I've done is a result of… No, I'm not going to blame Pres." The tears returned, and Sheila wiped her wet eyes with a shaky hand. "I saw that he was spiraling and I didn't try to help him. I was the one who sent him into another woman's arms."

"Pardon me?" A knot of anger and disbelief twined Hayden's insides together like a pretzel. Sheila was actually insinuating that her father had been the one to stray? Her dislike for the woman quickly doubled. That she could even accuse a man as honorable as Presley Houston of adultery was preposterous.

Sheila eyed her knowingly. "I guess he left out that part."

"I have to get going," Hayden said stiffly, her jaw so tense that her teeth were beginning to ache.

"I don't care what you think of me," Sheila said. "I only want you to take care of your father, Hayden. I think he's started drinking again and I just want to make sure that someone is looking out for him."

Without issuing a goodbye, Sheila pulled an Elvis and left the building.

Hayden watched as her stepmother disappeared down the busy sidewalk, swallowed up by Chicago's afternoon lunch crowd.

She couldn't will herself to move. Lies. It had to be lies. Her father would never break his marriage vows by hopping into bed with another woman. Sheila was in the wrong here. She had to be.

I think he's started drinking again.

The comment replayed in Hayden's brain, making her toy nervously with the hem of her thin blue sweater. She'd thought her father's eyes had looked bleary. Fine, maybe he *did* have a drink or two before coming here, but Sheila's remark implied that Presley's drinking went beyond today. That at some point in time he'd suffered from an alcohol problem.

Was it true? And if so, how hadn't she known about it? She might not visit often, what with her hectic schedule at the university, but she spoke to her father at least once a week and he always sounded normal. *Sober.* Wouldn't she have suspected something if he had a drinking problem?

Lies.

She clung to that one word as she pushed the strap of her

purse higher on her shoulder and stepped through the doors. Sucking in a gust of fresh air, she headed for her rental, forcefully pushing every sentence Sheila had spoken out of her mind.

BRODY LEFT the locker room after a particularly grueling practice, wondering if he'd made a big fat mistake by pretty much telling Hayden the puck was in her end, the next move hers.

It had seemed like the right play at the time, but today, after two hours of tedious drills topped off by a lecture from the coach, he was rethinking the action he'd taken. Or more specifically, regretting the action he wouldn't be getting. His body was sore, his nerves shot, and he knew a few hours in Hayden's bed were all the medicine he needed.

He also knew she wouldn't call.

You got cocky, man.

Was that it? Had he been so confident in his ability to turn Hayden on that he just assumed she'd want him to do it again?

Damn it, why hadn't he taken her home with him? He'd seen the lust in her gorgeous eyes, known that all he had to do was say the word and she'd be in his arms again, but he'd held back. No, pride had held him back. He hadn't wanted to go to bed with her knowing he'd coerced her into joining him for that drink. He'd wanted it to be her choice, her terms, her desire.

It was almost comical, how this conservative art history professor had gotten under his skin. She was so different from the women he'd dated in the past. Smarter, prettier, more serious, definitely more pigheaded. She annoyed him; she excited him; she made him laugh. He knew he should just let her go since she obviously didn't want to pursue a relationship, but his instincts kept screaming for him not to let her out of his sight, that if he blinked, she'd be gone, and someone very important would be slipping through his grasp. It made no sense to him, and yet he'd always trusted his instincts. They'd never failed him before.

He kicked a pebble on his way to the car, feeling like kicking something harder than a rock. His own thick skull, perhaps.

He pressed a button on the remote to unlock the doors, then swore when he realized his wrist was bare. Shoot. He must have left his watch back at the practice arena. He always seemed to misplace the damn thing. He hated wearing a watch to begin with, but it had been a gift from his parents in honor of his first professional game eight years ago. Chris and Jane Croft were ferociously proud of their son, and he witnessed that pride every time he went back to Michigan for a visit and saw them staring at that watch.

Sighing, he turned around and headed back to the entrance of the sprawling gray building. The Warriors practiced in a private arena a few miles from the Lincoln Center, a little unorthodox but Brody found it somewhat of a relief. It meant the media never filmed their practices, which took the pressure off the players to always be on top of their game.

The double doors at the entrance led to a large sterile lobby. A blue door to the right opened onto the rink. To the left were the hallways leading to the locker rooms, and when Brody strode into the arena he immediately noticed the two people huddled by the locker-room corridor. Their backs were turned, and Brody quickly sidestepped to the right, ducking into another hall that featured a row of vending machines.

"You shouldn't have come here," came Craig Wyatt's somber voice.

Brody sucked in a breath, hoping the Warriors captain and his companion hadn't spotted him.

He'd sure as hell spotted them, though.

Which posed the question: what was Craig Wyatt doing whispering with Sheila Houston?

"I know. I just had to see you," Sheila said, her voice so

soft Brody had to strain his ears to hear her. "That meeting with the lawyers today was terrible…" There was a faint sob.

"Shh, it's okay, baby."

Baby?

Deciding he'd officially heard enough—and that he'd return for his watch another time—Brody edged toward the emergency exit at the end of the hallway. He turned the door handle, praying an alarm wouldn't go off. It didn't. Relieved, he exited the side door of the building and practically sprinted back to his car.

The drive to his Hyde Park home brought with it a tornado of confusion that made his head spin. Craig Wyatt and Sheila Houston? The player rumored to be having an affair with the owner's wife was *Wyatt*? Brody would've never expected it from the straight-laced Mr. Serious.

If it was true, then that meant the idea of bribes exchanging hands in the franchise might not be a lie after all. Craig Wyatt might have the personality of a brick wall, but he was the captain of the team, as well as the eyes and ears. He frequently kept track of everyone's progress, making sure they were all in tip-top shape and focused on the game. If he suspected anyone had taken a bribe, he would've investigated it, no doubt about it.

Jeez, was Wyatt the source Sheila had referred to in that interview? Had he been the one to tell her about the bribes?

Or…

Shit, had Wyatt taken a bribe himself? No, that didn't make sense. Sheila wouldn't draw attention to the bribery and illegal betting if her lover was one of the guilty parties.

Brody steered into his driveway and killed the engine. He reached up and pinched the bridge of his nose, hoping to ward off an oncoming headache.

Damn. This was not good at all.

He didn't particularly care what or who Craig Wyatt did

in his spare time, but if Wyatt knew something about these rumors…

Maybe he should just confront the man, flat out ask what he knew. Or maybe he'd ask Becker to do it for him. Becker was good at stuff like that, knew how to handle tough situations and still keep a clear head.

He rubbed his temples, then leaned his forehead against the steering wheel for a moment. Lord, he didn't want to deal with any of this. If he had his way, this entire scandal would just disappear; he'd play out the rest of the season then resign with the Warriors or sign with a new team. His career would be secure and his life would be peachy.

And Hayden Houston would be right back in his bed. A guy could dream, after all.

"I WILL NOT WATCH porn," Hayden muttered to herself later that night, stepping out of the enormous marble bathtub in the master suite of the penthouse. She reached for the terry-cloth robe hanging behind the door, slipped it on and tightened the sash around her waist.

Not that there was anything wrong with porn. She wasn't a nun, after all—she'd watched a few X-rated videos in her twenty-six years. But she'd never used porn to get over a man before, and besides, she'd had six orgasms in two days. She should be thoroughly exhausted by now and not thinking about having sex at all.

Unfortunately, she *was* thinking about sex, and it was all Brody Croft's fault.

At dinner, Darcy had again pointed out that a fling wouldn't be the end of the world, but Hayden still wasn't sold on the idea. She got the feeling that if she gave Brody an inch, he'd take a mile. That if she suggested a fling, he'd show up with an engagement ring.

Barefoot, she stepped out of the bathroom into the master bedroom, pushing wet hair out of her eyes. She'd finally gotten around to unpacking her suitcase this morning, but the suite's huge walk-in closet still looked empty. She changed into a pair of thin gray sweatpants and a cotton tank top, brushed her hair and tied it into a ponytail, then headed for the kitchen.

Normally she hated hotels, but her father's penthouse at the Ritz-Carlton surpassed any ordinary hotel suite. He'd lived here before marrying Sheila, and the apartment had everything Hayden could possibly need, including a large kitchen that was fully stocked and surprisingly cozy. It reminded her of her kitchen back home, making her homesick for the West Coast. In San Francisco, she hadn't needed to worry about anything except how she was going to get her boyfriend into bed.

Here, she had her father's problems, her stepmother's lies and Brody Croft's incessant attempts to get *her* into bed.

Quit thinking about Brody.

Right. He was definitely on tonight's don't-think-about list.

After she'd made a bowl of popcorn and brewed herself a cup of green tea, she got comfortable on one of the leather couches in the living area and switched on the TV. She was totally ready to lose herself in that van Gogh biography. Since she was teaching an entire course on him next semester, she figured she ought to get reacquainted with the guy.

She scrolled through the channels, searching for the program, but couldn't seem to find it. The Biography Channel was telling the life story of a Hollywood actress who'd just been busted on cocaine charges. The History Channel featured a show on the Civil War. She kept scrolling. No van Gogh to be seen.

Great. Just freaking great. Could nothing go right in her life? All she'd wanted to do tonight was watch a show about her favorite artist and not think about Brody Croft. Was that really too much to ask?

Apparently so.

She skipped past a shocking number of reality shows, finally stopping on the Discovery Channel, which was playing a special on sharks. She sighed in resignation and settled the bowl of popcorn in her lap.

"The great white shark can smell one drop of blood in twenty-five gallons of water," came a monotone voice.

Hayden popped a few kernels in her mouth and chewed thoughtfully, watching as a lethal-looking shark swam across the screen.

"The great white does not chew his food. Rather, he takes massive bites and swallows the pieces whole."

Yeah, like Brody... *No Brody thoughts allowed, missy.*

"There have been reports of great whites exceeding twenty feet in length. They can weigh in at over seven thousand pounds."

Ten minutes and fifteen shark facts later, Hayden was stretching out her legs and wiggling her toes, wondering if she should apply some red nail polish. This shark documentary was getting old.

She pressed the guide button on the remote control, scrolled down, skipped the barrage of sports channels, stopped briefly on CNN, then scrolled again. She saw a listing for something called *The Secretary* and decided to click on it, but what came on the screen wasn't the sitcom her students at Berkeley were always raving about.

It was, of course, porn.

"You're a very fast typist, Betty."

"Thank you, Mr. Larson. My fingers have always been my biggest asset."

"I bet they have. Bring your hand a little closer."

"Ooh, Mr. Larson, that tickles."

"Do you like it?"

"Mmm, yes."

"What about this?"

"Mmm, even better."

Hayden had to bite her lip to refrain from bursting into laughter. On the screen, Betty and her boss began making out. Mr. Larsen's big hairy hand disappeared under Betty's conservative skirt. Loud moaning ensued.

She shook her head and pressed a button on the remote. Betty and Mr. Larson disappeared, replaced by a great white shark.

You want me, come and get me.

The sound of Brody's sandpaper-rough voice filled her head. She let out a long breath, exasperated. Why couldn't she stop thinking about the guy? And why couldn't she stop wanting him? She wanted him so badly she could practically feel those big muscular arms around her waist.

But sometimes the things you wanted weren't necessarily the ones you needed.

At the moment, she needed to concentrate on supporting her dad through his divorce and maybe finally call Doug back to tell him she'd slept with someone else and that it was time to turn their break into a breakup.

But what she *wanted* was one more night with Brody Croft.

It doesn't have to be black and white.

She sat there for a moment, chewing on her lower lip as Darcy's words buzzed around in her brain.

Was her friend right? Was she overanalyzing all of this? She'd always had the tendency to pick and prod at each situation until she'd sucked every last drop of fun or enjoyment from it. This wasn't an art history lecture she needed to plan for—it was just sex. Was there really anything wrong with delving into that gray area and enjoying a carnal ride with a man she found wildly attractive?

She turned off the television and reached for the phone.

6

THE CALL FROM HAYDEN came as a total shock. Brody had just stepped out of the shower, where he'd stood under the hot spray for a good half hour to get the kinks out of his muscles. He'd intended to grab a beer from the fridge and watch the highlight reel on ESPN, maybe give Becker a call to talk about Craig Wyatt, and then his cell phone began chirping out a tinny rendition of Beethoven's Symphony No. 9 and Hayden's throaty voice was on the other end.

Come over.

She'd only spoken those two words, then disconnected, leaving him both pleased and befuddled.

Obviously she'd finally changed her mind and taken him up on his offer to continue the fantasy she'd started two nights ago, but was it still just sex she craved? Or was she looking for something extra this time around?

Shit, he was getting ahead of himself here. Hayden was simply inviting him back into her bed for another wild romp, not offering to make a commitment.

He quickly put on a pair of jeans and pulled an old Warriors jersey over his head. Then he grabbed his car keys from the credenza in the hallway, shoved his wallet into his back pocket and left the house, breathing in the damp night air.

It was mid-May, which meant the nights were still cool and the chance of a thunderstorm or even a freak blizzard wasn't all that far-fetched, but Brody loved this time of year, when spring and summer battled for domination over Chicago's climate. He'd lived in this city almost eight years now, and he'd grown to appreciate and enjoy everything about it, even the indecisive seasons.

When he pulled up in front of Hayden's hotel, a light drizzle of rain was sliding across the windshield. He hopped out of the SUV and entered the lobby just as a bolt of lightning filled the sky. Thunder roared ominously in the distance, growing louder and louder until the rain became a steady downpour.

Shaking droplets of water from his hair, he approached the check-in desk and asked the clerk behind it to ring Hayden's suite. A moment later, the clerk walked him over to the elevator and inserted a key into the panel that would allow Brody access to the penthouse, then left him alone in the car.

The elevator soared upward, its doors opening into the suite, where Hayden was waiting for him.

"I have some ground rules," she said in lieu of a greeting.

He grinned. "Hello to you, too."

"Hello. I have some ground rules."

He tossed his car keys on a glass table beside one of the couches and moved toward her.

Even in sweats, she looked amazing. He liked how she'd pulled her hair back in a messy ponytail, how a few haphazard strands framed her face, which was devoid of makeup. He especially liked how her thin tank top didn't hide the fact that she wore no bra.

His mouth ran dry as he dragged his gaze across those gorgeous breasts, the outline of her dusky nipples visible through the white shirt.

Her fair cheeks grew flushed at his perusal. "Don't ogle. It's unbecoming."

He grinned. "Ah, I was wondering where Miss Prim and Proper had gone. Hello, Professor, nice to see you again."

"I am *not* prim and proper," she protested.

"Not in bed anyway…"

"Ground rules," she repeated firmly.

He released a sigh. "All right. Get it out of your system."

She leaned against the arm of the couch, resting her hands on her thighs. "This is only going to be sex," she began, her throaty voice wavering in a way that brought a smile to his lips. "Continuing the fantasy, or whatever it was you said. Agreed?"

"I'm not agreeing to anything yet. Is there more?"

"My father can't know anything about it." She paused, looking uncomfortable. "And I'd prefer if we weren't seen in public together."

His nostrils flared. "Ashamed of being linked to a hockey player?"

"Look, you already know the franchise is taking some heat, Brody. I don't want to make things worse for my dad by giving the media more fuel for the fire they're determined to start."

He had to admit her words made sense. After seeing Craig Wyatt whispering with Sheila Houston at the arena today, Brody had no interest in stoking the fire. Best-case scenario, if he was spotted with Hayden, the press would sensationalize the relationship the way they were currently sensationalizing everything else associated with the Warriors. Worst-case scenario, a jerk reporter would insinuate that the team owner's daughter knew of her father's guilt and was either trying to shut Brody up because he was involved, or sleeping with him to find out what he knew.

He didn't particularly like either of those scenarios.

Still, he wasn't about to let Hayden get her way entirely. He had a few demands himself.

"If I agree to your rules, you have to agree to mine," he said roughly, crossing his arms over his chest.

She swallowed. "Like what?"

"If you're in my bed, that's the only bed you'll be in." He set his jaw. "I won't share you, especially not with the guy waiting for you in California."

"Of course."

"And you have to promise to keep an open mind."

Interest flickered in her gaze. "Sexually?"

"Sure. But emotionally, too. All I'm saying is that if things between us get...deeper, you can't run away from it."

After a beat of silence, she nodded. "I can do that. And do you agree to keep whatever we do here to yourself?"

"I can do that," he mimicked with a grin.

"Then what are you waiting for?" she asked. "Take off your clothes already."

HAYDEN COULD barely contain her amusement as Brody pulled his jersey over his head and tossed it aside. He reminded her of a kid on Christmas morning. The eagerness practically radiated from his tall, powerful body, but when he pushed his jeans down his legs there was nothing comical about the situation anymore.

His cock sprang up against the material of his boxers, demanding attention and making Hayden's mouth grow dry.

No matter how unsettling she found Brody's terms, it was too late to reverse her decision. He wanted her to keep an open mind, fine. But she highly doubted things between them would get *deeper,* as he'd suggested. Their one-night stand may have turned into a fling, but she was confident it wouldn't go further than that.

Besides, right now she didn't want or need to think about the future, not when there were more important things to focus on. Such as Brody's spectacular body and all the things she wanted to do to it.

An impish grin lifted the corner of her mouth as she remembered what he'd done to *her* body the night before at the bar. Her next move suddenly became very clear.

"The keeping-an-open-mind part," she said mischievously. "It goes for you, too, right?"

Brody kicked aside his boxers and fixed her with an intrigued stare. "What do you have in mind?"

She didn't answer. Crooking her finger at him, she gestured for him to follow her down the hallway. They entered the bedroom, where she turned her finger to the bed and said, "Get comfortable."

Brody raised his brows. "Are you planning to join me?"

"Eventually."

He lowered himself onto the bed and leaned against the mountain of pillows at the headboard.

Fighting a smile, Hayden swept her gaze over Brody's long naked body sprawled before her.

"I'm feeling lonely," he murmured. "Are you going to stand there all night and watch me?"

"Maybe."

"What'll it take to get you to come here?"

She chewed on the inside of her cheek, thoughtful. "I don't know. You'd have to make it worth my while, give me a good reason to get into that bed with you."

He chuckled and grasped his shaft with his hand. "This isn't reason enough?"

She laughed. "God, you're arrogant." She stared at his erection, the way his fingers had curled around the base, and moisture gathered in her panties. There was something seriously enticing about watching this man touch himself.

"C'mere," he cajoled. "You don't really want to make me do this alone, do you?"

His gruff voice sent shivers through her, making her nipples poke against her tank top. "I don't know," she said again. "I'm getting pretty turned-on watching you right now…"

Still watching his hand, she strode toward the desk under the curtained window, pulled the chair out and lowered herself on it. "Tell me what you'd want me to do, if I was lying there with you."

Something raw and powerful flashed in his smoky blue eyes. "I think you already know."

"Humor me."

A hint of a smile lifted one corner of his mouth. Without breaking eye contact, he moved his hand up his shaft. From where she sat she could see a bead of moisture at the tip. Her sex throbbed.

"Well, I'd definitely encourage you to bring your tongue into play," he said, his voice lowering to a husky pitch.

He squeezed his erection.

Uncontrollable need raced through her body and settled between her legs.

"Some licking would have to be involved," he continued, propping one hand behind his head while his other hand continued stroking. "Sucking, of course."

"Of course," she agreed, shocked by the pure lust resonating through her.

Brody shot her a wolfish look.

She gasped when he quickened his pace. No man had ever done that in front of her before, and the sexual heat pulsating through her body was so strong she could barely breathe. There was something so kinky, so *dirty* about the way he was lying there, stroking himself while she watched. And that she was still fully clothed only made the situation hotter. It gave her the upper hand, reminding her of a fantasy she hadn't dared to think about in years. Scratch that—she'd thought about it only yesterday, when she'd seen Brody at the arena.

She licked her lips, debating whether or not to bring it up. "What are you thinking about?"

She was certain her embarrassment was written all over her face. And yet the pang of embarrassment was accompanied by a jolt of excitement, because for the first time in her life she was thinking about making that particular fantasy come true.

"Hayden?"

He stopped stroking and she almost cried out in disappointment. "No, keep doing that," she murmured, meeting his eyes again.

"Not until you tell me what's on your mind."

"I…you'll probably think it's silly."

"Try me."

She couldn't believe she was considering confessing her deepest, darkest fantasy to a man she'd known less than a week when she'd never raised the subject around guys she'd dated for months. That in itself said a lot.

Try him.

She swallowed and got to her feet. Eyeing her expectantly, Brody let go of his shaft and leaned his head against both hands, waiting. "Well?" he prompted.

"Promise not to laugh?"

"I won't laugh. Scout's honor." He held up his fingers in a sign that she was fairly certain did *not* belong to the Boy Scouts, but, hell, at least he'd promised.

She took a breath, held it, then released it at the same time she blurted out the words. "I've always wanted to tie a man to my bed."

He laughed softly.

"Hey!" Heat seared her cheeks. "You promised."

"I'm not laughing at the request," he said quickly. "You just took me by surprise."

Relief washed over her, dimming her humiliation. "You're not freaked?"

"Nope. I'm too turned-on to be freaked."

Her focus dropped to his groin, which confirmed his admission. He was thick and hard, a sight that caused every last drop of hesitation and embarrassment to drain from her body like water from a tub. That spot between her legs began to ache, pushing her to action.

"Keep your arms just like that," she ordered, drifting toward the walk-in closet. She grabbed what she needed from the top drawer of the built-in dresser and sauntered over to the bed.

Brody looked at the sheer panty hose in her hands and he grinned. "No fuzzy pink handcuffs?"

"Sorry, I left them in California."

"Pity."

Laughing, she looped the panty hose around his wrists, brushing her fingers over the calluses on his palm. His hands were so strong, fingers long and tapered. A thrill shot through her as she tied those sturdy hands to the headboard. That he let her do it, without moving, without complaining, only deepened the thrill.

She liked it, this feeling of control, something she'd never really felt in the bedroom before. She was all about control when it came to her life, her job, her goals. But sex? Not so much.

With Brody, she was discovering a part of herself she'd denied for a long time. That first night when she'd propositioned him, then letting him touch her in a public bar, now tying him up to her bed—how on earth had he managed to unleash this passionate side of her?

"So what now?" he said hoarsely. "How does this bondage fantasy of yours play out?"

"Well, the fantasy includes some payback actually." She made sure his hands were secure, then straddled him, still fully clothed. "You tortured me last night, Brody."

"You seemed to enjoy it," he teased.

"But you enjoyed it, too, didn't you? You loved having that control over me, driving me wild with your fingers and knowing I wasn't going to fight it." She arched one slim eyebrow. "It's my turn."

He tested the bindings. The headboard shook. "I could easily get out of this position, you know."

"But you won't."

"You sound sure of that."

She bent down and pressed a kiss to his jaw, then licked her way to his earlobe and bit it. He shuddered, his cock jutting against her pelvis. "You're dying for it," she mocked.

A crooked smile stretched across his mouth. "Do people out on the West Coast know how deliciously evil you are, Hayden?"

"They don't have a clue," she said with a self-deprecating sigh.

He threw his head back and laughed. The desire and awe dancing in his eyes sent a wave of confidence rushing through her. Brody made her feel that she could do anything she wanted, be anyone she wanted, confess to any naughty longing she wanted, and he wouldn't judge her.

"Well, it's your turn, as you said," Brody told her. "Let's see what you've got. I warn you, I don't lose control easily."

"We'll see about that."

She pressed both palms to his chest, relishing the hard feel of him, running her fingers through the light sprinkling of hair covering his golden skin. Dipping her head, she traced his collarbone with her tongue.

Brody chuckled. "You can do better than that."

She narrowed her eyes. Was he really convinced he could

stay in control? Arrogant man! She'd just have to show him, wouldn't she?

Not rising to his bait, she bent down and covered one flat nipple with her mouth.

He drew in a breath.

She ran her tongue down his chest, scraping her nails along his skin. He tasted like heaven—salty, spicy, masculine—and the hair leading to his groin tickled her lips as she kissed her way south. Her mouth finally reached his erection, but she made no move to wrap her lips around it. Instead she gently flicked her tongue against his tip then blew a stream of air over the moisture she'd left there.

Brody jerked and let out a soft curse.

"Everything okay?" she asked politely, lifting her head just in time to see the arousal creasing his rugged features.

"Is that all you've got?" he groaned.

"On the contrary." She licked her lips and sent him a heavy-lidded look. "I'm just getting started."

Oh, boy, there was nothing more empowering than driving a man as *manly* as Brody Croft into sheer and total orgasmic oblivion. Flames of arousal and satisfaction licked through Hayden's body as she circled the tip of Brody's cock with her tongue, savoring the taste of him.

Curling her fingers around his shaft, she licked him again, then sucked him into her mouth, trying not to smile when he released a low moan of pleasure. God, why hadn't she done this before? She wanted to berate herself for everything she'd been missing.

In the back of her mind a little voice suggested that perhaps she'd never admitted this fantasy because she hadn't found the right man to admit it to, but she forced the voice and its un-settling implications out of her brain. No more thinking. She didn't want to analyze anything about this.

She moved her mouth up and down his shaft, and when she reached one hand down to cup his balls, he shuddered and grew even harder. Her mind was spinning from the incredible feel of him against her lips.

Lightly stroking his rock-hard thigh, she kissed his sensitive underside, then pumped him with her hand while she took him deep in her mouth again.

"You're evil," he wheezed out.

She lifted her head. "What happened to the master of control?"

"He didn't stand a chance."

She laughed. With one final kiss to his tip, she moved up to straddle him. She could feel the heat of his naked body searing through her clothing, making her pants feel like a tight, hot nuisance. But she didn't undress. Not yet.

Leaning forward, she pressed her lips to his and deepened the kiss. He made a frustrated sound and yet again tugged at the bindings constricting his hands. He was right—one forceful tug and the knots would come apart—but he continued lying there at her mercy. His biceps flexed as he tested the knots again. He let out a soft curse.

"Damn it, Hayden, I need to touch you."

"Touch? Nope, sorry."

She lifted her tank top over her head and threw it aside, baring her breasts. "But I'll let you taste." Bending closer, she offered him a sampling, and drew in a breath when he captured one nipple in his mouth and began feasting. He sucked on the rigid bud, hard, biting it gently until she cried out with pleasure that teetered toward pain.

"More," he rasped, pulling away and staring at her pleadingly.

She laughed. "Define more."

His gaze lowered to her thighs, a clear message of what he

desired, and her sex instantly throbbed in response. If she gave him what he wanted, what *she* wanted, then the domination game would be shot to hell...but did she really care at this point? Could she last one more second without having this man's hands all over her?

The moisture between her legs provided the answer to that question—a big fat no.

As he inched down a little, so that his head was flat on the pillow, she quickly slipped out of her pants, tore off her panties and knelt over him.

His tongue darted out and flicked over her clit.

"Oh," she moaned, nearly falling backward at the jolt of excitement that ran through her. She was closer than she'd thought. The rippling wave of pleasure swelling inside her confirmed that she was on the brink, her orgasm about to crash to the surface.

Her thighs trembled as she tried to move away from his probing tongue, but he wouldn't let her.

"I want you to come in my mouth," he murmured, the husky sound reverberating against her flesh.

She reached for the headboard, gripped his bound hands and twined her fingers with his. Her heart thumped, her knees shook, and the moment she leaned into his warm lips again, the second he suckled her clit, she exploded.

Her climax tore through her, fierce, reckless. She gasped, sucking in oxygen as shards of colorful light danced before her eyes and prickled her flushed skin. Still shaking, she sagged against the headboard, struggling to regain her sense of equilibrium while she fumbled with the knots on his hands.

"I need you inside me. Now," she squeezed out, finally untying him.

With a grin, he rotated his wrists to get the blood flowing

again, but made no move to flip her over and plunge into her as she'd requested. "It's your show, remember?"

He curled his fingers around her waist and pushed her down so she was straddling him again. From the end table, he swiped a condom she hadn't even noticed him bring into the bedroom and handed it to her. "Do with me what you please."

Swallowing, she rolled the condom onto his erection and shifted her legs. She was wet and ready for him, more than ready, but she didn't guide him inside her. Instead, she brushed her nipples over his chest, enjoying the way his eyes narrowed with pleasure.

She ground her pelvis against him, teased him by pushing against his tip and then edging away from it. Feeling bold and wanton, she leaned forward, let her breasts graze his mouth, and murmured, "Tell me what you want, Brody."

His voice hoarse, he said, "You."

"Me what?"

A wicked gleam flashed in his eyes. "What was it you said to me that first night? Oh, right. I want you to fuck me."

Oh, my.

Without another word, she lowered herself onto him, taking him all the way in, and began to ride him. The pleasure cascading through her body was almost too much to bear. He felt so good inside, so right and perfect.

She increased her pace, moving over him faster, harder, his husky groans urging her on.

He lifted his lean hips and met her thrust for thrust. Then he grasped her ass and rolled her over, his powerful body covering hers as he drove into her. *Yes.* Her insides clenched, pleading with her for release.

"Will you come for me?" he murmured, slowing his pace.

She made an unintelligible sound.

He chuckled. "What was that?"

"Yes," she choked out.

With a satisfied nod, he plunged into her, hard, rough, stealing the breath right of her lungs. He reached down and stroked the place where they joined, continuing to pump inside her until she finally exploded again.

She gave herself to the orgasm that raced through her body. In the heavenly haze she heard Brody's deep groan, felt his fingers dig into her hips as he jerked inside her.

Struggling to steady her breathing, she ran her hands up and down his sweat-soaked back, enjoying the hard planes and defined muscles under her fingertips. "God, that was…" She trailed off.

He touched her chin, lightly dragging his thumbnail over her jaw. "That was what?"

"Incredible." A laugh flew out. "And to think I was going to spend the evening watching a documentary on a guy who cut his own ear off."

7

"LET'S ORDER room service," Brody said a few minutes later, slipping his boxers on.

He watched as Hayden put on her tank top and then attempted to fix the ponytail that had seen better days. Wayward strands of hair fell into her eyes and he smiled at the knowledge that her disheveled state was the result of rolling around in bed with him. She looked rumpled and beautiful and so damn cute he marched over and planted a kiss on her lips. She tasted of toothpaste and popcorn and something uniquely Hayden.

With a little whimper, she pulled his head closer and sank into the kiss, flicking her tongue against his in a tantalizing way that made him hard again.

Just as he lowered his hands to her breasts, she pushed him back. "What happened to room service?" she teased.

"Screw it."

"Knock yourself out. I, for one, am starved." With a grin, she brushed past him and left the bedroom.

He stared down at the erection poking against his boxers. Damn, how did this woman turn him on so fiercely? He felt like a horny teenager again.

He put on his jeans, used the washroom then drifted toward the living room.

"How do cheeseburgers sound?" she called when she spotted him lingering in the hallway.

His stomach growled with approval. "Great."

He joined her on the couch. As she dialed room service and placed their order, he noticed a stack of papers sitting on the table. Curious, he leaned forward and examined the first sheet. It looked like a biography on Rembrandt, neatly typed. The margins were full of handwritten notes.

"What's this?" he asked when she'd hung up the phone.

"Ideas for the Color Theory class I'm teaching in the fall. I plan to focus on Rembrandt for a few lectures."

"Rembrandt, huh? I thought all of his paintings were pretty dark and foreboding." The snippet of information stored in his brain came as a surprise to him. He hadn't thought he'd paid any attention during art history class his senior year of high school.

Hayden also looked surprised, but pleased. "Actually, that's what I want to focus on, the misconceptions about certain artists and their use of color. Did you know that Rembrandt's *Night Watch* is in fact a day scene?"

A vague image of the painting surfaced in his mind. "I remember it being very dark."

"It was—until the painting was cleaned." She grinned. "The canvas was coated with loads of varnish. When it was removed, it turned out to be daylight. A lot of his paintings ended up looking very different once they were cleaned or restored, proving that he definitely knew what he was doing when it came to color."

She grew more animated as she hurried on. "Same with Michelangelo. People didn't view him as much of a colorist, but when the Sistine Chapel was cleaned, it was so vivid, the colors so vibrant, that everyone was shocked."

"I never knew that."

"It took longer to clean that ceiling than it did to paint it," she added. "It was covered in so much soot and dirt that when they were removed the entire scene looked different. That's one of the things I want to talk to my students about, how something as simple as cleaning or restoring can change your entire view of a piece of art."

He nodded. "Sort of like when the Zamboni cleans the ice during second period intermission. Changes the entire playing surface."

He saw her mouth quirk and suspected she was trying not to laugh. "Yeah. I guess there's a similarity there."

Setting down the papers, he said, "You're really into art, huh?"

"Of course. It's my passion."

A smile reached his lips. He hadn't spent much time with women who were passionate about anything outside the bedroom, and the light in Hayden's green eyes tugged at something inside him. He realized this was the first time she'd opened up to him, engaged in a conversation that didn't include ground rules, and he liked it.

"So do you paint, or just lecture about painters?" he asked.

"I used to draw and paint a lot when I was younger, but not so much anymore."

"How come?"

She shrugged. "I was always more fascinated with other people's work than with my own. My undergrad was mostly studio work, but I did my master's in art history. I discovered I liked studying great artists better than trying to become one myself." She drew her knees up into a cross-legged position and asked, "What did you study in college?"

"Sports sciences," he answered. "You know, kinesiology, sports medicine. And I minored in athletic coaching."

"Seriously?"

He didn't respond. Her expression revealed nothing, but he got the feeling she didn't believe him, which made him feel like he was in high school all over again. The kid who'd been written off by his teachers as a big dumb oaf just because he happened to be good at sports. They'd stuck the jock label on him, and no matter how hard he'd tried to tear it off, the judgmental attitudes remained intact. One time he'd even been accused of cheating on an English test he'd spent hours studying for, all because his teacher had decided that a kid who spent all his time handling a puck couldn't possibly finish a book like *Crime and Punishment.*

Hayden must have sensed his irritation because she quickly added, "I believe you. It's just…well, most of the athletes I knew growing up only went to college for the athletic scholarship and just skipped all the academic classes."

"My parents would have killed me if I'd skipped class," he said, rolling his eyes. "They only allowed me to play hockey if I maintained an A average."

Hayden looked impressed. "What do your parents do for a living?"

"Dad's a mechanic, and Mom works in a hair salon." He paused. "Money was always tight during my childhood." He resisted the urge to glance around the lavish penthouse, which was an obvious sign that Hayden hadn't had the same problem growing up.

He wasn't quite sure why he'd brought up that money part, either. He hated talking about his childhood. Hated thinking about it, too. As much as he loved his parents, he didn't like to be reminded of how hard life had been to them. How his mom used to stay up at night clipping coupons and how his dad walked to work—even when Michigan's winter was at its worst—each time their beat-up Chevy truck broke down. Fortunately, his parents would never have to worry about money again, thanks to his lucrative career.

The phone rang, putting an end to their conversation.

Hayden picked up the receiver, then hung up and said room service was on its way.

As Hayden headed for the elevator to greet the bellhop with the cart, Brody turned on the television, flipped through a few channels, then finally stopped on the eleven-o'clock news.

Rolling the cart into the living room, Hayden uncovered their food and placed a plate in front of him. The aroma of French fries and ground beef floated toward him, making his mouth water. Funny, he hadn't even noticed how hungry he was when Hayden had had him tied to her bed. He'd been satisfying a different sort of appetite then.

He'd just taken a big bite of his cheeseburger when a familiar face flashed across the plasma screen. He nearly choked on the burger, as a wave of unease washed over him. Hayden had also noticed her father's image on the TV, and she quickly grabbed the remote to turn up the volume. They caught the Channel 8 newscaster in midsentence.

"—came forward this afternoon and admitted there is truth to the rumors surrounding the Chicago Warriors franchise. The player, who refused to be named, claims that the bribery and illegal betting activities Warriors owner Presley Houston is accused of are in fact true."

Brody suppressed a groan. Next to him, Hayden made a startled little sound.

"An hour ago, the league announced they will be launching a full investigation into these allegations."

The newscaster went on to recap the accusation that Presley had bribed players to throw at least two games, and that he'd placed bets on the outcomes. The divorce was also mentioned, as well as Sheila Houston's alleged affair with a Warrior, but by that point Brody had tuned out the news segment.

Who had come forward? It couldn't be Becker, because his friend would've called him with a heads-up before he did anything like that. Yeah, Becker would've definitely warned him.

Craig Wyatt, though, seemed like a likely candidate, especially after what Brody had witnessed at the arena earlier today. The reporters had been pretty rough on Sheila Houston, many of them holding the firm belief that she was lying. It made sense that Wyatt would step in and try to support the woman in his bed.

The headache Brody had tried to ignore before came back with full force. He reached up to rub his throbbing temples. Damn. He wished he knew which one of his teammates had confessed. Whoever it was, this probably didn't bode well for tomorrow's game. How would anybody be able to focus with a possible criminal investigation hanging over their heads?

"It's not true."

Hayden's soft voice jarred him from his thoughts, and he glanced over to see her big eyes pleading with him. "Right?" she said wearily. "It's not true."

"I don't know." He raked a hand through his hair, then absently picked up a French fry. Not that he had an appetite anymore. That news report had destroyed any desire he had for food. He dropped the fry and looked back at Hayden, who seemed to be waiting expectantly for him to continue. "I really don't know, babe. So far, there's been no proof that Pres bribed anyone."

"So far. But if that report we saw just now is true…"

Her breath hitched, and her pained expression tore at his heart.

"Were you… Did he…" She sounded tortured, as if saying each word took great effort. "Did he offer you a bribe?" she finally asked.

"Absolutely not."

"But he could have bribed someone else, another player."

"He could have," Brody said guardedly.

She grew silent, looking so achingly sad that he reached over to draw her into his arms. Her hair tickled his chin, the sweet scent of her wafting into his nose. He wanted to kiss her, to make love to her again, but it was totally not the time. She was upset, and the way she pressed her head into the crook of his neck and snuggled closer told him she needed comfort at the moment, not sex.

"God, this is such a mess," she murmured, her breath warming his skin. "Dad is already stressed-out because of the divorce, and now…"

She abruptly lifted her head, her lips set in a tight line. "I refuse to believe he did what they're accusing him of. My dad is a lot of things, but he's not a criminal."

The certainty in her eyes was unmistakable, and Brody wisely kept quiet. He'd always admired and respected Presley Houston, but experience had taught him that even people you admired and respected could screw up.

"Whoever came forward has to be lying," Hayden said firmly. She swallowed. "This will all get cleared up during the investigation. It has to."

She slid close to him again. "I don't want to think about this anymore. Can we just pretend we didn't see that newscast?" Without waiting for an answer, she went on. "And while we're at it, we can pretend I came home for a vacation rather than to deal with my father's problems." She sighed against his shoulder. "God, a vacation would be so good. I could really use some fun right now."

He smoothed her hair, loving how soft it felt under his fingers. "What did you have in mind?"

She tilted her head up and smiled. "We could go see a movie tomorrow—it's been ages since I've been to the movies. Or we could walk along the waterfront, go to Navy Pier. I don't know, just have fun, damn it!"

As much as he hated disappointing her, Brody smiled gently and said, "I would love to, but I can't. The team's catching a plane to L.A. at 9:00 a.m. There's a game tomorrow night."

The light drained out of her eyes, but she gave him a quick smile as if to hide her reaction. "Oh. Right. Dad mentioned something about an away game."

His arms felt empty as she disentangled herself from the embrace and inched back, absently reaching for a French fry on her plate. She popped it into her mouth, chewing slowly, not looking at him.

"How about Sunday?" he suggested, anxious to make things right and at the same time not sure what he'd done wrong.

"I have this party to go to." She pushed her plate away, apparently as uninterested in eating as he was. "It's important to my dad."

"Then another time," he said. "I promise you, I'll take you out and give you the fun you need."

Her expression grew strained. "It's okay, Brody. You don't have to indulge me. It's probably a silly idea to go out on a date anyway."

He bristled. "Why is it silly?"

She blew out an exasperated breath. "This is only supposed to be a fling. Playing out a few sexual fantasies."

A fling. Something inside him hardened at the word. Casual flings had pretty much been his entire life for the past ten years, serious relationships never even making a blip on his radar. And then he'd met Hayden and suddenly he wasn't thinking about casual anymore. He liked her. A lot. Hell, he'd actually experienced a flicker of excitement when she'd mentioned engaging in normal couple things like going to the movies or walking by the lake. He'd never felt the urge to do stuff like that with the previous women in his life. He hadn't cared enough, and that would have sounded awful if not for the fact that they hadn't cared, either.

Crazy as it was, Hayden was the first woman, aside from a reporter, who'd ever asked him about his parents or his college major. Mundane little questions that people asked each other all the time, and yet something he'd been lacking.

He'd seen the potential when Hayden had first walked up to him in that bar. Somehow, he'd known deep down that this was a woman he could have a meaningful relationship with.

And it was damn ironic that she only wanted a goddamn fling.

"What happened to promising to keep an open mind?" he asked quietly.

"I plan on keeping that promise." She shifted her gaze. "But you can't blame me for being skeptical about this becoming anything deeper."

"You don't think it will?"

"Honestly?" She looked him square in the eye. "No, I don't."

He frowned. "You sound convinced of that."

"I am." Pushing an errant strand of hair from her eyes, she shrugged. "I'm going back to the West Coast in a couple of months, and even if I were staying here, our lives don't mesh."

Irritation swelled inside him. "How do you figure that?"

"You're a hockey player. I'm a professor."

"So?"

"So, our careers alone tell me how different we are. I've lived in your world, Brody. I grew up in it. Dad and I had most of our conversations on airplanes on the way to whatever city his team was playing against. I lived in five states during a fifteen-year period. And I hated it."

"Your father was a hockey coach," he pointed out.

"And the travel requirements are not much different for

players. I had no say in the career my father chose for himself. But when it comes to what I want in a partner, I can choose."

"The guy in San Francisco, what does he do?"

Her discomfort at discussing the guy who Brody now thought of as the Other Man was evident as she began to fidget with her hands. She laced her fingers together, unlaced them, then tapped them against her thighs. "Actually, he teaches art history at Berkeley, too."

How frickin' peachy. "What else?" he demanded.

She faltered. "What do you mean?"

"So you're both interested in art. What else makes this relationship so delightfully rewarding?"

He almost winced at the sarcasm he heard in his tone. Damn it, he was acting like a total ass here, and from the cloudy look in Hayden's eyes, she obviously thought the same thing.

"My relationship with Doug is none of your concern. I promised to remain sexually exclusive, but I never agreed to sit around and talk about him."

"I don't want to talk about him," he growled. "I just want to get to know you. I want to understand why you feel I'm not a good match for you."

"God, don't you see it?" she sighed. "I want, I want. You said so yourself, you always get what you want. And that's why I feel the way I do. I've dated too many guys who *want*. But none of them want to give. They're too concerned with getting *their* way, advancing *their* careers, and I always come in second. Well, I'm sick of it. Doug may not be the most exciting man on the planet, but he wants the same things I do—a solid marriage, a stable home, and *that's* what I want out of a relationship."

A deafening silence fell over the room, stretching between. Brody felt like throwing something. He resented the fact that Hayden was projecting her frustration with her father and the previous men in her life onto him, but, hell, he'd opened this can of worms. Pushed her too far, too fast. Needled her about her on-hold relationship and demanded she give him a chance she wasn't ready to give.

Would he still get that chance now? Or had he blown it completely?

"I think asking you over here was a bad idea," she said.

The answer to his silent question became painfully clear.

He'd blown it, all right.

Big-time.

THE LAST THING Hayden felt like doing on Sunday night was attending a birthday party for a wealthy entrepreneur she didn't even know, but when she'd called her father to try to get out of it, he wouldn't have it. He'd insisted her presence was essential, though she honestly didn't know why. Every time she socialized with her father and his friends she ended up standing at the bar by herself.

But she didn't want to let down her dad. And considering how she'd left things with Brody on Friday night, maybe it was better to get out of that big penthouse and away from her thoughts.

It was just past eight o'clock when she neared the Gallagher Club, a prestigious men's club in one of Chicago's most historical neighborhoods. It had been founded by Walter Gallagher, a filthy rich entrepreneur who'd decided he needed to build a place where other filthy rich entrepreneurs could congregate.

The Gallagher Club was by invitation only, and it took some men decades to gain membership. Her father had inherited the membership when he'd purchased the Warriors from their previous owner, and he loved flaunting it. When Hayden was in town, he never took her anywhere else.

She drove down the wide, tree-lined street, slowing her rented Honda Civic when she spotted a crowd at the end of the road. As she got closer, she noticed a few news vans. The dozen or so people milling by the curb were reporters.

And since she couldn't think of anyone else currently involved in a possible criminal investigation, she knew the press was there because of her father.

This was not good.

Taking a few calming breaths, she drove through the wrought-iron gates leading to the Gallagher Club, turning her head and averting her eyes when a few of the reporters started to peer in at her. She exhaled as she steered up the circular cobblestone driveway and slowed the car behind the line of vehicles waiting near the valet area.

Had the reporters harassed her father when he'd driven in? Had he stopped to speak with them, to deny the absurd news report?

A voice interrupted the troubling thoughts. "Good evening, madam."

She lifted her head and saw a young man in a burgundy valet uniform hovering over the driver's window.

"May I take your keys?" he asked.

Her gaze flitted to the massive mansion with its enormous limestone pillars and the stone statues lining the marble entrance. Her father was probably already in there, most likely smoking cigars with his rich friends and acting as if the presence of the media didn't bother him. But she knew it had to bug him. Presley's reputation mattered to him more than anything.

With another sigh, she handed the valet her keys and stepped out of the car. "Davis will escort you inside," the young man informed her.

Davis turned out to be a tall, bulky man in a black tuxedo who extended his arm and led her up the front steps toward the two oak doors at the entrance.

He opened one door and said, "Enjoy your evening."

"Thank you," she answered, then stepped into the lavish foyer.

Miles of black marble spanned the front hall, and overhead a sparkling crystal chandelier dangled from the high ceiling. When she took a breath, she inhaled the scent of wine, cologne and all things expensive.

She paused next to the entrance of the coat check and quickly glanced down to make sure there were no wardrobe mishaps happening. She'd worn a slinky silver dress that clung to her curves, emphasizing her cleavage and bottom. Not to mention that it was slit up to the thigh, revealing a lot of leg. A light touch of eye makeup and some shiny pink lip gloss, and the ensemble had been complete.

Annoyingly, she'd thought about Brody the entire time she'd gotten ready. How much he'd probably enjoy seeing her in the dress—and how much he'd love taking it off her.

It still bothered her, how they'd left things Friday night. Brody hadn't spent the night, needing to catch his flight in the morning, and he'd headed for the elevator with the air of a man leaving a battlefield in defeat.

She'd felt pretty defeated, too. What had she been thinking, suggesting they go out on a real date? After all, she was the one who'd made it clear she wanted a fling. Yet she'd really enjoyed their conversation—talking to him about art, hearing about his parents. It had been really nice. Comfortable. And before she knew it, she was falling right back into her old ways, looking to embark on a new relationship.

That Brody had to be in L.A. the next day was just the wake-up call she'd needed. It reminded her precisely what she wanted—someone stable. Someone who wouldn't be out of town for half the year, while their relationship took second place. As wildly attracted to Brody as she was, she knew he couldn't be that someone.

"Quade has outdone himself this year," a male voice boomed, interrupting her thoughts and reminding her where she was.

Smoothing out the front of her dress, she followed the group of tuxedo-clad men into the large ballroom off to the left. It was a black-tie event, and she found herself surrounded by beautifully dressed people, some older, some younger, all strangers. A dance floor graced the center of the room, in front of a live band that was belting out an upbeat swing song. Before she could blink, a waiter handed her a glass of champagne.

Just as she was about to take a sip, a familiar face caught her eye.

"Darcy?" she called in surprise.

Her best friend's silky red hair swung over her shoulders as she spun around. "Hey! What are you doing here?"

"My dad demanded I make an appearance." She grimaced. "And to think, I almost believed he wanted to spend some time with me."

Bitter much?

Fine, so she was bitter, but really, who could blame her? She'd come here to support her father and bridge the distance between them, and yet he seemed determined to avoid spending quality time with her.

"What are *you* doing here?" she asked Darcy.

Her friend was clad in a white minidress that contrasted nicely with her bright red hair and vibrant blue eyes. "I know the birthday boy. He's a regular at the boutique and pretty much threatened to take his business elsewhere if I didn't make an appearance." Darcy snorted. "To be honest, I think he's dying to get into my panties. Like *that* will ever happen."

"Who exactly is the birthday boy? Dad neglected to mention."

"Jonas Quade," Darcy answered. "He's filthy rich, calls himself a philanthropist, and spends thousands of dollars on his many mistresses. Oh, and he's also a pompous ass, but I can't complain because those thousands I mentioned, well, he spends them at my boutique. He likes getting his lady friends to try on lace teddies and model for him, that sleazy bastar— Crap, here he comes."

A gray-haired man with the build of Arnold Schwarzenegger and a George Hamilton tan made a beeline in their direction. A plump, blond woman tagged on his heels, looking annoyed by her escort's obvious enthusiasm for Darcy.

"Darcy!" Jonas Quade boomed, grinning widely. "What a treat to see you here."

"Happy birthday, Mr. Quade," Darcy said politely.

Quade turned to his companion. "Margaret, this is the owner of the lingerie store where I buy you all those *intimate* gifts." He winked at the blonde. "Darcy, this is my wife, Margaret."

Hayden could see the barely contained mirth on her friend's face. Hayden had to wonder if Quade's wife was aware that her husband wasn't buying intimate gifts only for her.

"And who is your lovely friend?" Quade asked, peering at Hayden.

Since she didn't particularly enjoy being ogled, Hayden felt a flicker of relief when, before Darcy could introduce them, Quade's wife suddenly latched on to his arm and said, "Marcus is trying to get your attention, darling." She proceeded to forcibly drag him away from the two women.

"Enjoy the party," Quade called over his shoulder.

"That poor woman," Darcy said. "She has no idea…"

"I'm sure she knows. He might as well have *adulterer* tattooed on his forehead."

She and Darcy started to giggle, and Hayden decided this party might not be so bad after all. She hadn't spotted her father yet, but with Darcy by her side, she might not have such an awful time.

"Can I interest you in a dance?"

Damn, she should've known her best friend, with that indecently short dress, wouldn't be available for long.

The handsome, dark-haired man in a navy-blue pinstriped suit eyed Darcy expectantly. After a moment she shrugged, and said, "I'd love to dance." She handed her champagne flute to Hayden, adding, "I'll catch up with you later, okay?"

"Sure. Have fun."

Hayden's shoulders sagged as her friend followed Handsome Man onto the dance floor. Great. Seeing Darcy had been a pleasant surprise, but now her enthusiasm returned to its original level: low.

Then it swiftly dropped to nonexistent.

"Hayden, honey!" Her father's commanding voice sliced through the loud chatter and strains of music. He strode up to her, a glass of bourbon in his hand and an unlit cigar poking out of the corner of his mouth.

She stood on her tiptoes and pecked his cheek. "Hey, Dad. You look like you're enjoying yourself."

"I am, I am." He squeezed her arm and beamed at her. "You look gorgeous."

Something about his overly broad smile troubled her. She wasn't sure why—he was just smiling. And yet an alarm went off in her head. She examined her father more closely. His face was flushed and his eyes were a touch too bright.

Like an unwanted visit from the Avon lady, Sheila's words filled her head. *Your father's drinking again.*

"Are you okay?" she asked, unable to stop the wariness from seeping into her tone. "You look a little…tense."

He waved a hand dismissively. "I'm absolutely great."

"You sure? Because I saw those reporters outside and…" And what? *And I wanted to make sure that they're all just lying about your involvement in illegal sports betting?*

Presley's eyes darkened. "Ignore those bloodsuckers. They're only trying to cause trouble, conjuring up their delusional stories to sell papers." He took a slug of bourbon. "This isn't the time to discuss this. Martin Hargrove was just asking me about you. You remember Martin, he owns a chain of restaurants—"

"Dad, you can't just ignore this," she cut in. "What about the announcement that one of your players came forward? I tried calling your cell yesterday afternoon to talk about it but I kept getting your voice mail. I left you two messages."

He ignored the last statement and said, "I was golfing with Judge Harrison. No cell service out on the course."

She decided not to mention that she'd also called the house he was renting, knowing he'd probably have an excuse for not answering those calls, too.

God, why was he acting like none of this was a big deal? One of his players had admitted that Presley fixed games, and her father was brushing it off like a fleck of lint on his sleeve. Going to parties, smoking cigars, mingling with friends. Did he honestly think this would all just blow over? Hayden refused to believe her father had done the things he was accused of, but she wasn't naive enough to think they could just close their eyes and blink the whole mess away.

"Did you at least talk to Judge Harrison about what your next move should be?" she asked.

"Why the hell would I do that?"

"Because this is starting to get serious." Hayden clenched her fists at her sides. "You should give a press conference maintaining your innocence. Or at the very least, talk to your lawyer."

He didn't bother replying, just shrugged, then lifted his drink to his mouth. After swallowing the rest of the liquid, he signaled a passing waiter and swiped a glass of champagne.

Hayden took the opportunity to place her and Darcy's drinks on the waiter's tray, suddenly losing any taste for alcohol. Both times she'd seen her father this past week, he'd been drinking, but tonight it was obvious her father was drunk. His rosy cheeks and glazed eyes, the way he was swaying on his feet. The blatant case of denial.

"Dad…how much have you had to drink?"

His features instantly hardened. "Pardon me?"

"You just seem a little…buzzed," she said for lack of a better word.

"Buzzed? Is that California slang for drunk?" He frowned. "I can assure you, Hayden, I am not drunk. I've only had a couple drinks."

The defensive note in his voice deepened her concern. When people started making excuses for their inebriated state…wasn't that a sign of a drinking problem?

She cursed her stepmother for putting all these absurd ideas into her head. Her father wasn't an alcoholic. He didn't have a drinking problem, he hadn't had an affair, and he certainly hadn't illegally fixed any Warrior games to make a profit.

Right?

Her temples began to throb. God, she didn't want to doubt her dad, the man who'd raised her alone, the man who up until a few years ago had been her closest friend.

She opened her mouth to apologize, but he cut her off before she could. "I'm sick of these accusations, you hear me?"

She blinked. "What? Dad—"

"I get enough flak from Sheila, I don't need to hear this shit from my own daughter."

His eyes were on fire, his cheeks crimson with anger, and she found herself taking a step back. Tears stung her eyes. Oh, God. For the first time in her life she was frightened of her own father.

"So I made a few bad investments. Sue me," he growled, his champagne glass shaking along with his hands. "It doesn't make me a criminal. Don't you dare accuse me of that."

She swallowed. "I wasn't—"

"I didn't fix those games," he snapped. "And I don't have a drinking problem."

A ragged breath escaped his lips, the stale odor of alcohol burning her nostrils and betraying his last statement. Her father *was* drunk. This time there wasn't a single doubt in her mind. As she stood there, stunned, a tear crept down her cheek.

"Hayden…honey…oh, Lord, I'm sorry. I didn't mean to snap at you like that."

She didn't answer, just swallowed again and swiped at her face with a shaky hand.

Her father reached out and touched her shoulder. "Forgive me."

Before she could respond, Jonas Quade approached with jovial strides, clasped his hand on Presley's arm and said, "There you are, Pres. My son Gregory is dying to meet you. He's the Warriors' number-one fan."

Her father's dark green eyes pleaded with her, relaying the message he couldn't voice at the moment. *We'll talk about this later.*

She managed a nod, then drew in a ragged breath as Quade led her father away.

The second the two men ambled off, she spun on her heel and hurried to the French doors leading to the patio, hoping she could keep any more tears at bay until she was out of sight.

8

"I REALLY WISH you hadn't dragged me here," Sam Becker groaned as he drove his shiny silver Lexus in the direction of the Gallagher Club. "My wife is pissed."

"Come on, Mary doesn't have a 'pissed' bone in her body," Brody replied, thinking of the tiny, delicate woman who'd been married to Sam for fifteen years.

"That's what she wants you to think. Trust me, behind closed doors she's not very nice."

Brody laughed.

"I swear, she almost tore my head off when I told her I was going out with you tonight. It was last-minute, so we couldn't get a babysitter for Tamara. Mary had to cancel her plans. I'll never hear the end of this. Thanks a lot, kiddo."

Sam's words might have evoked guilt in some men, but Brody couldn't muster any. For two days he'd been trying to come up with a way to see Hayden and make things right. Sure, he could've just called her, but the way things had ended at the penthouse the other night left him cautious.

Hayden had mentioned she'd be at the Gallagher Club tonight, and he'd spent the entire afternoon wondering how he could show up there without appearing desperate. The answer had come to him during a call from Becker, who'd phoned to discuss a charity event they were participating in next month.

Brody wasn't a member of the Gallagher Club, but Becker was, so Brody had promptly ordered his best bud to brush the dust off his tuxedo.

He felt bad that Becker had been raked over the coals by his wife, but he'd make it up to him.

"Why didn't you get Lucy to watch Tamara?" Brody asked. He'd been over to Becker's house dozens of times, and had spent quite a bit of time with Becker's two daughters. Lucy was fourteen, ten years older than her sister Tamara, but it had been obvious to Brody how much the teenager loved her baby sister.

"Lucy has a—God help me—" Becker groaned "—boy-friend. They're at the movies tonight."

Brody hooted. "You actually let her leave the house with the guy?"

"I had no choice. Mary said I couldn't threaten him with a shotgun." Becker sighed. "And speaking of shotguns, she told me to put one to your head if you didn't agree to spend a week at our lake house this summer. She renovated the entire place and is dying to show it off."

Brody usually tried to spend the entire summer in Michigan with his parents, but for Becker, he was willing to alter his plans. "Tell your wife I'll be there. Just name the date."

Becker suddenly slowed the car. "Oh, shit."

A small crowd of reporters hovered in front of the gates of the Gallagher Club. A few turned their heads at the Lexus's approach.

Rolling up the windows, Becker turned to Brody and said, "Obviously the vultures are following dear old Pres."

Brody suppressed a groan. "Are you surprised? Someone on the team came forward and confirmed the rumors. The press is salivating."

Becker drove through the gate and stopped in front of the waiting valet. Lips tight, he got out of the car without a word.

The second Brody's feet connected with the cobblestone driveway, one of the reporters shouted at them from the gate.

"Becker! Croft!" a man yelled, practically poking his entire bald head between two of the gate's bars. "Any comment on the allegations that Presley Houston fixed Warriors games and…"

Brody tuned the guy out, choosing instead to follow Becker up the front steps toward the entrance of the club.

"Jeez, I hate this place," Becker muttered as they entered the foyer.

"How'd you get to be a member anyway?" Brody asked the question without caring too much about the answer. He'd much rather talk to Becker about Craig Wyatt and the possibility that he was the one who'd come forward, but Becker's body language clearly said he didn't want to discuss the reporters or the scandal. His massive shoulders were tight, his square jaw clenched. Brody could understand. He'd been feeling tense himself ever since he'd watched that news story with Hayden.

And yesterday's loss in Los Angeles hadn't helped. Losing a play-off game was bad, but losing 6–0 was pathetic. The Warriors had played like a team of amateurs, and though nobody had spoken about the scandal, Brody knew it was on their minds. He'd found himself glancing around the locker room, wondering which one of the guys had confessed to knowing about the bribes.

"My wife is involved with one of Jonas Quade's charity foundations," Becker was saying in response Brody's question. "When he offered to put in a good word for me with the members' committee, Mary pretty much threatened divorce unless I joined." Becker muttered a curse. "I'm telling you, man, she's not a nice person."

"You must have seen *something* good in her considering you married the woman."

"Yeah, I did see something." Becker's rugged features softened. "My soul mate."

The two men entered the massive ballroom, and Brody's eyes instantly began darting around the room.

"So what's her name?" Becker asked with a sigh.

He blinked. "What?"

"Come on, Croft. Only reason you dragged me here is because I belong to this pretentious society of snobs and you needed to score an invite. And since you're no social climber, that means you came here to see a woman. So what's her name?"

"Hayden," he admitted.

Becker accepted a glass of wine from a passing waiter. "Is she a member of Chicago's high society?"

"Kind of." He hesitated. "She's Presley's daughter."

Becker paused mid-sip. "As in the daughter of Presley Houston, the man who signs our paychecks?"

"Yep."

"Bad idea, man. You don't want to get involved with a Houston, not while this betting bullshit is going on."

Brody's tuxedo jacket suddenly felt too tight. "Hayden has nothing to do with that. She's just visiting from California."

"And if the media finds out you're sleeping with her, they'll start drooling. It'll be all over the headlines, how Pres's daughter is screwing one of the star players on the team in order to shut him up."

The hairs on the back of Brody's neck stood on end. "You say that as if you think there's something I need shutting up about. Sam…do you know something about this bribery crap?"

"No, of course not."

"You sure?" He hesitated. "You didn't…you didn't take a bribe, did you?"

Becker looked as if he'd been shot by a bazooka. His mouth dropped open, his cheeks reddened and a vein popped out in his forehead. "You actually think I'd take a fucking bribe? I've been playing in this league for half my life. Trust me, I earn enough."

Brody relaxed. "I didn't think you took a bribe," he said, trying to inject reassurance into his voice. "But what you just said…it sounds like you know more about this scandal than the rest of us. Did Pres tell you anything?"

Though he looked calm now, the vein on Becker's forehead continued to throb. He seemed uncomfortable, scanning the room like that of a prisoner scouting out an escape route. "I don't know anything," he finally said.

"Well, I think I might," Brody found himself confessing.

Becker's head jerked up. "What are you talking about?"

Although this was probably not the time, and definitely not the place, Brody told Becker about what he'd seen at the arena the other day. He spoke in a hushed tone, revealing his suspicions that Sheila Houston had confided in Craig Wyatt about whatever it was she knew, and that Wyatt was the one who'd spoken to the league. He finished with, "So do you think I should do something?"

The other man released a ragged breath. He looked a bit shell-shocked. "Honestly? I think it would be a bad idea."

"Why do you say that?"

"You don't want to get involved," Becker warned in a low voice. "You'll only cast suspicion on yourself."

He mulled over his friend's advice, knowing Becker did have a point. But then he thought of the team captain, and how subdued Wyatt had been lately. Wyatt had always been serious, but he'd barely spoken a word to anyone in weeks, and when he did, it was to yell at them for making a mistake out on the ice. Brody got the feeling Craig Wyatt might very well be in need of a friend, and as reluctant as he was to get involved, he wasn't sure he could watch a teammate struggle without doing a thing to help.

But Becker remained firm. "Don't confront Craig, kiddo. If it bothers you this much, I'll talk to him, okay?"

He glanced at his friend in surprise. "You'd really do that?"

With a playful punch to Brody's arm, Becker gave a faint smile and said, "Unlike my old-timer self, you've still got a lot of years ahead of you. I don't want to see your career tank just because Presley Houston might've decided he needed some extra cash."

"My two favorite players!"

Speak of the devil. Brody shot Becker a look of gratitude, then pasted on a smile as Presley approached them, holding a glass of champagne in his large hand. Considering there were reporters outside just dying to roast Pres for these bribery charges, the man seemed surprisingly jovial. Either the allegations didn't concern him, or he was doing a damn good job covering up his distress.

"Having a good time?" Pres asked.

"We just got here," answered Becker.

"Well, the party's just getting started." Pres lifted his glass to his lips and emptied it. A second later he flagged down a waiter and promptly received a full glass.

"Is your daughter here tonight?" Brody asked. His voice came out more eager than casual. His peripheral vision caught Becker's mouth creasing in a frown.

Pres looked distinctly ill at ease at the mention of Hayden. "I think she went out on the patio," he said.

And there was his cue.

Brody didn't feel bad leaving Becker in the clutches of the obviously plastered team owner. Sam Becker had been in the business long enough to know how to handle every situation thrown at him, and he usually handled them as well as he did the puck. The man was a pro, through and through.

Brody stepped away, glancing around the enormous ballroom for the patio entrance. Finally he spotted the French doors and made his way toward them.

His breath caught at the sight of Hayden's silver-clad figure. She was leaning against the railing overlooking the grounds of the estate, her long brown hair cascading down her bare shoulders, her delectable ass hugged by the silky material of her dress.

He paused at the doors, admiring her. To his surprise, she turned abruptly as if sensing his presence. Their eyes locked. And that's when he saw that her sooty black lashes were spiky with tears.

He was by her side in seconds. "Hey, what's wrong?" he murmured, resting both hands on her slender waist and pulling her toward him.

She sank into his embrace and pressed her face against his shoulder as she whispered, "What are you doing here?"

"I tagged along with a friend." He gently stroked her back. "And I'm glad I did. You look awful."

"Gee, thanks." Her voice came out muffled against the front of his tuxedo jacket.

"Oh, quit sulking. You know you're the sexiest woman at this party." He swept a hand over her firm bottom. The feel of her warm, curvy body made his pulse quicken, but he reminded himself that now was not the time.

"Now tell me the reason for *these*." He brushed the moisture from her lashes. "What happened?"

"Nothing."

"Hayden."

She lifted her head, chin tilting with defiance. "It's not a big deal, Brody. Just go inside and enjoy the party."

"Screw the party. I came here to see you."

"Well, I came here to see my dad." She turned her head away and stared out at the landscaped grounds.

The temperature had dipped drastically and the thick gray clouds littering the night sky hinted at a storm. Already the endless carpet of flowers on the lush lawn was starting to sway in the wind, sweeping a sweet aroma in the direction of the cobblestone patio.

It was the kind of night he usually enjoyed, the moistness of the air, the hint of rain and thunder, but he couldn't appreciate it when Hayden looked so distraught.

And beautiful. Damn, but she also looked beautiful. The slinky silver dress, the strappy heels, the shiny pink gloss coating her sensual lips. He wanted her, as strongly and as violently as he'd wanted her that first night in the bar. And not just sexually. Something about this woman brought out a protective, nurturing side in him he'd never known he possessed.

"Please, Hayden, tell me what happened."

She hesitated for so long he didn't think she'd say anything, but then her mouth opened and a string of words flew out like bullets spitting from a rifle.

"I think my father is drinking. He blew up at me when I questioned him about it, and then he made a few remarks about bad investments." She looked up, her eyes wide with anguish. "I'm worried he might have done some of the things everyone is accusing him of. God, Brody, I think there's actually a chance he might have bribed players and bet on games."

Brody's heart plummeted to the pit of his stomach. He shoved his fists into the pockets of his jacket, hoping to bring warmth to hands that had suddenly grown ice-cold. Damn it. He didn't want to have this conversation, especially with Hayden. Not when his own flags were raised.

So he just stood there in silence, waiting for her to continue and hoping she wouldn't ask him any questions that might force him to reveal something she probably wouldn't want to hear.

"I don't know what I should do," she murmured. "I don't

know how to help him. I don't know if he's guilty or innocent. I have no proof he has a drinking problem, but it's obvious after tonight that something is going on with my dad."

"You need to try talking to him when he's sober," Brody advised.

"I've tried," she moaned with frustration. "But he's determined not to be alone with me. And if by chance we *are* alone, he changes the subject every time I try to bring up my concerns. He won't let me in, Brody."

They stood there for a moment, silently, his arms wrapped around her slender body, her head tucked against his chest.

"I never thought my relationship with my dad would get to this point," she whispered. "He treated me like a stranger tonight. He snapped at me, *cursed* at me, looked right through me, as if I was just another headache he didn't want to deal with instead of his only daughter."

Brody threaded his fingers through her hair and stroked the soft tresses while he caressed her cheek with his other hand. "Did you two used to be close?" he asked.

"Very." She gave a soft sigh. "Nowadays, the team comes first."

"I'm sure that's not true."

She raised her chin and met his eyes. "Tell me, in all the years you've played for the Warriors, how many times has my father mentioned me?"

Discomfort coiled in his gut. "A bunch of times," he said vaguely.

Her eyes pierced his. "Really?"

"Fine, never," he admitted. "But I'm just a player to your father. He's certainly never treated me as a confidant."

"My dad is obsessed with the team," she said flatly. "He's always loved hockey, but when he was just a coach, it wasn't this bad. Now that he owns a team, he's almost fanatical. It used to be about the game for him. Somehow it's become about making money, being as powerful as he can be."

"Money and power aren't bad things to want," Brody had to point out.

"Sure, but what about family? Who are you supposed to rely on when the money and power are gone? Who will be there to love you?"

A cloud of sadness floated across her pretty face, her expression growing bittersweet. "You know he used to take me fishing a lot? Every summer we'd rent a cabin up at the lake, usually for an entire week. We moved around so much, but Dad always managed to find a place to go fishing. I hated to fish, but I pretended to love it because I wanted to spend the time with my dad."

She moved out of his arms and walked back to the railing, leaning forward and breathing in the cool night air. Without turning around, she continued speaking. "We stopped going once I moved to California. He always promised we'd go back to the lake during my visits home, but we never got around to it. Though we did go out on the yacht last summer." She made a face. "Sheila spent the entire trip talking about her nails. And Dad was on the phone the whole time."

The wistful note in her voice struck a chord of sympathy in him. Despite his busy schedule, he always made sure to return to Michigan a few times a year to see his parents. In the off-season he stayed with them for a month and spent every available moment with his folks. Although it irked him a little that his mom refused to quit her hairdressing job and take advantage of her son's wealth, he loved being home with his folks. And they were always thrilled to have him. He couldn't imagine his parents ever being too busy to hang out with their only son.

Presley Houston was an idiot. There was no other explanation for why the man would pass up the opportunity to spend time with a daughter as incredible as Hayden. She was intelligent, warm, passionate.

"I don't want to talk about this anymore," she burst out. "There's no point. Dad and I have been drifting apart for years. I was stupid to think he might actually value my support."

"I'm sure he does value it. It's obvious he's been drinking tonight, babe. It was probably the alcohol that made him snap at you like that."

"Alcohol is no excuse." She raked her fingers through her hair and scowled. "God, I need to get out of here. I want to go someplace where I can hear my own thoughts."

He glanced at the watch he'd picked up from the arena earlier in the morning, saw it wasn't that late, and threw an arm around Hayden's shoulders. "I know just the place."

She studied him warily, as if she suddenly remembered what had transpired between them two nights ago. He saw her hesitation, her reluctance to let him back in, but thankfully she made no protest when he took her hand. Instead, she clasped her warm fingers in his and said, "Let's go."

"THIS IS IT? The place where all my thoughts will become clear?" Hayden couldn't help but laugh as she followed Brody into the dark hockey arena twenty minutes later.

She'd let Brody drive her car, but hadn't thought to ask where he was taking her. She'd been content to sit in silence, trying to make sense of everything her father had said to her tonight. Now she kind of wished she'd been more curious about their destination.

The night guard had let them in. He'd seemed surprised at the sight of Brody Croft showing up at the practice arena way after hours, but didn't object to Brody's request. After digging up an old pair of boys' skates for Hayden from the equipment room, the guard had unlocked the doors leading out to the rink, flicked on the lights and disappeared with a smile.

"Trust me," Brody said. "There's nothing like the feel of ice under your skates to clear your head."

"Uh, I should probably mention I haven't ice-skated since I was a kid."

He looked aghast. "But your father owns a hockey team."

"We're not allowed to talk about my father anymore tonight, remember?"

"Right. Sorry." He flashed a charming grin. "Don't worry, I'll make sure you don't fall flat on your ass. Now sit."

Obligingly, she sat on the hard wooden bench and allowed Brody to remove her high heels. He caressed her stockinged feet for a moment, then reached for the skates the guard had found and helped her get a foot into one.

"It's tight," she complained.

"It belongs to a twelve-year-old boy. No figure skates here, so you'll have to make do."

Brody laced up the skates for her, then flopped down on the bench and kicked off his shiny black dress shoes. He'd retrieved a spare pair of skates from the bottom of his locker, and he put them on expertly, grinning when he saw her wobble to her feet. She made quite a fashion statement in her party dress and scuffed black hockey skates.

She held out her arms in an attempt to balance herself. "I'm totally going to fall on my butt," she said.

"I told you, I won't let it happen."

He stood, took two steps forward and unlatched the wooden gate that ringed the ice. Like the pro hockey player he was, he slid onto the rink effortlessly and skated backward for a moment while she stood at the gate and muttered, "Show-off."

Laughing, he moved toward her and held out his hand.

Body Check

She stared at his long, calloused fingers, wanting so badly to grab onto them and never let go. Yet another part of her was hesitant. When she'd picked him up at the bar five days ago, she hadn't imagined she'd see him after that first night. Or that she'd sleep with him again. Or that she might actually start to *like* him.

And she did like him. As much as she wanted to continue viewing Brody as nothing more than a one-night stand who'd rocked her world, he was becoming unnervingly real to her. He'd listened when she'd babbled about art, he'd let her cry on his shoulder, he'd brought her to this dark arena just to take her mind off her worries. One-night stands weren't supposed to do that, darn it!

"Come on, Hayden, I won't let you fall," he reassured her.

With a nod of acceptance, she took his hand. The second the blades of her skates connected with the sleek ice, she almost keeled over. Her arms windmilled, her legs spread open, and her skates moved in opposite directions as if trying to force her into the splits.

Brody promptly steadied her. "You're not very good at this, are you?"

"I told you I wasn't," she returned with an indignant glare. "Ask me to lecture you about Impressionist art, I can do that. But skating? I suck."

"Because you're trying to walk instead of glide," he pointed out. He clamped both his hands on her waist. "Quit doing that. Now, take my hand and do what I'm doing."

Slowly, they pushed forward again. While Brody's strides were effortless, hers were clumsy. Every few feet the tips of her skates would dig into the ice and she'd lurch forward, but Brody stayed true to his word. He didn't let her fall. Not even once.

"There you go," he exclaimed. "You're getting the hang of it."

She couldn't help smiling. Once she'd taken his advice and stopped treating the skates as shoes, her movements had become smoother. She felt giddy as they picked up speed, gliding along the ice like a pair of Thoroughbreds rounding a racetrack.

The boards, the benches, the bleachers—it all whizzed by her, the cool air in the arena reddening her cheeks. Although there were goose bumps dotting her bare arms, she didn't mind the cold temperature. The chill in the arena soothed her, cleansing her mind.

She cast a sideways glance at Brody and saw he was enjoying this, too. God, he looked delicious in his tuxedo. The jacket stretched over his broad shoulders and powerful chest, and the slightly loose trousers didn't hide his taut behind. She noticed his bow tie sat a little crooked, and resisted the urge to reach out and straighten it. She didn't want to move her arms and risk falling, so she tightened her fingers around his instead.

He looked down at their intertwined fingers, his mouth parting slightly, as if he wanted to speak but was being cautious. She knew exactly what was on his mind, because the same thing was running through hers. God help her, but she wanted this man in her bed again.

He was arrogant, yes, and pushy sometimes. But he also turned her on in the fiercest way, and every time he fixed those midnight-blue eyes on her, every time he wrapped those big arms around her, she melted.

They slowed their pace, and she forced her thoughts away from the dangerous territory they'd crossed into and tried to come up with a neutral topic of conversation. One that didn't make her think of Brody, naked and hard as he devoured her body with his tongue.

"When did you start playing?" she finally asked, deciding his career was as safe a subject as any.

"Pretty much the second I could walk, I was learning to skate. My dad used to take me to this outdoor rink near our house in Michigan." He chuckled. "Well, it wasn't much of a rink. Just a crappy pond that froze over every winter. My parents couldn't afford the membership fee for a real arena, so I used to practice my slap shots out on that pond while my dad sat on a folding chair in the snow and read car magazines."

"Did you play on a school team?"

"Uh, what team *wasn't* I on?" He dropped her hand and began skating lazy circles around her. "In high school I played hockey, rugby and baseball in the spring. Oh, and I was on the lacrosse team until the practices started to interfere with my hockey schedule."

"Huh. So you were one of *those* guys. I bet you were voted Most Likely to Become a Pro Athlete in your high school yearbook."

"Actually, I was."

He told her a bit about his early years in the league, then made her laugh with some anecdotes about his parents and their overwhelming pride in him. At times a twinge of bitterness seeped into his voice, giving her the feeling that his childhood was tougher than he let on, but she didn't pry. She remembered him telling her money had been tight for his family, and it was obviously something he didn't like talking about.

A few minutes later, a cramp seized her leg and she wobbled to a stop, leaning against the splintered sideboards as she rubbed the back of her thigh. On the West Coast she jogged every morning before heading over to the university, but she was obviously not in the great shape she'd believed herself to be in. Her legs were aching and they'd only been skating around for twenty minutes.

"Wanna take a break?" Brody offered.

"Please."

They stepped off the ice and climbed up to the bleachers. Brody was an expert when it came to walking on skates. She wasn't so fortunate. She almost pitched forward a half-dozen times before she finally sank down on the bench and exhaled with relief.

"I think I pulled a muscle in my butt," she grumbled.

"Want me to rub the kinks out?"

She stiffened, wishing his voice didn't contain that husky note of erotic promise. Damn it. She couldn't fall into bed with him again. As thrilling as it would be to continue exploring the sexual canvas they seemed so skilled at painting together, she couldn't help remembering what had happened the last time she'd given in.

As if sensing her concerns, Brody let out an unsteady breath. "I'm sorry about the other night, Hayden. I acted like an ass."

She didn't reply, just offered a pointed nod.

"I know I'm rough around the edges. I'm demanding, I like getting my way and I'm definitely not the kind of man who's content with playing second fiddle." He held up his hand before she could cut in. "I shouldn't have hassled you about, you know, *Doug*—" he said the name like it was contagious "—but damn it, Hayden, it drives me crazy knowing there's someone else in your life. I'm not used to sharing."

"You're not sharing. Doug and I are on a break."

"There's a giant difference between a break and a breakup." He frowned. "Do you think you'll go back to him?"

"I don't know." Deep down, though, she knew the answer to that question and it probably wasn't one Doug was going to like. But she couldn't talk about it, not now, and definitely not with Brody.

She could tell he wasn't happy with her answer, but instead of challenging her the way he had two nights ago, he simply nodded. "Guess I'll have to live it with then. And I *can* live with it, especially if it means I get to spend more time with you."

"But why? What do you see in me that makes you so sure we should pursue this?" She wasn't prone to insecurities, but she couldn't quite figure out why this sexy giant of a man wanted *her* and not some supermodel.

"What do I see in you?" He leaned closer. "You want a list? I can do that. I'll skip how beautiful you are. That's all just superficial."

"I'm not above superficial."

He chuckled. "So you'd like me to start with your wild green eyes that have been knocking me out since the second you strolled up to that pool table?"

She bit her lower lip. "Okay."

Carefully, he took a lock of her hair between his fingers. "Or should I start with this silky brown hair that keeps making me want to reach out and touch it?" His attention dropped to her chest. "Or these breasts I can't get enough of?" The fingers that had been toying with her hair moved to brush over her nipples, which were pushing against the thin fabric of her dress. "Or maybe these lips that keep begging me to taste them?" He brushed a thumb over her bottom lip.

Her lips parted, her eyelids grew heavy, and thankfully she was sitting down because she didn't think she could hold up the weight of her body in her weakened state. This man was one smooth talker.

"Any of those places are fine," she breathed.

Strong hands cupped her face. "Then there's the intelligence that practically radiates from you. Did I ever tell you smart women seriously turn me on?" His thumbs began caressing her cheeks and he bent to whisper close to her ear. "You're a walking contradiction, Hayden. Prim and proper one moment, wild and uninhibited the next. And the more I get to know you, the more I like what I find."

Each of his words softened her heart, and every warm wisp of his breath against her ear made her quiver with need.

"When I left the penthouse the other night you wouldn't let me kiss you," he said, his lips just inches from hers. "I promised myself I wouldn't kiss you again until you asked me to."

"Kiss me, Brody. Please…"

In an instant, his lips touched hers, unleashing a trickle of soothing warmth that rivaled a shot of fine brandy. She moved a hand to his cheek and relished the light prickles of his five-o'clock shadow. And despite his tender touch, the hardness of his chest and the roughness of his cheek reminded her he was all man.

He groaned softly, and deepened the kiss. She parted her lips, inviting him to explore. She wanted to surround herself in his protective embrace. Her father's behavior tonight had frightened her, hurt her, but Brody's kiss made her forget about everything except this moment, the feel of his mouth on hers, the flick of his tongue and warm caress of his fingers on her cheek.

She slid her hand to the nape of his neck, allowing the soft curls to tickle her fingers. She took hold and pulled the kiss deeper. His slow, heavy groan spoke of acceptance and thanks.

His hands moved down her sides, and he lightly caressed the sides of her breasts with his thumbs, sending a pulsing charge through her system. It was the most gentle he'd ever been with her, a stark change from his rough, drugging kisses and eager exploratory hands. And as much as she was enjoying the kiss, she wanted more. She lowered her hands to the growing bulge in his tuxedo trousers, but he moved her hand away and broke the kiss.

For a moment, her eyes wouldn't open and her mouth

wouldn't close. She was held in transition, her body still tingling from his touch. As she slowly raised her lids, she saw the deep sense of need in his eyes. Need that matched hers.

"Close your eyes," he murmured.

"Why?"

"Just do it."

Curious, she let her eyelids flutter shut. She heard a rustling sound, felt Brody move closer and lean forward, then gasped when his hand circled her ankle.

"Don't move." His voice was barely above a whisper.

She swallowed. Waiting. Sighing when he ran his big warm hand up her leg, bunching her dress between his fingers as he traveled north. His touch suffused her with heat, made her pulse race. He glided his fingers along her inner thigh, leaving a trail of fire in his wake. And then his palm was pressed against her lace panties.

"What are you doing?" she breathed out.

"De-stressing you." His tongue was suddenly on her ear, flicking against the tender lobe before suckling it.

Silent laughter shook her as her eyes popped open. "What's with you and your need to intimately touch me in public?"

He rubbed his palm against her mound, his breath hot against her ear as he whispered, "Want me to stop?"

"God, no."

"Good."

He moved his hand under her panties and pushed one long finger deep into her hot channel.

"You're always so ready, so tight and wet," he muttered.

Before she could tell him that *he* was the reason she was always ready, he covered her mouth with his. The kiss sucked the breath from her lungs, soft and warm and thrilling, his tongue matching the strokes of his finger. Long, deep, languid strokes. He slid another finger into her aching sex, kissing her, murmuring encouraging pleas against her lips, and then his thumb circled her clit and she exploded.

She cried out against his mouth, rocked against his fingers, her mind nothing but a big pile of mush while her body convulsed.

When she finally came back down to earth, she found Brody watching her with surprising tenderness. "You're gorgeous, Hayden," he murmured, withdrawing his fingers and fixing her dress.

Her heart squeezed. She opened her mouth to thank him— for the compliment, the orgasm, the shoulder to lean on— but he didn't give her the chance. "Will you let me come home with you tonight? No big deal if you say no. I just, uh, thought I'd ask."

He was so polite, so careful, when the heat in his eyes and his unsteady breathing told her he'd probably die from arousal if she said no. But it touched her that he'd asked instead of assumed.

"If we go to the penthouse," she began slowly, "what exactly will we do?"

A sensual twinkle filled his eyes. His voice lowered to a husky pitch as he said, "Well, I noticed there's a removable showerhead in the master bathroom."

She burst out laughing. "Do you make it a habit of scoping out the shower when you use other people's bathrooms?"

"Who doesn't?"

9

A FEW DAYS LATER Hayden was standing outside the lavish ten-bedroom home her father had bought for Sheila. It was only a few blocks from the Gallagher Club, in the heart of one of the wealthiest neighborhoods in Chicago.

Hayden had finally decided to talk to Sheila to learn more about her father's drinking problem. Although a part of her still didn't fully trust her stepmother, she knew this conversation was long overdue. If she had more information, maybe she could find a way to help her dad. And if his recent behavior was any indication, her father definitely needed some help.

Sheila answered the door wearing sweats, her expression clearly conveying her surprise at seeing her soon-to-be-ex-stepdaughter standing on the pillared doorstep.

"Hayden…what are you doing here?"

She fumbled awkwardly with the strap of her leather purse. "I think we should talk."

With a nod, Sheila opened the door wider so Hayden could step inside. The enormous front parlor, with its sparkling crystal chandelier, was as intimidating as it had been the first time she'd seen it. The white walls were devoid of artwork, a sight that made her frown. She'd encouraged her father to pick up pieces at auctions she had recommended, but it looked as if he hadn't bothered.

"So what's on your mind?" Sheila asked after they'd entered the living room.

Hayden sat on one of the fluffy teal love seats, waited for Sheila to sink down on the matching sofa, then cleared her throat. "I want you to tell me about my father's drinking."

Her stepmother raked one delicate hand through her blond hair, then clasped her hands together in her lap. "What do you want to know, Hayden?"

"When did he start?"

"Last year, about the same time the pharmaceutical company he'd invested in went bankrupt. He lost a lot of money, tried to recoup it by making more investments, and lost that, too."

Hayden fought back a wave of guilt, realizing that she'd had no idea any of this had been going on. Her father had always sounded so jovial on the phone, as if he had no cares in the world.

Was she a terrible daughter for not seeing through the lies?

"He didn't want to worry you," Sheila added as if reading her mind.

"So that's when he started drinking?"

Her stepmother nodded. "At first it was just a drink or two in the evenings, but the worse the situation got, the more he drank. I tried talking to him about it. I told him the drinking was becoming a problem, but he refused to hear it. That's when…" Sheila's voice drifted.

"That's when what?"

"He went to bed with another woman."

A silence fell between them, but this time Hayden didn't try to defend her father. That day at the law office, she'd believed Sheila to be a heartless lying bitch, accusing Pres of adultery, but after his blowup at the Gallagher Club, Hayden couldn't deny her dad had a problem. And if that problem had driven him to cheat, she needed to accept it. No point sticking her head in the sand and pretending things were okay, when they obviously weren't.

So she leaned back and allowed Sheila to continue.

"He told me what he'd done the next morning, blamed me for his infidelity, said my constant nagging forced him to do it." Sheila made an exasperated sound. "And he kept denying he had a drinking problem. I might have been able to forgive him for the affair, but I couldn't look away while he destroyed the life we'd built."

"What happened?"

"I confronted him again, ordered him to get help for his alcohol problem."

"I take it he didn't agree."

"Oh, no." Sheila's pretty features twisted in distress and anger. "He only got worse. A couple nights later, I came home from the gym and found him in the study, drunk out of his mind. That's when he confessed about the games he'd fixed."

A rush of protectiveness rose inside her. "It could have been the alcohol talking. Maybe he didn't know what he was saying."

"He knew." Her stepmother offered a knowing look. "And what he said was confirmed to me by a player on the team."

"The one you're sleeping with?" Hayden couldn't help cracking.

Two red circles splotched Sheila's cheeks. "Don't judge me, Hayden. I may have turned to another man, but only after your father betrayed me. Pres pushed me away long before I did what I did."

Her mouth closed. Sheila was right. Who the hell was she to judge? What happened within a marriage wasn't anybody's business but the people who were married, and she couldn't make assumptions or draw conclusions about a situation she hadn't been a part of.

And if she were to draw conclusions, it startled her to realize she actually believed Sheila. She might not approve of Sheila's contesting of the prenup or love for all things luxurious, but Hayden couldn't bring herself to brush off what her stepmother had told her.

If her father had really bribed players, what would happen to him if—when?—the investigation revealed the truth? Would he get off with a fine, or would she be visiting him in prison this time next year? Fear trickled through her, settling in her stomach and making her nauseous.

With a sympathetic look and a soft sigh, Sheila said, "Things aren't always as they seem. *People* aren't always as they seem." She averted her eyes, but not before Hayden saw the tears coating her lashes. "Do you want to know why I married your father, Hayden?"

For his money?

She quickly swallowed back the nasty remark, but Sheila must have seen it in her eyes because she said, "The money was part of it. I know, you probably won't understand, but I didn't have a lot of financial security growing up. My parents were dirt-poor. My father ran off with what little money we did have, and I was working by the time I was thirteen." She shrugged. "Maybe I was selfish for wanting a man who could take care of me, for wanting some security."

Sheila paused, shaking her head as if reprimanding herself. "But the money wasn't the only reason. If it was, I would have married one of the many rich jerks who showed up at the bar I waitressed at, pinching my ass and trying to get me into bed. But I didn't marry one of those guys. I married your dad."

"Why?" Hayden asked quietly, strangely fascinated by her stepmother's story.

"Because he was one of the good guys. I wasted so much time on the bad boys, the guys who light your body on fire but end up burning you out in the end. I was sick of it, so I decided to find myself a Mr. Nice—a decent, stable man who might not be the most exciting man in the world but who'd always be there for me, always put me first, financially and emotionally."

A wave of discomfort crested in Hayden's stomach, slowly rising inside her until it lodged in her throat like a wad of old chewing gum. She'd never thought she'd have anything in common with this woman, but everything Sheila had just said mirrored the thoughts Hayden had been having for years now. Wasn't that why she'd chosen Doug—because he was nice, decent and stable? Because he'd always put her first?

"But nice men aren't necessarily the *right* men," Sheila finished softly. "Nice men make mistakes, too. They can take you for granted and they can play with your emotions, just like those bad boys I wanted so badly to get away from."

She swiped at the tears staining her cheeks and lifted her chin. "Your father hurt me, Hayden. If he'd truly loved me, he would've seen that I was only trying to help him, that I wanted to be there for him the way I thought he'd be there for me. But he wasn't there for me. I feel awful about not being able to get him help for the drinking, I really do, but I couldn't take the way he was treating me. He went to another woman, he lied about his criminal actions, and now he's making me out to be a selfish gold digger."

With a bitter smile, Sheila leaned forward and stared at her with sad blue eyes. "How's that for Mr. Nice?"

HAYDEN LEFT with no real idea how to help her dad with his drinking problem, even more concerned about his possible criminal activities. She was just as confused and upset as she'd been when she'd rung the doorbell. Her cell phone rang the second she got into her car, and just when she thought this day from hell couldn't get any worse, it did. The number flashing on the phone's screen belonged to Doug.

Oh, God, she couldn't deal with this right now. But she couldn't keep avoiding her issues any longer, either. Today she'd finally opened her eyes to the downward spiral of her father's life, started to accept that her father might have become an alcoholic, adulterer and criminal.

Maybe it was time to face the other man in her life. She'd called Doug back last week, but she'd phoned in the afternoon knowing he would be in a seminar for one of the summer courses he was teaching. Maybe it made her a chicken but she hadn't been ready to talk to him yet, opting instead to leave a brief message on his machine.

She hadn't mentioned Brody in the message, either, mostly because the thought of telling Doug about Brody— on his answering machine no less—had made her palms grow damp. It would've been one thing if the situation with Brody hadn't gone beyond that first night, but it had. It'd been over a week since she'd approached him in the bar, and somehow, during that time, her casual fling had... changed.

She couldn't pinpoint when the change had occurred. All she knew was that since they'd gone skating after the Gallagher Club party, she and Brody had been having fun not only in the bedroom, but out of it. They'd gone back to the Lakeshore Lounge for dinner, gone skating at Millennium Park. Brody had even taken her to the Art Institute of Chicago, where he'd spent the entire day following her from painting to painting and listening to her rave about each one.

What *wasn't* fun, however, was having him fly to another city every other day. He'd had three away games this past week and each time he'd left to catch his flight she'd had to bite her tongue. Had to remind herself that no matter how much she was enjoying being with Brody, this was still a fling. And flings always came to an end at some point.

Her phone continued to chime, the ring tone speeding up to signal that voice mail would kick in soon.

Hayden took a deep breath.

She had to pick up. Doug had already left her three messages since she'd called him back, his voice growing more and more concerned with each call. He probably thought she was lying dead in a ditch somewhere, and she was disgusted with herself for her inability to deal with this Doug dilemma.

No more stalling. She'd already endured one unwanted confrontation today. Might as well make it two for two.

She hit the talk button on her cell phone.

"Thank God," Doug said when she answered. "I was beginning to think something terrible had happened to you."

His obvious relief caused guilt to buzz around in her belly like a swarm of angry wasps. She felt like total slime for making him worry like this.

"Don't worry, I'm fine," she replied, her fingers trembling against the phone. "Didn't you get my message?"

"I got it, but I've called you a few times since, Hayden."

"I know. I'm sorry I didn't return your calls. Things have been hectic."

"I can imagine." He paused. "Some of the papers here are running stories about your father, honey."

"Yeah, it's happening here, too. I'm starting to get worried," she admitted.

Confiding in him came as naturally as brushing her teeth in the morning. She'd always been able to talk to Doug about everything. Whether it was problems at the university or something as minor as a bad haircut, he was always there to listen. It was one of the things she liked about him.

Liked.

The word hung in her mind, making her tap one hand against the steering wheel. She *liked* everything about this man. His patience, his tenderness, his generosity. And she was certain that once he finally decided the time was right for them to get physical, she'd like that, too. And that was the problem. She wasn't sure she could spend the rest of her life with a man she simply *liked*. Sure, sometimes love took time to develop, feelings could grow, friends could realize they were soul mates…at least that's what she'd always believed.

After meeting Brody, she was starting to reconsider.

She didn't just *like* sleeping with Brody. The sex was wild, passionate, all-consuming. When Brody kissed her, when he wrapped those big muscular arms around her, the ground beneath her feet fell away, her body sizzled like asphalt in a heat wave, and her heart soared higher than a fighter jet.

When Doug kissed her…none of those things happened. His kisses were sweet and tender, and she really did *like* them—damn, there was that word again.

"Honey, are you there?"

She forced her mind back to the moment, to this conversation she'd been putting off for too long. "Sorry, I just spaced out for a second. What were you saying?"

"I want to come visit you."

She nearly dropped the phone. "What? Why?"

There was an annoyed pause. "Because I miss you." Another beat, this time strained. "I was hoping maybe you missed me, too."

"I…" She couldn't bring herself to lie, but she couldn't quite tell the truth, either.

Fortunately, Doug continued speaking. "I keep thinking about what you said before you left, Hayden. I know you asked for space, but…" A heavy breath resonated from the other end of the line. "I think space will only lead to distance, and the last thing I want is distance between us. Maybe if I come out there, maybe if we sat down together and talked this through, we could figure out why you're feeling the way you are."

"Doug…" She searched for the right thing to say. Was there even a right thing? "This is something I need to figure out on my own."

"I'm part of this relationship, too," he pointed out.

"I know, but…"

Tell him about Brody.

Damn it. Why did her conscience have to chime in right now? She already felt terrible enough, sleeping with a man a few short weeks after telling her boyfriend she needed space. Could she really confess her sins, *now,* when Doug was so eager to patch things up between them?

You don't have a choice.

As much as she wanted to fight her conscience, she knew that little voice was right. She couldn't hide something this important from him. He needed to know. No, he *deserved* to know.

"I've been seeing someone," she blurted out.

Dead silence.

"Doug?"

A muffled cough sounded from the other end. "Pardon me?"

"I'm seeing someone. Here, in Chicago." She swallowed. "It's only been a couple of weeks, and it's nothing serious, but I think you should know."

"Who is he?"

"He's… It doesn't matter who he is. And I want you to know that I didn't plan on this. When I asked for space, the last thing I wanted was to jump into another relationship—"

"Relationship?" He sounded distressed. "I thought you said it wasn't serious!"

"I did. I mean, it's not." She tried to control her voice,

feeling so unbelievably guilty it was hard to get out the next words. "It just sort of…happened."

When he didn't say anything, she hurried on. The pretzel of guilt in her chest tightened into a vise around her heart. "Are you still there?"

"I'm here." He spoke slowly, curtly. "Thank you for telling me."

Her throat tightened. "Doug…" She trailed off, not sure what to say. Not sure there was anything else *to* say.

"I have to go, Hayden," he said after a long pause. "I can't talk to you right now. I need time to digest all this."

"I understand." She gulped, bringing much-needed moisture to her arid mouth. "Call me when you're ready to…"

To what? Forgive her? Yell at her?

"To talk," she finished awkwardly.

He hung up without saying goodbye, and she sat there for a moment, listening to the silence before her cell phone finally disconnected the call. She shoved the phone back into her purse and leaned against the plush driver's seat, raking both hands through her hair.

Between Sheila and Doug, she felt as if she'd spent the afternoon waving a red flag in front of a bull determined to gore her to pieces.

At least nobody could call her a coward.

10

THE ATMOSPHERE in the locker room was subdued, the usual pregame chatter absent as the players changed into their gear and spoke in hushed voices to one another. Brody would've liked to blame the serious mood on nerves; the series was 3–2, and if they won tonight's game they'd move on to the second round of play-offs. But he knew it wasn't the pressure that was weighing everyone down.

Fifteen minutes earlier, a league executive had informed the team that an investigation into the bribery claims was officially under way. Players would be interviewed privately throughout the week, and if the allegations bore any weight, proper disciplinary actions would be taken.

And possible criminal charges executed.

Lacing up his skates, Brody glanced discreetly over at Craig Wyatt, who was adjusting his shin pads. Wyatt hadn't spoken one word since the announcement, his sharp features furrowed with silent concern, his big body moving clumsily as he dressed. He was definitely worried about something.

Damn, winning this game tonight was going to be seriously tough. The morale was lower than the murky depths of the ocean, the players behaving as if individual axs were hovering over their heads.

Which one of them had taken a bribe? And was it only one? For all he knew, half the guys could be involved. The notion caused his blood to boil. You had to be a real son of a bitch to deliberately throw a game. The media had claimed only one or two games had been fixed, and early in the season, but it didn't matter to Brody when or how many. All it took was one game. One game could be the difference between making the play-offs and ending the season in defeat. It was a good thing they'd played well enough to make up for those early losses.

"Let's give them hell tonight," Wyatt said quietly as everyone began shuffling out of the locker room.

Give them hell? That was the big pep talk for the night?

From the wary looks on the other men's faces, Wyatt's words of encouragement were about as effective as dry glue.

"Craig, wait a second," Brody said, intercepting the team captain before he could exit the room.

"We've got a game to play, Croft."

"It can wait. I just need a minute."

The captain tucked his helmet under his arm. "Fine."

What now? Did he come out and ask Wyatt about the bribery bullshit? Bring up the affair with Sheila Houston?

Brody realized that maybe he should've come up with a game plan before he initiated this conversation.

"Well?" Wyatt said, looking annoyed.

He decided to take a page out of his mom's policy book: honesty. "I saw you with Sheila at the arena last week."

Wyatt's face went ashen. Then he swallowed. "I don't know what you're talking about."

"Don't bother with denial. I *saw* you." The collar of Brody's jersey suddenly felt hot and the padding underneath his uniform became tight. Sucking in a breath, he added, "How long have you been having an affair with Presley's wife?"

The air in the locker room grew tense, stifling. Wyatt's face was still white, but his eyes flashed with anger and indignation. Shoving his helmet onto his head, he shot Brody a frown. "This is none of your business."

"It is if you're the player who came forward and confirmed Sheila's accusations."

A long silence fell, dragging on too long for Brody's comfort. Wyatt's face was completely devoid of emotion, but it didn't stay that way for long. After several more beats, a look of weary resignation clouded Wyatt's eyes.

"Fine. You win. It was me." The captain's large hands trembled as he fumbled to snap his helmet into place. "I went to the league, Brody. I'm the reason this damn investigation is starting up."

Brody swallowed. His gut was suddenly burning, but he couldn't figure out if he felt angry, betrayed or relieved. He studied Wyatt's face and quietly asked, "How did you know Sheila was telling the truth?"

"I had my suspicions at the beginning of the season, when we lost a couple of games we had no business losing. And Sheila confirmed it."

Wyatt exhaled slowly, his breath coming out shaky. "I can't play on the same team as a few assholes that would sabotage us for money. I can't play for an owner who is willing to cheat."

Brody couldn't help but believe him. Wyatt seemed legitimately torn up about all this.

"You know who took the bribes then?" Brody asked.

Wyatt quickly averted his eyes. "Just drop it, Brody. Let the league conduct its investigation. You don't want to get involved in this."

"Wyatt…"

"I'm serious. It'll all get cleared up eventually. Just…drop it," he said again. Wyatt stepped toward the door. "Now get your ass out there. We've got a game to win."

Brody watched the other man stalk off. A part of him

wanted to run after Wyatt and shake some names out of the guy, but another part was telling him to let it go. Trying to force Wyatt to confide in him wouldn't achieve anything. Craig would just get angrier, more volatile, and the last thing Brody wanted to do was piss him off. Wyatt was a gifted athlete, one of the best in the league, and with play-offs happening, Brody wanted the Warriors captain focused on the game, not personal junk.

And he needed to focus on the game, too. Lately he'd spent too much time worrying, doubting his fellow players, wondering if his career would be blown to hell by the scandal. He had the truth on his side, the knowledge that he'd played clean and hard all season, but that didn't mean squat. Guilty by association, or whatever the hell they called it.

He would be a free agent in a few months, but another franchise might be loath to pick him up knowing he'd been investigated for bribery. All he could hope was that the investigation was quick, painless, and that his name wouldn't be dragged through the mud for something he hadn't done.

Cursing softly, he left the locker room and headed down the hallway leading out to the Warriors bench. As he entered the arena, the deafening cheers of the crowd assaulted his eardrums. The Lincoln Center was filled to capacity tonight, the bleachers a sea of silver and blue. Seeing the fans supporting the team by donning their jersey warmed Brody's heart, but it also renewed his anger.

All these fans who'd come out here tonight—the people yelling words of encouragement, the kids clapping their hands wildly—deserved a team they could be proud of.

Unfortunately, there was very little to feel proud about, especially when ten minutes into the first period the Warriors were already down by two goals.

And it was one of those games that went from bad to worse.

The Vipers cleaned the ice with the Warriors. By the second period, Brody was drenched in sweat, gasping for air and wanting to bodycheck everyone from the ref to his coach. It didn't even seem to matter how fast they skated, how many times they rushed the net, how many bullets they slapped at the Vipers' goalie. The opposing team was faster, sharper, better. They had the advantage of good morale on their side.

When the third period rolled around, Brody could tell most of his teammates had given up.

"This game blows," Becker sighed once they'd sunk down onto the bench after a line change.

Brody squirted a stream of water into his mouth then tossed the bottle aside. "Tell me about it," he muttered.

"So did you take the advice I gave you?" Becker asked, his eyes still on the game in front of them.

"Advice?"

"About staying away from Presley's daughter," Becker reminded him.

Stay away from Hayden? Brody almost laughed out loud. He was tempted to tell his friend that at the moment he was doing everything in his power to stay *close* to her. And he was succeeding. For the most part, anyway.

No matter how often Hayden called their relationship a fling, Brody couldn't view anything between them as casual. For the first time in his life, he was with a woman he actually liked hanging out with. Sure, he liked the sex, too—fine, he *loved* the sex—but there had been moments during the past week when he was shocked to realize there were other things he enjoyed just as much. Such as watching art documentaries with her. Holding her while she slept. Teaching her to ice-skate even though she wasn't much of a student.

She was funny and smart and her eyes lit up when she talked about something she loved. And it troubled him how that light left her eyes whenever an away game came up. He'd had to leave town three times this week, and although Hayden never said a single word about it, he could tell it bothered her. But he had no idea how to make it better, short of retiring from hockey—and he wasn't about to do that.

Yet he had to do something. Hayden seemed determined to keep him at a distance, at least when it came to admitting they were in a relationship, and he desperately wanted to bridge that gap, make her realize just how important she was becoming to him.

"Are you even listening to me?" Becker's loud sigh drew him out of his thoughts.

Brody lifted his head. "Huh? Oh, right, Pres's daughter. About that… As much as I value your advice, I…I can't stay away from her, man." He shrugged sheepishly. "I'm seeing her tonight, in fact."

Becker frowned, but before he could respond, the ref's whistle pierced the air and both men looked over to see who'd taken a penalty. Wyatt. Big surprise there.

There was no more time for chatting as Stan tossed them both back onto the ice for the penalty kill, and although Becker scored a ridiculously incredible shorthanded goal, it wasn't enough. The buzzer went off indicating the end of the third period and the game. The final score was a pathetic 5–1, Vipers.

IT DIDN'T TAKE a genius to figure out the Warriors had lost the game. Hayden could see it on every face that left the Lincoln Center. Her father was probably dreadfully disappointed.

She was tempted to go up to the owner's box and offer some sort of condolences, but she was in no mood to see her dad right now. If she were, she'd be inside the arena instead of loitering in the parking lot and waiting for Brody.

She leaned against the back of his SUV and scanned the

rear entrance of the building, willing him to come out. God, this day had been hell. Listening to Sheila's awful tale of Presley's drinking, hearing Doug's heart break on the other end of the telephone line. She didn't want to think about any of it anymore. That's why she'd left the penthouse and driven over here. The need to see Brody and lose herself in his arms was so strong she'd been willing to wait for over an hour.

When he finally emerged from the building she almost sobbed with relief. And when his midnight-blue eyes lit up at the sight of her, she wanted to sob with joy. Maybe their lives didn't mesh, maybe their careers were colossally different and their goals weren't aligned, but she couldn't remember the last time a man had looked so happy to see her.

"Hey, this is a surprise," he said, approaching her.

"Hi." She paused. "I'm sorry about the game. Does this mean the team is out of the play-offs?"

"No, the series is tied. We've got another chance to win it tomorrow."

"That's good."

For some reason, she couldn't tear her eyes from him. He looked good tonight. His hair was damp, his perfect lips slightly chapped. He'd confessed to licking them too much during games and the first time she'd seen him rubbing on lip balm she'd almost had a laughter-induced coronary. But she liked moments like that, seeing Brody out of his manly man element.

Tonight, though, he was all man. Clad in a loose wool suit that couldn't hide the defined muscles underneath it. The navy-blue color made his eyes seem even brighter, more vivid. Brody had told her that with play-offs around the corner, the league expected the players to look professional on and off the ice and, she had to admit, she liked seeing him in a suit as much as she enjoyed his faded jeans and ab-hugging T-shirts.

Unable to stop herself, she stood on her tiptoes and planted a kiss square on his mouth.

"What happened to not being seen together in public?"

She faltered, realizing this was the first time they'd ever engaged in a public display of affection and startled that she'd been the one to initiate it. "I…had a bad day" was all she could come up with.

Brody grinned. "That's all it takes for us to come out of the closet, you having a bad day? Damn, I should've pissed you off a long time ago." His expression sobered. "What happened?"

"I'll tell you all about it later. Let's get out of here first."

"Meet you at the hotel?"

She was about to nod when something stopped her. "No. How about we go to your place tonight?"

He seemed baffled, and she honestly couldn't say she blamed him. Since she'd agreed to explore this…thing…between them, they'd been doing things her way. Brody had asked her over to his house a dozen times but she'd always convinced him to stay at the penthouse instead. She'd felt that being on her own turf, sticking to familiar surroundings, would stop things from getting more serious than she wanted.

Yet suddenly she found herself longing to see Brody's house, to be with him on *his* turf.

"All right." He unlocked the door of his SUV. "You want to follow me in your car?"

"Why don't we just take yours? We can come back for my rental tomorrow."

His eyebrows soared north again, while his jaw dipped south. "You're just full of surprises tonight, aren't you? You do realize your father will see your car in the lot and know you didn't go home?"

"I don't live my life to please my dad." She sounded more bitter than she'd intended, so she softened her tone.

"Let's not talk about him. All I want to think about tonight is you and me."

He gently tucked an unruly strand of hair behind her ear. "I like the sound of that."

The drive to Brody's Hyde Park home was a short one. When they pulled up in front of his place, Hayden was pleasantly surprised to see a large Victorian with a wraparound porch and a second-floor balcony. Flowers were beginning to bloom in the beds flanking the front steps, giving the house a cheerful, inviting air.

"Weren't expecting this, were you?" he said as he shut off the engine.

"Not really." She smiled. "Don't tell me you actually planted all those flowers yourself?"

"Heck no. I didn't choose the house, either. My mom flew out here when I was drafted by the Warriors, and she found the house. She did all the gardening, too, and she visits once a year to make sure I haven't destroyed her handiwork."

They got out of the car and drifted up the cobbled path toward the front door. Inside, Hayden's surprise only grew. Decorated in warm shades of red and brown, the interior boasted a roomy living room complete with a stone fireplace, a wide maple staircase leading upstairs and an enormous modern kitchen with two glass doors opening onto the backyard.

"Want something to drink?" he offered, crossing the tiled floor toward the fridge. "I don't have that herbal tea you like, but I can brew you a cup of Earl Grey."

"How about something stronger?"

He gave a faint smile. "You really did have a bad day, didn't you?"

He moved to the wine rack on the counter and chose a bottle of red wine. Grabbing two glasses from the cupboard over the sink, he glanced over his shoulder. "Are you going to tell me about it or do I have to tickle it out of you?"

"Hmm." She chewed on her bottom lip. "I'm kind of leaning toward the tickle." Her expression sobered when he shot her an evil look. "Fine, fine… I'll tell you."

Brody poured the wine, handed her a glass and then led her to the patio doors. The backyard was spacious, adorned with more flowers that Brody's mom must have planted. The fence surrounding the area was so high she couldn't see the neighboring yards, not even from the raised deck on the patio. At the very far corner of the lawn stood an idyllic-looking gazebo surrounded by thick foliage.

They stepped onto the deck, where a surprisingly warm breeze met them. It was a gorgeous night, the warmest she'd experienced since coming home, and she breathed in the fresh air and tilted her head to admire the cloudless sky before finally releasing a long breath.

"I paid a visit to my stepmother today," she said.

She filled him in on the details, leaving her conversation with Doug for the end. Brody's jaw tensed at the mention of Doug's name, but as he'd promised her that night they'd skated at the arena, he didn't freak out about it. When she'd finished, he set his wineglass on the wide rail ringing the deck and gently caressed her shoulders.

"You didn't have to tell him about us," he said.

The remark surprised her. "Of course I did. I told *you* about *him*. Doesn't he deserve the same courtesy?" She lifted her glass to her lips.

"You're right." He paused. "So it's over between you and Doug?"

"Yes," she admitted. "He hung up on me, which is very uncharacteristic of him. I don't think he's happy with me at the moment."

When Brody didn't answer, she put down her wine and reached up to cup his strong chin with her hands. "You're not happy with me, either, are you?"

He looked her in the eye and said, "I *am* happy, babe."

"You are?"

"I love being with you, Hayden." He blew out a ragged breath. "And I'm glad it's over with Doug. It was frustrating sometimes, knowing there was another man in your life. And not just any man, but a man who works in your field, who shares your passion for art and is probably much better at those intellectual conversations you're always trying to have with me. I feel like a dumb oaf in comparison."

A pained look flashed across his handsome face, and it took her a moment to realize it wasn't really pain she saw in his eyes, but vulnerability. The idea that Brody Croft, the most masculine man she'd ever met, could be vulnerable stole the breath from her lungs. God, did he actually feel inadequate? Had *she* made him feel that way?

Her heart squeezed at the thought and she found herself reaching for him. She twined her arms around his strong, corded neck and brushed her lips over his. "You're not a dumb oaf," she murmured, running her fingers over the damp hair curling at the nape of his neck.

"Then you won't mind if I make an intelligent, rational point about how difficult you're being."

She raised her chin. "And what on earth am I being difficult about?"

Brody let out a breath. "Come on, Hayden, you think I don't see that look in your eyes whenever I have a plane to catch? Every time I left town this week you withdrew from me. I felt it."

Discomfort coiled inside her belly, causing her to drop her arms from his neck. Why was he bringing this up?

"See, you're doing it again," he pointed out, smiling faintly.

"I just…" She inhaled slowly. "I don't see why it's an issue."

"If it keeps you from entering into a relationship with me, then it *is* an issue."

A tiny spark of panic lit up inside her. "We agreed to keep things casual."

"*You* agreed to keep an open mind."

"Trust me, my mind is very open."

"Your heart isn't." His tone was so gentle she felt like crying.

She drifted over to the railing, curling her fingers over the cool steel. Brody moved so they were standing side by side, but she couldn't look at him. She knew exactly where this conversation was going, and she had no idea how to proceed.

"I think we have something really good here," he said quietly, resting his hand on hers and slowly stroking her knuckles. "You've got to admit we're good together, Hayden. Sexually, sure, but in other areas, as well. We never run out of things to talk about, we enjoy each other's company, we make each other laugh."

She finally turned her head and met his eyes. "I know we're good together, okay?"

It was incredibly hard admitting it, but it was the truth. Brody made her body sing, he made her heart soar, and she couldn't imagine any other man doing that. But she also couldn't imagine them ever having a stable life together.

"But I want someone I can build a home with." Tears pricked her eyelids. "I want to have kids, and a white picket fence, a dog. I did the whole hockey-lifestyle as a kid. I don't want to be sitting on airplanes for half the year, and when I have children, I don't want to be home alone with them while their father is gone."

He was silent for a moment. "I won't play hockey forever," he said finally.

"Do you plan on retiring soon?"

After a beat of hesitation, he said, "No."

Disappointment thundered inside her, but really, what was she expecting? That he'd throw his arms around her and say, *Yes, Hayden, I'll retire! Tomorrow! Now! Let's build a life together!*

It wasn't fair to ask him to give up a career he obviously loved, but she also wasn't willing to give up her own goals and dreams. She knew what she wanted from a relationship, and no matter how much she loved being with Brody, he couldn't give that to her.

"I wish you'd reconsider," he murmured. He shifted her around and moved closer so that his body was flush against hers. "Damn, we fit so well together."

She rubbed her pelvis against his. They did fit. Even though he was a head taller, their bodies seemed to mesh in the most basic way, and when he was inside her… God, when he was inside her she'd never felt more complete.

A soft moan escaped her lips at the delicious image of Brody's hardness filling her, and suddenly the tension of the day drained from her body and dissolved into a pool of warmth between her legs. Suddenly everything they'd just been talking about didn't seem to matter. Brody's job, her need for stability—it all faded away the moment he pressed his body to hers.

"Let's not talk anymore," she whispered. "Please, Brody, no more talking."

Her arousal must have been written all over her face because he ran his hands down her back and squeezed her buttocks. "You've got a one-track mind," he grumbled.

"Says the man who's fondling my ass," she murmured, relieved that the tension had eased. The heavy weight of the painful revelations they'd just shared floated away like a feather.

Brody bent his head and covered her mouth with his. The

kiss took her breath away, made her sag into his rock-hard chest as his greedy tongue explored the crevices of her mouth. Keeping one hand on her ass, he moved the other one to the front of her slacks, deftly popped open the button and tugged at the thin material.

Pulling back, he pushed her slacks off her body, waited for her to step out of them, then tossed them aside. Goose bumps rose on her thighs the second the night air hit her skin. She wore a pair of black bikini panties that Brody quickly disposed of.

"Your neighbors can see us," she protested when he reached for her blouse.

"Not where we're going." He quickly removed her shirt and bra, then lifted her into his arms and headed for the steps of the deck.

She wriggled in his embrace, self-conscious about her naked body being carried around in his backyard, but he kept a tight grip on her. Quickening his strides, he moved across the grass toward the gazebo, ascended the small set of stairs leading into it and set her on her feet.

Her heels made a clicking noise as they connected with the cedar floor of the little structure. She looked around the gazebo, admiring the intricate woodwork and plush white love seat tucked in the corner. When she turned back to Brody, he was as naked as she was.

She laughed. "Let me guess, sex in the gazebo is one of *your* fantasies?"

"Oh, yeah. I've wanted to do this since the moment this damn thing was built."

"What, none of your hockey groupies ever wanted to do it in the wilderness of your backyard?" she teased.

"I've never brought a woman home before."

She forced her jaw to stay closed. He'd never brought a

woman home before? The implications of that statement troubled her, but she didn't feel like dwelling on them now. As she'd said, no more talking.

At the moment, all she wanted to do was fulfill this gorgeous man's fantasy.

11

HE'D STARTLED HER with his admission. He'd seen it in Hayden's eyes the moment he'd confessed to never having brought a woman home, but fortunately that flicker of wariness had faded. Her eyes now glimmered with passion, and he loved that she wasn't complaining about the way he'd stripped her naked and carried her out to the gazebo.

Lord, she turned him on in the fiercest way. He'd sensed the untamed passion in her the moment they'd met, experienced it that first night when he'd made love to her on the hallway floor, reveled in it the night she'd tied him up to her bed and devoured his body. She was full of surprises, and he couldn't get enough of her. He loved her sass and her intelligence and her dry humor, the way she challenged him and aroused him and made him feel like more than just a hockey player.

"So what does the fantasy involve?" she asked, resting her hands on her bare hips.

He swept his gaze over her curvy body, trying to put his needs into words. He had no idea how the fantasy played out, only that his hands tingled with the urge to fondle her full, perky breasts and slip between her shapely legs.

The night breeze grew stronger, snaking into the gazebo and making his cock swell and thicken as the warm air caressed it. The wind also succeeded in hardening Hayden's small, pink nipples, which were now standing up as if demanding his attention.

But instead of reaching out to touch her, he cleared his throat and said, "Lie down on the love seat."

There was no objection. Her heels clacked against the floor as she walked over to the small couch and draped herself over the cushions. When she reached for the clasp on her right shoe he held up his hand. "Leave them on," he ordered.

"Why do men always get turned-on by a naked woman in high heels?"

"Because it's damn hot," he replied with a roll of his eyes.

"So are you just going to stand there and watch me, or do you plan to join me?"

"Eventually."

They were the same words they'd spoken to each other the night she'd admitted her taste for bondage, only this time he was the one in charge. He leaned against the railing of the gazebo and crossed his arms over his chest. "You've gotta give me some incentive, babe."

"Hmm. Like this kind of incentive?" She slid her hands to her breasts.

His breath hitched when she squeezed the lush mounds with her palms, the motion making her tits look bigger, fuller. With an impish smile, she stroked the underside of each breast, circling her nipples with her fingers and then dragging her thumbs over each hard bud.

He almost fell over backward at the sight of Hayden fondling her own breasts. His mouth was so dry he could barely swallow. He allowed her to play for a bit, then narrowed his eyes and muttered, "Spread your legs."

She did, and his breath caught in his throat again. From where he stood he could see every tantalizing inch of her glistening sex. He wanted to lick those smooth pink folds, shove his tongue inside that sweet paradise and make Hayden scream with pleasure, but he held back. His erection throbbed as he curled his fingers over his shaft.

Making slow, lazy strokes to his cock, he gave her a heavy-lidded look and said, "Touch yourself."

"Sure you don't want to do that for me?" Her voice came out throaty, so full of unbridled lust he almost came on the spot.

"Humor me," he squeezed out.

"It's your fantasy." She shrugged, grinned, and promptly lowered her hand between her legs.

Oh, man, this woman was incredible. His eyes nearly popped out of his head as she dragged her index finger down her slick folds and rubbed her swollen sex.

"That's it," he said hoarsely. "Get yourself nice and hot, Hayden."

She replied with a soft whimper. Her cheeks grew flushed the more she kept stroking herself. The hazy look in her eyes told him she was close, but her fingers continued to avoid the one place he knew would drive her over the edge.

She lifted her hand. "Brody," she murmured anxiously.

He chuckled. "Uh-uh. You won't be getting any help from me."

Agitation flickered in her eyes but still he remained on the other side of the gazebo. After a moment she gave a strangled groan and her hand returned between her thighs.

And then she came.

His hand froze over his erection. He was one dangerous stroke from a release he wasn't ready for, but for the life of him he couldn't tear his eyes from the gorgeous woman climaxing in front of him. Arching her back, Hayden cried out, moan after moan filling the warm night. Any neighbor by an open window could've heard her, but she didn't seem to care, and neither did Brody. He was a professional hockey player; his neighbors probably expected female moans of ecstasy to drift out of his house.

He leaned back against the rail and relished every moment, from the contented sighs that slipped out of her throat to the way she'd spread her legs even wider, her heels still strapped to her feet.

When she finally grew still, he crooked his finger at her. Despite the sluggishly sated look in her eyes, she stumbled from the love seat and made her way over to him.

"Has anyone ever told you you're the sexiest woman on the planet?" he murmured before dropping a kiss on her lips.

She responded with a lethargic smile. The remnants of orgasm he saw flashing across her delicate face only made him harder. Suddenly impatient, he bent down and grabbed a condom from the pocket of his jeans, then smoothed it over his throbbing shaft. Without giving her time to recover, he gripped her hips with both hands, maneuvered her around so her ass was pressed against his hard-on and drove his unbelievably stiff cock inside her damp sex.

She moaned, leaning forward and clutching at the railing with her hands. The move caused her bottom to raise, allowing him even better access. He withdrew slowly, rotated his hips the way he knew she liked, then plunged right back in to the hilt.

"This is going to be fast," he warned, his voice sounding gruff and apologetic to his ears. He wanted to make it last for her, but the way his cock kept pulsating, he knew it wouldn't be long before he toppled over that cliff into oblivion.

"I love everything you do to me. Fast, slow, hard, I don't care. Just make love to me."

The whispered reply brought a smile to his lips, but it was the phrase *make love* that caused his chest to tighten. It was the first time she'd referred to what they were doing as making love, and hearing the words brought a rush of pleasure so great his knees almost buckled.

He suddenly felt the primal need to claim this woman. Quickening his pace, he thrust into her, again and again, until his orgasm slithered down his spine, clutched at his balls, and the world in front of him fragmented in shards of light. He shuddered, palming a sweet breast with one hand while stroking the small of Hayden's back with the other, wanting to hold on to her for as long as possible.

He wrapped his arms around her from behind and nuzzled her neck, inhaling the scent of her vanilla and lavender body lotion. She gave a breathy sigh and murmured, "Your fantasies are almost as good as mine."

"Almost as good?" He laughed. "Wait until *I* tie *you* up. Then we'll see who has the hottest fantasy."

She disentangled herself from his embrace and turned to kiss him. Then she drifted to the entrance of the gazebo. "Think any of your neighbors will see me streaking through the yard?"

"*Now* you're self-conscious?"

She offered a rueful look. "I guess you're right. The whole neighborhood probably heard me, huh?"

"You are kinda loud…"

He bent down and grabbed his wool trousers, pulling them up his hips. Finding his shirt and jacket, he tucked them under his arm, walked over to Hayden and extended his arm. "Shall I walk the unclothed lady to the house?"

"You could at least let me wear your shirt."

"Nope. I want to experience the splendor of your body during this evening stroll."

"Screw strolling. I'm running."

Before he could blink she bounded down the gazebo's steps and tore across the yard, her firm ass pale in the moonlight. Laughing, he took off after her, hoping to keep her naked just a little bit longer, but she was already slipping her sweater over her head when he reached the deck.

"Spoilsport," he grumbled.

She put on her panties and slacks, then gestured to the back door. "You still have to give me a tour of the upstairs," she reminded him.

"Any room in particular you'd like to see?"

"Definitely one that features a bed. Or a removable showerhead."

With a grin, he grabbed their wineglasses from the railing and followed her inside. "Do you want more wine?" he asked.

"No, thanks."

She suddenly went quiet as he placed the glasses in the sink, and when he turned to look at her he saw her expression had grown somber.

"You okay?" he asked.

"I'm fine." She let out a breath. "I was thinking about my dad."

Brody made a face. "We just had mind-blowing sex and you're thinking about your dad?"

"It's just…the wine." She gestured to the bottle still sitting on the cedar counter. "It made me think about what Sheila told me today. You know, about my dad's drinking…" Her voice trailed, the distress in her eyes unmistakable.

"Are you going to talk to him about it?"

"Yes. No." She exhaled again. "I don't want to confront him right now, not when he's smack in the middle of this scandal."

"We're all in the middle of it now. We were told today that the investigation is under way. All the players are being interviewed this week."

Her green eyes glimmered with distress. "What kind of questions will you be asked?"

Brody shrugged. "They'll probably ask us what we know

about the allegations, try to coax confessions out of us, quiz us about whether we know if another player was involved."

"Are they going to ask about my dad?"

He nodded.

Resting her hands against the counter, she went silent for a moment, her pretty features shadowed by worry. He could tell she was upset by all of this, especially with everything she was learning about her father, and though he had no intention of making her feel worse, he unwittingly did so with his next statement.

"It was pretty much confirmed to me today that your dad fixed those games."

Her gaze rose to meet his, her mouth forming a startled *O*. "You're saying you know for sure that he did it?"

Damn. Maybe he shouldn't have spit it out the way he had, but the confrontation with Wyatt had been troubling him all night and he'd been hoping to talk it through with Hayden before the league's investigator interviewed him. He knew he'd have to tell the truth if asked, but he'd wanted her advice, wanted her to tell him how to handle the time bomb in his hands without looking like he was betraying his teammates or the team owner.

But he hadn't realized confiding in Hayden meant confirming her doubts about her father. Up until now she'd only suspected Presley had fixed those games, but with that one sentence he'd turned those suspicions into reality, and the crestfallen look on her face tugged at his insides in the most powerful way.

He wanted to comfort her, but he didn't know how.

So he kept his distance, leaned against the counter and released a slow breath. "Yes, he did it. I'm ninety-nine-percent sure of it."

"Ninety-nine percent," she repeated. "Then there's still a chance Dad wasn't involved."

"It's unlikely."

"But there's still a chance."

"Look, Hayden, I know you want to see the best in your father, but you're going to need to accept that he's probably guilty."

Her eyes widened, the color in her cheeks fading fast. "Are you going to tell the investigator that? You're going to say my dad is guilty?"

"I don't know what I'm going to say yet."

He could see her legs shaking as she walked across the tiled floor toward him. Eyes wild with panic, she placed one palm on his bare arm and tilted her head to look up at him. "You can't do it, Brody. Please, don't turn against my father."

HAYDEN DIDN'T KNOW where the words were coming from but she seemed to have no control over her vocal cords. In the back of her head she knew what she was asking of him was wrong, that if Presley was truly guilty he deserved to pay for his crimes. But this was her father, the only parent she had, the only constant in her life.

"You want me to lie?" Brody said flatly.

She swallowed. "No, I...maybe if you just didn't say anything..."

"Lying by omission is still lying, Hayden. And what if they straight out ask me if Presley bribed anyone? What do I do then?"

Desperation clawed up her throat. She knew she had no right asking him to do this for her, but she couldn't watch her father's entire life shatter before her eyes. "He's my only family," she said softly. "I just want to protect him."

Compassion flickered in Brody's eyes, but it quickly faded into annoyance. "What about me? Don't I deserve to be protected, too?"

"Your career isn't at stake," she protested.

"Like hell it isn't!" His eyes flashed. "My integrity and reputation are on the line here, Hayden. I won't throw away my career by lying to protect the team owner, not even for you."

She nearly stumbled backward, assaulted by the force of his words.

She suddenly felt so very stupid. What the hell had she been thinking, asking him to lie for her dad? Her only defense was that she *hadn't* been thinking. For a split second there, the fear seizing her insides was so strong it had overpowered her ability to think logically. Suddenly she'd been the lonely little girl who'd grown up without a mother, who didn't want to see her father carted off to jail even if it meant breaking the rules to keep him out of a cell.

What was the matter with her? She wasn't the type of woman who broke rules. And she didn't condone lies, either.

God, she couldn't believe she'd just asked Brody to throw away his honesty and honor.

With shaky steps, she walked over to him and pressed her face against his chest. She could feel his heart thudding against her ear like a drum. "I'm sorry. I shouldn't have asked you to lie. It was unfair of me to do that. I'm..." She choked on a sob. "I can't believe I just did that."

His warm hand caressed the small of her back. "It's okay. I know you're concerned about him, babe." Brody pressed a kiss to the top of her head.

"I just wish... Damn it, Brody, I want to help him."

"I know," he said gently. "But your dad is the one who got himself into this mess, and I hate to say it, but he's the one who'll have to get himself out of it."

HAYDEN'S CELL PHONE woke her early the next morning, rousing her from a restless sleep and making her groan with displeasure. She was on her side, her back pressed against Brody's big warm body, one of his long arms draped over her chest. She squeezed her eyes shut, waiting for the ringing to stop. A second of blessed silence, and then it rang again. And again. And again.

With a sigh, she disentangled herself from Brody's arms and slid out from under the covers. The sight of the alarm clock on Brody's nightstand made her grimace. Six o'clock. Who on earth was calling her this early?

"Come back to bed," came Brody's sleepy murmur.

"I will after I murder whoever keeps calling," she grumbled, padding barefoot to the armchair under the window. Her clothes and purse were draped over the chair, and she rummaged around in the pile until she found her cell.

Looking at the display, she immediately recognized Darcy's number. Uh-oh. This probably wasn't good. Not if Darcy was giving up her own beauty sleep to make a call.

Hayden flipped open the phone and said, "What's wrong?"

"Have you seen the morning paper?"

"That's what you woke me up to ask?" Hayden edged to the door, not wanting to disturb Brody. She leaned against the wall in the hallway and added, "And what are you doing up early enough to read the morning paper? Do you even subscribe to the paper?"

"I never went to bed last night." Hayden could practically see the grin on her best friend's face. "And, no, I don't get the paper. But Marco does. Marco, by the way, is my new personal trainer."

"At the rate you're going, you'll never be able to find a permanent gym, Darce." She let out a breath. "Now tell me what's so important about today's newspaper."

"You."

"Me?"

"You're in it, hon. Front page of the sports section, with your hockey player's tongue in your mouth and his hands on your ass."

She nearly choked. "You're making it up!"

"I'm afraid not."

Horror lodged in her throat. Darcy sounded serious. And if Darcy couldn't make a smart-ass remark about it, then it must be bad.

"I'll call you back in a minute," Hayden blurted, disconnecting the call.

The T-shirt Brody had given her to sleep in hung all the way down to her knees, but her arms were bare and goose bumps had risen on her skin. She wrapped her arms around her chest and hurried down the stairs two at a time. In the front hall, she unlocked the door and poked her head out, darting forward when she saw the rolled-up newspaper on the porch. The wooden floor was cool under her feet, making her shiver. Snatching up the newspaper, she headed back inside, pulling the paper from its protective plastic as she wandered into the living room.

She sank down on the couch, found the sports section, and gasped. Darcy was right. The first page boasted a large photograph of her and Brody in the Warrior arena parking lot. It must have been taken the moment she'd stood up on her toes to kiss him, and there was no mistaking it, his hands really were on her butt.

The caption read, "Warriors forward cozies up to team owner's daughter."

But it was the article beneath it that drained all the color from her face. She read it twice, not missing a single word, then set the paper on the cushion next to her and dropped her head into her hands.

"What happened?"

She jerked up at the sound of Brody's drowsy voice, to see

him standing in the doorway wearing nothing but a pair of navy-blue boxers and a concerned expression.

Without a word, Hayden pointed to the newspaper beside her. After a second of hesitation, Brody joined her on the couch and picked up the section.

She watched his face as he read the article, but he gave nothing away. Blinked a couple of times, frowned once, and finally rose slowly to his feet. "I need coffee," he muttered before walking out of the room.

Hayden stared after him in bewilderment, then shot up and rushed into the kitchen. Brody was already turning on the coffeemaker, leaning against the counter with a look of utter disbelief in his gorgeous blue eyes.

"They're saying I took a bribe," he said softly.

She moved toward him and rested her hand on his strong bicep. "It's just speculation, Brody. They don't have any proof."

"They have a *source!*" he burst out, his voice resonating with anger. "Someone actually told that reporter I took bribes from your father. This isn't a tabloid, where the so-called reporters make up sources to suit their story. Greg Michaels is an award-winning sports journalist—and someone on the team told him I took a goddamn bribe!"

Hayden's mouth went completely dry. She could barely keep up with the range of emotions flashing across Brody's face. Anger and betrayal and dismay. Shock and disgust. Fear. She wanted desperately to hold him, but his posture was so tense, his shoulders stiff, his jaw tight, every aspect of his body language screaming *back off!*

"Someone is trying to ruin me," he snapped. "Who the hell would do that? I know Wyatt is up to his ears in this mess, but I can't see him casting suspicion on me. He told me to stay out of it."

His eyes were suddenly on her, focused, sharp, as if

realizing she was in the room with him. "They think you're sleeping with me to shut me up about your father's part in it." He laughed humorlessly.

Sympathy welled up inside her, squeezing her heart like a vise. "It's going to be okay, Brody. Everything will get cleared up when you meet with the interviewer."

Another chuckle, this time laced with bitterness. "All it takes is one black mark on your name and teams look at you differently."

The coffeemaker clicked, and Brody turned his attention to it. Grabbing a mug from the cabinet over the sink, he slammed it down on the counter, filled it to the brim with coffee and swallowed a gulp of the scalding liquid, not even wincing.

Hayden had no idea what to say. How to make this better for him. So instead she just stood there, waiting, watching his face, trying to anticipate the next outburst.

But she wasn't ready for what he said next.

"I think maybe we should cool things off for a bit."

Shock slammed into her. "What?"

Setting down his mug, Brody rubbed his forehead. "I can't be dragged down along with your father," he said, so quietly she barely heard him. "If you and I are seen together, the rumors and suspicions will only grow. My career…"

He let out a string of curses. "I've worked my ass off to get to where I am, Hayden. I grew up wearing secondhand clothes and watching my parents struggle to afford anything. And finally, finally, I'm in a position to support myself, to support them. I can't lose that. I *won't* lose it."

"You're breaking up with me?"

He dragged his fingers through his hair, his eyes tortured. "I'm saying maybe we should put…us…on hold. Until the investigation concludes and the scandal blows over."

"You want to put us on hold," she echoed dully.

"Yes."

She turned away, resting her hands on the kitchen counter to steady herself. He was breaking up with her? Sorry, putting things on *hold*. Not that it made a difference. Regardless of the way he wanted to word it, Brody was pretty much telling her he didn't want her around.

Everything he'd said last night about how good they were for each other, how well they fit…what had happened to all that, huh?

The memory of the words he'd spoken only yesterday caused the bitterness swimming through her body to grow stronger. It was like a current, forcing all reason from her mind and pushing her into an eddy of resentment she knew too well. How many times had her father chosen his hockey team over her? How many times had the men in her life let their careers take the front seat while she sat in the back begging to be noticed?

"All right. If that's what you want," she said, unable to stop her tone from sounding clipped and angry. "I guess you need to look out for yourself, after all."

His eyes clouded. "Don't make it sound like that, Hayden. Like I don't give a damn about you. Because I *do* give a damn. You can't fault me for also giving a damn about everything I've worked so hard for."

She edged away from the counter, suddenly wanting to flee. Maybe it was for the best, ending it now. They'd already reached an impasse yesterday, when she'd told him his life-style didn't fit what she wanted in a relationship. Maybe it was better to break things off now, before it got even harder.

But although it made sense in her head, her heart couldn't stop weeping at the idea of not being with Brody.

Silence stretched between them, until Brody released a frustrated curse and raked his hands through his dark hair. "I care about you, Hayden. The last thing I want to do is end this." He shook his head, looking determined. "And I don't see it as an ending. I just want this mess to go away. I want my name cleared and my career unaffected. When it all dies down, we can pick up where we left off."

She couldn't help but laugh. "Because it's that easy, right?" Her laughter died, replaced with a tired frown. "It would have ended anyway, Brody. Sooner or later."

Anguish flooded his gaze. "Come on, don't say that. This break doesn't have to be permanent."

"Maybe it should." A sob wedged in her throat and it took every ounce of willpower she possessed to swallow it back. "We're probably doing ourselves a favor by letting go now. Maybe it will end up saving us both a lot of heartache in the future."

He opened his mouth to respond, but she didn't give him the chance. Blinking back the tears stinging her eyelids, she headed back to the bedroom to find her clothes.

12

THE CAB RIDE to the arena, where she'd left her car, was probably the most mortifying experience of Hayden's life. Somehow, while she'd gotten dressed, called the cab, murmured a soft goodbye to Brody, she'd managed to rein in her emotions. But the second she slid into the backseat and watched Brody's beautiful house disappear in the rearview mirror, she'd burst into tears.

Looking stunned, the taxi driver handed her a small packet of tissues then promptly ignored her. Despite the tears fogging her eyes she noticed the man shooting her strange looks in the mirror. Apparently it wasn't every day that a brokenhearted woman in tears rode in his cab.

And *brokenhearted* was the only word she could come up with to describe how she felt right now. Although she'd told Brody the breakup was for the best, her heart was aching so badly it felt like someone had scraped it with a razor blade. All she wanted to do was go back to the penthouse, crawl under the covers and cry.

The cab driver dropped her at the arena, where she got into her rental car, swiped at her wet eyes and took a few calming breaths.

Fifteen excruciatingly long minutes later, she was walking into the hotel, hoping nobody noticed her blotchy face. In the lobby, the clerk behind the check-in desk gestured at her. She reluctantly headed over and was surprised when he said, "There's a man waiting for you in the bar."

Hope and happiness soared inside her. Brody? He would've definitely had time to get here before her, since she'd had to pick up her car. Maybe he realized how foolish it was to end things because of something a reporter had written.

She hurried across the marble floor toward the large oak doors leading into the hotel bar. Only a few patrons were inside, and when she searched for Brody's massive shoulders and unruly dark hair, she came up empty-handed. Disappointment crashed into her like a tidal wave. Of course he wasn't here. He'd made it clear back at his place that he couldn't risk his career by being seen with her.

She glanced around again, then gasped when her attention landed on a man she'd dismissed during her first inspection.

Doug.

Oh, God. What was *he* doing here?

"Hayden!" He walked toward her with a timid smile.

She stared at him, taking in the familiar sight of his blond hair, arranged in a no-nonsense haircut. His pale blue eyes, serious as always. That lean, trim body he kept in shape at the university gym. He wore a pair of starched tan slacks and a crisp, white button-down shirt, and the conservative attire kind of irked her. Everything about Doug was neat and orderly and unbelievably tedious. She found herself longing for even the tiniest bit of disorder. An undone button. A coffee stain. A patch of stubble he'd missed while shaving.

But there was nothing disorderly about this man. He was like a perfectly wrapped gift that only used three efficient pieces of tape and featured a little bow with the same length tails. The kind of gift you hesitated to open because you'd feel like an ass messing it up.

Brody, on the other hand... Now he was a gift you tore open

the second you got it—the exterior didn't matter because you knew what it contained inside was a million times better anyway.

Tears stung her eyes at the thought.

"Hi," Doug said gently. "It's good to see you."

She wanted to tell him it was good to see him, too, but the words refused to come out. They stared at each other for a moment, and then he was pulling her into an awkward embrace. She halfheartedly hugged him back, noticing that the feel of his arms around her had no effect on her whatsoever.

"I know I shouldn't have come," Doug said, releasing her. "But after the way we left things…I thought we needed to talk. In person."

"You're right." She swallowed. "Do you want to come up?"

He nodded.

Without a word, they walked out of the bar and headed for the elevator. Silence stretched between them as they rode the car up to the penthouse. Hayden wanted to apologize to him again, and yet she wasn't sure she felt apologetic anymore. She and Doug had been on a break when she'd started seeing Brody, and though she regretted hurting Doug, she couldn't will up any regret about what she felt for Brody.

"I was shocked when you told me that you were seeing someone else," Doug began when they stepped into the suite.

"I know." Guilt tugged at her gut. "I'm sorry I just dropped it on you like that, and over the phone, but I had to be honest."

"I'm glad you were." He stepped closer, his eyes glimmering with something she couldn't put a finger on. "And it was the kick in the behind I needed, Hayden. It made me realize how much I don't want to lose you."

He reached out and tenderly stroked her cheek.

Discomfort crept up her spine.

"I love you, Hayden," Doug said earnestly. "I should have

said it a long time ago, but I wanted to go slow. I guess I was going *too* slow. I'm sorry."

He moved closer, but he didn't touch her again, or kiss her, just offered an affectionate smile and said, "I decided we've waited long enough. I want us to cross that bridge. I want us to make love."

No, not the intimacy bridge. Hysterical laughter bubbled inside her throat. "Doug—"

"It's finally the right time, Hayden."

Maybe it's the right time for you, she wanted to say. But for her, that perfect moment she might've shared with Doug had slipped away the second Brody Croft had walked into her life.

He reached out for her again, but she moved back, guilty when she saw the hurt in his eyes.

"It's not the right time," she said quietly. "And I think there's a reason we never got to this point before, Doug. I think…it wasn't meant to be."

He went still. "I see," he said, his voice stiff.

She took hold of his hand, squeezing his fingers tightly. "You know I'm right, Doug. Would you honestly be saying all of this, now, if I hadn't met someone else?"

"Yes." But his voice lacked conviction.

"I think we got together because it was comfortable. We were friends, colleagues, two people who liked each other well enough…but we're not soul mates, Doug."

Pain circled her heart. She hated saying these words to him, but there was no other choice.

Being with Brody had made her realize that she wasn't going to settle for a man just because he happened to be nice and dependable. As wild and sexy and unpredictable as Brody was, he was also honest and tender, more intelligent than he gave himself credit for, strong, funny, generous… Oh, God, had she fallen in love with him?

No, she couldn't have. Brody was just a fling. He might have some wonderful traits, but his career would constantly keep him away from her. She wanted someone safe, someone solid. Not someone who was so big and bold and arrogant and passionate and temporary and— Damn it!

She loved him. And wasn't it ridiculously ironic that she'd figured it out the day he broke up with her.

"Hayden? Please don't cry, honey."

She glanced up to see Doug's worried expression, then touched her cheeks and felt the tears. She quickly wiped them away. "Doug…I'm sorry," she murmured, not knowing what else to say.

He nodded. "I know. I'm sorry, too." He tilted his head, looking a bit confused. "But I don't see what's so wrong with comfortable."

"There's nothing wrong with it. But I want more than comfort. I want…love and passion and…I want *earth-shattering*."

He gave her a rueful smile. "I don't have much experience in shattering a woman's world, I'm afraid."

No, but Brody did.

Unfortunately, he also had plenty of experience in shattering a woman's *heart*.

TWO DAYS LATER Hayden woke up feeling confused, devastated and angry. The anger surprised her, but most of it was directed at herself anyway. She'd tossed and turned all night, thinking about what a mess she'd gotten herself into since she'd come back to Chicago. She'd propositioned a stranger, then proceeded to fall in love with him. She'd hurt Doug. Discovered her father had a drinking problem and was probably a criminal.

And what exactly are you doing to fix any of it? a little voice chastised.

She forced herself into a sitting position, her anger escalating. What *was* she doing to fix it? She'd spent all day yesterday lying on the couch in her sweatpants. She'd watched the Warriors play the Vipers, trying to catch glimpses of Brody. And when the team had lost, her heart ached for him. The Warriors were officially out of the play-offs, and she knew how disappointed Brody must be. She'd been so tempted to call and tell him she was sorry. Instead, she'd devoured a carton of ice cream and gone to bed at ten o'clock.

How was that going to help anything? She wasn't the type to let problems pile up without looking for solutions, and although she might not be able to "fix" Doug's broken heart or Brody's decision to stay away from her, she sure as hell could do something about her father.

Jumping out of bed, she threw on some clothes, headed for the bathroom to wash up, then stepped into the elevator with renewed energy and determination.

Enough was enough. She needed to look her dad in the eye and demand the truth from him. This scandal was affecting her, too, and she deserved to know whether or not the trust and faith she'd placed in her father was justified. Presley's mess had taken her away from Doug and brought her to Chicago, it had broken up her and Brody, caused stress to tangle inside her. It was time to quit avoiding her father and try to make sense of everything that had happened.

She drove to the Lincoln Center with a heavy heart, knowing her dad was scheduled to be interviewed by the league investigator today. Come to think of it, Brody was being interviewed, too. She hoped she wouldn't run into him. If she did, she'd be tempted to hurl herself into his arms, and she had no desire to be pushed away again.

Ironic that she'd been fighting this relationship from day one, set on keeping it a fling, and in the end he'd been the one to break things off.

And she'd been the one to fall in love.

Forcing the painful thoughts from her mind, she parked the car and walked to the arena's entrance. After greeting the woman at the lobby desk, she rode the elevator up to the second floor, which housed the franchise offices.

Her father's office was at the end of the hall, through a pair of intimidating wood doors more suited for a president than the owner of a hockey team. Tucked off to the right was the desk of her dad's secretary, a pleasant woman named Kathy who was nowhere to be found.

Hayden walked up to the doors, but stopped when her dad's voice practically boomed out of the walls. He sounded angry.

She slowly turned the knob and inched open the door, then froze when she heard her dad say, "I know I promised to cover your ass, Becker, but this is getting out of hand."

Becker...Becker...hadn't Brody shown up at the Gallagher Club with a player named Becker?

Her blood ran cold. She knew she shouldn't stand there and listen, but she couldn't bring herself to announce her presence.

"I don't give a damn about that...they won't trace the money..."

Enough. She'd had enough.

Feeling sick to her stomach, Hayden pushed open the door and strode into her father's office. He was standing behind his desk, clutching the phone to his ear, and he nearly dropped the receiver when he saw her enter.

"I have to go," he said into the phone, hanging up without giving the other person—Becker?—a chance to respond.

Hayden inched closer, fighting the urge to throw up as she stared into her father's eyes. His face had gone pale, and she could see his hands trembling as he waited for her to approach.

"So it's true," she said flatly, not bothering with any pleasantries.

Her dad had the nerve to feign ignorance. "I don't know what you're talking about, sweetheart."

"Bullshit!" Her voice trembled with anger. "I heard what you said just now!"

Silence hung over the room. Her father looked stunned by her outburst. After a second, he lowered himself into his leather chair, gave her a repentant look and released a heavy sigh. "You shouldn't have eavesdropped, Hayden. I didn't want you involved in any of this."

"You didn't want me involved? Is that why you asked me to come home? Is that why you practically forced me to give a deposition in your divorce? So I wouldn't be involved? Too late, Dad. I already am."

Her legs barely carried her as she stumbled over to one of the plush burgundy visitor's chairs and sank into it. It was hard to think over the roar of her pulse in her ears. Anger and disgust and sadness mingled in her blood, forming a poisonous cocktail that seared through her veins. She couldn't believe this. The signs and suspicions had been there from the start, but hearing her father confirm his criminal actions was like a switchblade to the gut.

If someone had told her that the father she'd loved unconditionally, whose flaws she'd always ignored, whose attention she'd always craved, could be capable of such dishonesty, she would've laughed in their face. And yet it was true. Her father had broken the law. He'd lied. He'd probably cheated on his wife.

When had this man become a stranger to her?

"Honey…" He gulped. Guilt etched into his features. "At least let me explain."

"You committed a crime," she said stiffly. "What's there to explain?"

"I made a mistake." He faltered. "I made some bad investments. I…" Desperation filled his eyes. "It was only two games,

Hayden. Only two. I just needed to recover the losses, and…I…I screwed up."

Her belief in him slowly began to shatter, tiny jagged pieces of trust and faith chipping away, ripping into her insides as they sank down to her stomach like sharp little razor blades. How could he have done this? And why hadn't she seen it, damn it?

"Why didn't you call me?" she whispered.

"I was too ashamed." His voice cracked again. "I didn't want you to know I'd destroyed everything I'd built." His eyes looked so tortured Hayden had to turn away. "I never wanted another woman after your mother died. None of the ones I met even compared to her. So I focused on my job instead, first as a coach, and then as an owner. Money was tangible, you know? Something I didn't think I could lose."

When she looked at him again, she was stunned to see tears on her dad's cheeks. "But I did lose it. I lost it and I got scared. I thought I'd lose Sheila, too." He swiped viciously at his wet eyes. "I know part of the reason she married me was for my money. I'm no fool, Hayden. But Sheila and I also loved each other. Sometimes I think I still love her. She's so full of…*life,* I guess. And after so many years of feeling dead, I needed that. I didn't want to lose her. I started drinking too much, trying to forget about what was happening, I guess. Sheila tried to help me, but I wouldn't listen. I didn't want her to think I was weak…"

His voice drifted, his eyes glistening with pain, shame and unshed tears. Tears sprang to Hayden's eyes, too.

She'd never seen her father cry before. It broke her heart. And it hurt even more knowing that she hadn't even noticed while his life was spinning out of control. She knew how much his career and reputation and, yes, his wealth, mattered to him. The threat of losing it had driven him to make such hideous decisions. And she'd been so busy living her own life that she'd failed to be there for her father. Because no matter how dishonorably he'd behaved, he still was her father, and she couldn't write him off just because he'd screwed up.

She rose slowly from the chair and rounded the desk, placing her hand on her dad's shoulder. His head jerked up, his eyes wide with surprise, and then the tears flowed in earnest down his cheeks.

"I'm sorry, Hayden," he choked out.

She wrapped her arms around him and hugged him tightly. "I know you are, Daddy. Don't worry. We're going to get you some help." She swallowed. "And you're...you're going to have to tell the truth today, okay?"

Dropping her arms, she stared into her father's eyes, seeing the remorse and guilt flickering in them. After a moment, he nodded. "You're right," he whispered. "I know I need to face the consequences of my actions."

"I'm here for you, Dad. And if you want me to go to the interview with you, I will."

He shook his head. "It's something I need to do alone."

"I understand."

Her father rubbed his cheeks, then looked up at her and sighed. "Don't you think it's time for *you* to explain?"

"Explain what?" she asked in bewilderment.

"I do read the newspapers, Hayden." He shook his head. "How long have you been seeing Croft?"

Heat flooded her cheeks. "Not long."

"And this affair...you think it's a good idea? Croft isn't your usual type, sweetheart."

"It's not an affair," she blurted out. "I...I love him." She couldn't fight the tears that stung her eyelids. "I want to be with him, Dad."

She paused as the words settled between them. *I want to be with him.* And then she thought of what she'd told her father, just a moment ago. *I'm here for you.*

Why was it so easy for her to say that to her father, but not to Brody? He might not have the stable life she'd always longed for, but didn't he have so many other incredible qualities that more than made up for having to travel every now and then?

She suddenly realized how unfairly she'd treated him, wanting to keep everything on her terms. Fighting him when he tried to make her see they were good for each other.

Well, he was right. They *were* good for each other. Brody was the first man she'd ever been truly herself with. He made her laugh. He drove her wild in bed. He listened.

God, she didn't deserve Brody. All she'd done since the day they'd met was set boundaries, have expectations, find reasons why he wasn't right for her. Yet he'd stayed by her side. Even when she came up with silly rules, or told him he was nothing but a fling. Wasn't that what she claimed to want in a man? Someone solid to stand by her?

And didn't Brody deserve the same thing, a woman who stood by him? He cared about her, she *knew* he did, and if he thought putting their relationship on hold until the scandal blew over was best, maybe she needed to trust him.

She stumbled away from the desk, suddenly knowing what she had to do.

"Hayden?" her dad said quietly.

"I need to take care of something," she answered, inhaling deeply. "We'll talk after your interview, okay? We'll talk about everything."

Her father nodded.

She was halfway out the door when she glanced over her shoulder and added, "And, Daddy? I hope you remember to do the right thing."

BRODY STOOD outside the conference room, anxiously tugging at his tie as he waited. Damn, he hated this tie. It was choking the life out of him. Or maybe he found it so hard to breathe because any minute now he'd be sitting in front of three people who could very well destroy his career.

Both explanations were logical, but deep down he knew there was only one reason for the turmoil afflicting his body—Hayden.

He hadn't thought it was possible to miss someone this much. He hadn't been able to stop thinking about her from the second she'd left his house two days ago. Which was probably why his performance during that final game against the Vipers had been less than stellar. But even though the team was out of the play-offs, Brody's disappointment wasn't as great as it should have been. His season had officially ended, and yet he hardly cared. How could he, when his entire body ached for Hayden? Although his brain insisted he'd done the right thing by distancing himself from her, his heart refused to accept the decision. In fact, his heart had been screaming such vile things at him for two days now that he was beginning to feel like the biggest cad on the planet.

Had he made a mistake? He hadn't wanted a permanent break, hadn't intended to end the relationship; he'd just wanted the investigation to be done with, the scandal an unpleasant blip on his memory radar. But Hayden, well, she'd gone and made it permanent. Reverted to her belief that a relationship between them could never have lasted anyway.

Yet he couldn't bring himself to agree. She was wrong about them. If she'd only let down her guard and open her heart she'd see that the two of them could be dynamite together. Not just in bed, but in life. So he traveled for work. He'd have to retire sooner or later, and when he did, he planned on settling down in one place and opening a skating arena that didn't require a membership fee, so that kids from poorer families would have access to the same facilities as those who were better off. He might even coach a kids' team. It was an idea he'd been tossing around for years now.

But instead of planning a future with Hayden, he'd lost her. Maybe he'd never really had her to begin with….

"Croft."

He raised his head, frowning when he spotted Craig Wyatt walking toward him.

Wyatt's massive frame was squeezed into a tailored black suit, his shiny dress shoes squeaking against the tiled floor. The captain's blond hair was gelled back from his forehead.

"What's up?" Brody couldn't stop the twinge of bitterness in his voice.

A muscle twitched in Wyatt's square jaw. "I saw the article about you and Presley's daughter, Brody. You have no reason to be nervous. We both know you didn't do anything wrong."

"You're right, I didn't." He couldn't help adding, "But how did you know?"

Wyatt jerked his finger to the left and said, "Follow me. We need to have a chat."

Brody glanced at his watch, noting he had another twenty minutes before they called him in for his scheduled interview.

They walked silently toward the lobby, then exited the front doors and stepped into the cool morning air. Cars whizzed by in front of the arena. Pedestrians ambled down the sidewalk without giving the two men a second look. Everyone was going about their day, cheerfully heading to work, while Brody was here, waiting to be questioned about something he wanted no part in.

With a strangled groan, Wyatt ran one hand through his hair, messing up the style he'd obviously taken great care with. "Look, I'm not going to lie. I've been seeing Sheila, okay?" His voice cracked. "I know it's wrong. I know I have no business sleeping with a married woman, but, goddammit, I was a goner from the moment I met her. I love her, man."

"Sheila told you who took bribes, didn't she?"

Wyatt averted his eyes. "Yes."

"Then who, damn it? Who the fuck put us in this position, Craig?"

There was a beat of silence. "I don't think you want to know, man."

Another pause. Longer this time. Brody could tell that the last thing Craig Wyatt wanted to do was name names.

But he did. "Nicklaus did. And—" Wyatt took a breath. "I'm sorry, Brody, but...so did Sam Becker."

13

THE GROUND BENEATH Brody's feet swiftly disintegrated. He sagged forward, planting both hands on his thighs to steady himself. Sucked in a series of long breaths. Waited for his pulse to steady.

"Those are the only two Sheila knows about," Wyatt was saying. "There could be more."

Brody glanced up at Wyatt with anger. "You're lying. Nicklaus maybe, but not Becker. He wouldn't do that."

"He did."

No. Not Becker. Brody pictured Becker's face, thinking back to the first day they'd met, how Sam Becker had taken Brody's rookie self under his wing and helped him become the player he was today. Becker was his best friend on the team. He was a stand-up guy, a champion, a legend. Why would he throw his career away for some extra pocket money?

"He's retiring at the end of the season," Wyatt said, as if reading Brody's mind. He shrugged. "Maybe he needed a bigger nest egg."

Brody closed his eyes briefly. When he opened them, he saw the sympathy on Wyatt's face. "I know you two are close," Craig said quietly.

"You could be wrong about this. Sheila could have lied." Brody knew he was grasping at straws, but anything was better than accepting that Becker had done this.

"It's the truth," Wyatt answered.

They stood there for a moment, neither one speaking, until Wyatt finally cleared his throat and said, "We should go back inside."

"You go. I'll be there in a minute."

After Wyatt left, Brody adjusted his tie, wondering if he'd ever be able to breathe again. His head still spun from Craig's words. And yet he couldn't bring himself to believe it. Damn it, he needed to talk to Becker. Look his friend in the eye and demand the truth. Prove Wyatt wrong.

Then he looked up and realized he was going to be granted his wish sooner than he'd expected. Samuel T. Becker had just exited the arena.

Becker spotted him instantly, and made his way over. "You done already?"

"Haven't even gone in yet." He tried to mask his emotions as he studied his old friend. "Are you scheduled to be interviewed today?"

"Yep," Becker said. "And as a reward, I get to take Mary shopping afterward. What fun for me."

Brody smiled weakly.

"What the hell's up with you?" Sam demanded, rolling his eyes. "Don't tell me you're still gaga over Presley's daughter. I told you, man, you shouldn't be seeing her."

Yeah, he had told him, hadn't he? And Brody now had to wonder exactly where the advice had stemmed from. Had Becker really been looking out for him, or had he wanted to keep him away from Hayden in case Presley decided to confide in his daughter? In case Brody learned the truth about Becker's criminal actions. The thought made his blood run cold.

"Let's not talk about Hayden," he said stiffly.

"Okay. Whatcha want to talk about then?"

He released a slow breath. "How about you tell me why you let Presley bribe you?"

Becker's jaw hardened. "Excuse me?"

"You heard me."

After a beat, Becker scowled. "I already told you, I wasn't involved in that crap."

"Someone else says otherwise."

"Yeah, who?" Becker challenged.

Brody decided to take a gamble. He felt like a total ass, but still he said, "Presley."

The lie stretched between them, and the myriad of emotions Brody saw on his friend's face was disconcerting as hell. Becker's expression went from shocked to angry. To guilty. And finally, betrayed.

And it was all Brody needed to know.

With a stiff nod, he brushed past his former mentor. "I'm needed inside."

"Brody, come on." Becker trailed after him, his voice laced with misery. "Come on, it wasn't like that."

Brody spun around. "Then you didn't sell out the team?"

Becker hesitated a little too long.

"That's what I thought."

"I did it for Mary, okay?" Becker burst out, looking so anguished that Brody almost felt sorry for him. "You don't know what it's like living with a woman like her. Money, power, that's all she talks about. She's always needling me to be better, richer, more ambitious. And now that I'm retiring, she's going nuts. She married me because of my career, because I was at the top of my game, a two-time cup winner, a goddamn champion."

"And you could've retired knowing that you *are* a champion and a two-time cup winner," Brody pointed out. "Now you'll go out a criminal. How's Mary going to like that?"

Becker said nothing. He looked beaten, weak. "I messed up, kiddo, and I'm sorry," he whispered after several moments had passed. "I'm sorry about the games and the article and—"

Brody's jaw tightened. "The article?"

His friend averted his eyes, as if realizing his slipup.

Brody stood there for a moment, wary, studying Becker. The article...the one that had been in the paper two days ago? The one that featured a source who insinuated Brody had taken a bribe?

His blood began to boil, heating his veins, churning his stomach, until a red haze of fury swept over him.

"You spoke to the reporter about me," he hissed.

Becker finally met his eyes. Guilt was written all over his face. "I'm sorry."

"Why? Why the *hell* would you do that?" Brody clenched his fists, knowing the answer before Becker could open his mouth. "To take the blame off yourself. You were too close to being caught, weren't you, Sam? You thought my relationship with Hayden would get the press going, put some pressure on me instead of you."

The sheer force of Brody's anger was unbelievable. He wanted to hit the other man, so badly his fists actually tingled. And along with the rage came a jolt of devastation that torpedoed into his gut and brought a wave of nausea to his throat.

"I'm sorry," Becker murmured for what seemed like the millionth time, but Brody was done listening to his friend's apologies. No, not his friend. Because a true friend would never have done what Sam Becker had.

Without another word, he brushed past Becker and stalked into the arena.

He felt like slamming his fist into something. Becker, his best friend, had betrayed him. Becker, the most talented player in the league, had cheated. And why? For money. Goddamn *money*.

Money. Power. Ambition. She married me because of my career.

And suddenly Brody found himself sagging against the wall as the truth of his own stupidity hit him. Didn't he, too, place importance on financial success? Hadn't he just thrown away the woman he loved because of his damn career?

And, God, but he did love Hayden.

He loved her so damn much.

Maybe he'd fallen for Hayden when she'd first strolled up and proceeded to wipe the pool table with him. Or maybe it happened the first time they'd kissed. Or the first time they'd made love. It could've been the night she'd put on the pair of skates and stumbled all over the ice, or the day she'd dragged him around the museum talking passionately about every piece of art.

He didn't know when it happened, but it had. And instead of clinging to the woman whose intelligence amazed him, whose passion excited him, whose soft smiles and warm arms made him feel more content than he'd ever felt in his life—instead of hanging on to her, he'd pushed her away.

And why? Because he'd been implicated in a crime he hadn't committed? Because his family never had money when he was growing up? So what? His parents loved each other, and their marriage had thrived despite their financial difficulties. What did money and success really matter when you didn't have someone to share it with, someone you loved?

A laugh suddenly slipped out of his mouth, and he noticed the receptionist giving him a funny look. Releasing a shaky breath, he crossed the lobby toward the hallway off to the left and walked back in the direction of the conference room. Lord, he was an ass. He'd been searching for a woman who'd look at him and see past the athlete, and, damn it, but he'd found her. Hayden didn't care if he was a star and she didn't care how much money he made, as long as he was there for her.

He wasn't willing to lie to protect Hayden's father, but he should have told her he'd stand by her no matter what happened with her dad. His relationship with the team owner's daughter might place a negative spotlight on him, but wasn't it worth it if it meant keeping Hayden in his life?

"Brody?"

He almost tripped when he saw Hayden standing at the end of the hall, right in front of the conference-room door.

"What are you doing here?" he asked.

She stepped toward him, and he noticed her red-rimmed eyes. Had she been crying?

"I came to talk to my dad," she murmured. "And then I remembered that you were being interviewed, too, so I thought I'd find you before you had to go in…" Her voice drifted, and then she cleared her throat. "I'm sorry the team didn't make it to the second round."

"So am I… But to be honest, it doesn't seem all that important anymore, considering everything else that's going on."

"I know." She gave him a sad smile. "A criminal investigation kind of casts a shadow over things, doesn't it?"

The pain in her eyes tore at his insides. He hated seeing her this way, and he knew why she'd been crying.

Resting his hand on her arm, he slowly pulled her away from the conference-room door and led her to the end of the hall. "I'm not going to lie," he said softly.

She tilted her head to meet his eyes, her gaze confused, then opened her mouth to speak.

"Wait," he cut in. "I want you to know that just because I won't lie doesn't mean I won't be there for you. Because I will, babe. I don't care what the papers write about us, I don't care how my career is affected. I don't care about anything but you. I'll stay by your side, Hayden. I promise, I'll be here for you, as long as you need me."

He blew out a breath, waiting for her to reply, praying she didn't say, *Well, I don't need you, Brody. It was just a fling.*

But she didn't say that. She didn't say anything, in fact.

Instead, she burst out laughing.

HAYDEN COULDN'T STOP the giggles from escaping. She'd come down here to tell Brody she was willing to wait until the investigation ended, that she would do anything it took to keep him in her life, even if it meant staying apart for a while. And here he was, telling her he wanted to stay by her side.

"You think it's funny?" Brody said in annoyance, raking both hands through his dark hair. "Remind me never to make a grand romantic gesture again."

She chuckled. "I only think it's funny because I came to tell you I'll stay away from you until the investigation is finished."

"What?"

"I respect your decision. If you want to lie low until this blows over, I'll do that." She curled her fingers over his arm and looked at him imploringly. "But I don't want it to be permanent. I don't want us to end, Brody."

His features softened. "Neither do I." He paused. "I also don't want us to lie low."

"Are you sure?"

He moved closer, bent down and planted a soft kiss on her mouth, right there in the hallway. Then he pulled back, smiled, and dipped his head to kiss her again, this time slipping her a little tongue.

Flushed, she broke the kiss and stepped back before she gave in to the urge to pull him into the restroom and fulfill yet another kinky fantasy. "Come to the hotel when you're done," she said, her voice coming out breathy.

He grinned. "I'll be there with bells on."

"No bells. But naked would be good." Her heart did a crazy

little somersault. "And don't keep me waiting too long." She drew in a breath. "There are definitely a few things I still need to say to you."

AN HOUR LATER, Brody stepped into the elevator at the Ritz. He waited for the bellhop to turn the key that gave him access to the penthouse floor, and when the guy left, Brody sagged against the wall of the car, feeling as if he'd just run the Boston Marathon and followed that up by climbing Everest. The interview with the league investigators had been pure torture. He'd sat there in his suit, with his oxygen-depriving tie, and had had to sell out a man he'd once considered a friend and another he'd respected as a boss.

Thank God this day from hell was over. He didn't know what the investigation would turn up, how it would all end, but a load had been lifted off his chest. One load, at least. He still hadn't quite faced the fact that Becker had betrayed him. He knew it would take more than one afternoon to come to terms with it. But he'd walked out of that conference with his conscience clear, and now he couldn't wait to lose himself in Hayden's arms and forget about everything except the love he felt for her.

"Hayden?" he called as the elevator doors swung open and he entered the living room.

Her voice drifted out from the bedroom. "In here."

He found her in the bedroom, sitting cross-legged in the center of the bed, still clad in the flowy green skirt and yellow silk top she'd been wearing earlier. Damn. He'd been hoping to find her naked.

Ah, well, that could be easily amended.

She slid off the bed, her skirt swirling around her firm thighs as she moved toward him. "How was the interview?"

"Terrible. But I think I convinced them I wasn't guilty of any wrongdoing."

Relief flooded her features. "Good." Then, looking somber, she added, "I found out something about Becker that you're not going to like."

He swallowed. "I know already. Who told you?" he asked after exhaling a shaky breath.

"I overheard my dad talking to him on the phone. So it's true? He really did do it?"

"Yes." He swallowed. "Nicklaus took a bribe, too—he's our goalie." His anger returned like a punch to the gut. "I can't believe they would do that. Especially Sam."

"I'm sorry," Hayden said again, reaching up to touch his chin with her warm fingers. "But I think forgiveness will come in time. If I can forgive my dad, maybe you'll be able to forgive your friend."

Brody faltered. "And if I can't?"

"I'll help you." She smiled glibly. "I'm good at forgiveness. After all, didn't I forgive you for dumping me?"

"I panicked, okay? And I only suggested we put things on hol—" He stopped when he saw the amusement in her eyes. "You're not mad," he said.

"Of course not." She ran her index finger along the curve of his jaw. "I can't stay mad at the man I love."

He held his breath, not daring to give in to the sheer bliss threatening to spill over. "You mean that?"

"Yes." She lifted her other hand and cupped his chin with both her hands. "I love you, Brody. I know I kept fighting you whenever you said we were perfect for each other, but…I'm not fighting anymore." She exhaled slowly. "I've fallen for you, hockey star. The earth moves when we're together and I love it. I love you."

The joy in his heart spilled over, warming his insides and making his pulse skate through his veins like a player on a breakaway.

"I'm willing to be part of the hockey lifestyle for as long as it takes," she added, certainty shining in her eyes. "I'll even go to your games." She chewed on her bottom lip. "But I'll probably bring some lecture notes to work on, you know, because I still don't particularly like hockey, but I'll make an effort to—"

He silenced her with a kiss, but pulled away just as she parted her lips to let him in.

"I won't play hockey forever, Hayden," he said softly. "And I'm already trying to work on the possibility of signing with a West Coast team next season. That way you can keep teaching at Berkeley, and we could—" his voice cracked "—we could get started on building a life together. A *home*."

As he said the words, he knew without a doubt that's what he wanted. A home with Hayden. A life with the one woman who looked past his uniform and saw the man beneath it. He'd been searching for her for so long, and now that he'd found her, he wasn't about to let her go. Ever.

"I love you, Hayden," he said roughly. "More than hockey, more than being successful, more than life. I want to wake up every morning and see one of your sleepy smiles, go to bed every night pressed up against you, have kids with you, grow old with you." He put his hands on her slender hips and pulled her toward him. "Will you let me do that?"

Twining her arms around his neck, she leaned up and kissed him, a long, lingering kiss that promised love and laughter and hot, endless sex. Pulling back, just an inch, she whispered, "Yes," and then raised her lips to his again.

"Should we seal the deal?" he murmured against her hot, pliant mouth.

"God, yes."

Deepening the kiss, he untucked her shirt from the waistband of her skirt and slid his hands underneath, filling his palms with the feel of her silky skin. His tongue sought hers. His hands found her breasts.

Hayden moaned. "No, not here." Breaking contact, she darted over to the nightstand and pulled out a condom. Without another word, she grabbed his hand and dragged him out of the bedroom to the middle of the narrow hallway.

"Here," she said, a playful light dancing in her eyes.

He looked at the spot she'd chosen, chuckling when he realized this was the first place they'd made love. On the hallway floor, while Hayden writhed beneath him and squeezed his ass and pushed him into her as deep as he could go.

"Here is perfect," he answered huskily.

He drew her into his arms, claiming her with his mouth, and they were both breathless by the time the kiss ended. Gently stroking her cheek, he gave her another soft kiss, then began peeling her clothes from her body. First her shirt, then the bra, the skirt, the panties, until she was standing naked in front of him, a vision of perfection. He marveled at her silky curves and perfect skin, those beautiful breasts, the shapely legs… God, he couldn't believe she was his. All his.

"I love you, Hayden," he said, his throat thick with emotion. "I love everything about you."

She gave a soft sigh of pleasure as he cupped her breasts, tenderly stroking the swell of each perfect mound.

He hastily removed his own clothes, kicked them aside, then dropped to his knees and peppered little kisses on her flat abdomen before moving to nip at her inner thigh. He loved the sweet little moan she responded with, loved the way she tangled her fingers in his hair and guided him to the spot between her legs that he knew ached for his touch.

He kissed her sensitized nub, flicked his tongue over her sweetness. He would never be able to get enough of her, even if he spent the rest of his life trying. With a small groan, he planted one last kiss on her soft folds and then pulled her down to the carpet.

With a look of pure contentment swimming in her forest-green eyes, Hayden lay back, spread her legs and offered him a wicked smile.

"Don't keep me waiting," she said with just a hint of challenge in her throaty voice.

"I don't intend to."

He covered her body with his, his shaft, hot and hard, pressed up against her belly. He shifted so that his tip brushed her wet sex, but didn't plunge inside.

First, he kissed her again, a long, lazy kiss, and then he pulled back and said, "No ground rules this time."

Her eyelids fluttered open. "What?"

"That second night, you said there were ground rules." He nipped at the hot flesh of her neck. "No rules this time. You're getting not only my body, but my heart and my soul, every night for the rest of your life. Got it?"

She raised her brows. "Again with the demands, huh?"

"You got a problem with that?"

With a laugh, she gripped his hair with her fingers and pulled his head down. Slipping her tongue into his mouth, she kissed him until he could barely see straight, then reached between them, circled his shaft and guided it to her opening, pushing herself down over his length.

He gasped.

"I don't have…" she moaned as she took him in deeper "…a single problem with that." With a breathy sigh, she wrapped her arms around his neck and pressed a kiss to his collarbone. "I love you, Brody."

He slowly withdrew, then plunged back in, filling her to the hilt. "It drives me wild when you say that," he squeezed out.

"What, I love you?"

His cock jerked in response. "Yes, that."

She lifted her hips off the ground, and hooked her legs around his lower back, holding him prisoner with her wet heat. "Good, because I plan on saying it often. I love you, Brody Croft."

Staying true to her word, she brushed her lips over his ear and said it again. And again. And again. With a groan, he buried his head in the crook of her neck, inhaled her sweet scent and sent them both to heaven.

And when they were sated and happy and lying there on the carpet, Brody could swear that the earth had moved.

Epilogue

One year later

"SERIOUSLY, BABE, we need to do something about that shower," Brody grumbled as he stepped out of the bathroom.

Hayden couldn't help but laugh at the aggravation on his ridiculously handsome face. "The plumber will be here on Monday, *babe*. Quit getting your panties in a knot."

He strode into the recently painted master bedroom of their San Diego home, his frown deepening. "It really doesn't bother you?"

"No, Brody. It doesn't. It's just a removable showerhead, for Pete's sake. We'll live without it for a couple more days."

She rolled her eyes and rose from the bed. They'd purchased the house two months ago, at a bargain since the rambling three-story Victorian was in desperate need of renovations. So far, they'd painted every room, gutted the living room, retiled the kitchen—and Brody was worrying about a showerhead. Her husband definitely had a one-track mind. Of course, she'd known that when she'd married him.

"We should head over to the restaurant," she said, swiftly putting an end to the subject Brody refused to drop. "Darcy will be wondering where we are."

Brody snorted. "Darcy is probably having sex with one of the waiters as we speak."

She wagged her finger at him. "Be nice. She's taken a vow of celibacy, remember?"

Another snort. "Yeah, and I'm sure that'll last for, oh, ten seconds. No, make that five."

Hayden laughed, knowing he was probably right. Leopards couldn't get rid of their spots, lions weren't about to grow horns and Darcy White certainly couldn't "quit" men. But Hayden was glad her friend was finally able to take time off and visit them. Darcy was actually considering moving to the West Coast, and Hayden was avidly encouraging her friend to do so. She would love having Darcy around on a more regular basis, especially since she wouldn't be able to travel with Brody to his away games for much longer.

Although the Warriors hadn't made it far in the play-offs last season, Brody's standings had impressed the Los Angeles Vipers' general manager, who'd made him an offer, to both Hayden and Brody's relief. It put an end to the "where do we live" dilemma that had been plaguing them since the engagement. Brody signed with the Vipers, and since the commute to San Francisco had been too much for her, she'd agreed to teach courses at Berkeley during the hockey season as well as a few summer courses. The arrangement worked for both of them; the online seminars gave her the time to work on her Ph.D. at the University of San Diego, and getting to L.A. from San Diego would be easier for Brody.

They'd married in Chicago, though, deciding it was fitting to say their vows in the city where they'd met and fallen in love. Brody's parents had flown in for the wedding; Darcy had been the maid of honor, and the guests were a mixture of academics and athletes, including Brody's former captain Craig Wyatt, who'd brought Hayden's ex-stepmother. Shockingly, Wyatt and Sheila were now engaged, and Sheila was happily planning the wedding and enjoying the money she'd gotten from her divorce; she'd eventually settled for half of Presley's estate.

Hayden's dad hadn't been able to make it to the wedding—the rehabilitation facility he'd checked himself into hadn't allowed it—but he'd sent her a beautiful letter that stated how happy he was she and Brody had found love. He'd also thanked her for supporting him through everything, and Hayden had been in tears when she'd read his heartfelt words.

"Hey, you okay?"

Brody's concerned voice drew her from her thoughts. She managed a nod. "Yeah. I was just thinking about my dad."

Brody moved closer and wrapped his strong arms around her. "I know you wish he would move out here, but you can't monitor every move he makes, Hayden. He's sober now. Just have faith that he'll stay that way."

"I know." She sighed. "At least he's not in jail."

Last year's league investigation had resulted in criminal charges being brought up on her father, as well as the players he'd bribed, but Presley had gotten off with a fine and four years' probation. Since her dad hadn't been involved in a gambling ring or organized crime, he'd been lucky with his punishment. He'd lost the team, though, and Hayden knew that had been a big blow for her dad. The Warriors were now owned by none other than Jonas Quade, the man of many mistresses and that god-awful tan.

Sam Becker had wound up with probation, too, but Brody still couldn't seem to forgive his former friend. Hayden hoped that in time the two men might reconcile.

"Last time he called he mentioned he's thinking of buying a place by Lake Michigan," Brody was saying, still talking about her dad. "Did he tell you that?"

"No, he didn't mention it." She suddenly smiled, wondering if maybe there was hope for her dad after all. He might have lost the team, but he seemed much happier lately, and the two of them were on their way to regaining the close relationship they'd had when she was younger.

"I told you he used to take me fishing when I was a kid, right?" she said.

Her husband kissed her on the cheek and took her hand. "Come on, we should go."

"You're right. Darce will freak out if we don't show up soon. She's been really bitchy lately. You know, the lack of sex and all."

They headed for the doorway. "Actually, I think she'll freak out when she sees *this*." Brody rubbed her protruding belly with his palm.

Hayden sighed. She was only five months along, and already she felt huge. "Remind me again how you knocked me up when we'd decided to wait a couple years?"

He shot her a cocky grin. "I told you. I never miss. It's my fatal flaw."

"No, your fatal flaw is not getting me the ice cream I asked for last night."

They left the bedroom and walked down their brand-new winding staircase. The floor in the front hall still needed to be laid down, but Hayden didn't care as long as the renovations were done before the baby came. She grabbed her purse from the hall table and slipped into her flat sandals.

She followed Brody out on the porch, lifting her head to the late-afternoon sun and breathing in the warm San Diego air.

"I told you why I didn't pick up the ice cream," Brody grumbled. "You've got to eat healthy, babe. You're carrying a future champion in that belly of yours. Our son needs proper nourishment."

Oh, brother. Not again.

"I only need one champion in my life, thank you very much." She shot him a sweet smile. "Our *daughter* is going to be a Nobel Prize winner."

"It's a boy," he said confidently with a charming smile of his own. "Haven't you figured out by now that I always get what I want?"

"God, you're arrogant."

"Yeah, but you like it." His grin widened. "And if it weren't for me, you'd still be hiking across some intimacy bridge—"

"I should never have told you about that!"

"And deprive me of endless bridge jokes?"

She tried to scowl but ended up laughing. "Fine. I surrender. The intimacy bridge is funny. Now let's go before Darcy really does sleep with a waiter."

Brody held her arm as they walked to the car. He opened the door for her, then rounded the vehicle and got into the driver's seat.

She stretched the seat belt over her stomach and buckled up, then tucked a strand of hair behind her ears. Suddenly she became aware of Brody watching her, and when she turned her head, her breath caught at the awe, love and passion she saw shining in his eyes.

"Have I told you today how beautiful you are?" he asked.

"Twice, actually." Warmth suffused her body. "But feel free to say it as many times as you'd like."

"Believe me, I will." He shifted closer and stroked her cheek. "You know, the happiest day of my life was when you walked up to that pool table and asked me back to your hotel."

"You're not going to tell our daughter that, are you?"

"Nah. We'll tell *our son* we met at a museum and it was love at first sight."

He cupped her jaw and ran his thumb over her lower lip, sending a wave of heat and desire through her. She could never get enough of Brody's touch, not even if she lived to be a hundred.

"Let's skip dinner," he murmured, then dipped his head to kiss her.

Her pulse raced as his tongue teased hers with long, sensual strokes.

It took all her willpower to pull back. "We can't." When he grumbled, she added, "Come on, it's one little dinner. I'll make it worth your while…"

His eyes lit up. "How?"

She laughed. "You'll just have to wait and see."

"For you, I'd wait forever. In fact, I'd do just about anything you asked." His gaze softened. "I love you that much, Mrs. Croft."

She leaned closer and brushed her lips over his. "I love you, too…so let's get this dinner over with so I can get you home and show you *exactly* how much."

* * * * *

Playing To Win
Taryn Leigh Taylor

Taryn Leigh Taylor likes dinosaurs, bridges and space, both personal and of the final-frontier variety. She shamelessly indulges in clichés, most notably her Starbucks addiction (grande six-pump whole-milk no-water chai tea latte, aka: the usual), her shoe hoard (I can stop anytime I... Ooh! These are pretty!) and her penchant for falling in lust with fictional men with great abs. She also really loves books, which is what sent her down the crazy path of writing one in the first place.

Want to be virtual friends? Check out tarynleightaylor.com, facebook.com/tarynleightaylor1 and twitter.com/tarynltaylor.

Books by Taryn Leigh Taylor

Harlequin Blaze

Kiss and Makeup

To get the inside scoop on Harlequin Blaze and its talented writers, be sure to check out BlazeAuthors.com.

All backlist available in ebook format.

Visit the Author Profile page at millsandboon.com.au for more titles.

Dear Reader,

I usually don't remember how ideas get from my brain to the page, but this novel's origin story can be traced back to a cold, snowy evening while watching *Hockey Night in Canada*. (What? A Canadian who likes hockey? It's true. I'm also a woman with way too many pairs of shoes. Embracing clichés is good for the soul, eh?)

At one point in the game, the TV announcer was talking about a defenseman and actually said, I kid you not, "He's a big, strong farm boy with good hands."

Um...yes please! I'll take one of those.

And the Women's Hockey Network was born. My friend and I joked endlessly about *Sexy Sports Coverage for Her*, complete with play-off beard analysis ("As you can see from this graph, peak attractiveness was reached here, when he was sporting six days' worth of stubble in game three of the first series."), and some risqué, double-entendre commentating ("I really admire the way he keeps such a firm grip on his stick. That kind of control is going to result in some great scoring opportunities.").

Our inside joke was a romance novel waiting to happen, and Luke and Holly were the perfect duo for the job. They're both incredibly career-focused, and it was a blast to bodycheck them out of their comfort zones and into each other's arms.

By the way, do you like the internet? I hang out there sometimes at tarynleightaylor.com, facebook.com/ tarynltaylor1 and on Twitter @tarynltaylor. You should totally swing by if you're in the neighborhood.

Keep on dreaming out loud,

Taryn Leigh Taylor

DEDICATION

This one's for my Women's Hockey Network cohost, and the best amanuensis in the business. Cool Crystal, I owe you a slab of cake with a cupcake on top.

To Adrienne, who always makes my stories better. I don't have the words to thank you enough. (But editors like irony, right?)

My love forever to Uncle Don and Auntie Shirl for keeping it real and staying true to the home team amidst a sea of red.

Mimsy, Dadoo and the man behind Grammataco— I'm so lucky to have you guys in my corner. High fives and secret handshakes all around.

And to my Palisades Crew: Michele, Michelle, Lori, Carolyne, Marilyn and Laura. The kind of women, and writers, who inspire me even now.

1

"QUIT SQUIRMING, HOL. You look totally porn-hot."

Holly Evans glared at her friend and cameraman. "Well, thanks, Jay. I feel so much better now. After all, 'porn-hot' is just what we professional sportscasters aspire to, right, Corey?"

She immediately regretted throwing the question to the reporter setting up a few feet down the rubber-floored hallway. Corey Baniuk was Portland's favorite on-the-scene sports authority...at least for now.

Rumor had it that Jim Purcell, the longtime sports anchor at *Portland News Now*, was contemplating retirement and that Corey had a lock on the in-studio position. That meant Holly's dream job might soon be up for grabs—and Holly intended to do the grabbing. Provided she hadn't screwed up all her credibility by playing Sports Reporter Barbie for the next three months, of course.

"Sure." Corey shot her the familiar, good-natured grin that was a staple of both the six and eleven o'clock news. "Someone will be by to oil my chest any minute."

His camera guy chuckled and heat prickled up Holly's

cheeks, no doubt rivaling the fire-engine-red color of her outfit. She forced a wan smile—small thanks for him taking the high road, but it was all she could muster. God, she envied him his conservative gray pinstripe suit. And he was even wearing a shirt under his jacket. She would give up her firstborn for a shirt.

"How did this happen?" she lamented in Jay Buchanan's general direction. "I am an intelligent, educated woman who is passionate about all things sports." She glanced down at her brazen skirt suit, but with her boobs pushed up to her chin, not much of it was visible to her.

Damn Victoria and all her secrets.

"When did I become the Hooters girl of broadcasting?"

Jay rolled his eyes. "Hey, you knew what you were signing up for. Hell, I'll bet Lougheed had dollar signs circling his head when he saw your audition tape."

Holly cringed at her friend's choice of words. "It wasn't an audition tape," she protested weakly. "It was a favor for you. And a fight against injustice."

When she'd agreed to shoot the joke video with Jay's fledgling production company, she was aiming for satire, intending it to be biting commentary on how female sports reporters were perceived. It was an attempt to show people the stereotypes she fought against every day in pursuit of her dream. Instead, she was now the star of a bona fide viral video, sporting a teased-out helmet of blond hair and freezing her butt off while she pretended to be hockey-impaired.

It had caught the attention of Ron Lougheed, the GM of Portland's professional hockey team, and the ditzy routine was now, sadly, the best on-camera experience she'd been offered since she'd graduated broad-casting school.

"No one cares what it *was*. What the Women's Hockey Network *is*, is a YouTube sensation! People are eating it up and coming back for seconds. To the suits, you're the living, breathing, high-heel-wearing crowbar they're gonna use to pry into the coveted female demographic."

"And they somehow figure short skirts are going to help me accomplish that lofty goal?" she asked snidely, tugging said skirt back down her thighs.

"Hell, no! That's to keep the guys interested while you're talking about girly stuff like player hairdos."

With a deep breath of arena—rubber and concrete and sweat and ice—Holly called upon the stupid yoga class she'd suffered through two years ago at her best friend Paige's behest. Something about a mind/body connection, and inner peace, and deep breaths, and—ah, screw it.

Time to suck it up, Princess.

Jay was right. She'd accepted the job as the Portland Storm's web reporter for the duration of their play-off run, and if dressing like someone's too-slutty-to-acknowledge cousin was the price of breaking into her dream career, then that's what she'd do. She gave a determined nod at the thought, slamming a mental door on the last remnants of her doubt.

The buzzer sounded to hail the end of the game, and Holly's newly minted courage took a nosedive. This was it. Her debut.

She watched with mounting nerves as twenty massive men in skates and full equipment stalked toward her.

And speaking of porn-hot...

There he was: Luke Maguire, team captain, number eighteen, a premier left-winger with a career-best thirty-seven goals in the regular season this year. Not to mention sexy as hell and in possession of all of his teeth—no rare feat after six years in professional hockey. The man looked incredible, all tall and sweaty and pissed off over the loss of their first play-off game against Colorado.

When she caught his eye, she was torn somewhere between lust and duty. Then his gaze dropped to the straining top button of her suit jacket, and she felt extreme mortification enter the mix. He slowed his pace, lifted his beautiful blue eyes from her cleavage to her face and stepped out of the single-file line of burly hockey players to take a question. *From her.*

This was it. Her big moment. Thirty seconds with one of the elite players of the game. But instead of being able to ask something pertinent, like his thoughts on the lackluster performance of the Storm's players, or his musings on the unprecedented twenty penalty minutes they'd accrued, she was contractually obligated to say:

"This is Holly Evans of the Women's Hockey Network, and with me tonight is the captain of the Portland Storm, Luke Maguire! Luke, it's play-off season, a time when superstitions run rampant and hockey players all over the league stop shaving, even though a recent study shows that women prefer the clean-shaven look to a full beard by a margin of almost four to one. Do you think tonight's loss had anything to do with the fact that you chose to shave today, and do you plan on reconsidering your stance on facial hair as the play-offs progress?"

One straight, brown eyebrow crooked up, the only indication he'd even heard her "question." (She was willing to concede that she was using the term loosely.)

He shoved the nightmarish memory back into the mental penalty box where it belonged, barely aware he'd reached for his helmet until he caught himself brushing his thumb across the number ten sticker he'd placed inside it—a talisman to keep him focused. With a sigh, he reached up and set his helmet on the shelf above his head.

He was the team captain now, he reminded himself. He had a job to do and he couldn't afford to wallow in personal issues. You couldn't lead a team to victory if they didn't trust you to take care of business. And yet he didn't seem to be leading the team anywhere but to an early play-off exit. They all needed to get their heads out of their asses.

"We won't be in the play-offs for long if we keep playing like we just did. I know there are some nerves in the room. This franchise has never been in the play-offs before, and no one here has ever won a championship. None of that matters. We need to play our game, stay hungry and determined.

"And we can't get sidetracked by the increased media scrutiny. Especially now that even the non-sports media are hunting for stories and interviews. The blonde out there actually asked me if I thought we lost because I'm not growing a play-off beard."

The entire dressing room went silent as Luke untied his skate. He glanced around at his eerily quiet team-mates. "What?"

"Well, we *did* lose…"

Luke's face twisted with disgust. "Are you kidding me? It's the first game! None of you even have beards yet. You guys really buy into this 'no shaving' bull?"

The rookie stroked his pitiful day's worth of stubble.

"All I know is that I'm in this to win this, and if sportin' a Grizzly Adams gets me closer to a championship, then I'm on it like STDs on a hooker."

"You realize that three out of four women hate beards, right?" Luke pulled his skate off, hating that he'd actually reduced himself to quoting stats from that reporter.

Sillinger got a philosophical look on his face. "Shave and you get laid for a night. Do what it takes to score a championship ring, and you'll be up to your balls in puck bunnies for the rest of your life. I mean, seriously, Mags. A woman with a body like that reporter's names me her 'hockey hottie of the month,' and I'll answer any stupid question she asks."

Luke paused in the act of loosening his other skate. "What are you talking about?"

"Are you serious?" Sillinger's surprise was obvious. "Holly Evans? The Women's Hockey Network?"

Luke gave a bewildered shrug.

"Dude, she's all over YouTube! She does this girly hockey-analysis show that's gone viral. And in it, she named *you* the hottest hockey player in the league. The top brass practically begged her to be our web reporter during the play-offs! Do you guys believe this? Hot Stuff here doesn't even know who Holly Evans is!"

The announcement set off a round of catcalls and ribbing. Luke turned to his linemate, Eric Jacobs. The stoic centerman gave a shrug of his big shoulders and shook his head. Luke was relieved he wasn't the only one out of the loop on this.

"Okay, okay." Luke waited for the dressing room to quiet. "Let's stay focused, guys. The game might be over, but we've still got work to do."

Work that involved hours of ripping apart the carcass

of the worst game they'd played all year. The assembled jackals—uh, *reporters*—were going to eat him alive, Luke thought soberly. He shed the rest of his equipment and headed for the showers.

But that was the price of the *C* on his jersey. The price of earning a living doing what he loved. Which was an honor and a privilege, considering some people never got that chance. And others had it stolen from them. Luke sighed.

At least the evisceration wouldn't have anything to do with beard statistics and superstitious nonsense. And yet somehow Luke sensed that Holly Evans was a bigger threat than all the other sports reporters combined...

2

"THE STORM ESSENTIALLY played an entire period short-handed, which, given the dismal play of your PK unit, definitely contributed to tonight's loss. Can you give us any insight as to what led to this unprecedented number of penalties for the Storm?"

Holly hit the pause button on last night's broadcast and whirled on the couch to face her best friend, Paige Hallett. "Did you hear that? That was my question. Corey Baniuk just asked Luke Maguire *my* question. And did the dumb jock walk away without a word? No. He stood there and answered it, the jerk!"

"You asked him that question and he ignored you?" Paige looked offended on her behalf.

"Well, no. I asked him if he thought he might grow a play-off beard—then he ignored me. But that's the question I *wanted* to ask him. That was a great question!"

Paige turned back to the magazine she was perusing. "I'll take your word for it. He lost me when he started talking about China. Besides, why would the Storm play a whole period shorthanded? Seems kind of counterproductive to me."

Holly sighed and set the remote on her coffee table. "They didn't play an actual period shorthanded, they got twenty penalty minutes, so over the course of the game, they essentially played a man short for the length of a period. And he didn't say Peking, he said *PK* unit. When a team gets a penalty, they put out their best penalty killers, their *penalty kill* unit."

"Oh. Well, why didn't he just say that?"

"He did! He *did* say that, and Luke Maguire answered him, because it was a relevant question asked by a serious sports reporter."

Paige shot her a sympathetic look. "*You're* a serious sports reporter."

"No, *I'm* a traitor to my gender. Last night I wore a tiny suit and high shoes and made a mockery of everything I love."

"Would you cut yourself some slack? Those were some seriously great shoes I picked out for you to wear. Besides, the only way you're truly a traitor to your gender is the complete lack of readable magazines in your house." Paige held up the *Sports Illustrated* she was flipping through as proof. "Seriously. If these guys weren't shirtless, I'd throw this across the room in protest. Oh, wow." A dreamy smile spread across Paige's pretty face. "Who is *that*? Come to momma."

Holly glanced over at the glossy, two-page spread featuring a certain hot, shirtless hockey player. His brown hair was the perfect length between shorn and shaggy, his blue eyes intense as ever. He was sitting in the dressing room, kitted out in hockey gear from the waist down—pants, socks and skates—and all muscle and beautiful bronzed skin from the waist up. Behind him, his last name and a big number 18 gleamed white against the navy of his Storm jersey.

"That's *Luke Maguire*. The topic of my diatribe for the last twenty minutes? The man currently paused on my television?" Holly gestured at his stupid handsome face in HD.

"Well, why didn't you tell me he was so yummy? I would have paid better attention." She glanced at the television, presumably for the first time since her arrival. "*Mmm.* Maybe you were right. I should watch more hockey."

Holly couldn't help but smile. She had been trying to open Paige up to the wonders of sports for the better part of a decade now. How had Holly not realized the best way to turn Paige on to sports was to *turn Paige on*? "You're incorrigible, you know that?"

Paige smiled sweetly. "I'm a divorcée with no serious relationship prospects on the horizon. I have to take my thrills where I can get them." She flicked her gaze back to the TV. "And that man looks like he gives good thrill."

Holly couldn't argue. Irrationally, it made her even angrier at him. At one of her favorite hockey players. One day of playing dress-up and her view of the sports world was already starting to become skewed. So far, a steady paycheck was the only thing she enjoyed about this gig. Especially after such a mortifying first night. She'd taken the job because it was her chance to get on camera. One step closer to her big dream of talking sports on TV. But now...

"I'm wondering if taking this job was a mistake," she confessed.

Since she'd graduated, she'd been plugging away,

ghostwriting sports pieces for a bunch of online sports
blogs. Hockey, basketball, baseball, football, golf…you
name it, she wrote it. Not that anyone knew, since all
her painstaking work was credited to "staff writer."
But it was the only way she could continue to write for
enough outlets to make a living. She spent what little
free time she had busting her butt trying to get one of
her sports op-eds picked up.

That was the kind of writing she really loved—not
spewing facts and stats and scores, but interpreting
them, putting them in context, figuring out what was
making a team successful, suggesting what they could
do to become more so, having a go at dumb managerial
decisions and underperforming athletes.

That sort of in-depth analysis was the key to getting
where she really belonged—on television, just like her
mom used to be. She wanted to read her pieces aloud,
share them with people who loved sports as much as she
did. Anyone could read a teleprompter; Holly wanted
to make an impact.

"I mean, Jay and I made the Women's Hockey Network video as a joke. And now it's gotten me closer to
my goal of being on camera than any article I've ever
written." Holly looked down, picking at the red lacquer
Paige had insisted on slicking over her stubby nails.
"But instead of feeling great about that, I feel like I've
sold out. I'm a joke. I mean, can you even imagine what
my mom would think of all this?"

"Woah. Back up the pity bus. I will not let you go
down the mom road. She loved you and she would want
what's best for you. But Hols, even if your mom was
still alive, what's best for you would be your choice,
not hers."

Holly flopped onto the couch. "I know. But I still worry about letting her down. When I accepted this gig, I thought it was going to be a case of 'all publicity is good publicity.' Now I'm not so sure."

She ran her hands down her face. "Luke Maguire believes I'm a total idiot! How can I ever do an in-depth interview with him now? And I don't even get to travel with the team! That's how dumb the questions I ask are supposed to be. I'm not worth a seat on a chartered plane that's already been paid for."

Paige glanced up from a picture featuring a shirtless LA Laker. "Lighten up, would you? It's been one day. This job is a stepping-stone—one with over a hundred thousand hits on YouTube so far. You never know where this opportunity could take you. Besides, what do you think the rest of your former sports broadcasting class-mates are doing right now? Interviewing team mascots and reporting on who scored the most baskets in soc-cer games played by twelve-year-olds? I'll bet you're closer to a real gig than any of them." Paige shut the magazine and tossed it onto the coffee table. "You're working with a real hockey team, interviewing some of the best players in the game. And yeah, it's not per-fect, but it could be a hell of a lot worse. So to quote a good friend of mine—" Paige arched one perfectly winged eyebrow "—*suck it up, Princess*. Go out there and do the job."

Holly sighed. "I hate it when you're right."

"Then you must hate me all the time," her friend lamented with a grin. It faded after a moment. "Was that enough of a pep talk? Because I'll bail on my date and we can go out for a drink if you want to talk this out some more."

"Oh, right! You have a date." Holly shook her head. "I keep forgetting since you've been so secretive about this mystery man of yours."

"It's new. We're still feeling each other out. Once we start feeling each other *up*, then I'll have some details to share." Paige was the only person in the world Holly knew who could pull off a wink with such aplomb.

"Of that I have no doubt. Now go and have fun. Besides, I'm already in the middle of a sports-related crisis. There's no way I can muster the fortitude and patience it would take to teach you that you don't score baskets in soccer right now."

Paige laughed at the jab.

Holly squared her shoulders. "Like you said, I made this choice. I'm going to honor this contract. Maybe I can even convince them to let me do some real reporting. Wow 'em so they give me a chance to document the Storm's first time in the play-offs with the gravitas and seriousness that it deserves."

"That's the spirit! You show those men who's boss." The phone rang just as Paige stood to leave. "See? That's probably some titan of the hockey world, impressed with your journalistic integrity and calling to poach you for his own team."

"Who else could it be?" Holly agreed drolly. "Say hi to your date for me."

"No way. Get your own man, which I hope you do soon. You're in desperate need of some hunky distraction in your life," Paige advised, heading for the door. "At the very least, this job will be great for that."

Holly rolled her eyes in a silent goodbye as she grabbed the handset of her phone, recognizing Jay's number on call display. Paige didn't like him very much,

but Holly and Jay had hit it off immediately in broadcasting school.

When the Storm offered to let her pick her own cameraman, she'd eagerly snatched Jay away from filming
weddings and local stories. It was a relief not to have to
fake sports stupidity with at least one person.

"Hey. The footage looks great." Embarrassing as it
might be for her personally, she had to admit that Jay
had edited her interviews with Luke and the rest of the
team into a professional-looking comedic montage that
could now be viewed by the world at portlandstorm.com.

"I'm glad you think so, because the boss man agrees."

"What?"

"That's why I'm calling. Check your texts."

"Or you could just tell me since we're, you know, *on
the phone*," she pointed out.

"Okay, smart-ass. It seems your big-haired alter ego
can do no wrong. Hits on the Storm's website have increased twenty percent since your interview was posted
last night. Usually after a loss, website traffic goes
down. They've decided to give us an extra assignment."

"Oh, God." Holly cringed. She couldn't help it. A
twenty percent uptick? That did not bode well for Operation: Journalistic Integrity. She'd be stuck asking
about favorite childhood breakfast cereals for the rest
of her career while important stories, like Luke Maguire's scoring drought that had now entered its twelfth
game, went unmentioned.

On the upside, at least the team captain was so annoyed with her about the play-off beard thing that she
could focus her insipid questions on the rest of the players. "What do they want us to film?"

"Some fluffy pregame interviews with the guys, to-

morrow after their morning skate. The brass plans to
air them as teasers between periods to help drive up
website traffic. We're starting with the big three, then
we'll try to fit in as much of the rest of the team as we
can manage."

The big three: goaltender Jean-Claude LaCroix, centerman Eric Jacobs, and, because sometimes life sucked
with a vengeance, captain and left-winger Luke Maguire. Holly couldn't bring herself to speak through
the impending sense of doom.

THWACK.

Luke's slap shot missed the net completely.

God—*thwack*—damn—*thwack*—mother—
thwack—fuc—

"Mags!"

Luke looked up from the line of pucks he was sys-
tematically assaulting to see Jean-Claude LaCroix—
J.C. to his teammates—standing in the players' box. He
was dressed in a navy T-shirt that mimicked the Storm's
home jersey, this year's standard issue for doing press.

With another muttered curse, Luke skated over to
the bench.

"I just finished with the reporter, and Eric's in the
hot seat right now. Someone can cover for you with her
if you want to grab a shower, but to avoid the wrath of
the higher-ups, I'd suggest you get a move on."

Luke pulled off one of his gloves so he could remove
his helmet and set them both on the boards. "Yeah, I'll
be there in a minute."

"You okay, man?"

He ran a hand over his sweaty hair. "Sure. What
could be wrong?"

J.C. gave him a look. "You're the one who snapped two sticks in practice and is still out here pounding the boards. You tell me."

Luke appreciated his friend's tact. It wasn't like his problem wasn't obvious.

He couldn't hit the net.

It had been twelve games since he'd scored a goal—the longest dry spell of his hockey career. But no matter how hard he practiced, how much extra time he logged out here working on his shot, when he was in the game, he froze up. And people were noticing. He'd read the grumblings in the paper, heard the callouts on television. Hell, people were even tweeting him to say he sucked. If he didn't get his act together soon, he'd be headed for some obligatory couch time with the sports psychologist. And that meant talking about Ethan, a fate he tried to avoid at all costs.

"It's nothing." Luke brushed it off, hoping his buddy would let it go.

J.C. shook his head, rejecting the lie. Luke should have known he would. They'd been playing hockey together on and off since they were fourteen years old. At this point, his goaltender could read him just as well off the ice as on.

"It's *not* nothing, man. Don't overthink it. Besides, scoring isn't the only way to help the team."

"Easy for you to say. Your save percentage was .916 this season. You're doing your part, but we won't win if we don't put pucks in the other guys' net." Luke's shoulders tightened under the weight of expectation—from management, the fans, his teammates… "I haven't scored in over a month. What am I supposed to do about that?"

"Just relax and play the game."

Luke rolled his eyes at the Zen advice. "This is the reason people hate goalies, you know? You're all a bunch of pretentious assholes."

J.C. just grinned. "I'll see you up there, okay?"

With a nod, Luke grabbed his helmet and glove and headed to the dressing room to shower and change, hoping he could clear his head before he faced Holly Evans. His brain conjured the memory of the curvy blonde in the siren-red outfit. Yet another complication he didn't need right now. Because last night, he'd done something stupid.

With a self-directed curse, he'd opened a new browser window and typed "The Women's Hockey Network" into the search field on YouTube.

And there she was, Holly Evans, all big blond hair and big brown eyes and big, beautiful breasts. In fact, she was damn near perfect...until she got to the Hockey Hunk of the Month segment.

He wanted to be pissed.

Instead, he was oddly flattered.

Sure, he wasn't wild about the fact she'd used that damned shirtless picture of him from last month's *Sports Illustrated*, but after his on-ice struggles over the last month, he found his battered self-esteem had sort of appreciated the boost from those pouty, shiny lips of hers.

She'd even managed to make the award about more than his pectorals, citing his work with his pet charity, Kids on Wheels, and explaining its focus on providing wheelchairs and wheelchair-friendly sports programs for kids in need. Hell, she'd even brought up his role as a goodwill ambassador for ice sledge hockey, a cause near and dear to his heart.

If he wasn't so firmly anti-reporter, he might have approved of the way she'd so beautifully shifted the focus from the nonsensical to something that actually mattered. But in the end, what mattered most was winning, and ogling the pretty reporter wasn't going to help him put the puck in the net.

Now, Luke stood outside the dressing room, temporarily set aside this morning so that she could make a mockery of the sport he loved, willing himself to man up and walk in.

He scratched his chin self-consciously, wishing to hell that he'd shaved this morning. He didn't want to give her the satisfaction of assuming his decision not to shave had anything to do with her. If he'd been given any kind of heads-up about being locked in a room with Little Miss Play-off Beard today, he definitely would've given a big middle finger to all the doubts she and his teammates had planted about their loss. But there'd been no warning until just before practice. No doubt about it, karma was a stone-cold bitch.

With a deep breath, he stepped through the door to find his linemate was just finishing up his interview.

"That was great, Eric." Holly's voice, warm and sexy, called to mind the drizzle of honey on cream. Luke subconsciously turned toward it.

God*damn*, the woman was gorgeous. She was rocking the painted-on suit again, but this time the color was the same teal as the stripes and the cresting wave on the Storm jersey. (A color which, according to the Women's Hockey Network color chart, indicated a driven personality whose inner turmoil was often masked by an outward appearance of calm.)

She was sporting mile-high heels, a barely there skirt, plenty of cleavage and that big, tousled hair that probably felt like a helmet of straw in real life, but always managed to look kinda sexy on TV. And yet, now that she wasn't just a caricature on his computer screen, but a living, breathing woman, smiling and putting the notoriously shy Eric Jacobs at ease as they finished up their interview, he found himself wondering what she'd look like in jeans and a T-shirt.

The thought irritated him. He just wanted to get this whole thing over with so he could concentrate on the important stuff. Like winning hockey games. He made himself take a step forward. "So I guess that means I'm up?"

With obvious relief, Jacobs flashed him a thankful smile, said a quick goodbye and fled the scene.

Holly whirled around, tugging at her skirt as though willing more fabric to appear. "Luke! Uh, Mr. Maguire, I—"

"Luke's fine."

They lapsed into an awkward silence.

She bit her lip.

Damn, her mouth is amazing. And he really needed to stop noticing that.

He pulled a frustrated hand down his face, cursing inwardly as he realized his mistake. Satisfaction sparked in those coffee-brown eyes of hers—he and his day's worth of stubble were busted. But to his surprise, her dawning smile was more teasing than mocking, and it made him want to wipe it off her face in a way that would be pleasurable for them both.

"You guys want to get started, or what?"

The cameraman's sudden intrusion jerked Luke out of a mental image in which he and Holly were long past "started" and well on their way to "finished."

What a hypocrite! He kept telling his guys to focus and here he was, distracted by a pretty face.

Except he sensed she was more than that. Something about her ditzy act wasn't quite right. There was more going on underneath the glossy surface she presented to the world, he just knew it. He trusted his instincts—his livelihood depended on them. His shot might be off, but his gut wasn't. And if Holly Evans had another agenda, she was a danger to him and his team. Then again, just the sight of her in that outfit was dangerous.

"What? Yes! Of course, Jay, thanks!" Holly's voice was about an octave too high and a six-pack of Red Bull too perky. She gave Jay an overly bright smile and snatched her interview cards from the stool. "Luke, if you'll take a seat?"

Like a good little soldier, Luke walked over and sat down.

"We'll start with a quick Q and A with just you on camera, and then I've got a couple of more in-depth questions that we'll shoot with the two of us on-screen."

"Yeah, sure." He tried to appear casual and nonchalant.

She gave Jay a nod and waited until the little red light on the camera flicked on and the boom was in place. Then she turned back to Luke, fixed him with a look of professional interest and got down to business.

"What's the last thing you watched on YouTube?"

The question was like being cross-checked from behind, leaving him momentarily stunned. No way in hell he was going to admit he spent his evening re-inflating his ego by watching her call him hot.

"Are you serious?" He'd meant to sound casually mocking, but was afraid it had come out somewhat closer to defensive. "That's the hard-hitting lead issue? You've got to have something better than that. What's the next question?"

She looked flustered by his outburst, and he hated the fact that he felt badly about it. He should be out on the ice, working on his slap shot, not in here trying to hide his guilt. She glanced down at her note card and closed her eyes, just for a second, before opening them and meeting his gaze. She looked focused, determined and a little defiant, if he wasn't mistaken. She cleared her throat.

"Boxers or briefs?"

All his composure deserted him. He held up a hand and glanced over at the camera. "Turn that off."

He waited until Jay lowered the boom mic and stepped toward the tripod before he rounded on the woman who had the singular ability to distract and frustrate him beyond measure.

"Look, I get that you have a job to do, but what's going on here, it's a big deal. This team is in the play-offs for the first time in its five-year history. Not a single player on our roster has ever won a championship. We've got a chance to do something great."

He took a deep breath and unclenched his fist.

"The problem is, two nights ago we handed Colorado a shutout victory on a silver platter. This team is now skating on thin ice, and if we're going to get out of the first round intact, I need my guys focused on winning hockey games, not talking about their underwear

Then he grabbed the logoed towel some *Sports Nation* lackey had slung on his shoulder, wiped the sweat from his face and turned and walked away.

"BUCK UP, CAP. Why so down?"

Luke took a deep breath and started pulling off the tape wound around his socks and shin pads. "You mean aside from getting shut out in our own building, setting a franchise record in penalty minutes and the looming press conference I have to spend assuring reporters that we know we sucked out there?"

As far as Luke was concerned, the only upside to their spectacular 5–0 loss to Colorado was that Coach Taggert had been so pissed that he'd refused post-game media access to the dressing room. At least they could shower, change and lick their wounds in relative peace.

Brett Sillinger, the Storm's eighth-round draft pick, ran a hand through his sweaty curls. "Well, sure. When you put it that way. But look at the bright side! We're loaded, and women throw themselves at us! We've got the best goddamn job in the world, bar none. And we're in the play-offs, baby!"

Luke's stomach lurched. "Trust me, rookie, I know we're in the play-offs."

Did he ever. It was a pretty big deal to some very rich people in some very high places, people who were...*eager* to see the team perform well in the franchise's first run for the cup since joining the league five years ago. That fact had been made abundantly—and repeatedly—clear to him in the month since they'd clinched their play-off spot.

It was also Luke's first time in the play-offs since the worst night of his life. Three years had passed, but the wound was still as fresh as ever.

and eyeing your cleavage. Everyone else thinks you're cute and harmless and charming, but I don't buy it. So if you're just using us to make a name for yourself, then you've picked the wrong team. We don't have time for distractions right now. I'm done here."

With that, Luke stalked away from her. Again.

3

"LUKE! HOW DID it go? I was just going to stop in and get a behind-the-scenes peek at the interviews."

Luke pulled up short at the familiar booming voice. You didn't stalk past Ron Lougheed, general manager of the Portland Storm, no matter how frustrated you might be. Besides, this was the perfect opportunity to bring up his concerns.

"Yeah, about that, sir... As team captain, it's my job to make sure that my guys are centered, that hockey is the top priority. We've been through a lot this season and now it seems we're finally gelling at the right time. I'm worried that Holly Evans is a distraction we can't afford right now."

"Nonsense! Holly Evans and her delightful brand of infotainment is exactly what the franchise needs in order to make some headway into the hearts and minds of hockey fans."

Ron Lougheed was a heavyset giant of a man and despite his gregarious demeanor, everyone in the hockey world knew that when he made up his mind, there was no changing it.

Still, Luke had to try. "But sir, our time is better spent if we—"

"Let me tell you a little something about the business of hockey, Mr. Maguire. For the last five years, our merchandising and ticket sales have consistently ranked in the bottom third of the league's teams. Since we made the play-offs, we've seen a fifteen percent jump in merchandise revenue and we've almost sold out tonight's game. That's after *one* post-season game. We need to ride this wave, and the Women's Hockey Network is helping us do that. That clip of you walking away from her the other night has half a million likes. I'm not exactly sure what that means, but it's good."

Luke nodded. Shut his mouth. Braced for impact.

"I trust I don't need to tell you how *eager* we are to see results in the postseason?"

"No, sir."

"Excellent. Now, what were you saying about concerns?"

A headshake was the best Luke could muster. "Nothing, sir. Nothing at all."

"That's what I thought. I'm looking forward to watching your interview footage from this morning. After all, a captain sets the tone for his team, and I know I picked the right man to keep these boys on track. And put a couple of pucks in the net, while you're at it. Understood?"

"Perfectly."

Ten minutes of fuming and a chicken and pasta lunch later, Luke was back in front of the doors emblazoned with the stylized cresting wave of the team's logo. The doors burst open just as he reached for them, but instead of revealing his sexy, skirt-suited nemesis, he came face-to-face with the rookie.

"Dude, you up next?"

"Yeah." He glanced over the kid's shoulder, but the doors swooped shut before he could catch even a glimpse of teal. "Yeah, I'm up next."

"Cool. Word of advice? If you stand close enough during the part where she's on-screen with you, you can see all the way down her shirt."

When his tip failed to elicit any reaction from Luke, Sillinger's cocky grin faded. "Look, Cap, I want to apologize for what I said after the game the other day. Cubs explained why you're so tense and everything."

The kid glanced away as he said it, so he missed Luke's look of surprise at the mention of Eric Jacobs, or Cubs, as everyone on the team referred to him. "Exactly what did he tell you?"

"Oh, you know. All the pressure you're under from the higher-ups. And dealing with the media. And about your shot being off and stuff."

Luke exhaled. He should have known Jacobs would have picked up on all of Luke's behind-the-scenes crap. The guy was eerily intuitive—it was what made him so great out there on the ice.

"Um, you ever consider that maybe your shot's off because, um…" The kid leaned conspiratorially close and murmured, "I'm just sayin', maybe it would help if you changed the oil."

Luke stared blankly at the right-winger. He didn't like where this conversation was going, mostly because he'd been thinking about it a lot since he'd watched that damn video last night. Holly Evans was beautiful, and she'd made him think about something other than hockey for the first time in a long while. And she could certainly get him riled up. Not to mention she didn't give a damn about hockey. All things he found way too appealing at this very moment.

"Sometimes things get rusty when the pipe's not clean, you understand? I mean, how long's it been, man? In my experience, a good lube job can really help work out the kinks. And lucky for you, right through that door is a smoking-hot woman who told the entire internet that she considers you a certified Grade-A cut of beef. Plus, when I made my move, she told me she's looking for a guy with more maturity. That's your in, dude! She totally wants someone *old*. You should hit that."

Luke was pretty sure he'd never felt more ancient than he did having this particular conversation and he was only twenty-six. "Thanks for the advice, rookie."

"Hey, no problem, Cap. I got your back." Brett glanced at the door to the interview room. "You need a wingman in there, or you good?"

"I think I got it," Luke assured him.

Their conversation was interrupted by the infamous "Charge" anthem, a staple of sporting events everywhere. The rookie yanked his phone out of his back pocket. He glanced at the screen and grinned like he was on the cover of *Hockey Digest*. "Yes! It's the car dealership. You are not even going to believe the sweet ride I just bought!"

He was bouncing up and down like a Chihuahua that was about to pee on the floor. "The guys won't be able to give me a hard time about my wheels anymore. I gotta take this, Cap. Good luck in there."

Luke waited until Brett disappeared around the cor-

ner before he stepped inside for his mandated face-off
with Holly Evans, intrepid reporter.

"ARE YOU KIDDING ME, Jay? You took Salt Lake City
over Vancouver in the first round? That's ridiculous.
No wonder you always lose your hockey pool. I mean
honestly. I expected better of you. Vancouver clearly
has the edge and—Luke!" Holly bolted off the interview stool.

She hadn't been expecting *him*.

Like the rest of the team, he was wearing the navy
T-shirt that mimicked his jersey, with the cresting wave
on the front and his last name and number on the back.
His T-shirt even had a white *C* on the front.

But unlike the rest of the team, the sight of Luke in
his T-shirt and jeans did funny things to her hormones.
Seriously, is it hot in here?

"I thought you were…not coming back…ever. How
long have you been there?"

"Not long," he said, shoving his hands in his pockets
as he sauntered farther into the room. His cocked eyebrow and smug half grin said otherwise. Holly worried
that her attempt to appear innocent was failing miserably, because her thoughts were anything but G-rated.

"What are you guys talking about?"

"You know," she said, so brightly that she could have
sworn he squinted a little. "This and that."

Luke nodded, glancing over at Jay, who avoided
meeting his gaze. "Sounded like hockey talk to me."

"What? No."

"Yes," he countered, matching her wide-eyed tone.
"It really did. I'm a bit of an expert on the subject. Salt
Lake City, Vancouver, first round. Definite hockey talk."

Luke had already nailed the fact that she was using this job to angle for a promotion. If she confirmed it by dropping the shtick, he could have her fired before she even got started. The best way to reassure him that she was harmless was to *be* harmless.

Holly's laugh was both forced and slightly manic as she shooed his words away with the dainty flick of her hand. "Oh, that. I was just telling Jay about…uh—" *Think, Holly. Think!* "—the numerology class I took." She nodded, warming to the story. "Yeah, really interesting stuff. I was explaining how it can help you make decisions about important things. Like which handbag to buy. Or in Jay's case, he's doing some hockey thing with his friends and I was showing him how he could use it to pick teams."

"Cool. I'd love to see how it works." He raised an eyebrow to punctuate the challenge, and she couldn't quite hold back her frown. But she'd come this far. Might as well go all-in.

Holly could almost swear she saw something like respect in his blue eyes as she lifted her chin and squared her shoulders.

"Uh, yeah. I just added up the letters in Vancouver—A is one, B is two and so on, your typical cipher—and then you take whatever the sum is, add those numbers together if it's more than a single digit and you have it. And in this case, *it* was equal to nine. Jay's birthday is September ninth, so obviously Vancouver is the luckier team for him."

Luke smiled, but it didn't quite reach his eyes. "So it has nothing to do with the fact that Vancouver is a team with enough depth and experience that it's pretty

470 <i>Playing To Win</i>

much a foregone conclusion that they'll knock Salt Lake out of the first round?"

Holly shrugged. "What can I say? The numbers don't lie."

"Sorry to interrupt…whatever *this* is, but I gotta use the can," Jay announced. "Down the hall and to the left?" he confirmed, and Luke nodded. The members of the Portland Storm were so superstitious that she and Jay had been asked to trek all the way to the building's public washrooms because no one but the team was allowed in the dressing-room bathroom on game day.

The two of them watched Jay leave, and she used the silence to regroup. She felt much more formidable when her adversary's baby blues swung back in her direction.

Until he said, "What is your game?"

"Game?"

His laugh was derisive, but kind of sexy for all that. "You're not fooling anyone. I know something's up with you and I intend to figure out what it is."

Oh great. That was all she needed, this handsome bastard messing up the most real-life, on-camera experience on her résumé. She might not like this job, but it was good experience, and she certainly wasn't going to lose it by making him suspicious on the second day.

"Up to something?" She placed a hand on her chest like a Southern belle. "Me?"

His parry was a narrowing of his pretty blue eyes. "Something has been bugging me about your act since the moment we met."

"Oh, you mean that time you were so unchivalrous as to walk away from me without answering my question?"

"So I asked myself," he continued, without missing

a beat, "why would someone who disliked sports so
much that she asked about beards instead of the game
bother to make a fake sports show? And the only answer I could come up with was, she wouldn't. The way
I see it, you have your own agenda, and it's not going to
do any of the members of this team any good."

Holly shook her head, eyes wide like an ingenue.
"I don't know what you mean. The Women's Hockey
Network is all about asking the kinds of questions we
girls find important, such as what kind of cologne do
you wear?"

He smelled so good she *was* actually a little curious.

"Oh, really? You're gonna keep up the act?"

Luke stepped closer. His big body sucked up all the
oxygen, and her breath came faster to compensate. Who
knew having a man accuse you of being smart was
such a turn-on?

"That's the only question you want to ask me? I'll
give you a free pass, on the record. Ask me anything.
No holds barred. Nothing's off-limits. And I guarantee
you a real answer. I promise not to say 'no comment.'"

Holly's hand clenched into a fist.

Any question. On the record. The reporting equivalent to winning the lottery.

She could ask about his brother's accident. Be the
only reporter ever to get a statement on the one topic
that was off-limits when interviewing Luke Maguire.
Hear in his own words how it felt to be back in the
play-offs for the first time since tragedy struck.

And she wanted to. She wanted to ask more than
she wanted her next breath. But she wasn't supposed
to know anything about hockey, so she restrained herself. Because if she took the bait, she would confirm

that when given the opportunity, she'd put her ambition before the team. And she'd be done here. He could not only get her fired, but ruin her career. She had to keep her eye on the prize. She had to believe that one day, she would earn that story from him on her own merit, not as blackmail, and it would be worth the wait.

So she did what was best for her career and took a deep, centering breath. *Man, he really does smell amazing.* "Seriously, is that the new Hugo Boss fragrance?"

He narrowed his eyes and the crease between his brows deepened. It made him look even sexier, if that was possible.

"I've got my eye on you, Evans."

Not exactly the part of him she *wanted* on her just then, but probably the safest of the available options.

"I'm going to figure out what you're doing here and I'm going to expose you."

Geez. Everything sounded sexual when he was standing this close. She upped the ante and took a half step closer to him—she definitely wasn't going to let him intimidate her in this sexy game of cat and mouse they'd embarked on. If he thought she was going to let him be the cat, he was so very wrong. She'd been holding her own in a man's world for a long time.

"You can try, but there's nothing to expose. What you see is what you get."

"Oh, I very much doubt that, Ms. Evans. The truth is hiding somewhere behind that big hair and tiny suit."

"Look at me, Mr. Maguire. You honestly think there's room to hide anything under this suit?"

Her breath stuttered at the sudden fierceness in his eyes, the predatory gleam that pinned her in place. Were their lips getting closer because he was leaning in, or had she swayed toward him?

She was drawn to his body, hard as iron and just as magnetic. Her fingers brushed his biceps as his hands made first contact with her waist. She didn't want to stop looking at him, but her eyelids grew heavy as their breaths comingled and his lips moved closer, closer still...

"Okay, I'm back. What'd I miss?"

"Nothing!" Holly and Luke sprang apart at Jay's intrusion. Her heart thumped with a cocktail that was one part adrenaline and two parts unassuaged lust. She tugged at the bottom of her blazer, sneaking a quick glance in Luke's direction. He exhaled and rubbed a hand across the back of his neck.

Guilty. They looked as guilty as a couple of teenagers who'd been caught making out. Which they probably would have ended up doing if not for Jay's poor timing.

"Geez, Jay. You've been gone long enough. Let's get this interview going, shall we?" Her hand went to her hair—a classic Holly-ism that gave away her nerves. Good thing Luke didn't know that, she decided, dropping her hand. Luke lifted an eyebrow and Holly was sure she was blushing. Damn it.

"My pleasure," Luke said.

Jay, however, was not fooled in the least, and the look he shot her said she owed him an explanation. She waved him behind the camera and directed Luke back to the stool where their interview earlier had gone so wrong.

This one went a lot better. She had to hand it to him—he was as consummate a professional off the ice as he was on it. Charming, funny, quick with a witty answer. No one who saw this footage would dream for a minute that he believed her to be a threat to the team. In fact, the only question that tripped him up was "Do you have a secret talent?" She could have sworn he blushed a little before he stammered some nonsense about speaking a little French.

Then she sent him off to shoot some B-roll with Jay, which involved posing and puck tricks in the hallway.

For the first time all day, she was alone in the Storm's dressing room with a microphone in her hand. It was a pretty surreal experience, both as a hockey fan and as an aspiring sports reporter.

She'd watched it on television all her life, a reporter interviewing some member of the team or other, a bunch of bare-chested, sweaty-haired men talking about a big win or a battle-weary loss. The locker room looked different now, empty and quiet, all the jerseys clean and hanging number-side out, equipment neatly arranged on the shelves above each player's designated spot. Holly tried to just enjoy the moment, but her stupid heels were pinching her feet, reminding her that she was only living a fun-house version of her dream. But one day, she vowed. One day she'd be here, wearing pants and asking serious, in-depth questions.

And then Luke Maguire wouldn't be the only guy on the team who suspected that she was an expert on this stuff. Everyone on the roster would know she could hold her own.

She set the mic on the stool Luke had sat on for part of their interview and headed for the forbidden bathroom. Jay and Luke would be occupied with filming for at least five minutes. What harm would it do to sneak a peek?

It contained all the typical male bathroom accoutrements—urinals, stalls and a ginormous gang shower. But it was elevated to luxe standards by the details: gleaming navy and white tiles, stainless steel fixtures and enough accents of Portland Storm teal thrown in to pull it all together. Calculatedly masculine and very *go, team, go*!

Bracing a hand on either side of the sink, she stared into the mirror. She barely recognized herself. Gone were the usual blond ponytail and unadorned brown eyes. No T-shirt and jeans. She flexed her feet against the stiff leather of her heels—definitely no sneakers.

She wanted to splash some water on her face to assure herself the reflection in the mirror was just a mirage. But the sad reality was that the made-up, well-coiffed woman who was staring back at her now was the version of herself that had scored the biggest deal on her résumé by far.

This was the Holly Evans that was being invited to appear on local morning talk shows and well-respected podcasts. Hell, she'd even gotten a call about turning the Women's Hockey Network into a weekly comedy-sports show on satellite radio. And if fancy suits and a little lipstick were what it took to fulfill her dream of being a sports reporter, then it was a small price to pay. *Right?*

Holly sighed. This was who she was now, at least for the duration of the Storm's play-off run, and a splash of water wasn't going to change that. Besides, Paige had done such a lovely job with the goop on her face that she didn't dare. She settled for another sigh and tugged a few stray pieces of hair back into place before she headed for one of the navy stalls.

"Whatever it takes," she muttered to herself.

She'd just locked the stall door when the sound of footsteps made her freeze.

4

AW, CRAP.

The footsteps were coming closer. Honestly. What were the odds? The bathroom had been deserted all day, and now someone decided to come in? Stupid hockey superstitions.

How could a bunch of grown men be this ridiculous? She was just wondering if perhaps there was a story in the naive belief wins and losses had anything to do with who used which freaking toilet, when her line of thought was interrupted by the "Charge" fanfare echoing off the tiled walls. The sudden burst of noise made her heart jump.

There was a muttered curse, followed by a hoarse, angry whisper: "Why are you calling me? It's game day. You know I'm not alone."

Her reporter instincts piqued, Holly abandoned all thoughts of superstitious nonsense and redirected her attention into eavesdropping.

"I'm very aware of that! But there's only so much I can do."

She frowned. She couldn't distinguish the voice, despite all the interviews she'd conducted today. All she could tell was that whoever had her trapped in a bathroom stall didn't have an accent. There were at least fourteen guys on the team proper who fit the bill. And that wasn't including coaching staff, cleaning staff, anyone who—

"I know we have a deal!"

Whoa. Holly flinched at the anger in his voice. She glanced down at her stilettos. Could she climb up on the toilet quietly enough to not blow her cover? Because from that height, she could peek over the top of the stall and see who the guy on the phone was. Not an ideal solution, but at least it would give her a lead.

Excitement brewed in the pit of her stomach. Now *this* was a story. Sure, she'd resigned herself to her fate of asking moronic questions and wearing short skirts, but maybe this was going to turn out to be a right place, right time kind of serendipity. She lifted her knee to test how high she'd need to hike up said skirt to make the big step.

"No. No! You can trust me. I've got it under control. You'll get your money's worth. We'll win tonight. Yes. By two. I got it."

There was another loud curse and the sound of shoes slapping tile as the man stormed out. Holly did an about-face in the stall and unlatched the door, hoping to catch a glimpse of the man, but she saw nothing. *Damn it, I missed him.*

But there, in the middle of the tile floor beside the sinks, was a folded piece of yellow legal paper. Holly rushed over and picked it up. It was a list of letters and numbers in stark black ink. L2+, W2+, W1, W1, W2 and on it went. And suddenly the cryptic conversation made a lot more sense.

Well, well, well. It looked like someone was partaking in a little over/under betting. But who was stupid enough to do that?

Not only was it illegal for someone affiliated with a professional sports team to bet on themselves, but it would get you banned for life from the sport, and that was on top of whatever criminal prosecution was handed down. And to risk all that on point-shaving? It was dicey at best, because no one player had full control over a hockey game. And yet, if you were favored to win anyway, there were subtle things you could do to make the game a little closer than it needed to be. Someone could have gotten cocky.

The Storm had already weathered a scandal earlier in the season, when the not-so-secret affair between captain Chris Powell and GM Ron Lougheed's trophy wife had become front page fodder. Lougheed and his soon-to-be-ex were currently fighting a pretty nasty custody battle in the courts—and in the media. This was the last thing the organization needed on its résumé, tainting its inaugural play-off run. But for Holly, it was perfect.

This was the windfall she'd been waiting for. Because breaking a story like this was the key to making herself the front-runner, not just for Corey Baniuk's position, but an on-air sports position at almost any station in the country. It was a first-class ticket to reporter legitimacy. All she had to do was figure out who the guilty party was.

She liberated her phone from her bra—she'd had to stow it there earlier because skirt suits like this one didn't come with pockets—and snapped a photo of the questionable list so she could inspect it more closely when she got home.

The key to a good investigation, her mother had told her once, was to let the action go on around you. If you disturbed things too early, you'd never get the answers you were looking for. To that end, she refolded the paper and placed it back where she'd found it.

It was the first time during this entire sham that Holly felt she might have made her mother proud.

Her head whipped around at the sound of a door swinging closed. Getting caught now would ruin everything.

She hurried back into the bathroom stall as quietly as her heels would allow. Was it her perp returning to the scene of the crime? Had he realized he'd dropped his list? Maybe this time she could catch a glimpse of whoever was striding into the bathroom.

She'd just pulled the stall door shut and was about to navigate her way up onto the toilet—no easy feat since there was only a toilet seat and no lid—when an indecipherable noise made her stop. There was a beat of dead silence, and then, "Holly, I know you're in there. I can see your shoes."

Busted.

She unlatched the door and did her best to appear sheepish. "Luke. Hey. I didn't hear you come in. You look nice. When did you get a chance to change? I thought you were filming puck tricks with Jay."

The surge of adrenaline at getting caught morphed into a surge of something else as she took in the sight of Luke Maguire looking big and handsome and powerful in the most beautifully tailored charcoal suit she'd ever seen. His silk tie was a deep plum and his blue eyes were flashing. "We finished up a while ago. I've already changed and done a pregame interview. Things move fast on game day. That's why I thought you were *gone*." He put particular stress on the last word.

Geez. How long had she been staring in that mirror? No wonder Paige was always late.

"Now maybe you can explain what the hell you're doing in here?"

She shot him a look that was all smart-ass. "It's a bathroom, Luke. Do I have to spell it out for you?"

He frowned at the joke, and she resisted the sudden urge to smooth his brow. Why was he so serious all the time?

"You need to get out of here, right now. Only the team can use the bathroom on game day." If she wasn't mistaken, he looked a little embarrassed when he explained. "It's a good luck thing."

"It's a stupid thing," she countered. "I'll never understand why elite athletes aren't more enlightened than medieval man."

"Well, you don't have to understand it. You just have to respect it. And keep your voice down! Guys are in and out of the dressing room this close to game time." He ran a hand through his close-cropped hair. "Jesus. Not even the cleaners are allowed in today. We've got to get you out of here before someone sees you. Come on." He reached out to cup her elbow, an old-fashioned gesture that took her by surprise. Holly was dismayed at the way her skin thrilled at the warmth of his fingers, even through the sleeve of her blazer.

She shrugged her arm from his grasp, an act of self-preservation.

Luke sighed, obviously interpreting it as an act of defiance.

"Holly, you remember all that stupid stuff you asked me earlier? I gave you the benefit of the doubt and I answered all your dumb questions because you were just doing your job. Now I'm trying to do mine, and part of me doing my job is making sure my guys are ready to play. Focused. And if maintaining a stupid superstition is what it takes to ensure we bring our A game tonight, then that's what I have to do. So do me a solid, okay? Even though it's silly, and inconvenient and probably makes no difference at all, *please* let's get out of here before anyone sees you?"

Holly had to look up at him, despite her four-inch heels and his lack of skates. When had he gotten so close? God, he was handsome, all tall and stubbly, his ocean-blue eyes pleading.

"Fine. Let's—"

"Shit. Someone's coming!"

Holly wasn't sure exactly how it had happened, but suddenly she was chest to chest with Luke inside the tiny bathroom stall, made positively miniscule by his large frame. She heard the telltale footsteps a moment later.

Luke scooped her into his arms, one hand around her back, his other forearm under her knees. He'd literally swept her off her feet, and the suddenness of it stole her breath. Her arms flew around his neck in self-preservation, and she was vividly aware of every inch of her body, especially the parts of her that were plastered against his broad chest.

She could feel his muscles beneath his suit jacket, enough to tell that they were barely straining under her weight. She shot him her best "what the hell?" glare through the onslaught of yum, and he gestured with his chin in the direction of her feet.

"Your shoes. That's how I knew you were in here."

He breathed the words quietly, his mouth so close that she could feel the exhalation against the sensitive skin beneath her ear. It tickled, and she turned her head to protect her neck. Suddenly there was nothing but a fraction of an inch's worth of air separating their lips.

His muscles flexed then, pulling her tighter to his chest and her breath came fast and shallow. Heat prickled over her skin and pooled in her belly. Her fingers clenched against the soft material of his jacket.

Holly had never experienced lust at first sight before, but man, Luke Maguire made her lust. She ran her hand up his chest, and he shifted his stance, but before their lips met, he banged his elbow against the stall. The thump reverberated through the bathroom, snapping them back into the present, and they froze, eyes wide.

They both cocked their heads toward the sink side of the stall, listening intently for any sign that they'd blown their cover.

After another moment of silence, Luke set her carefully on her feet. The lust hangover made Holly a little wobbly on her heels. He stepped forward and lifted onto his toes so he could see over the edge of the stall. "He's gone," he said, the words tinged with relief. They hadn't even heard him retreat.

Holly unlatched the door, and with a covert glance to assure herself they were, in fact, alone, took some tentative steps toward the sink. She paused for a moment, but the piece of paper wasn't on the floor, nor had it been kicked under the sink.

"No time for sightseeing, Evans." Luke's hand at the small of her back was warm and insistent. "Let's get out of here before you get caught."

They snuck back out to the dressing room, Holly letting Luke precede her so he could make sure the coast was clear. She wasn't four steps out of the bathroom before several members of the team strutted into the dressing room, bedecked in expensive suits and pregame gravitas. Luke sent her a "See? You really lucked out," kind of look.

Ass.

Then the "Charge" anthem sounded to her right. Holly's spine snapped straight as she watched Luke fish his iPhone out of the breast pocket of his suit jacket.

He glanced at the caller ID and that serious expression of his descended over his handsome face like a shutter. Holly decided she might prefer his pompous expression after all.

"I gotta take this," he said. She watched with interest as he turned away from her, shielding the call with his broad shoulders. "Why are you calling again? Seriously? Hold on." Was it her imagination, or did Luke glance in her direction. "Let me get somewhere I can talk."

The "Charge" fanfare? Why are you calling *again*? Pieces were falling into place and she didn't particularly like the picture they were forming.

Had it been Luke in the bathroom earlier? She'd just assumed that whoever had inadvertently held the two of them hostage had come back for his list. But now that she thought about it, Luke had definitely had enough time to pick up the wayward paper before he'd gone all foot fetishist on her and blown her hiding place.

That could be the reason he'd even noticed her shoes under the stall in the first place—he was bending over to pick up the list.

Holly strained to hear more of his conversation, but he pointedly disappeared back into the bathroom. To her dismay, there were too many team members in the swanky locker room now for her to follow. Still, the reporter buzz—that's what her mother used to call it— was zinging around her gut. She was on to something. Obviously Luke's regular deep baritone had sounded nothing like the whispered panic she'd heard earlier, but that ringtone was an indisputable clue, and one that she had to follow up on.

LUKE WALKED OVER to stand by the sinks, hating that his gaze went immediately to the stall he and Holly had hidden out in only moments ago.

But he couldn't afford to be distracted by sex right now. Harding Lowe was the kind of law firm that charged in the triple digits for phone calls like these, and with money as tight as it was, Luke had to pay close attention and cut to the chase. "What's so important?"

"I was going to wait until tomorrow to tell you this, but I'm worried it might hit the papers and I didn't want you to find out like that," Craig Harding informed him.

Luke's blood turned to ice. It was never good when someone started a phone call that way, but when it was your lawyer? Infinitely worse.

"What?" The word was flat, more demand than question.

"Brad Timmons is filing for bankruptcy."

Luke's face went numb. The asshole who'd put Ethan in a wheelchair, put his parents in debt, strained his family to the emotional breaking point time after time over the last three years, was going to screw them over again.

"Fuck."

The word echoed hollowly in the vast expanse of shiny white tile and empty navy stalls.

Luke wanted to punch something, but it wasn't worth the fine the Storm would levy against him if he did.

Jesus Christ, how had things come to this? He made almost two million dollars a year with his new contract and still it was all he could do to keep himself and the people he loved financially afloat.

Loans, renovations, lawyers, specialists, physio—it had all added up after the accident. His paycheck was all but spent before it got deposited. He was grateful he had the means to keep his family living a comfortably middle-class life despite their exorbitant bills, but the idea that the coward who'd put his little brother in a wheelchair wasn't going to have to contribute a dime to Ethan's recovery made Luke nauseous.

Timmons had already lucked out with his criminal charges. He'd been convicted of assault with a weapon for the crosscheck, but ended up with an eighteen-month conditional discharge, which meant he hadn't served any jail time and he wouldn't have a criminal record once his probation was complete. Now he'd found a way to punk out on financial restitution, too.

"Thanks for the heads-up, Craig. I'll take care of telling my family."

"Understood. I'll be in touch."

Luke hung up the phone. He would deal with the personal stuff later. Right now, he had to focus on his team. They were only two hours away from puck drop.

He reached into the inside breast pocket of his suit, exchanging his phone for a folded-up piece of yellow legal paper. He'd found it on the floor of the bathroom and recognized instantly what it was. That 5–0 loss had been brutal. The fact that it was predetermined made it cut even deeper. Luke shook his head against the proof clutched in his hand.

He couldn't believe any of his guys would do this. They'd battled too hard to get to where they were.

And yet…the entire premise of point-shaving and over/under betting was predicated on having an inside man, someone out there on the ice who could impact the game.

This was the last thing they needed right now. He'd only just put this team back together after losing their last captain in a blaze of scandal and lies. It had taken months of work to get all twenty-three players over the shake-up and focused on making the play-offs.

And look at them now.

The only bright spot in this rotten situation was that he'd been the one to find the betting sheet. At least this way he could deal with it internally—protect his team.

He didn't even want to think about how this would have played out if Holly had found it instead. She could've ruined their chance at winning the championship before it even began.

And he wanted that championship, not just for himself but for the team.

Each and every one of those guys deserved to hoist sports' greatest trophy above their heads, and he'd do whatever it took to make sure that happened.

For them. For himself. For his brother.

5

"WE'LL WIN TONIGHT. Yes. By two."

The words still echoed in Holly's brain, hours after the final buzzer had sounded.

The Storm had handled their opponents with relative ease tonight, up 3–0 after two periods. Then at the start of the third, Sillinger had taken a bone-headed roughing penalty, Luke had fumbled the puck and failed to clear the zone, and seconds later, LaCroix had lost his chance for a shutout.

For a while, things settled down a bit, until Colorado scored to make it 3–2 with seven minutes left in the game. Things were looking grim for the list's prediction, and then Jacobs came out of nowhere, stripping one of his opponent's defensemen of the puck. He deked out the goaltender and put a wrister top-shelf to make the final score 4–2.

And the Storm won by two with eight seconds left in the game.

"You'll get your money's worth."

The eavesdropped whisper haunted her.

It could just be coincidence, she reminded herself. It

wasn't like 4–2 was an outlandish hockey score. And this was the first prediction on the list that had come true. She had nothing but suspicion at this point. Still, the words were on her mind as she conducted post-game interviews with the guys.

"Hi, everyone. This is Holly Evans of the Women's Hockey Network, reporting live from the Storm's dressing room after a big 4–2 win over Colorado tonight. I'm with Portland defenseman Doug Kowalchuk." She turned and held her mic in his direction.

"Doug, what do you think of the new jersey colors?"

On the ice, the burly D-man was a force to be reckoned with, but off ice, he reminded her of a big cartoon bear—imposing but nonthreatening. His grin was goofy and genuine. "They're great. Red and black is a really classic combination, you know?"

Holly couldn't quite mask the withering look on her face at his answer. She hoped Jay had zoomed in on the navy and teal jersey behind Doug instead of her face. *Seriously, this was her life now?*

"No, Doug. Not New Jersey's colors—I meant the Storm's redesigned jerseys."

"Oh right. Yeah. They're awesome. Go Storm!"

Holly forced a smile as she turned back to the camera. She could see Jay's shoulders shaking with laughter. "You heard it here, folks. Go Storm!"

When she was sure the camera was off, she let out a frustrated sigh.

"You're doing great," Jay assured her. "Who's next?"

Holly glanced around the scrum in the dressing room. She'd been hoping to sneak in an interview with anyone who'd made a direct contribution—be it positive or negative—to the final score tonight. She wanted to get an idea of their demeanors, a sense of their moods. But unfortunately, all four players that had risen to the top of her list—Eric, J.C., Luke and the rookie—were all big draws for reporters and had press queued up and waiting for them.

"I think we've got enough. Kowalchuk's was interview number five, and I'll do some highlight voice-overs later to cut with it. They only wanted a three-minute piece about the game, right?"

Jay nodded as he removed the camera from the tripod. "Yeah, that should be plenty."

"Okay. I'll catch you in about half an hour."

"Sure thing, Holly."

Now that she was off duty, she angled her way through the bustling dressing room toward the crowd around Eric Jacobs. He was known to be a little shy and incredibly humble considering the breadth of his talent, but he was always exceedingly polite to reporters and smiled easily. Holly hadn't seen him smile once tonight.

She listened in as Corey Baniuk asked Eric about his spectacular goal, but the handsome centerman seemed disinterested in the recap, a little tired maybe.

And though he made the Storm's PR department proud by saying all the right things—"Colorado played a great game and were worthy opponents," "I saw an opportunity and fortunately I was able to capitalize on it," "I couldn't have done it without my teammates"—there was none of the quiet intensity that he usually brought to an interview and his gaze wandered, like he was preoccupied.

Then the "Charge" anthem played, and panic flashed across Eric's handsome face. He turned away from the cameras and microphones being shoved in his direction and dug his phone out of the pocket of his jacket.

What the...? Eric and Luke have the same ringtone?

Eric's expression darkened when he glanced at the caller ID, as if he was expecting bad news from whomever was on the line. "Excuse me, please, I have to take this," he said to the group of reporters.

After Eric left, the reporters dissipated quickly, rushing off to grab quotes from other players before their allotted time in the dressing room was up.

Holly pulled out her phone and typed her observations into the memo she'd titled *SUSPECTS*. This investigation was the key to parlaying this farcical job into something she could be proud of, and every clue counted. To prove it, she added a note about the dark circles under Eric's eyes and the fact that his last-minute goal corresponded to the +2 win predicted by the list. And the ringtone, obviously.

"Texting or 'Candy Crush'?"

Holly started, almost dropping her phone at the sound of a voice so close behind her. "Oh, geez. Luke, you scared me!"

He jutted his chin in the direction of her phone. "Your thumbs were really burning up the keyboard."

She tucked the phone back in her bra, trying not to notice that his eyes tracked her hand, making the move feel far more suggestive than she'd meant it. "Oh, you know. Reporter notes," she said vaguely, hoping she was pulling off nonchalance. "So what's the story with the matching ringtones? You and Eric have some kind of 'linemates for life' pact or something?"

"Team building. Everyone on the team is using it,

kind of a 'keep hockey your top priority during the play-offs' type of thing."

"Your idea." It wasn't really a question so much as a statement. That was exactly the type of hands-on captaincy she expected from the man standing beside her. And also a huge hit to finding her guilty party, since it put everyone on the team back on the suspect list.

"Yes."

"That's great! Do you mind if I talk about that in the piece we're putting together? People love fun little details like that."

"Sure. I know you're all about the fun little details," he said pointedly.

Man, he was tenacious. Even after the sexually charged moment in the bathroom stall earlier, he wasn't about to let her off the hook. Holly had to admit, she liked that about him. And she really liked that this battle of wills they had going on made her feel as if he was talking to the real Holly Evans, not the persona she'd agreed to play. It restored her faith in men to see that Luke Maguire wasn't about to be derailed by some off-the-charts sexual tension. For the first time all evening, her smile was completely genuine.

"Well, I should probably go help Jay pack up. Good game tonight."

"No, it wasn't."

His candor stopped her.

It really hadn't been, but while she admired his honesty, she wasn't going to get tricked into revealing her cover. He might be a worthy opponent—his entire life was predicated on it—but when she put her mind to something, she wasn't to be underestimated.

Except in this case, she reminded herself, since her

entire goal was to convince him to underestimate her. To that end, she scrunched her face in a way she hoped might convey bewilderment. "What? But you guys won. Aren't you happy?"

"It'll do," he said simply.

"Well, I thought you guys were awesome." She couldn't tell if he was buying her enthusiasm.

Meanwhile, his big sweaty body and mussed-up helmet hair were making her remember those stolen moments in the bathroom earlier.

Focus, Holly! She made a point to slow her steps to a reasonable pace as she walked away, even though her thoughts continued to race.

Luke cared about his team. That was obvious. The question was, did he care enough about them to cheat? For some reason, Holly hoped that her investigation turned up nothing incriminating. At least, not on Luke Maguire.

LUKE WATCHED HOLLY walk away.

Normally, he would have been glad for the team's win, but since it had come at the price of the list being correct, he wasn't able to let himself enjoy it.

And Holly had sidled right up to Eric, the one who'd fulfilled the list's prophecy.

Luke had planned on talking to the centerman, too. Eric had seemed really down lately—quiet as ever, but in a different way. Like something was wrong. Like his heart wasn't in the game.

What were the odds that Holly "I'm not that into hockey" Evans had randomly chosen Eric to target... Luke didn't like the way their instincts were lining up. And her whole demeanor had changed when she thought no one was watching—the set of her shoulders, the look in her eye. It was as though she'd flipped the switch from bubbly to...almost predatory.

He recognized that look. It was the one reporters always gave him before they sank their teeth into him. The way they'd looked after Ethan got hurt. The way they'd come at the team after Chris Powell had been traded. Luke had learned many times over that you couldn't trust anyone whose livelihood depended on uncovering secrets.

So he'd circled up behind Holly, trying to see what she'd been typing so furiously. But she'd bobbled her phone when he'd spoken, and he hadn't managed a good look at the screen.

And then she'd turned to him, a little bit breathless, slightly flushed, and his hormones had surged like they had back in that bathroom stall. His objectivity had been effectively drowned in a tidal wave of good old-fashioned lust.

"What's up, Mags?"

Luke looked over at goaltender Jean-Claude La-Croix. Despite a long history together in the minor leagues, it wasn't until Luke had been traded to the Portland Storm after Ethan's accident that the two of them had really cultivated a friendship.

"Hey, J.C. Nothing. Just trying to get the inside scoop on what stupid interview questions we'll be enduring tomorrow. Because distraction is just what a team in play-offs needs," he added. The bitterness that laced his voice was genuine.

"Ha. Yeah, she's pretty hot, huh? If you're gonna be distracted, she's the way to do it."

Luke's head whipped toward his friend. He didn't

like the way that comment bothered him. It felt almost like…jealousy? "Do you trust her?"

J.C. seemed genuinely surprised by the question. "What's to trust, man?"

"You don't think she's up to something? As if she's putting on an act so she can snoop around?"

"Luke, be serious. Her latest question was, 'name the last show you binge watched.' I really doubt there's much to worry about here," J.C. told him. "Management hired her to be comic relief. Ask us softball questions to make us look charming and funny so we can sell more jerseys. It's not as if she's a real reporter."

"I guess. But doesn't it seem odd to you that someone with no apparent hockey knowledge would even bother to apply for this position?"

His friend chuckled. "Dude, she's a YouTube phenomenon looking to cash in on her fifteen minutes. And management is taking advantage of it. Don't overthink it."

"You're probably right." Luke frowned. "I just can't shake this feeling that she's more of a reporter than anyone gives her credit for."

"We all have enough trouble without searching for more. So keep your focus on the game and forget about this inconsequential stuff. We tanked the first game. Tonight we were out for redemption. There's a lot of series left. Keep your eye on the prize."

Luke nodded. J.C. was right. But for some reason, he couldn't get Holly out of his mind.

He *wanted* to see her again. He wasn't quite sure when it had happened, but he realized in that moment that sparring with her had become the best part of his day.

6

"CAN I TALK to you for a sec?"

Holly looked up from her notes about her latest piece—she was headed to the parking lot so the Storm players could answer silly questions and show off their sweet rides—to find J.C., hands shoved in his pockets, looking sheepish.

"Is this car tour optional? Because I'd rather not do it."

"Oh. You mean, ever? Or did you just want me to reschedule?"

"I mean ever. I just…there's some family stuff going on right now. I know you usually don't get through the whole roster when you're doing interviews, so I was hoping you could skip me for the car tour today. I'm happy to do the other part—the teammate question stuff."

"Okay, that's fine. I can pick someone else."

The relief on his face was almost comical, except that it was a little too extreme for someone who'd just dodged the fluffiest interview of all time.

"LaCroix! Quit flirting and go do your tour so the rest of us can get on with ours."

The rest of her interviewees were milling about the dressing room, waiting to head outside with her.

"Bite me, Kowalchuk. I'm not doing the car stuff."

"Ha! Of course you're wussing out!" Sillinger laughed. "Have you seen the piece of crap he's driving lately? Some low-end, old-man SUV. It's almost as bad as Luke's truck!"

"You got rid of the Porsche?" Luke sounded genuinely surprised to hear. Weird, considering he and J.C. seemed quite close. Holly made a mental note to add J.C.'s vehicle downgrade to his suspect file.

"Back off, guys. You do your interviews and let me do mine."

There was a bite to the usually affable goaltender's voice, and judging by the looks on his teammates' faces, Holly knew she wasn't the only one who found it odd.

Sillinger wasn't cowed. "Hey, don't take it out on us just because you're cruising around town in an old guy's ride."

"Yeah, well, sometimes you gotta make sacrifices. Dads have to think about safety, not flash."

There was a long moment of silence as the not-quite-an-announcement sank in. Luke was the first to wade into the breach.

"Tania's pregnant? Congratulations, man! That's great!" Luke and J.C. shook before Luke pulled him in for a laudatory slap on the back.

"Yeah. Not quite the plan, but what are you gonna do?"

Holly watched as the Storm gathered around their goalie, congratulating him on the big news. A new baby on the way. That was a pretty good reason to sell your sports car, she supposed. Guess she didn't need to update the suspect file after all. Maybe she could score an exclusive on potential baby names, though...

"See?" crowed the rookie. "Dad vehicle. Just like I said. Come on, Holly. I'll show you what a real man drives."

"Says the guy who rolled up to his first practice in a Ford Fiesta," J.C. shot back.

"That was my old life. Now my ride lives up to my standards. Wait until you see it," he promised, bouncing like a toddler on a sugar high. "Cherry-red Lamborghini with black leather interior. It's so sweet, you might get diabetes just looking at it."

"Jesus, rookie," Luke warned. "You remember the first three years of your contract are flat-rate, right? Pace yourself or you're going to outspend your bank account before you start raking in the big bucks."

Holly hadn't even considered that. Sillinger was only making about three hundred thousand a year. Not chump change by any means, but it made it tight to rock two-hundred-thousand-dollar cars and a place to live, on top of day-to-day expenses. And the kid was not rolling in endorsement deals. Not yet, anyway.

"Don't you worry about me. If you got the fame, there's always a way to bring in the money."

Holly tried not to react outwardly to the sentiment, but she filed it away for parsing later. Under the guise of sending a text, she typed it into the Sillinger file on her phone, but when she glanced up, it was to find Luke watching her with narrowed eyes. She shot him a bright, innocent smile and followed the rookie out to his car. .

LUKE INHALED DEEPLY and let the cool scent of arena ice soothe him. The lights were off, except for a few spotlights shining down from the press catwalk high above and all the seats in the building were bathed in shadows. No one clapped, no one jeered, there was just the rhythmic sound of the cut of his blades echoing through the empty rink as he skated a slow, easy lap. To Luke, it was heaven, a balm to his battered nerves.

There was nothing better than a moment alone on the ice. It reminded him of his early childhood, before his family had moved to Oregon when he was nine. He'd spent many a Michigan winter outside, whiling away the hours pretending he was Gretzky or Hull or Lemieux on the patch of ice his dad had made for him in the backyard.

He'd needed this, a minute to himself, so he'd bailed on Holly's car tours, suited up and come out here under the guise of breaking in his new gloves. Truth was, he wanted to clear his head. Thanks to a neatly folded piece of yellow legal pad and a certain blonde in sky-high heels, everything was too complicated right now. One of his guys was putting himself ahead of the team by playing the inside man on a point-shaving operation.

And if Holly was aware of it and just waiting until she had enough evidence to expose one of his guys, he needed to beat her to it. It was imperative that he deal with this quickly and quietly. The Storm couldn't weather another scandal.

He snagged the puck he'd brought out with him as he skated past and bounced it off the boards to himself. He'd dreamed of winning hockey's ultimate prize for as long as he could remember. But now that he was finally back in the play-offs, his play was lackluster, at best. He needed to do better, play better.

He owed that to his team, who were counting on

their captain and looking to him to set an example. He owed it to his parents, who had sacrificed so much to support him on his hockey quest. And he owed it to Ethan. His little brother had always been the better hockey player, much as Luke had hated to admit it. But it had become obvious by the time the little punk turned ten that he was destined for big things. Even through his jealousy, Luke had always been proud of Ethan, cheering him on, pushing him harder.

And since Ethan couldn't be in the play-offs himself because of the accident, it was Luke's duty to succeed on his behalf.

Yet despite the pressure, and the hoopla, and his messed-up shot, Luke was having a hard time focusing on anything but Holly.

She was ballsy. He liked that about her. Most reporter types, though dogged, kept a reverential tone when they talked to the players, as if they were trying to butter them up. Not Holly. She was a straight shooter, which he appreciated. But it was also the reason he couldn't quite buy her ditzy routine. He'd met plenty of women who couldn't care less about hockey during his lifetime, and she wasn't quite pulling it off.

He'd been unwillingly impressed that she hadn't taken the Ethan bait, though. Despite all the red flags, he *liked* her. What was that about? He hadn't been "in like" with a woman since, well, since ever. "In like" was for mooning high school students.

All his recent relationships had been about good fun, good conversation and good sex…not necessarily in that order. But when it was time for him to suit up, hockey reigned supreme. So why was she always creeping into his thoughts now?

Luke stopped at center ice and sent the puck sliding toward the net, watching until it crossed the goal line and came to a stop at the back of the net.

Maybe Sillinger was right. Maybe it was just lust and he should get it out of his system. Maybe if he spent some time with her, he could break this ridiculous and ill-timed crush on the infuriating woman who kept popping into his mind at the most inopportune of moments.

He turned to leave the ice but stopped short. As if he'd conjured her, Holly Evans was standing in the players' box, arms crossed over her chest, waiting for him. And every single reason that he should stay away from her left his brain.

"You can't hide from me forever."

Luke skated over. "Who says I'm hiding?"

"You're the one out on the ice, avoiding the interview we're supposed to do. I'm the one who's here, questions at the ready, reporting for duty."

"You calling me a coward?"

"Hey, if the skate fits…"

He smiled at that, and her heart stuttered. She'd never seen him smile for real before. He'd flashed his PR smile on a couple of occasions during their on-camera stuff, but his real grin was something to behold. It was the first time he'd looked carefree. Like he didn't have the weight of the world on his shoulders. And it suited him. She had the irrational urge to make that smile come out more often.

"You think I'm gonna fall for some thinly veiled reverse psychology? I play hockey for a living. Trash talk doesn't faze me. You'll have to do better than that."

Luke stepped off the ice and over the boards like

they were nothing—God, why was that so hot?—and sat down on the bench. Holly turned her back to the ice and leaned against the boards, facing him. He set his stick against the side of the box and divested himself of his hockey gloves and his helmet. Then he ran a hand back and forth over his helmet hair. Somehow, after just a few careless swipes, his short brown coif looked photo ready. Holly lamented the hour and a half it had taken to make herself camera presentable.

"You don't like me very much, huh?" she asked.

"I don't like that you take the team's focus off the game and disrupt our routine. We need to be at our best, mentally and physically. I have to trust that every man on that ice is playing for me, and they have to believe I'm playing for them, too."

"Admirable sentiment, Captain Maguire, but there's really only one person you have complete control over. Sometimes you just have to keep it simple and play the game for you."

"I know exactly who I'm playing for," he countered. Then he went on the offensive. "So, Ms. Reporter, what kind of hard-hitting questions do you have for me tonight?" he asked, pulling his elbow pads off and setting them beside him. "What I ate for breakfast? The last song I downloaded?"

Luke pulled off his shoulder pads and jersey together and set the amorphous mound on the bench. Just like that, he was stripped down to a T-shirt—a T-shirt that was damp and clinging to his muscles. Suddenly his leg seemed very close to her bare thigh, and the fact he was wearing shin pads and hockey socks didn't deter a warm tingling from spreading through her body.

"Favorite sexual position?" he continued.

Oh geez. That warm tingling upgraded to hot throbbing in a split second.

He stood up. His skates made him incredibly tall. He loomed over her, but she didn't feel threatened. On the contrary, she felt sort of powerful—like she wanted to tame the beast. The smoldering look in his eyes said he'd let her. Somewhere, in the deep recesses of her brain, a warning light flashed.

She was here to do a job. She shouldn't get romantically involved with a story. Especially not a top suspect in a betting scandal that had the potential to rock the sports world. Her head knew walking away was the smart play right now, but her body overruled the call, especially since he'd provided the perfect opening. "So what *is* your favorite sexual position?"

His eyes darkened like a stormy sky. "Off the record?"

"Of course." Her words were a breathless rush.

"I like all of them." He reached for her, his big hands biting into her hips. She wrapped her arms around his neck as he hoisted her onto the edge of the boards and stepped between her legs. Her short skirt slid farther up her thighs, but she barely noticed the cold plastic against her skin. His mouth came down on hers, stealing her breath and wringing a moan from her.

God, she wanted him. Something about Luke Maguire called to every cell in her body.

Screw journalistic integrity, she decided. Finding out hockey players' favorite colors barely counted as journalism anyway. Then she stopped thinking altogether.

There was nothing but his lips against hers, his hands tugging her blouse from the waistband of her skirt and the sexy thrill of knowing that he was the only thing keeping her from falling onto the ice. Despite that imminent danger, she trusted he'd keep her safe.

He groaned as he slid his warm palm under her shirt and up the bare skin of her back. She returned the sound. The dichotomy of the cool, icy air and the warmth of his skin was a delicious push deeper into the sensual spell he'd cast.

She resented the T-shirt he was wearing and she tugged it up, revealing those washboard abs Paige had been so enamored with in the pages of *Sports Illustrated*. They were even better in real life, and Holly took pleasure in revealing each ridge, the definition of his pecs, his beautiful big shoulders and the flex of his muscles as he raised his arms so she could divest him of the shirt entirely. And then he was all naked torso and harsh wanting.

Holly couldn't get enough.

LUKE WAS OVERWHELMED by the desire inside him, clawing to get out. He was used to being in charge, but something about Holly unleashed the beast in him, made him want to lose control.

He let go, let himself drown in the lust, because he needed the escape. He needed her.

He wished he hadn't suited up, because there was no way he could shuck his skates, shin pads and hockey pants, but he wanted inside her too much to resist the desire. He ran his hand up under her skirt, groaning when he found her most intimate place.

He brushed his knuckles against the damp swath of her panties. She gasped and buried her face against his neck, her arms tightening around him.

Luke was certain he'd never felt more turned on in

his entire life while wearing so many clothes. There was something so amazingly sexy about the feel of her warm, smooth skin and the sounds of pleasure that escaped her throat, juxtaposed with the cool air and the familiar scent of ice and concrete that he loved so much. The heady scent of passion mixed with the comforting smell of the rink.

"Just so we're clear, this doesn't change anything," he panted. He pulled her underwear down her thighs. The first touch of his fingers on her clit made her stiffen. "I still hate that you interview my team like we're appearing in a teen magazine."

Slowly, he eased a finger inside her, and his gentle invasion was almost his undoing as he imagined himself sliding into her the same way. Her body, which had been tense, relaxed as he built her pleasure up. After a few strokes, he used two fingers to give her the friction she was craving so badly. His hips mimicked the thrust of his hand, increasing the pressure on her clit.

"Fair enough. And just so we're crystal clear," she breathed, arching toward him, unable to hold back any longer, "I'm still going to do it."

He could tell when he found her G-spot because she bit her lip and her fingernails dug into his back, pulling him closer. The sound of her breath grew choppy and it was the sexiest thing he'd ever heard. Until she moaned his name.

It short-circuited his brain and he sped the pace of his fingers, rubbing his thumb against her clit, moving his hand to the rhythm of her desire until she came apart in his arms, her cry of release echoing through the arena.

She sagged forward, her forehead resting on his

shoulder. He took a deep breath to calm his racing heart, but all he got was a lungful of her, a scent that was warm and female and sweet...like apples.

"That was amazing." Her smile was radiant, free.

He fought back a flood of testosterone that hit him so hard it was tough to think straight. He hadn't seen a smile like that maybe ever, and definitely not after sex.

The women he'd been with usually tried to act coy, or feigned modesty, or seemed embarrassed. Holly looked like a satisfied lioness who'd gotten exactly what she wanted.

"Paige was right. I definitely needed that."

He needed deep breaths and to not think about all the things they hadn't done together yet. "Who's Paige?"

"My best friend. She's been threatening to hire me a male escort because she's worried that my 'special flower' is crying out for some water. Her words, not mine."

Okay. Well, that *was as good a mood killer as any.* "She sounds like something else."

"Oh, she's something else all right."

A sudden crack followed by a loud hum echoed through the arena, and one by one, the big overhead lights fired up.

Luke swore as he, half-naked, and Holly, barely dressed, both instinctively dropped down behind the boards. It took him a moment to process what had happened.

"It's just the cleaning crew," he explained. He was about to get up, but when he looked over, instead of the panicked or angry woman he expected to find, Holly had both hands clamped over her mouth. "Holly?"

He was about to ask if she was okay when a giggle

slipped out from behind her fingers. Her shoulders were rocking and she was laughing so hard that Luke couldn't help but join her. God, she was pretty.

He leaned in conspiratorially. "Why are we still hiding?"

"Because my contract specifically states I'm not supposed to fraternize with members of the Portland Storm franchise. A clause, may I point out, that does not appear in my cameraman's contract."

Her put-out frown made him chuckle. "Well, they may not be a very enlightened bunch, but in management's defense, I've never seen Buchanan's practical white cotton panties." He grabbed said underwear from the ground beside his hip and held them out to her.

"Hey, these are really comfortable," she said, snatching them from his fingers. With a pretty blush, she glanced over at Luke's naked torso. "And touché. But I'd rather not get fired for engaging in an illicit affair with a member of the team because we were stupid enough to let the cleaning staff catch us."

"Is that what this is?" Luke asked, grabbing his T-shirt from the bench and pulling it back on. "An illicit affair?"

"This," she said, "was a mistake. A big one."

She had a point. He'd let her goad him into losing control. And boy, had he lost it. Yet he couldn't quite bring himself to regret it. Or stop himself from imagining Holly in his bed.

"I still owe you an interview. I'm going to head back to the dressing room and grab my stuff. Give me a couple minutes' head start so that no one suspects anything, and I'll meet you at the exit to the player parking lot."

"Aye, aye, captain."

She made a face at him before she hurried out of the

box and down the hallway with speed and stealth, despite her high heels.

As she disappeared around the corner, Luke leaned back against the boards, relishing the bracing sensation of cold plastic against his overheated skin. He'd never admit it aloud, but that had been the most genuine fun he'd had in a hockey arena in ages.

HOLLY WALKED THROUGH the parking lot beside the man who was responsible for her first non-self-induced orgasm in over a year. And thanks to his prowess, she found him even more attractive, something she wouldn't have thought possible before he'd unleashed a tsunami of delicious endorphins in her system. She'd forgotten how freaking fantastic sex could be. Holly vowed in that moment she'd never let herself forget again.

She couldn't help stealing glances at his handsome profile as they headed toward his black Ford F-250 pickup truck. Holly knew it was his because it was the last vehicle left in the fenced-in players' parking lot. He walked her over to her side of the vehicle and pulled the door open for her, and she crawled up into the black leather cab, waiting as he headed around to the driver's seat.

Get it together, girl. Time to focus.

"So," he said, crawling into the bucket seat beside her, "this is my truck."

He looked nervous, like he cared what she thought. She smiled and let him off the hook. "It's nice."

His answering grin was tinged with equal measures of relief, pride and embarrassment. The combination was utterly adorable.

"It's my one real indulgence. Money's been tight, so I try to keep the extravagances to a minimum."

Holly frowned. She was trying to keep it light and in standard Women's Hockey Network territory, and he just kept dumping incredible openings in her lap. Luke's latest contract was for just south of six million dollars over three years. How tight could money be? "Not a sports car kind of guy?"

Luke shrugged. "Can't haul a wheelchair in a two-seater."

Luke and Holly both froze at his slip. The blatant reference to Ethan hung there for a long moment. And after what they'd just shared, Holly felt she couldn't ignore it. "I read about what happened to your brother. I'm incredibly sorry for what your family has been through. What you've been through."

A weird pressure filled the cab. It was like she could feel Luke withdrawing into himself, but also fighting not to. She wasn't at all sure which part of him was going to win until he rolled his shoulders and tipped his head from side to side, like a boxer loosening up for a match.

After a deep breath, he finally spoke. "Yeah, it's been a tough couple of years. But Ethan's a fighter. And you don't want to hear the sob story. So how exactly does this work? You're just going to ask me some questions?"

Oh right. The interview.

"Yeah, if you can turn on your interior light, I'll just ask you about the truck, your first car, your favorite song to cruise to, that kind of stuff." She gave him the rundown while she pulled her phone out. Once she switched it to video mode, they were ready to roll. He was a good sport, and they sped through the questions.

Holly was just leaning toward him to show him the playback when the "Charge" anthem struck again.

"Sorry." Luke pulled out his phone. She couldn't quite read the expression on his face when he read the screen. "I have to take this."

She nodded, surprised to find he didn't leave the truck to answer the call. "Hey, Dad. How are you? Oh. Yeah, I heard. I was going to call and fill you in, but… uh…" He snuck a glance in her direction and flushed. "Practice ran late."

The G-rated reference to her amazing orgasm made her flush a little herself.

"Yeah, yeah. Don't worry about the money. It's covered. No problem. How's Ethan doing? Really? Well that's good, right?" He listened for a bit longer and then said his goodbyes.

He sighed and turned to her. "Sorry. That was my dad."

"Yeah, I got that." She smiled.

"Are you parked around here?" he asked, searching the near deserted parking lot.

"No, I caught a ride with Jay because my car's in the shop. It's okay, though. I'll just grab a cab."

"I'll drive you."

He looked as surprised as she was by the offer. "Oh. Well, if you're sure it's no trouble."

Holly told him her address and the big engine rumbled to life as he turned the key. She fastened her seat belt as the black behemoth rolled out of the parking stall under Luke's guidance.

"Sounds like you and your dad are close."

He shot her a look of surprise as he pulled out of the lot and onto the road. Night had fallen, and the roads around the arena had cleared.

Luke nodded. "Yeah, he's great." There was a smile in his voice that let her know he meant what he said.

The distance ticked by in ribbons of light and dark as they sped past streetlight after streetlight. There was something soothing about the calm quiet of the evening. It seemed to invite conversation, and Holly found herself saying more than she meant to, as though the residual physical intimacy they'd shared earlier was still lurking, searching for another outlet. "I'm jealous. My pop and I don't really get along that well."

"Nothing in common?" he asked.

Not for lack of trying, she thought, not proud of the bitterness that seeped in as she remembered the hours of her childhood she'd spent camped out on the couch, watching sports with her father, learning player names and stats, anything that might engage him in a more meaningful dialogue than, "What should we order for supper tonight, kids?"

"Well, he really loves his hockey."

"Is that why you took this job?" he asked, and she wondered at that.

Indirectly, she supposed, it was the reason behind every job she'd ever held. It was definitely the reason she strove to succeed in sports reporting. She craved her father's acceptance so blatantly that she was sure any psychologist worth her salt could pick her out of a lineup. Add that to her mother's long shadow, and it was pretty clear what drove Holly.

"Yes. Mostly. I stop by his place once a week to make

him dinner. I'd hoped maybe it would give us something to talk about."

It didn't work any better now than it had then, though, which was why she always timed dinner duty to coincide with a game she was covering for one of her freelance writing gigs—hockey, basketball, baseball—didn't really matter.

Keeping track of the game and taking notes for her articles always made the uncomfortable silence pass more quickly.

"I thought this job would impress him," she confessed. "But it hasn't. I'm not sure what the problem is. Maybe he hates the questions as much as you do. Before my mom died, I remember doing a lot of stuff with him. I miss that."

Holly often found herself wondering if her earliest memories were actually memories, or just dreams she made up of what a great family they'd been before cancer had stolen so much from her. "I want to ask him why we don't hang out or talk the way we used to, but I always chicken out."

Luke nodded as they took the exit that led to her neighborhood. "That's not just you. For the most part, my dad and I get along great, but family emotions can be tough to navigate. There's stuff I can't bring up with him, either." He paused. "Sometimes I worry that my parents blame me for what happened to Ethan."

Oh, God. Holly hadn't seen that coming, and it hit her like a kick to the gut. Did Luke really harbor that much guilt over an event that had been completely out of his control?

"The whistle blew. The game stopped. There was no warning when the hit came," he whispered.

He did a double take when she put a comforting hand on his arm. The startled look on his face, like she'd pulled him out of a memory, made her wonder if he'd meant to say that aloud.

He cleared his throat, motioning toward the upcoming turnoff. "This is the one?" he asked, effectively shifting the rest of their drive to a strictly navigator/ navigatee dynamic.

When they rolled up to the curb in front of her house, she did her best to remove any pity from her smile, despite her breaking heart. "Thanks for the ride."

"No problem." To her surprise, he switched off the truck. "I'll walk you to the door."

They sauntered in silence up to the porch, side by side, in the chill of the night air. Their footsteps and the faint sound of distant cars were the only break in the quiet until they arrived at the front step. Her keys jangled as she pulled them from her purse and unlocked the door.

"Thanks so much for the ride, Luke. I really appreciate it."

"Not a problem. I just wanted to make sure you got home safe."

"And here I am," she said, motioning at her surroundings. "Safe."

"I guess I'll see you when we get back from Colorado then."

She nodded, and there was a weird moment where she wasn't sure if he was going for a hug or a handshake, and somehow it morphed into a bit of both, with a surprise cheek kiss thrown in for good measure.

"Good night, Holly."

"Good night."

With a smile, Holly stepped inside and pushed the door closed behind her. She dropped her purse and keys on the small table in the entranceway. Tonight had been...incredible. From the sexy encounter in the players' box, to laughing with Luke without a care in the world, to navigating some emotionally dense daddy issues while he drove her home.

Even the awkward cheek kiss had been kind of perfect. In a way, it was representative of this crazy friend-or-foe relationship they had going on. And suddenly, and with complete clarity, she knew that if she didn't do something, right then and there, to foster whatever fragile, new thing had bloomed between them tonight, then it would be lost forever.

She yanked the door back open with two hands, ready to run down the street after his truck if she had to.

Instead, she found him standing on the step, arm arrested in knocking-position.

HE'D BEEN ABOUT to rap on the door when she'd suddenly pulled it out of the way.

Luke had meant to leave, he really had, but he'd barely made it down the steps before he'd turned around. The prospect of being alone tonight was too much. Not with all that family stuff bubbling up in his brain.

He'd told her things he'd never said to anyone on the drive to her house. And the crazy part was, he was glad it'd been her.

She was addictive. A life raft in the midst of the sea of hockey that had overtaken his world. And tonight he wanted to be selfish. He wanted to do what he wanted, not what he should—consequences be damned.

"I can't stop thinking about you." He stepped toward her. And then his hand was buried in her hair, and his lips were devouring her lips, and she was pulling off his jacket as he pushed the door shut behind them. And for the first time since the Portland Storm had made the play-offs, Luke felt like he could breathe.

He was vaguely aware of the slap of his leather jacket hitting the floor, but suddenly her arms were around his neck and she was kissing him. His mind went incredibly, deliriously blank. With a growl of need, he grabbed the backs of her thighs and hoisted her into his arms, reveling in the press of their bodies as she wrapped her gorgeous legs around his hips.

"Which way's the bedroom?" he managed to ask when they finally came up for air.

"Over there," she said with a vague motioning of her head. He interpreted the gesture to mean he should turn down the hallway to their left. "Then last door on the right."

Their mouths met deeply, frantically, as he did his best to navigate without bumping into anything. He was eager to arrive at their destination but not willing to miss any part of the journey. There was something so elemental about carrying a woman to bed, kissing and touching and driving each other crazy. Luke couldn't get enough of it.

But inevitably, even through the halcyon buzz and the rushing hormones, Luke's responsible side made its presence known as they rounded the corner into her bedroom. "Please tell me you have condoms."

"Um..." She pushed her hair back from her face, brown eyes glazed with lust, lips swollen with his kisses and the rasp of his stubble.

He'd never wanted anyone so badly in his life.

"I don't think so. But I'm on the pill. So if you're…"

She trailed off, and he nodded reassuringly. "I am. In my line of work, we get tested for everything—and I mean *everything*—regularly."

"I am, too," she said. "Clean, I mean."

Luke stood there, with Holly wrapped around him, and there was a breath of anticipation in the air as they enjoyed that split second of awareness that what they both so desperately wanted was about to happen.

And then that moment of restraint erupted into all-consuming flames. He crushed her mouth with his own, lowering her onto the mattress and following her down. They tugged off each others' clothes, revealing the bend of an elbow, the curve of a hip, the camber of a thigh until finally they were both naked.

She was as beautiful as he'd imagined, as he'd remembered, as he'd hoped. The kind of beauty that brought a man to his knees.

He pushed inside her, one long, deep stroke, and then, because he couldn't wait, he did it again. And again. Losing himself in the rhythm, taking everything he'd craved since they'd gotten down and dirty on the rink boards, loving that the reality of their bodies together was putting his fantasy to shame.

He braced himself on his elbows, trying to tell if she was as turned on as he was, if she liked it, if she was pissed that he'd gone straight for the main event and cheated her out of foreplay. But when he slowed the pace of his hips, she opened her eyes and whispered, "Don't stop. Just like that, Luke. Just like that."

His cock surged inside her and he increased his pace,

loving the soft, startled gasps of her pleasure and the bite of her fingernails against his back.

He buried his face in her neck and breathed, "You feel so good, baby. You make me feel so good."

HOLLY WAS BEWITCHED. Luke Maguire at peak concentration was a powerful force. It was like every cell of his body was focused on her, a visceral awareness that crackled in the air. Missionary was not usually enough to build such a powerful arousal in her, but already she could feel the telltale heat growing, throbbing. She dug her heels into the bed and met him thrust for thrust, ensuring she was taking every inch of him inside her.

She'd thought his fingers had been magical, but this, the heat of him between her thighs, the weight of him against her breasts, this was so much better.

The orgasm at the arena had been sharp, tingly and shallow, racing along her skin like flash paper. In short, nothing compared to the savage need that was building inside her with every stroke of his cock, every brush of his hands. She wanted more, and when she couldn't bear the scorching heat of it a second longer, she let go, reveling in the dark pleasure that erupted, thick and hot like lava, through her veins. All she could do was hold on, clutching Luke against her as their bodies shuddered with the aftershocks of the explosion.

7

"I THINK I HAVE a crush on my arch-nemesis," Holly confessed to Paige a few days later.

Holly did not add the fact that her arch-nemesis was a virtuoso in the sack and might be involved in illegal betting. Just because some of the Storm's games had correlated with the list didn't mean they all would. And this was not an accusation that could be made lightly.

"First of all, thank God. It's been a shockingly long time since you've had man problems." Paige popped the last bit of her cupcake in her mouth and pushed the plate to the edge of their usual table at Piece of Cake, a cute little bakery just down the street from Paige's salon. Holly had originally dragged Paige to the shop in a moment of pure fangirlism, because it was owned by none other than Eric Jacobs's grandma, but the legendary vanilla bean cupcakes kept them coming back time and time again. "And second of all, who?"

"Just this guy at work. He's trying to catch me in the charade. Thinks I know more about hockey than I'm letting on and he wants to figure out my angle. It's awful."

"Then why are you smiling?" Paige asked.

"What? I'm not smiling." But she was. Holly did her best to neutralize her expression.

Sure, Luke was gorgeous, but she shouldn't feel so infatuated. She knew it was a trick—the result of her parent issues. After she'd lost her mom, her father had never thought she was good enough, no matter how much sports trivia she memorized, no matter how insightful her comments. He'd never taken her seriously. And as for her mom...it was really hard to impress someone who wasn't even on this corporeal plane.

So to have this hockey god, a player she deeply admired and respected on the ice, with a body and a face that made her melt, to have him see through the facade that she was presenting, well...of course she was infatuated.

Still, she couldn't get too carried away. He'd been sweet the next morning, even made her breakfast. On his way out, he'd kissed her and said he'd see her after the team's away games in Colorado. But he hadn't exactly professed his undying love, or even promised to call.

Besides, she was the one who'd insisted it was a mistake. And then there was that pesky contract thing...

"Okay, now you're seriously frowning. What's up?"

"I dunno, Paige. It was just really hot."

Paige gave her a skeptical look. "What kind of hot? Taming-the-rebel hot? Corrupting-the-innocent hot? Wrestler hot?"

"What? Ew. No. What is wrestler hot? That doesn't even exist."

"Wrestler hot is when the guy is loud and confident and is kind of pulling off fringe. Besides, you know I love it when men glisten."

Holly took a sip of her macchiato. "It was black-and-white movie hot. Sexy banter, witty repartee..."

"Everyone was wearing all their clothes..." Paige joked.

Rarely had Holly hated her fair skin and propensity for blushing more than she did in that moment.

"Oh my God! Someone watered your special flower? Holly, I'm so proud of you!"

She winced. "Geez, Paige. Decorum much? Would you keep your voice down?"

"Fine, but only if you tell me *everything.*"

"He's the only person who doesn't treat me like a complete idiot. He basically accused me of stepping on the Storm to get ahead and that he's sure I know more about hockey that I'm letting on."

"Ooh. I like a man who gets to the point. So what did you do?"

Holly shoved a hand through her hair with a sigh. It felt so much better when it wasn't teased and sprayed into submission. "Swore up and down that I definitely *was* an idiot and then doubled up on the act. I can't let him win! Besides, why does he care so much whether I'm asking his team some joke questions? What's he hiding?"

Besides, of course, a potential windfall of ill-gotten cash for selling out his team.

"Oh, my! Sex *and* intrigue? This is more serious than I thought! Give me every detail about the man who swept you into bed."

Holly tamped down the blush as best she could. She was not getting into the down and dirty in the middle of a crowded bakery. "He's tall, and handsome and serious, but in this appealing, cares-about-something kind of way. And he's built. Good God, the body on that man." Holly took a long, restorative gulp of caffeine.

"So what's the problem? You deserve to blow off some steam. I know this job has been a little tough on you. So if he's into it, have at him!"

"It's not that simple. We both work for the team."

Paige sighed. "Stupid ethics. They get in the way of all the best stuff. Can't you guys have a secret affair or something?"

Holly laughed at the wording, so similar to her own. "That's what I love about you, Paige. You're always full of ideas."

She smiled back. "Please. You held my hand throughout my divorce. Getting you laid is the least I can do."

"You don't think it's wildly unprofessional of me?"

Paige shook her head so hard that her ponytail swung side to side. "No way! First of all, they called you because you're a YouTube sensation and they wanted to hitch a ride on your star. They know they're beyond lucky to have you. And secondly, this is a temporary job, not your career. So if there's a hot guy who will get you back in the game, then I see nothing wrong with that."

"Back in the game?" Holly laughed as Paige took a dainty sip of espresso. "What, you're sporty now?"

"*My* inspirational speech, *my* metaphor. All the men I work with are gay. I'm living vicariously through you here."

"Excuse me?" said a voice from above them.

Holly and Paige glanced up to find a woman standing beside their table, a young girl in tow. Holly pegged the girl at around nine. She looked very nervous, the pen and napkin clutched in her fingers shaking enough to betray the tremor in her hands. "Aren't you Holly Evans?"

"Yep, that's me. Can I help you?"

The woman's smile turned radiant.

"I'm Lydia, this is my daughter, Teagan. We just love your show! Teagan was actually hoping to get your autograph." Lydia gave her daughter a little shove, and the girl held the napkin and pen out in front of her.

"Of course!" Holly made herself speak through the shock. She accepted the napkin and smiled at Teagan. "So you like sports?" she asked, scrawling a quick little message and adding her signature to the bottom. The girl just shrugged shyly and took the napkin Holly held out to her.

"Can I get a picture of you two?" Lydia asked, holding up her phone.

"Oh, sure!" She leaned in closer to Teagan, surprised when the little girl tucked right in beside her.

"Oh, that's a nice one! Thank you so much. Teagan, say goodbye to Holly."

Teagan threw her little arms around Holly's neck, and Holly was so surprised, it took her a moment to hug the girl back.

"Thank you for making my mom yell less about my daddy watching sports," she whispered. "I want to be just like you when I grow up." Then Teagan pulled away and gave Holly a timid smile before she hurried to her mom's side again.

"How adorable was that?" Paige gushed. "What did she say to you?"

"She said she wants to be like me when she grows up."

Paige placed a well-manicured hand over her heart. "I think I just died a little from cuteness!"

The shrill ring of her phone shook Holly out of the surreal moment, and she grabbed it from the back pocket of her jeans. "Jay, what's up?"

Her tablemate made a face and Holly rolled her eyes at the childish gesture. *Grow up*, she mouthed, and then said into the phone, said, "I'm just having breakfast with Paige—hey. Be nice."

Paige frowned at the unheard insult.

"What? Are you serious? When? Oh my God. Thanks for the heads-up! Yes, of course I'm going to submit my résumé right now. Yeah. I'll talk to you later. Thanks again."

"What? What's going on?"

"Jim Purcell finally retired!" The announcement came out a little high-pitched and squealy, but Holly was so stoked she didn't even care.

"Oh my God!" Paige seal clapped with glee. "Who is that and why do we care?"

Holly laughed. She and Paige might be polar opposites, but she couldn't ask for a better, more supportive friend. "Jim Purcell is the sports anchor on *Portland News Now.*"

"Right! The old guy with the bad toupee."

"Exactly. And if he's retiring, that means that the one and only Corey Baniuk is most likely getting promoted to the anchor desk as we speak. And that means…"

"That they will be looking for an amazing, knowledgeable, well-spoken replacement—who is you!" Paige's seal clap was genuine this time. "We have to get you home immediately," she exclaimed, downing the rest of her espresso. "You need to email that stellar résumé of yours to them at once. At once, I say! And then later, I'll take you out for dinner and we can celebrate this big step in your quest for nightly news dominance."

Holly smiled, appreciative of Paige's enthusiasm. "A lovely offer, but I'm having dinner with my dad tonight."

"Fine. I'll eat alone. But I'm having champagne in your honor and you can't stop me."

Paige's over-the-top zeal was a nice little ego boost, but Holly couldn't afford to lose sight of the truth. There were a lot of résumés out there far more stellar than hers.

But, she rationalized, if she could be the one to break a certain hockey scandal wide open at just the right moment… that was exactly the sort of thing that could make her stand out from a crowd.

"Hey, Pop. How's it going?"

"I'm still alive."

The gruff response was a typical one, and Holly sighed as she stopped at her father's recliner and pressed a kiss to his forehead. "Well, at least you've got that going for you. Tacos okay tonight?" she asked, heading toward the kitchen.

"I could eat a taco or two."

"Perfect. Put the game on and turn it up so I can hear it from in here." Holly hefted the bag of groceries onto the counter and set about unpacking. She put the hamburger in a skillet, sliced up some toppings and dumped the cheese in a bowl, glad she'd sprung for pre-shredded.

The third game of the series had ended with an uninspired 1–0 win for Portland. She knew that because she'd ghostwritten no less than seven articles about it. Not that she was complaining. Play-offs were always a nice bump to the bank account. Tonight they were playing the second of their two-game road trip. Which meant that, except for televised interviews, she hadn't seen a certain hot captain in a few days. She missed him.

But tonight she had to focus on the game and on Pop. Judging by the announcers' lack of enthusiasm, the Storm seemed to be headed for a scoreless first period. She hoped the second period would bring more excitement, because she had another seven articles due bright and early in the morning.

What could she say? Freelancing was not the most glamorous lifestyle. You wrote what people wanted, when they wanted it. That was why she preferred op-eds. It was nice to inject a little personality and analysis into a piece every now and again. But she couldn't afford to be too choosy. It was the no-frills assignments that paid the bills.

Whenever the cooking permitted, she snuck a glance at the big TV, her father's only real indulgence. Everything else in the small bungalow was almost exactly the same as it had been when she'd grown up here. Same oatmeal-colored carpeting, same dated brass lamps, same crystal knickknacks sitting in exactly the same spots, as evidenced by the dust.

It was a house full of good memories and dismal reality. Before her mother had died, the place had been cheery and full of love. Since her passing, it had gotten stuck in time, and there was a palpable desperation to a house that seemed to just be waiting for someone who was never coming back.

With a sigh, Holly served up two plates of soft tacos

and headed into the living room to join her father. She took her usual place on the threadbare couch after she handed him his supper, which he accepted with a grunt. "Pop, you think maybe it's time to get some new furniture?" she asked, noticing that he'd finally given in and duct-taped the armrest on his recliner. "You know, spruce the place up a little?"

"It doesn't need sprucing."

"Your chair is falling apart. It's older than I am."

"I fixed it, didn't I?"

Holly sighed. There was no budging him when he was being stubborn. "Like trying to charm a pig outta mud," her mother used to say, although to Holly's recollection, Diane Evans had always managed to get her husband to come around to her way of thinking.

Holly hadn't inherited that particular gift, so instead of arguing with her father, she dug in to her taco.

As they waited for the second period to get underway, the station was showing highlights from another game being played that night. A San Jose player tipped the puck into the opposition's net, and the home crowd went wild.

"Montana's gonna blow it. Those guys can't get their defense in order." Her dad's words were muffled by a mouthful of taco.

"I don't know. Federov and Rogers are a pretty good duo when their forwards are hot."

"Your brother thinks they should trade 'em both."

Holly shook her head. "No way. If they're going to trade anyone, it should be Powell. He's not living up to his potential because they don't have anyone good enough to play with him. But he's had a decent enough season, so they'll get something in return for him. Plus, he's got a real attitude. He's not gelling with the team."

No comment. Of course. Instead of acknowledging the brilliance of her strategy, he took another giant bite of his taco.

She watched and reported on sports for a living. Her brother was an electrician. Why *wouldn't* Neil's comments hold more weight?

Holly took a sip of her beer. It wasn't unexpected, but it always stung. She couldn't figure out why she kept setting herself up for the TKO, but at some point on these visits, she always brought up sports and always got shut down.

You'd think I'd have learned by now.

For a long time, Holly had figured her father's distance had something to do with her being a girl. Maybe he couldn't relate to her without her mother there as a buffer. And that sucked. But then her niece Melissa had come along and wound her grandpa around her little finger. He went to her hockey games and cheered louder than anyone. It hurt.

As they settled into watching the second period, Holly grabbed the notebook she'd set on the small table next to her dad's chair and began taking her usual game notes. It didn't take long before she found herself nitpicking the game, though. Well, not the game so much as the players. More specifically, the players she most suspected of game tampering.

Holly started an impromptu plus/minus tally on all the potential suspects from the last game. Brett Sillinger, for a boneheaded penalty, Luke for coughing up the puck, Eric Jacobs for a heroic play that had maintained the two-goal lead. It was more in-depth stat keeping than she usually bothered with, but then again, this was about more than a couple of "last night in hockey" reports. This was about making a name for herself in the world of sports.

Each time one of them was on the ice and the Storm scored, she gave them a plus sign. If one of them was on the ice and Colorado scored, she marked a minus sign. When the final buzzer scored to herald a 3–2 win for the Storm, Eric was +1 and Luke and the rookie were both sitting at -2. Not up to the season's standards for any of them. Which wasn't to say that bad games didn't happen. Still, trends were tracked for a reason.

"I thought these guys would walk all over Colorado. None of them are playing up to snuff."

Holly nodded at her father's summation. "You're right. Even when they win, they're performing statistically worse than I'd have suspected."

Her father harrumphed. "I'm going to get another beer. You want one?"

"I'm good, thanks."

And for once, Holly actually was.

She glanced at the stats filling the left side of her notebook—the list had been right about the spread again tonight.

She might not be great at family stuff, but she was a damn good reporter. And soon, she'd have the evidence to prove it. Even if that evidence pointed at Luke.

LUKE LOOSENED HIS tie and tried to rearrange himself in a more comfortable position in the posh airplane seat. Both games had turned out just like the list in his pocket had predicted.

He glanced around the dimly-lit cabin. In fact, the

mood was pretty low-key, despite their back-to-back wins in Colorado. Probably because they'd eked out some pretty ugly victories against a team they should have crushed. He was still surprised they'd held on to a 3–2 win tonight.

J.C. was snoring beside him. Most everyone else was plugged into a movie or talking with seatmates. Except for Eric, who was sitting toward the front of the plane, all by himself, reading a book, as usual.

He liked Eric Jacobs. He was a great hockey player, and the game really mattered to him.

And he was low-key off the ice—no tabloid stories of drunken debauchery or chronic womanizing. He didn't love being on camera, but he didn't complain about the obligatory interviews, either. Still, he'd seemed particularly aloof lately.

With the weight of his *C* heavy on his chest, Luke got up and walked over to him.

"Mind if I sit down?"

Jacobs glanced up from his book. "Sure." He opened his right hand to reveal a chain looped through two expensive-looking rings. Luke watched as he placed the necklace reverently between the pages of his spy thriller like a bookmark before shoving the book in the pocket in front of him. "What's up, Mags?"

"Actually, I was going to ask you the same thing," Luke confessed, taking a seat.

"Nothing really." Eric ran a hand through his dark blond hair. "I'm fine."

"Cubs, we both know that's bullshit. How long have we been playing together?"

"Two years."

"Exactly. You think I can't tell when something's up with my linemate?"

Eric was toying with the bottom of his matte gray tie and refused to meet Luke's stare.

"Let's not make this any worse than it has to be. Just be straight with me. You know I've got your back. Are you in some kind of trouble?"

There was a long, ominous stretch of silence. The piece of yellow legal paper weighed heavy on Luke's mind.

Then Eric heaved a sigh of defeat. "It's nothing like that. It's just…family stuff."

Luke kept his gaze steady and waited.

Cubs dropped the end of his tie and turned to face him. "My grandma's in the hospital. She had a heart attack."

"Jesus. Eric, I'm really sorry to hear that." Eric's parents had died when he was really young, and his grandmother, Stella Jacobs, had raised him ever since. She'd become the unofficial grandma of the Portland Storm and when she was in the stands to cheer them, a round of cupcakes from her bakery always made their way to the dressing room to announce her presence. "Is she going to be okay?"

Eric shrugged, and the gesture had an air of helplessness about it. "The doctors won't say. She seems to be doing better. She pretty much forced me to come on this road trip." He smiled a little when he said it, and Luke had a vivid vision of tiny, white-haired Stella bossing her six-foot grandson around, even from the confines of a hospital bed.

"Why didn't you tell anyone?"

"I don't want to talk about it. And I definitely don't want reporters asking."

"I understand wanting to keep the family stuff under wraps. I won't object if you're sure you want to keep playing."

There was no hesitation in Eric's nod. "It's the play-offs. And I get that this is stupid, but I want to win for her, you know?"

Oh, Luke knew all right. It was what drove him every single day. He wanted that championship, wanted to win it so badly. Not for himself, but for the brother who'd lost his shot at the dream they'd shared their whole lives. "Yeah," he said quietly. "I get that."

And he did. Which was why he was so shocked when Holly's voice echoed in his mind. *Sometimes you just have to keep it simple and play the game for you.*

THE TEAM WAS already out on the ice for practice when she arrived at the arena the day after the Storm had knocked Colorado out of the play-offs with a 4–2 win at home. Because of the celebration and the increased media interest, the team captain had been too busy for her to snag an interview last night, but today, well, it was only a matter of time before they ran into each other, and her nerves were on edge for the reunion.

Holly was standing in the players' bench—Orgasm Central, as her dirty mind had taken to calling it. She was trying to keep her voice even, her blush under control and her eyes from wandering over to the practice happening on the ice behind her. Not because she cared about the practice but because of the overwhelming desire to check if maybe Luke was having as much trouble concentrating as she was.

It took three tries before she managed to get through the intro to the car interview montage without messing up. She could tell Jay was relieved when she finally nailed it by the speed at which he was gathering his video equipment. "Okay, I'm just going to run upstairs to get a few more angles on the practice. Give me ten minutes and we can go for lunch."

Holly nodded. "Okay. I'll text Paige and tell her we'll be at the restaurant in about half an hour."

"Aw, Paige is coming?" Jay whined.

"Suck it up, Buchanan. You know she is."

"Fine. Not sure why we have to ruin a perfectly good lunch, though. I'll meet you at the car in fifteen minutes."

She pulled her phone out of her bra, its usual storage space when she was dolled up in a skirt suit, and texted their ETA to Paige.

Her friend immediately returned the text with one that predictably read: Aw, Jay is coming?

"Holly."

She almost dropped her phone at the sound of the familiar deep voice saying her name. With a deep breath to restore her composure, she turned around. Luke, sweaty and gorgeous in his Storm practice jersey, was standing on the other side of the bench. Her stomach lurched at the sheer handsomeness of him. Clearly her body was ready to start on Orgasm Central: The Sequel.

"Hey. I didn't know we had interviews scheduled for today."

"Oh, we don't. Jay wanted to get some practice footage, and we filmed a quick intro to the car interview bit."

Luke's eyes darkened in a way that shot heat right

through her core. So apparently she wasn't the only one haunted by the sexy ghosts of lovemaking past.

He shook his head slightly, as if to clear it, and when his eyes met hers, he had the air of a man who'd come to a decision. His next words confirmed what that decision was.

"Look, I wanted to ask, do you think maybe I could buy you dinner tonight?"

Holly wouldn't have been more shocked if a hockey-stick-wielding alien had burst through the logo on his broad chest.

"As per my contract, we can't really be seen cavorting about town," she reminded him.

He nodded. "I remember. I was going to suggest takeout at my place. I'll pick you up around five thirty?"

Holly cocked an eyebrow at the time.

"Play-offs," he reminded her with a grin and a shrug. "I've got curfew, so we'll have to get an early start."

Holly couldn't help but laugh. "Didn't I go on this date in the seventh grade?"

"Yeah, well. You pick a career that twelve-year-old boys dream of, turns out that sometimes you get treated like a twelve-year-old boy."

"So there is justice in the world after all," she joked. "It's not all big paychecks, fast cars and constant adoration."

"It's definitely not all that," Luke agreed, and she caught a somber note in his deep voice. Before she had a chance to examine it, he barged through the moment. "So I'll see you tonight?"

"Sure."

His smile was endearingly self-conscious. Not the smile she'd expected from a professional athlete blessed with a big salary and the good looks to back up some swagger. "I gotta get to practice. Five thirty. Don't forget."

Holly watched him skate off to rejoin his team, her phone clutched to her heart and a single thought running through her head.

Oh, shit.

8

"HE ASKED ME OUT."

"Who?"

"Luke Maguire."

The answer brought two very different reactions from her lunch companions. Jay stopped in the middle of eating his nachos, his mouth agape. Paige continued the act of buttering her roll and barely glanced up as she repeated, "Who?"

Holly took a bracing chug of Heineken. "The shirtless hockey player from the *Sports Illustrated* magazine your eyes were glued to a couple of days ago."

"The superhot dreamy one with the bedroom eyes and the washboard abs?"

"He's not *that* hot," Jay countered gruffly.

"Please. That man is a god."

Jay took a huffy bite of nacho.

"Wait a minute! Is Abs Maguire your sex crush?"

Jay cringed. "Do I really need to be here for this?"

"Hush, Jay. This is important lady business. So what did you say?"

"I'm not an idiot, Paige."

"Great. So if you said yes, then I don't understand the problem."

That was the more complicated part. "The problem is that a high concentration of shame is eating through my stomach lining as we speak." Holly took the final swig of Dutch beer. "I'm contractually obligated to lie to him...about my hockey knowledge," she hedged. She hadn't told either of her best friends about her suspicions of illegal betting, and the realization that she was lying to everyone she cared about made her feel worse. "I have a guilt ulcer."

"What's to feel guilty about? You're a beautiful, single woman, and he's a rich, single man who looks like he knows how to wield his hockey stick. Let's not kid ourselves, Hol. You need to get laid. Jay and I, mortal enemies that we are, have actually discussed hiring a male escort just to put you out of your misery."

Jay winced. "No, we haven't."

Paige's raised eyebrow confirmed that they had.

"I swear, you guys. How is it even possible to be so close to your dream job and yet light-years away?"

She reached over and took an unladylike gulp of Paige's red wine, then did her best not to spew it across the table. "Oh, *gawd*! How do you drink this stuff?" she demanded, gratefully tearing the bottle of Pilsner Jay held in her direction from his hand and drowning out the obnoxious taste of merlot with luscious, cold beer.

Shrugging, Paige took a perfect, dainty sip of her wine. "Well, I'm proud of you for putting your lady bits first for once."

"Oh, man! I'm trying to eat here," Jay complained.

"And vaginas disgust you?" Paige asked. "You can't possibly ingest food around women who are discussing them, even though men talk about their penises constantly?"

"What? How did my junk get brought into this conversation? Nobody said anything about dicks."

Holly groaned. "Would you two just sleep together already and get rid of the sexual tension? It's *exhausting*."

"Ewww!" Their disgust was expressed loudly and simultaneously. "That would be like kissing my—" The words "sister" and "dog" overlapped.

Their affronted expressions were almost identical, not that Holly would offend either of them by saying so.

"Seriously, Jay? Your sister? She has a mustache."

"Kissing me is like kissing a dog?"

"Except for the fact that I could muster some enthusiasm for kissing an adorable dog, yes, I imagine so."

Jay cocked an eyebrow. "So you *have* imagined kissing me, then?"

"You. Wish." Paige held up a hand. "I'm going to pretend you're not here." To Holly, she said, "I'm still not seeing the problem."

"Paige, game analysis isn't just criticism. There are a lot of moving pieces to a game. Line matchups, hot streaks, underperforming players, team morale. And when you get millions of dollars to play a game, you have to understand that there will be some scrutiny. But I'm a professional, and that means I can't let my personal feelings interfere with my ability to do my job."

Something that she would do well to remember, Holly decided.

Paige nodded, but Holly didn't like the sly smile on her face. "Tell me more about these personal feelings you're having."

"And now *I'm* going to pretend *you're* not here."

"You'd better be thanking your lucky stars that I'm here. Otherwise you'd probably end up wearing some ripped jeans, a ratty T-shirt and a ball cap on your date tonight."

Holly looked down at her stupid skirt suit. "Well, I'm definitely not wearing this."

Paige smiled. "I'm sure we can find a happy medium. Hurry up and finish your nachos, Jay. We've got work to do."

THERE WERE BUTTERFLIES in her stomach as she crawled into Luke's truck. He'd rolled up to her curb at five thirty sharp, just as he said he would.

"Wow. You look great."

The compliment meant a lot, because it was the first time she'd hung out with Luke feeling even remotely like the real her. Paige had sanctioned Holly's pick of a pair of dark-wash skinny jeans and a white T-shirt. But in exchange, Holly had relented and worn the strappy nude heels and the jade statement necklace Paige had insisted upon.

"Thanks. It feels like I haven't worn pants in ages."

"Well, to celebrate the Portland Storm making it through the first round of play-offs and your long-awaited return to wearing pants, we can have any kind of takeout you want."

"Wow. Living the high life."

Luke nodded as he pulled away from the curb. "Tonight, the world is ours."

Two hours later, Luke, Holly, two mostly decimated pizzas and two bottles of beer were spread out across the living room floor of Luke's swanky—but not quite as swanky as she'd been expecting—apartment. They'd just finished watching a chase movie that was heavy on explosions and fast cars and light on plot. Holly was pretty sure she'd never been on a better date. Until he said—

"I have a confession to make."

Holly's stomach bottomed out and she choked on her beer.

Luke's brow creased with concern. "You okay?"

She nodded, coughing as she set her bottle back on the coffee table. "Yeah. Just went down the wrong way. Sorry. You were saying?"

The nervous look on his face made her gut twist into knots. Her palms prickled with moisture.

No. Please don't let it be Luke who's throwing games.

"I had a bit of an ulterior motive for inviting you for dinner."

The beat of silence scraped across her nerves. She hadn't realized how much she was hoping Luke was innocent of point-shaving. And now, here they were, after an amazing couple of hours together, and it was all about to fall apart.

"Tomorrow I'm heading home to Millerville for the sledge hockey finals," he said, reaching for his own beer. "These kids have worked so hard. And if they win this weekend, they're going to the state finals. I told them I might not be able to make it, but now that we've wrapped up the series and I have a week off, I asked for two days' leave," he explained.

He picked absently at the label on the bottle in his hands and took a deep breath. "And I was wondering if you'd come with me."

Holly couldn't quite process the words. There was a buzzing in her ears as she reexamined the last few minutes. "You plied me with pizza and beer because you want me to go to your hometown with you?"

Luke nodded before draining the last of his drink and leaning forward. "I was kind of hoping you'd do a little story on the team. You know, interview them, give them a taste of what it's like to deal with the media. They'd love that."

Holly couldn't hold back a smile at how animated Luke was at the mention of the kids who were part of his pet charity. She'd done a lot of research about it for her Hockey Hottie of the Month shtick.

Kids on Wheels was a top-notch organization that did an amazing job assisting kids with physical disabilities. She admired the genuine joy on Luke's face when he talked about it. It made her want to say yes, except…

"I don't have anywhere to stay. And Jay's filming a wedding this weekend."

"My parents have plenty of room. And we can just film the interviews on my phone. It doesn't have to be fancy. I just wanted to give the team some professional hockey league experience, you know?"

Holly shook her head to clear it. *Did he just say what I thought he just said?*

"You want me to stay at your parents'?"

"Yeah, well, my mother would kill me if I rented a hotel room, so consider Casa Maguire like a bed-and-breakfast, but with more parental interference."

"You had me at breakfast." The words were out of her mouth before she'd realized she said anything. Because she liked Luke. She wanted to go with him. And it scared her that, for the first time in her life, she was willing to put her job—even one as banal as asking hockey players what kind of underwear they wore—on the line for someone else.

Thankfully, Luke's dazzling smile was enough to shore up her resolve against the doubt that was trying to trickle in.

"That's great. I was really nervous about bringing this up, but the kids are going to be so excited to meet you."

"Me?"

"Yeah, they've all watched your show. They give me a hard time about my answers to your interview questions. The second your videos get posted to the Storm's site, the text messages start pouring in."

"Ah. So this isn't a nice perk, this is revenge," she joked, before downing the last sip of her own beer.

"You caught me. Gotta keep those little punks in line or they'll be out of control before you know it."

"Ooh. You're such an authority figure. That's actually kind of hot."

"What can I say? It's dangerous when things get out of control," he said, and the proof was in the way his eyes darkened.

"It can be," Holly agreed. She shivered as he moved closer. His leg came into light contact with hers. Her body flooded with warmth and sweetness, like she had syrup coursing through her veins. He increased the pressure of his knee against her thigh.

"You done with dinner?" he asked, and his voice was low and rough.

She licked her lips involuntarily. "I could be talked into starting the dessert course."

"I was hoping you'd say that."

THE JOURNEY TO his bedroom was a hazy, erotic blur of kissing and touching and haphazard stripping. Now he was standing shirtless beside the bed, marveling at how damn sexy Holly looked in her pale-pink lace lingerie. He watched with slack-jawed appreciation as she crawled onto the mattress, giving him a perfect view of her incredible ass.

God, he'd never seen her in anything but sensible white cotton, and the idea that she'd picked the sexy lace out just for him was blowing his mind and his restraint. And that was *before* she rose up onto her knees, her back still toward him and sent him a coy glance over her shoulder. She reached behind her back and unclasped her bra, tugging it off in the most delectable little peep show he'd ever seen.

Shucking his jeans and boxer briefs in one move, Luke joined her on the mattress, pulling her against his chest. He nuzzled at her neck, kissing the curve of her soft shoulder. She turned her head to grant him easier access, raising her arms to run her fingers through his hair. The movement made her breasts lift, and Luke couldn't resist the pretty sight. She sighed her pleasure as he ran his hands up the smooth skin of her torso and cupped her breasts.

He pressed his erection against the small of her spine and she pressed back, as if she was testing how ready to go he was. She wouldn't be disappointed.

"I want you," she said.

Luke wanted her, too. He loved her abandon, the way she went after what she wanted, be it the answer to her question, or his body.

Her breath came in soft little pants, and he reveled in how responsive she was to every brush of his fingers, every kiss of his lips. He ran his palm down the front of her stomach, his fingers flirting with the elastic of her panties. She leaned back against his chest, encouraging him to explore. He accepted her invitation, sliding his fingers down to find her wet and ready for him.

"Jesus, Holly. I want you, too. So damn bad."

Her throaty, sensual laugh made his hips jerk. "So do something about it," she challenged, reaching forward so that she was on her hands and knees in front of him. She wiggled her ass, looking back at him over her shoulder.

Luke let himself take what he wanted. With a growl, he yanked her underwear down her thighs and, anchoring his hands on her hips, plunged into her.

Oh, God. She'd never felt anything like this.

Holly had to remind herself to breathe, the pleasure was so intense. What was it about this man that could take her so high, so fast? She'd released the beast, and there was something so empowering about making a man known for his steely control lose all sense of restraint. He was stroking her G-spot with every thrust of his hips, and the sensation that was building inside her was all-consuming.

She dropped down to her elbows, almost screaming with pleasure as the angle changed. Heat streaked through every nerve in her body, culminating in a tingling starburst of bliss that moved through her body like a wave. Luke was only a few strokes behind, and she could feel him pulsing inside her as he joined her in the most intense orgasm she'd ever experienced.

Sweaty and satisfied, she flopped onto her side. Luke lay down beside her, gathering her close so that her cheek rested against his shoulder. She reached out to trace her finger around his nipple, loving the way his pec jumped at her touch. "So much for your curfew."

"What are you talking about? I was in bed by nine."

She laughed. "You always play this fast and loose with the rules?"

"Rules were made to be broken."

She snuggled up closer to his big naked body. "After that deft display, I can't help but agree."

He ran his hand up and down her arm, and the soft, rhythmic stroking made here eyelids flutter closed.

"I'm glad you're coming with me tomorrow."

"Mmm. Me too."

"Are you falling asleep?"

She smiled as he shifted, pulling the blanket from the end of the bed up to cover them. "Maybe."

He pressed a sweet kiss to her forehead. "'Night, Holly."

She wasn't sure if she answered or not as she drifted into the best sleep she'd had in ages.

9

SINCE SHE'D STAYED the night, they'd ended up getting a much earlier start than they'd anticipated—despite the fact that their tandem shower had turned into an hour and a half of fun distraction that had necessitated another shower.

Luke grabbed the bag he'd packed, and they swung past her place so she could throw some weekend supplies into a small suitcase. One more quick stop at her brother's house—Holly needed to pick something up, and Luke was nice enough to indulge her in the last-minute errand—and they were on their way out of town.

In a scant hour and twenty minutes, they pulled up in front of a house that was small but cozy. The kind of house that any kid would be lucky to grow up in. It boasted big trees that were perfect for climbing, lots of driveway space, which, considering two hockey stars had grown up here, had probably hosted its fair share of ball hockey grudge matches and an attention to detail—potted flowers, freshly painted trim—that said the owners cared.

The idyllic scene made her a little wistful. She couldn't

remember even a handful of family memories that could match the cheerfulness of Luke's childhood. She bet he could think of hundreds without trying.

Luke slipped the keys from the ignition and unbuckled his seat belt, but he paused after that, staring at the house for such a long time that Holly didn't know what to make of it.

"Luke?"

She'd startled him, but he tried to cover it with a smile. "Sorry. Lost in thought." He scrubbed a hand across his stubbly face.

Despite the question she'd asked him the day they'd met, Holly was glad he wasn't growing a proper play-off beard. That whole "lumberjack chic" look that was sweeping the magazines didn't do much for her.

He sat there for another long moment, as if he was psyching himself up to go inside. When he finally turned to her, his smile was dimmer than she was used to and it didn't quite ring true. "Ready?"

Holly did her best to seem peppy and normal, ignoring the part of her that wanted to wrap her arms around him and soothe the pain she hadn't expected to find in his eyes. "Ready," she agreed.

She followed Luke into the small bungalow where he'd grown up. She'd never considered meeting the parents to be the big deal everyone else seemed to make it, but suddenly her stomach seemed to think it was on a roller coaster.

"Holly! It's so nice to meet you!"

She found herself caught up in a hug that blindsided her. It took her a moment to relax into the other woman's maternal embrace. She couldn't remember the last time a woman had hugged her—*really* hugged her—as opposed to the cursory, two-second greeting hugs that were all the rage these days. It was…a little unnerving, actually.

"Thank you, Mrs. Maguire. It's great to meet you, too."

The tiny dynamo of a woman flicked her fingers, shooing away the notion. She was casually dressed in jeans and a yellow T-shirt with flowers on it. Her short brown hair was streaked with gray and cut in a no-fuss style that suited her kind face.

"Please. I'm just me. You're the famous one! I watch all your shows on the internet. Luke gave me an iPad for Christmas. I even saw your interview on *Good Morning Portland*. And we don't stand on formality here. Call me Cathy. This is my husband, Ross."

Holly smiled as she shook the man's hand. He had only a hint of white at the temples of his dark hair. It made him look very distinguished. She could see Luke in him: the strong nose, the kind eyes, the rugged jaw.

Luke's smile, though—his real smile—that was all Cathy.

"Well, let's not just stand in the doorway! Luke, you take Holly's bag up to my knitting room." She turned to Holly. "It's actually a little suite over top of the garage, so you'll have lots of privacy and your very own bathroom. I already made up the bed for you."

Luke caught Holly's eye and grinned at the way Cathy had subtly stressed that the room was for her and her alone. "Sure thing, Mom." Grabbing both their bags, he leaned over and kissed Cathy's cheek, and Holly was enchanted at the joy sparkling in his mom's eyes.

As Luke headed back outside and toward the detached garage, Cathy tucked Holly's arm into hers and pulled her into the kitchen.

The highly varnished wooden table was littered with official-looking envelopes emblazoned with the logo of a prominent bank in the top left-hand corner. Some of them had ominous red stamps that said *Final Notice* on them.

"Oh my. Please excuse the mess!" Cathy rushed over to the table and began stacking the notices into a disordered pile, but not before Holly noticed that Luke's name appeared on some of them, along with his parents'. *Huh.*

"Ross and I were just paying some bills before you arrived." Cathy dumped said "bills" into the shoebox on the table and replaced the lid. Only then did her smile regain its genuine warmth of earlier.

"Now let's get some food into you. I just finished making coconut gumdrop cookies—they're Luke's favorite."

The afternoon sped by. The Maguires were warm, attentive hosts, and although Ethan did not make an appearance, Holly was drawn in by their obvious closeness. Luke seemed more relaxed here, and she liked knowing that this side of him existed—that he wasn't uptight and serious all the time.

And yet, she couldn't help but notice the blatant hockey void in the conversation. Hours of chatting had gone by with no mention of Luke's play-off run, or anything hockey related whatsoever. Considering Luke's entire world revolved around the sport right now, she found the omission very odd. She found herself growing indignant on his behalf that his parents didn't make more of a fuss about him.

"I'm going to go check on dinner," Cathy announced. "Luke, why don't you show Holly to her room, in case she wants to freshen up before we eat. I've practically held her hostage all day. I'm sure she'd appreciate a moment to herself."

Holly smiled at the false summation of their day, but the prospect of stealing a few moments alone with Luke was too great to pass up.

"Actually, Luke, I'd rather see your old room."

LUKE LED HER down the hallway to his childhood bedroom. There was still a wooden sign on the door with a hockey player and his name printed in primary colors. He'd picked it out himself in the second grade. A normal kid probably would have taken it down when he was thirteen or fourteen, but at fourteen, Luke had already been billeting with other families and playing in the minor leagues, trying to become the best.

Ethan had been coming up fast on his heels, a definite hockey superstar in the making, and it had pushed Luke to excel. He was proud of his little brother, but he was also competitive enough that he didn't want to be surpassed, either.

As always, his room was just how he'd left it. His parents had talked about turning it into a reading room, but they'd never gotten around to it. Maybe that was something he should do for them for Christmas…send his parents on a trip somewhere and get the room renovated. Just a little something to put a smile on their faces. God knew they deserved it.

"Wow, check it out. A glimpse into the life of a young Luke Maguire." She meandered around the room, staring at inscriptions on trophies and titles on book spines.

He spent the moments looking at her. He liked casual Holly, barefoot and clad in jeans and a black T-shirt, her blond ponytail swinging behind her as she snooped around his room.

He thought it'd been the short skirt and push-up bra and teased-out hair that had pulled him in, but if he was being honest with himself, he found her much prettier and more alluring today than ever before.

He was curious about the attraction they shared. It burned hot and bright and yet it wasn't all passion. They'd had a great trip down, conversing easily and laughing the entire hour and change that it had taken to get here. He enjoyed her company, both in and out of the bedroom.

"Yearbook!"

"What? No!" Luke did his best to mask the panic in his voice, knowing that would only encourage her. "You don't need to look at...too late."

She was already nose deep in the glossy pages, in search of childhood embarrassment.

"Is this you? Oh my God, you had a mullet!" She flipped the yearbook around to show him, pointing gleefully at his photo, as if he didn't remember what he'd looked like.

"I did not have a mullet."

Her pretty mouth hitched up on one side, and he was a goner. "Photographic evidence begs to differ."

"I had a flow. It's totally different. That is a well-respected and timeless hockey haircut. Jaromír Jágr had that exact hairdo."

She laughed as she shut the book and set it on the end table. "Check out this place. You ate, slept and breathed hockey, huh?" He followed her gaze around the room—

old hockey trophies and medals dominated the shelves above his desk, along with a couple of hockey biographies and an impressive collection of *Don Cherry's Rock'em Sock'em Hockey* videos.

"Wayne Gretzky, Mario Lemieux and Bobby Hull." She pointed at each of the faded, curling posters he'd tacked to the wall so very long ago. "Dreaming of the day when you'd have a poster of your own?"

"You know it." Luke tried to keep the frown out of his voice as he crossed his arms over his chest.

Wayne Gretzky, sure, his 99 was showing after all, and Mario Lemieux's name was printed on the poster. But Bobby Hull? Would someone who didn't have the first clue about hockey recognize him? He seemed a little too niche.

It was on the tip of his tongue to call her out on it, but he swallowed his retort. He wasn't going there. No, he was done being suspicious. He liked this girl. She was funny and beautiful and he enjoyed her company. He was done looking for flaws and investigating her every move.

Being home always reminded him that things could change for the worse in a split second. And it would be a disservice to forget to enjoy the things he had. Because he was all too aware that it could all disappear in an instant.

"Instead of posters, I had a signed picture of Barbara Walters on my wall," she said.

Luke smiled at the odd choice. "Really?"

Holly nodded. "It was my mom's. She was an anchor on the six o'clock news. Barbara was her hero, too. Every weeknight, my family would eat dinner in front of the TV and watch Mom tell us about the day's events. And at the end of the hour, she'd tuck her hair behind her right ear and that was our signal. Her little code that she loved us and she knew we were watching."

Her smile was sad, but beautiful, and Luke was glad she'd trusted him with it.

"When she died of breast cancer, my father let me hang the Barbara picture in my room. I'd look at it every night and promise my mom that one day I'd be a reporter on TV, just like her, and then I'd tuck my hair behind my right ear so that she knew I was thinking about her."

"And that's why you do what you do," he said, adding a few more pieces to the puzzle that was Holly.

"That's why."

"I'm sorry about your mom."

She shrugged as she sat on his childhood bed. "It was a long time ago. And it's nice to remember the good stuff."

"Kids! Dinner's ready! Wash your hands."

Luke and Holly shared a smile at his mother's summons, and he took comfort in the fact that, even in the midst of constant flux, some things never changed.

"TAKE A SEAT! Holly, you can sit beside Luke over here," his mom directed. She set a roast chicken on the table.

"Everything looks fantastic, Cathy. Thank you so much for having me."

His mother preened under Holly's praises. Luke hadn't seen his mom this animated in a long time. "Oh, it's our pleasure. It's just so nice to see Lucas happy."

Luke didn't have a chance to be embarrassed, because the hum of the back door made everyone freeze. His father walked in first, and behind him, Ethan navigated his wheelchair into the kitchen with such ease that it made Luke realize just how long he'd been using it.

Sometimes it felt like only yesterday they'd been camped out in the hospital, waiting for the swelling to go down, hoping against hope that Ethan would walk again. Other times it felt like aeons had passed since that fateful night.

"The prodigal son returns," Ethan muttered when he spotted Luke.

Luke forced a smile, trying not to be hurt by the lackluster greeting. "Hey, little brother. Looking fit." Ethan's arms bulged against the fabric of his Nike T-shirt. He must be up at least a couple of pounds of muscle since they'd seen each other last. "Katie must be putting you through your paces."

Ethan nodded at the mention of his physiotherapist. "Yeah. She's tough." He grabbed his plate and started dishing out some food.

"This is Luke's friend, Holly," his mother offered, wading into the tension.

"Hey," he said without glancing up.

"Ethan! Manners." There was a warning note in Cathy Maguire's voice that not even a sullen twenty-two-year-old could ignore. Hell, even Luke still flinched when she marched it out.

Ethan sighed and Luke watched him physically regroup. When he raised his eye, Luke recognized the battle-weary look of a man engaged in a tireless fight. "It's very nice to meet you, Holly."

Holly's smile was warm, despite the fact that the greeting had been decreed rather than given sincerely. "You, too, Ethan."

Taut silence settled over the room then, broken only

by the clank of utensils as everyone served themselves portions of chicken and stuffing and gravy and veggies.

"If you'll all excuse me, I'm going to eat in my room."

"Ethan, we have company." Ross Maguire's voice held a hint of desperation that made Luke wonder how many nights he and his mother ate at the dinner table alone.

"Oh, that's fine." If she was hurt by his brother's abruptness, Holly didn't show it. "I understand better than most what it's like to want to avoid small talk," she joked.

"Thanks." It was, by Luke's count, Ethan's most sincere moment of the night.

The world deflated when he left.

Luke could feel his mother's heart break just a fraction more, see the way his father's shoulders sagged under the weight of his youngest son's misery. He wanted to punch his brother in the face for doing this to them, and yet...

And yet, Luke's own shoulders and his own heart were just as affected at the sight of Ethan's struggle to make sense of the devastating blow he'd been dealt. His little brother was the strongest man he knew. Ethan's dedication to his recovery was beyond incredible, and even the doctors were amazed by his progress. Luke was jealous of how ripped he'd gotten and in awe that Ethan had taught himself to walk again.

But he could only stand for short periods, and his walk was a slow shuffle. Neither was good enough for his brother, who was aiming for nothing less than full recovery. But three years later, the odds of that were dwindling at an alarming rate. And his brother was angry.

Luke couldn't blame him for that, even when he wanted to.

Holly broke the ice. "I can't wait to dig into this chicken."

His mom smiled and encouraged everyone to eat. Holly was wonderful through the entire meal. She did her best to carry the dinner discussion and after the meal, helped his mom clean up the dishes so he and his father could figure out why the power opener on the back door wasn't functioning properly. Then they all sat outside on the deck with his mother's famous lemonade and talked until it was time for bed.

"Thanks," he said, as he and Holly sauntered toward the garage. The evening air was warm and damp and tinged with the scent of spring flowers.

"For what?" she asked, like she honestly didn't know.

"For handling today like a pro."

"Nothing to thank me for. Your family was incredibly kind."

He put a hand on her hip, tugged her forward a step and brushed a soft kiss to her lips. Her sigh was sweet and dreamy, and he leaned his forehead against hers. "Good night, Holly."

She smiled up at him. "Good night, Luke."

He kissed her once more before he pulled himself away, glancing behind him to watch her ascend the small staircase and disappear into the guest suite.

He waited until she'd pushed the door shut before he headed back to the house.

He had every intention of heading straight for his

own room, but instead, he found himself standing outside his brother's.

Luke rapped his knuckles against the door before he pushed it open.

Ethan didn't look up from his physio log book. "Hey."

"Hey." It was weird, seeing the wheelchair beside the bed. Unlike his own room, Ethan's reflected the passage of time. All his trophies and posters and hockey paraphernalia had been packed up and hidden away—probably in the attic, if he knew his mother. Cathy Maguire couldn't bear to throw away memories.

"I just dropped Holly off in the guest room. I'm glad Mom's still protecting our virginities," Luke joked.

A ghost of a smile played over Ethan's lips.

"Some things never change."

Luke didn't mean for his gaze to dart to the wheelchair beside the bed, but it did, and the moment of camaraderie disappeared with the blank expression that overtook his brother's face.

Luke wasn't about to let his brother shut him down that easily. Not again. "And some things change a lot."

"Yeah, well. Be thankful you're the one who got out of this mess unscathed."

Luke ran a frustrated hand over his hair. The ever-present guilt chewed at the lining of his stomach. He ignored his brother's dig and tried to take the high road. "Do you want to come to the sledge hockey game with Holly and me tomorrow? The kids would love to meet you. They keep giving me a hard time that you haven't come."

"I have physio."

"Ethan—"

"I have physio," he repeated in a tone that brooked no opposition.

"Okay, fine." Luke didn't know what to do to reach his brother anymore. Every time he came home, he felt like they grew further and further apart. "You wanna have some ice cream?" he asked. It was a last-ditch effort to connect, a ritual from back in the day. Whenever there was company staying at the house, they'd wait until midnight and sneak downstairs for makeshift ice cream sundaes, thinking they were pulling one over on their parents.

It wasn't until years later that they'd realized it couldn't be coincidence that whenever they had visitors, there was always ice cream in the freezer and an array of toppings in the cupboard. Luke didn't doubt for a second they were there now.

"I think I'm just going to go to sleep. Hit the light on your way out?"

Even though Luke had braced himself for the impact of rejection, his brother's dismissal stung more than he'd expected. "Yeah, sure. Good night, Ethan."

Luke flipped the switch and headed for his own room. He unceremoniously stripped down to his underwear and crawled into bed, but he didn't sleep. It wasn't just that he'd outgrown the bed, either. The whole house was uncomfortable. The whole family was stuck in the middle of a nightmare.

Luke was still wide-awake come midnight. He slipped out of bed and pulled the door shut behind him. Once in the kitchen, though, he decided ice cream didn't sound all that appealing.

A glance out the window showed a light burning

brightly in the suite above the garage. Suddenly, he was in the mood for a different kind of sweet.

Luke grabbed the extra key from the hook in the entryway and was careful to close the door silently behind him—a trick he'd mastered by the age of twelve. In no time, he'd crossed the small expanse of grass between the house and the garage and climbed the stairs to the door.

He knocked before he used the key. Holly looked up from her phone as he pushed the door shut behind him. She was sitting on top of the covers, her back against the headboard, feet flat on the mattress, wearing nothing but a T-shirt and another pair of those sensible white cotton panties. She was absolutely perfect.

"To what do I owe the honor?" she asked, her eyes tracking down his bare chest, boxer-briefs and thighs. If he hadn't already been up for the main event, that once-over would have done the trick.

"This is a booty call."

She licked her lips. "You don't say."

"But it's not just any booty call," he explained, crossing the carpeted floor until he stood beside the bed. "This is a booty call twelve years in the making."

She set her phone on the end table. "Oh? Sounds epic."

Luke nodded as he crawled across the bed. "Since I was fourteen years old, I've dreamed of sneaking a woman up to this bed. Tonight, the fantasy has finally presented itself. So whad'ya say, Holly Evans? Want to make a man out of me?"

"I don't know," she told him, and the uncertainty on her face made him pause. She'd seemed into it a second ago.

"I don't want to get in trouble." She cocked a wicked eyebrow. "We'll have to be really quiet."

Jesus. Lust ignited in his belly as if her words were gasoline. He understood she was just playing along, teasing him, but damn if the role play wasn't working for him in a big way.

She twirled a piece of hair around her finger. "And you have to promise not to gossip to all your friends about this at school tomorrow."

"I promise." She was so damn perfect in that instant that the words came out in a growl. He hooked his arm beneath her knees, tugging her toward him so that she was flat on her back. She let out a cute little shriek, surprised by the move, and he swooped in to kiss the giggles from her lips.

"Shhh. Wouldn't want someone to figure out that I sneaked in here."

Her eyes shone with humor as she wrapped her arms around his neck and pulled him down on top of her. "Oh right. Well, I guess I should warn you, I'm a bit of a moaner, so you'd better think up some way to keep me quiet."

Up for the challenge, Luke pressed his mouth to hers. God, he ached to be inside her. Everything around here felt so wrong, but when he was alone with her... he could turn off his brain. He could just shut it down, run on pure instinct and lose himself in her embrace. It was almost magical the way she made him forget all the pressures that dogged him when she wasn't around.

He poured everything into that kiss, his whole self, and when she pulled away from him, things were spinning so fast that it took him a moment to reorient himself.

"Luke?"

He caught his breath, braced himself on his elbows. Her smile was so pretty it made his chest ache.

"I think I'm ready to go all the way," she teased.

He grinned down at her, unable to resist dropping a kiss to the end of her nose. It was the perfect thing to say. She'd kept things light, pulling him back from the spiraling emotional abyss of moments before.

He got to his feet beside the bed and shoved his underwear down his thighs. "I'm the luckiest fake high school kid on the planet," he said, watching as she sat up and tugged her T-shirt off. He enjoyed the gentle sway of her breasts as she wiggled out of the white cotton panties. At this point, those damn panties had some kind of Pavlovian hold over his body. Just the thought of them made him hard.

"Oh, you're about to get lucky, all right."

She reached for him as he joined her on the twin bed. But he misjudged the distance, swearing when he banged his head on the headboard as he pushed her back against the pillows.

"Oh, are you okay?" she asked, giggling as she ran her hand over his hair to soothe the wound. "I'm sorry. It's not funny," she said, but she was still laughing a little, and he couldn't help but join her, even though his head stung almost as much as his pride.

"If I die, it will be from embarrassment and not head trauma," he assured her. She scooted over to the edge of the mattress so he could lie down.

"Awww. Poor thing. Don't worry. Nobody's first time goes smoothly," she reminded him, reverting to their role play. It brought a smile to his face. "Maybe you'd better let me kiss it better," she offered, leaning over and pressing her lips to his.

Her mouth tasted heavenly. She ran her tongue across his bottom lip, and he reached up to bury his hand in her hair, pulling her toward him so that he could return the kiss with more urgency. He was panting when she pulled away.

"Did that help?"

He nodded. "That definitely helped…a little."

"Only a little? Hmm. We might have to up our treatment level." She pushed herself up and straddled his hips.

He could do nothing but watch in awe as she lowered her body slowly toward his erection. He was so turned on by the time his body finally made contact with the apex of her thighs, he was crazy with wanting.

She continued moving down, trapping his cock against his stomach before rocking her hips forward and back, her wet heat sliding along his length, driving him to madness.

"How about now?" she asked. There was a breathy quality to her voice that confirmed she was just as aroused as he was.

"What head injury?" he managed to ask, his hips pumping involuntarily in an effort to maintain the sensation that had wrung a groan from deep in his chest. She was going to kill him with pleasure, Luke decided.

"Shhh. You're going to get us caught."

She pressed a finger to his lips and he sucked it into his mouth. She threw her head back at the sensation and sped up the pace of her hips. It was incredible, but he wanted more. He wanted all of her.

As if she was reading his mind, Holly reached down and placed her hand on his heart, bracing herself so she could reach between them and when she finally slipped him inside her, his world shrank to raw sensation and a string of swearwords on loop in his head, because he couldn't form anything more coherent through the bliss.

Then she started fingering herself as she rode him, and he'd never seen anything so perfect in his whole life. It was all he could do not to explode. But he needed to hold out until he was sure she was getting at least as much pleasure out of this as he was.

"Come for me, Holly."

"I'm so close…so close."

He grabbed her hips, pushing himself as high and deep as he could. He thrust once, twice, and then she fell forward, hands on either side of his head, kissing him as the contractions of her body ignited Luke's own fierce orgasm.

10

"GOOD MORNING, HOLLY. Did you sleep all right?"

Surely the heat prickling across her face wasn't as obvious as it felt? This was another parental milestone she'd never endured. She'd already moved out of the house by the time she'd lost her virginity.

"I did, thank you, Cathy." She accepted the mug of coffee the other woman held in her direction and took a grateful sip.

"I'm glad to hear it. Come, sit down. I'm making bacon and eggs. I hope that's okay."

"Sounds delicious."

"Oh, wonderful. There's fresh fruit on the table, please help yourself. I'll bring the rest out as soon as it's ready."

"Can I help at all?"

"Nonsense! You're our guest. Besides, that's what Luke is for, right, son?"

Holly turned to find Luke padding into the kitchen in a rumpled T-shirt, gray sweats and a seriously sexy case of bedhead and stubble. "I live to serve," he agreed.

Her pulse sped up as he stepped toward her and pressed a kiss to her cheek.

Holly ducked her head to hide her blush. Cathy's smile of approval was too much to deal with right now. She hurried into the dining room, joining Ross at the table.

"Morning, Holly. Sports section okay?"

"Perfect. Thank you." She set her coffee down and sat next to Ross, accepting the newspaper he handed to her. Combined with the incredible spread of strawberries, pineapple, kiwi and grapes piled high on the platter in the middle of the table, Holly was hard-pressed to remember a lovelier morning. It was idyllic, the kind of scene she'd imagined so many times since her mother had died.

Seemed that Luke was not the only one living out childhood fantasies this weekend. The problem was, her fantasy was a dangerous one. This family wasn't hers and never would be. Still, she couldn't help but let herself be swept up in the idle chatter and homey sounds that came with eating breakfast with people who loved each other.

"You should see that apple tree your mother and I planted beside the ramp in the backyard last year, Lucas. We'll deal with these plates and then I'll show you how much it's grown."

"No, you two go," Holly insisted. "Take Cathy with you. Spend some time with your son. I'll take care of the breakfast dishes. It's the least I can do."

"That's very sweet of you, Holly." Cathy stood, but started gathering up plates as she did. "You boys go on outside. I'm going to relish the joy of having another woman in the house. And don't you argue with me, missy," she warned, cutting Holly's protest off before she could make it. Instead, Holly stood and grabbed the rest of the plates, oddly flattered that Cathy wanted to spend this time with her.

In the kitchen, Cathy stopped at the sink. She set the dishes down before leaning forward to gaze out the window that overlooked the backyard. As Holly approached, she could see father and son, standing at the edge of the wheelchair ramp. Ross was pointing at the small, flowering tree as Luke nodded.

"I'm just so happy you're here," Cathy said, grabbing the plates from Holly's hands and adding them to the pile. Holly's eyes widened in surprise. She didn't think she'd ever received such a warm reception.

"It's such a relief to see him happy. My Lucas has always been serious. And I've been worried about him. Always takes the weight of the world on his shoulders. My little Atlas, I used to call him. Still do, just not to his face anymore," Cathy said with a wink. "I'm glad that he's smiling again." Cathy's warm fingers found Holly's and she gave her hand a quick squeeze. "And I'm glad he found you."

The warm, maternal gesture stunned Holly into immobility.

"How long have the two of you been dating?" Cathy asked.

"Oh, uh. We're not really...we're not very far into things. We only met a few weeks ago."

"Really?" Cathy looked surprised. "Well, I'm relieved Luke hasn't been hiding you from us. But you two seem so comfortable together, so in sync, that I just assumed you'd known each other for longer."

She wasn't wrong. Holly had been pleasantly surprised at just how much they had in common. The drive down had been a blast. Easy conversation, lots of laughs, they'd even established some inside jokes. If she wasn't lying outright to his face and he wasn't the prime suspect in the betting scandal she was investigating, then hey, they might actually have a future together.

The joke sobered her. Luke was a really great guy. He was completely devoted to his family, who were totally worth it, as far as she'd seen. He was confident without being cocky, serious without being stodgy and despite his intense image, he was still able to relax and make her laugh. The sex was pretty incredible, too.

He was the total package. And, she reminded herself, innocent until proven guilty, despite her suspicions. So really, *she* was the problem in this relationship. Fortnight of fun. Spring fling. Whatever you wanted to call it, she was the only verified liar in their midst.

And for what? For a job? But it was more than a job. And not just because the story she was investigating was career making. She was actually starting to come around to the Women's Hockey Network stuff. It was kind of fun.

And she'd gotten a few really nice emails forwarded to her from the Portland Storm site that said stuff like, "You saved my marriage," or, "I get why my boyfriend is into this stuff now," or just, "Your show makes us laugh." It made her feel good to know that this wasn't just three months of career limbo. She was getting exposure and she was touching people's lives.

And she was sitting on a sports scandal that would propel her into the big leagues. Especially now that Corey Baniuk's old job was up for grabs. Besides, she and Luke hadn't agreed to anything. They weren't even dating. Like the Women's Hockey Network, their time together was temporary, and it would be lunacy to put her future in the hands of a man she was having a tryst with, no matter how skilled and sexy those hands might be.

Holly glanced at him through the kitchen window.

Especially since Luke didn't trust her. And with the evidence mounting, she couldn't quite trust him, either.

The sound of rattling dishes pulled Holly back to the present, and she was surprised to find that Luke's mom had completely finished loading the dishwasher while Holly had done little more than stare starry-eyed out the window at her son.

"There, all done," Cathy said, pushing the door to the machine closed and wiping her hands on the tea towel she'd plucked off the counter. "Can I tell you again how much I love your show?"

"Aw, thank you, Cathy. That means a lot. Especially since I would imagine you know everything there is to know about hockey, whether you like it or not."

Luke's mom grinned. "I am a bit of an expert. Job hazard of being the mom of two sports-obsessed boys. I thought Luke might be the most hockey-crazed kid ever, but along came Ethan, every bit as hockey crazy. That child came out of the womb ready to outdo his older brother at anything he possibly could."

She folded the red-and-white checkered towel into perfect thirds and hung it on the oven door.

"For a while, Ross and I used to worry that it would impact their relationship. But Lucas…he's just got a special temperament, I guess. They've been thick as thieves their whole lives, until…well. We've all struggled since

Ethan's accident. But I hope one day that we'll find our way back. I catch glimpses of it sometimes, when Ethan forgets to be angry. My boy's still in there."

Holly's eyes stung, but she did her best to hold back the tears. Cathy's words were not for her—they were the words of a mother who'd come to the aching realization that her son's happiness was out of her control and it was a fact that she resented the hell out of. Holly had never missed her own mother more than she did right then, witnessing the strength and the heartache in Cathy's face, the duality of maternal love.

The Maguire men were a very lucky bunch.

Wiping her eyes, Cathy made a shooing motion with her other hand. "Oh, listen to me. We old people are always going off on tangents! I will not waste this beautiful day blathering when I could be learning all about you. I'm going to make us a pot of tea, and we're going to go enjoy some girl chat out on the deck."

LUKE FOLLOWED HIS dad around the backyard, taking in his latest updates. The old man had done a lot of work. Installed wheelchair ramps to make both the front and back doors accessible, widened all the sidewalks and his car was parked outside because he'd revamped the garage into a physio studio for Ethan. As they stopped to admire the apple tree, Luke could hear the muffled banging of weights behind the door.

Luke glanced at his dad. "How's he doing?"

Ross Maguire shook his head. "He's still so angry. But determined. He's in there every day, does his exercises religiously. Everything that made him such a great hockey player—the focus, the drive—he pours into his recovery. The physiotherapist is astounded by his progress, but Ethan has a hard time accepting praise because he's not where he wants to be. I don't know how to break it to him that he might never be."

The pain on his father's face was unbearable.

"I've never had to do that before, Luke. I've raised two extraordinary men who've accomplished everything they've put their minds to. No one's explained the protocol for when dreams don't come true."

"You're doing fine, Dad. Better than fine. Look at this place. You remortgaged the house to make every inch of it accessible. Ethan's gone to the best doctors, the best rehab clinics. His physiotherapist is practically part of the family, she's here so much. And as much as it sucks, there's nothing more we can do. The rest is up to Ethan."

Ross Maguire nodded. "I know you're right, son. But it doesn't make standing on the sidelines any easier."

Luke raked a hand through his hair. He hated himself just then, because even as he bore witness to his father's hurt, Luke had the overwhelming urge to yell, "No one's asking you to be on the sidelines of *my* life! I'm your son, too. I got named captain, my team made the play-offs and I'm struggling, playing worse than I ever have. And you haven't asked me about a single one of those things! I'm not even sure you watch my games on TV."

But he couldn't say any of those things without being a completely selfish bastard, so instead, Luke said, "I'm going to see if Ethan needs a spotter for his workout," and then he headed toward the garage.

"Got room for one more?" he asked as he entered.

Ethan barely glanced up at the intrusion. He was on the lat pull-down machine, doing heavy weights and high reps. Luke watched the sweat drip from his brother's determined brow. He was going to hurt himself if he kept up this demented pace. And yet Luke respected the hell out of him for sticking to it. For believing.

Luke stepped between the parallel bars, the spot where Ethan had willed himself to walk again. First one step, then twenty, then a few more. In that moment, Luke had wanted to believe, too, that Ethan would one day be free of the wheelchair. But after that, his brother's progress had stalled. And with each passing day it became less and less likely that he would ever fully recover. Ethan refused to accept that. But as Luke had learned as the captain of the Portland Storm, somebody had to be the voice of reason.

He understood that his parents couldn't bring themselves to dash the hopes of their little boy. And that meant that Luke would have to raise the possibility.

Stalling, he anchored a hand on each of the waist-high bars. He pushed up until his feet left the floor and his arms were straight. Then he launched into a quick round of tricep dips, pounding them out until his arms started to burn a little.

The clank of weights dropping let Luke know that he had an audience. He swung his feet back and forth a few times before dropping to the ground.

"What do you want, Luke?"

"I was hoping if my boys win this afternoon, that maybe you could attend the sledge hockey state championships with the team for me. If our series against Montana goes well, I'll be out of town."

Ethan was shaking his head before Luke had even finished speaking. "I can't. I'm training."

"You're always training, E."

"If I can't walk, I can't skate. I need to keep working. I can't afford to lose focus now."

Luke watched as Ethan pulled the pin and raised the knee pad on the lat machine. Slowly, carefully, he pushed himself into a standing position. He waited a moment, hand on the machine, to make sure he was stable. Then he backed up a step, then another, then another.

"No one's more determined than you. I know that better than anyone."

It was all Luke could do not to rush over and help him, to push the wheelchair closer, to swear at the injustice that had left this young, virile kid with the walking skills of a decrepit eighty-year-old man.

But he didn't.

Ethan made it, slowly but surely, back to his chair.

"You might be four years younger than me, Ethan, but you've always been right on my heels. Anything I ever did, you did faster and better, including hockey. And I know you miss it. But it's been three years since the accident. Three intense years, and you've been training nonstop."

Now Ethan did look up at him, and Luke could read betrayal in his brother's eyes. "You don't think I can do it? You don't believe I'll skate again?"

"I have no doubt that you will accomplish all kinds of great things in your lifetime, Ethan. You've always done anything you put your mind to. But I'm wondering at what price. As powerful as your single-minded focus is… We're just worried about you, little brother. Mom, Dad, me. You're in here for hours every day. You're only twenty-two years old. I don't want life to pass you by."

Ethan's laugh was bitter. "And what kind of life do

you think is passing me by, Luke? I spent a whole year barely able to take a piss by myself. People have to open the door for me. I can't drive. I can barely reach the damn stove. Physio is the only thing that makes me feel even halfway normal. Working out is the only thing that's helped me get better."

His voice broke. Ethan swiped at his cheek, erasing any sign of weakness. "And I fought through it. I fought through the pain and I won. I went from not being able to stand, to being able to walk five steps and then ten. It's measurable. I can see myself improving and I need that. Because that's what's going to make my life better."

Ethan shook his head. "That hit took everything from me, Luke. It took my body. It took my career. It took my dream. You can't understand what that's like because you're still playing. You're in the goddamn play-offs!"

"And I hate every minute of it! I can't concentrate, I can't score. Because I wish you were there instead of me."

"You want me to feel sorry for you? You want me to give up? Well, I won't. I'll do whatever it takes to walk again." His brother said the words like a vow.

"You're right," Luke said quietly. "This isn't about me. I want you to walk again, Ethan. I do. But I also want you to have a life. To enjoy yourself sometimes. To smile again."

"I'll smile when I can get rid of the chair and the crutches."

Luke scrubbed a hand down his face. "It's been three years."

His brother flinched like he'd punched him.

"Nobody wants to say it, but what if this is it, Ethan? What if this is as good as it gets?"

"Get out."

"C'mon, man. I just—"

"Stop treating me like I'm one of your damn charity cases, Luke. What are you even doing out here? Jesus Christ! Don't you understand? If this doesn't work out, I've got nothing!"

Luke shook his head at the injustice of that. "That's not true."

"Spare me the platitudes and get the fuck out."

With a sigh, Luke walked over to the door. He stepped outside and pulled the door closed behind him, but he hesitated to walk away.

There was a long pause, but then he heard the clank of metal that meant Ethan had resumed his workout. Luke headed back to the house.

He couldn't wait to find Holly and hit the road.

"You ready to go?"

Holly could tell something was on Luke's mind. He'd been distant since he'd come back to the house. Reading the signs, she'd packed up her suitcase and brought it down to the kitchen, anticipating his need for a speedy exit after his shower. She glanced over to where he stood, making jeans and a sledge hockey sweatshirt look good.

"Just about," she responded. "I wanted to say good-bye to Ethan before we go."

Luke tugged nervously at the brim of his black cap, and she could tell he wasn't wild about the idea. Neither were his parents, if their identical deer-in-headlights expressions were any indication. Little did they know, that was exactly the reason she was doing it.

She grabbed the bag she'd purposely left out of her luggage and headed for the back door.

With a deep breath for courage, she walked down the lovingly crafted wheelchair ramp and knocked on the garage door before stepping inside.

"Hi, Ethan. I hope I'm not intruding. My niece, Melissa, is your biggest fan and when she found out I was coming here, she asked me to see if you'd sign her jersey."

He'd looked pissed when she'd first walked in, but now there was only surprise in his eyes as she pulled the Team USA jersey from the bag, complete with "Maguire" and a big number ten on the back.

Ethan rolled his chair from the modified bicep curl machine he'd been using and approached her. He hesitated before he took the marker she held in his direction and even longer before he took the jersey itself.

"No idea why she'd want this," he muttered, scribbling his signature on the crest on the front.

"Are you kidding? You're her favorite player. Your goal in the gold medal game is what made her want to play hockey."

"That was a long time ago." Ethan clicked the lid back onto the Sharpie.

"Not so long," Holly countered. "People still remember. Just like they remember the dirty, after-the-whistle hit that took it all away."

Ethan's head snapped up at her bluntness.

"What happened to you was awful, completely unfair. But you can't let it define you. You can't spend your life focused on what you've lost."

"Did Luke put you up to this?"

Holly shook her head. "Nope. This is all me."

"You're going to walk into my house and tell me how to live my life? Like I give a fuck what my brother's new girlfriend thinks of me?"

"Oh, I'm not Luke's girlfriend. We're just sleeping together."

The expression on Ethan's face was almost comical, but Holly didn't pause to enjoy it. She had too much to say. "I'm just an outside observer, a hockey lover, someone who was sitting with Melissa when you scored that golden goal—one that will grace highlight reels for the rest of time. I saw the way you inspired my niece to try something new and the way your memory still inspires her to be the best at something that she loves."

Holly took a seat on a nearby weight bench.

"Your family loves you. They want to help you through this. And they're devastated every time you turn your back on their help."

"Leave my family out of this!"

Holly ignored him. "Luke's in the longest scoring drought of his professional career. He's playing like shit in the play-offs and beating himself up over it every single second. All because he feels like he's letting you down. But he straps on those skates every day and tries to do better, because he holds on to the hope that you might be watching.

"It kills him a little bit more with every game that you're not in the stands to cheer him on, but he'd never tell you that. Just like he'd never tell you that he's got a number ten sticker plastered to the inside of his helmet."

Holly shook her head. Her eyes prickled with unshed tears, but they were for Luke, not for Ethan, so she didn't let them fall.

"You know, I wanted to play hockey my whole life,

but I wasn't any good. I washed out. I was a horrible skater and I couldn't keep up with the other kids, so I decided to pursue hockey in a way that I *was* good at. I changed my focus to something more realistic. I took up sports journalism and broadcasting and now I get to be close to the game I love.

"There are opportunities to be part of hockey that don't involve playing. Television stations would kill to have you as a commentator or an analyst. Hell, Luke would love your help with the sledge hockey foundation. But if you're not into that, there are hundreds of sports-related charities dying for big names to bring them some much-needed press and support. There are also a ton of hockey teams out there, from the underprivileged ones all the way to the pros, who need mentors, or assistants, or coaches. And all of them would consider it an honor to have you aboard."

Holly got up and walked over to stand in front of Ethan. "So I guess what I'm trying to say is, the only one who thinks you're stuck in that chair is you." She grabbed the jersey from his slackened hands and held it up. "Thanks for the autograph, by the way. My niece is going to love it."

AFTER WARM HUGS with his parents and a promise that she'd come back to visit soon, Holly and Luke and their luggage were back in his truck and headed for the arena.

The game was amazing. Holly had never watched sledge hockey before and she was in awe. The kids were strapped into their sleds and propelled themselves around the ice with what looked like elongated miniature hockey sticks in each hand. Luke did his best to commentate for her, explaining how the butt end of the sticks had little metal teeth that gripped the ice and how a flip of the wrist was all it took to go from shooting the puck to speeding down the ice.

The logistics of the game hardly mattered as the game progressed. These kids were playing their hearts out, loving every minute of it, and by the time the Millerville Sled Dogs vanquished their opponents 3–1, Holly was cheering as loudly as anyone in the arena.

She followed Luke down to the Sled Dogs's dressing room, and they stood outside the open door waiting for the coach's cue.

"Great job today, boys! So good, in fact, that somebody special wanted to stop by and congratulate you on your big win!"

From the moment Luke stepped into the dressing room, it was obvious the kids loved him. Holly stood just outside the door, watching as he high-fived everyone. She couldn't help but be impressed. These kids weren't excited to see a premier hockey player—this wasn't a hero-worship, get-an-autograph type of joy. The bond went deeper than that. They were excited to see an old friend.

"Luke! You came!"

"Of course I did. You guys think I'm gonna miss watching you play such a big game? Not for anything. And you were fantastic! You guys just made the state finals! That's a really big deal."

"Says the man in the middle of a play-off run."

Luke brushed off the comment, and Holly really admired the way he kept the focus on the kids. "I'm proud of you guys. You've worked so hard this season, and all the practices and the focus is paying off. You have a real shot at winning the state championship, and that's why I brought an extraspecial surprise guest to get you ready for all the media and interviews you guys are going to be doing! Please welcome Holly Evans!"

She waved as she stepped into the dressing room, laughing at the excitement and all the hoots and hollers that greeted the announcement.

For the next few hours, she and Luke had a blast filming the kids, asking silly questions and watching them emulate the interview styles of their favorite hockey stars.

Holly was so caught up in talking with the kids, taking photos and answering questions, that she didn't even notice when Luke slipped out of the room. She found him sitting alone at the top of the bleachers, hands in the pockets of his hoodie, staring out at the ice as the Zamboni circled slowly, erasing the game they'd just witnessed.

"Wow. Those kids really love you."

Luke shook his head modestly, but a flush crept up his neck. His embarrassment was so endearing Holly's insides went all squishy. "I get more out of it than they do."

"Oh yeah?" she asked, taking a seat next to him. The painted wood was cold through her jeans. "How do you figure?"

"It's just awesome to see their joy. Their genuine love of the game. Lots of guys lose that by the time they go pro. The people I play with, the people I play against, there's not too many who still love it the same way they did when they were kids. Too much bullshit creeps in. Contracts, ice time, money and constant criticism from the media, armchair athletes.

"But these kids are still pure. They still play for the love of the game. And when I see them happy, it just…"

"It just what?"

Luke shook his head. "Nothing. It's stupid."

She placed a hand on his shoulder. "Luke?"

He kept his eyes firmly on the ground for so long that she was sure he wasn't going to tell her. She squeezed his shoulder to let him know that was okay, but when she pulled her hand away, he met her gaze.

"It makes me hope that maybe, someday, Ethan will find a way to be happy again, too, y'know? Some of these kids have never been able to walk, and some of them were injured, like him. But this game, this team, it makes them smile, despite all the shitty stuff they've been through. I want that for my brother. Even for a second, I want him to remember that life can be good. That we can be good. Like we used to be."

Luke pulled his hands from his pockets, tugged on the brim of his cap and continued.

"Ethan was a superstar. One of those kids that you knew was destined for greatness. Scouts were sniffing around him by the time he was twelve, keeping track, asking questions. He was just so goddamn good that you couldn't help but notice him."

Luke shook his head. "At seventeen, my little brother scored the goal that won our country a gold medal. At eighteen, he got drafted first overall to the league. People had big hopes. And even though I was jealous as hell of the kid, at how it all came so easily for him, I was proud, too.

"Anyway, as fate would have it, he and I both ended up on the Wisconsin Blades that year—his first year as a professional hockey player. Because of our age gap, we'd never officially played hockey together. Some pickup at the local rink, ball hockey in the driveway, sure, but we'd never had matching jerseys, or been on the same line. And it was awesome."

Luke laughed, and Holly realized that he'd left her. He was back in that moment, reacting to some inside joke she couldn't hear.

"Seriously, I loved every second of that season, him down the center, me on the left wing. We dominated. The Blades breezed through the regular season and right into the play-offs. We thought nothing could stop us. That championship had our name on it."

He was wringing his hands together, picking at his thumbnail, bouncing his heel on the concrete beneath his foot. Agitation that would have warned her the story was about to take a turn for the worse, had she not already known.

"And then we hit the fifth game of the second round. We were up three-one in the series, winning two-nothing in the second period. The whistle blew and I headed for the bench. Then there was this thud behind me, and it sounded like every fan in the building gasped, as if they'd all gotten punched in the stomach at the same time."

There were tears in his eyes now, and he bent over, elbows on his knees. And she knew that for him, just telling the story was a punch in the gut.

"Everyone in the Blades bench was standing up, craning to see what had happened. And when I turned, there was my little brother sprawled out on his stomach on the ice, not moving at all. Still. Deathly still. I dropped my stick and gloves and moved. I don't think I've ever skated so fast or so slowly in my life.

"It took forever to get over there, and I was screaming his name. People grabbed me, held me back. I remember them yelling, 'Don't touch him! You can't move him!' but at the time, the words meant nothing. I just wanted to get to him. I just wanted him to wake up."

The tremble in his voice stole her breath.

"Then there were team doctors, and ambulance crews and spine boards. And they took him away, and there was absolutely nothing I could do to help him. He's my little brother, Holly. I was supposed to protect him!"

Luke scrubbed his hands over his face and she could feel his struggle to pull himself together. With a sigh, he sat straight and tall on the hard wooden bench, eyes still glassy with the old pain. She doubted he knew there were tears streaming down his face.

"It was the worst fucking moment of my life. And it haunts me every single day. It's always there. And it makes me feel like an asshole. Because if that's how it feels for me, I can't even imagine how much worse it is for him."

Holly knew the chain of events, of course. She'd watched the career-ending hit. And the aftermath. But hearing Luke tell his story, to actually see his pain, still so close to the surface, it made her heart bleed.

And all she could do in that moment, high in the dimly lit bleachers of the chilly, small-town arena, was put her head on his shoulder and cry with him.

11

HOLLY STOOD AT the counter of her father's kitchen, dicing onions, while Luke Maguire chopped peppers. It was like playing a surreal version of house, and Holly had to remind herself that the domesticity was just an illusion. After their trip to Millerville, they'd both wanted to continue seeing each other. But they agreed on very clear rules for their dalliance. Just sex, no commitments. Still, the lines kept getting blurred.

Like how he'd dropped her off at home at four o'clock, and by six she was on her way to his place, with only a quick stop to drop off her niece's newly signed Team USA jersey to slow her down.

Like how she'd spent the next two days at his fancy condo with him, having sex and watching movies and eating takeout.

Or how it had taken everything she had to keep her standing Tuesday night dinner date with her father and leave Luke behind. But when she told Luke why she was leaving, he'd volunteered to come with her.

Things were getting very complicated.

"Do you know what I enjoy about this?" He gestured back and forth between them with the knife.

Holly raised an eyebrow. "About the fact that I have boobs and you don't? I could take a wild guess."

Luke winced with annoyance. He was so easy to bait. "No. And keep your voice down. We're at your dad's house."

He was *adorable*, she decided. "Yeah, but he's not here," Holly reminded him, glancing at her watch. 6:20. He always ate at 6:30 on the dot. *Where on earth is he?*

"Besides," she added, "what else am I supposed to guess with you waving that blade around at chest height?"

"I was gesturing to signify us." He lowered his voice. "Our illicit affair."

"What do you like about us?" she asked, ignoring the way her heart stuttered at the topic.

"That we don't talk hockey."

She hoped her face didn't give away her disappointment at that answer. "Oh?" She turned back to the onions, dumping them into the pan on the stove. They sizzled as they hit the hot oil, releasing their fragrance almost immediately.

"Everyone in my life wants to talk about hockey. About Ethan. About the Storm. My thoughts on our last game. My thoughts on our next game. My thoughts on games I'm not even part of. Sometimes it feels like I don't talk about anything else. It's actually kind of a relief that you don't care about it."

Holly added the peppers Luke had cut to the pan, as well as the bag of stir-fry veggies she'd left in her dad's fridge last week.

She knew he meant it as a good thing. He was trying

to say he was comfortable with her, and it was a lovely sentiment. But it made her gut hurt. Because that thing that he liked about her? It wasn't her at all. She was dying to debate hockey with him. Ask him his thoughts on all those things he was tired of talking about and share hers.

She gave the veggies a halfhearted stir, forcing a smile when he stepped up behind her and kissed her neck. "I'm glad," she lied.

And it reminded her that their entire relationship was based on lie after lie. Luke might be comfortable with this woman who didn't exist, but it was Holly's real heart on the line.

There was a big commotion at the front door and while it was right on time, it was much too big to be *just* her father.

Holly groaned inwardly. Her brother and niece must've decided to come over for stir-fry. Karen was probably working a stretch of nights at the hospital, and Neil was a notoriously lazy cook when his wife wasn't around to supervise.

Holly's suspicion was confirmed a moment later when a hungry eight-year-old girl came rushing into the kitchen. "Smells good, Auntie. Dad and I were going to have McDonald's but…" Melissa trailed off, eyes round as hockey pucks as she started to hyperventilate. "You're Luke Maguire. Ohmygosh, you're Luke Maguire!" By the end of the sentence, Melissa's voice was so high-pitched only dogs could hear her.

Holly laughed. "Breathe, monkey."

"Dad, Luke Maguire is at Grandpa's house! Are you staying for dinner, Mr. Maguire?"

Luke nodded. "That's the plan."

"That is so awesome! Your brother is my favorite player of all time. No offense."

"None taken," Luke assured her.

"Aunt Holly got my Team USA jersey signed by him. How cool is that?"

"She did?" Luke's raised brow held questions she didn't want to answer.

"Luke, will you sign my hat? Aunt Holly, is there a marker around here so I can get my hat signed?"

Saved by the autograph seeker. Holly rooted through the junk drawer as Melissa flitted around like a butterfly drunk on excitement. "My team's in the play-offs, too, you know. Just like yours."

"Is that so?"

"Yep. And we're gonna win, too. Dad! Luke Maguire is in Grandpa's kitchen. He's gonna sign my hat. Dad?" Melissa disappeared back into the living room in search of Neil.

Thank you, she mouthed at Luke, tossing him the marker she'd found. He caught it easily, but he waved off her appreciation like it was no big deal. Considering he'd finished explaining to her how much he'd been enjoying his hockey reprieve, she found his kindness toward her niece even more touching.

"So that's why you went to see Ethan before we left. Why didn't you tell me?"

"Oh, you know," she said, nudging the drawer shut with her hip. "I was worried your fragile ego might not be able to handle that Melissa's heart belongs to your brother."

Luke made a halfhearted effort at a laugh, but his preoccupation was obvious. "He actually signed it, though?"

"Yeah. He signed it."

The relief on Luke's face was heartbreaking.

"I'm really sorry about all this craziness. I understand that you were trying to escape hockey. I didn't realize it was going to be a full house."

Whatever Luke was about to say was cut off as Melissa marched back into the kitchen, pulling her dad along by the wrist.

"Nice try, monkey. You expect me to believe a hockey superstar is hanging out in Grandpa's kitchen and…"

"Told you." Melissa pulled off her ball cap and handed it to the hockey superstar hanging out in the kitchen.

Holly suppressed a laugh as her brother lost all ability to speak. His complexion, every bit as fair as her own, flamed red as he recognized their guest.

"Neil, meet Luke. Luke, this is my older brother, Neil."

"Hi. Wow. Hi."

Luke grinned as he signed Melissa's hat and handed it back to her. "Nice to meet you, Neil."

"You, too. Wow. Just…wow. Why didn't you warn me, Hols?"

"Or me," added her father. "When you said you were bringing someone home for dinner, this was definitely not who I was expecting," her father said gruffly, extending a hand. "Frank Evans. It's a pleasure to have you in my home."

Luke shifted the marker to his left hand so he could return the handshake. "Thank you for having me, sir."

"Okay, dinner's almost ready. How about everyone who just got home goes and washes their hands so they can help set the table."

"The table?" her father scoffed. "The first game of

the Buffalo-Wisconsin series is on TV right now and you want us to eat at the table?"

Holly shook her head in defeat. "Why do I even bother?"

TEN MINUTES LATER, Holly was sitting on the couch, sandwiched between Luke and her brother, with Melissa on the floor at Luke's feet. Pop, as always, was comfortably ensconced in his recliner. All of them were enjoying heaping bowls of teriyaki chicken stir-fry.

The first period featured some pretty intense hockey, and her family was in fine form, heckling the refs and players alike, hypothesizing the trades they'd make if they ruled the hockey world.

"Hey, Luke?"

He grinned down at the star-struck girl at his feet, and Holly hated her traitorous heart for noticing how good he was with her.

"Hey, Melissa?"

"Um, remember the time you scored that goal against the Wyoming Stallions back on October seventeenth? You stole the puck from Alfredsson at the blue line and then you skated so fast and scored right through the five-hole? And the goalie was just lying there 'cause he couldn't even believe it?"

Luke chuckled at the description. "I have a vague memory of that, yes."

"I was at that game," Melissa told him. "It was awesome. Aunt Holly took me for my birthday."

Oh my God. As if her "I don't speak hockey" cover wasn't tenuous enough *before* the last few hours. Now a witness had placed her at the scene of the crime. Holly jumped to her feet. "Okay. I think that's enough hockey talk for today. Who wants dessert?"

The answer was a unanimous yes. When Luke tried to help her gather up the supper dishes, she shook her head firmly. "I got it," she said, hurrying into the kitchen.

Thankfully, her family was too caught up in the on-ice battle to notice Holly's odd behavior. Luke, however, followed her into the kitchen before she'd even finished unwrapping the store-bought brownies.

"You sure you're okay? You seem a little distracted tonight."

She reached into the cupboard to grab a stack of napkins. "It's fine." She tried to smile. "I just feel badly for you. You were saying earlier how nice it was not to talk hockey every moment."

"Sure, but that?" He thumbed in the direction of the living room. "That brings back memories. Yelling at the television, armchair coaching and that instant connection you can have, even with a stranger, as long as he's wearing the same jersey as you. I'd forgotten how great the game could be from this side of the boards. It's a lot different than watching game tape."

Holly was touched by his kindness. He was trying to fit in and put her family at ease.

He stepped closer to her and his hands came to rest on the small of her back. "But somehow, I don't actually believe that's the reason you're so distant tonight."

"Oh no? What, are you a mind reader now?" she joked, resting her hands on his chest.

"Maybe I am. Are you thinking of the number... four?"

She shook her head, not understanding. "Four?"

"It's numerology," he said. Holly had to forcibly remind herself to breathe during the pause that followed. "If you add up all the letters in Vancouver, you get four. Not nine, like you said. Not nine, like Jay's birthday. Four."

Uh-oh. That was not an auspicious start to the conversation. Dread seeped through her stomach lining, and the stir-fry soured in her belly. "You've known for that long?"

"I did the math that night, when I got home."

Busted. On the bright side, it was probably the nicest way she'd ever been called a liar.

"I told you the day we met that I was on to you. Hockey is not a sport for the weakhearted. You're either all in, or all out. And I had a hunch you were all in. But now... I just wanted you to know that I know. You don't have to pretend with me anymore. Okay?"

Holly nodded. "Yeah. Better than okay."

He leaned in and the kiss was sweet and filled with relief. It was nice to be assured that she didn't have to hide that part of her around him anymore. That some part of what they had was based in truth.

"Great. So let's go watch some hockey." He grabbed the plastic tray of brownies and stack of napkins she'd set on the counter.

Her phone rang, and she recognized the name of one of her freelance clients, *Sports Nation*, on the caller ID. "Right behind you. I just have to take this first."

"More brownies for me, I guess," Luke joked, heading back into the living room.

She was smiling when she answered the phone.

"Holly? It's John Marshall from *Sports Nation*."

"Hey, John." That was odd. He was the senior editor

at one of the biggest blogs she wrote for. Except for the day he'd called to offer her the freelance job, he usually stuck to email, and even then his messages tended to come through lackeys. "I'm just waiting for the final buzzer so I can finish up tonight's game wrap-up. Should have it to you within the hour."

"That's great, Holly, but it's not why I'm calling. I actually wanted to talk to you about publishing one of your op-ed pieces."

Holly's heart revved, thudding against her rib cage. "I'm sorry, what?"

"Don't play coy with me," John joked. "Every second week, you submit an article about something going on in the world of sports and beg me for a byline. I'm finally going to give you what you want."

"Oh my God! John, that's amazing. Seriously. I couldn't be happier." Holly was practically bouncing. This was a big deal. She couldn't wait to tell her dad.

"Which article finally convinced you? The one about the evolution of goaltending equipment? No, it's my analysis on the new hybrid icing rule, isn't it?"

"Actually, it's neither. Those were solid pieces, but I could publish them any time, interchangeably. There's no *oomph* to them. The one that really impressed me is not only provocative and well-argued but incredibly timely. It's the perfect storm of sports articles."

"Don't leave me in suspense! Which article are you…"

Oh no. Holly's shoulders hunched even as all her muscles braced for bad news. *He doesn't mean…*

"How Luke Maguire Is Hurting His Team."

Holly's stomach bottomed out.

"It's fantastic, Holly. Obviously, I'll have to update it a bit since you wrote it at the beginning of the play-offs—his scoreless streak has hit sixteen games now—but all in all, it's got huge potential for our site. If it does as well as I think it will, who knows? I'm always on the lookout for insightful staff writers."

The line between dream and nightmare blurred. She'd been sending in articles for two years without a word from John, and the minute she got hired by the Portland Storm, the minute she and Luke were, well, whatever they were, *this* happened? She'd written that article two months ago. Before the Women's Hockey Network had even existed.

"You can't publish it, John."

"Yes, I can, Holly. The submission guidelines clearly state that once you send it in, I own it. And I will publish this article—"

She didn't have time for legalese right now. "Fine. Publish it, but I need you to pull my name off it."

"What are you talking about? You've been begging me for a byline since the day I hired you."

"John. The article is yours, but no names, okay?"

"I guess we can go with Anonymous. Might give the article more legs if everyone is speculating about who wrote it."

Great.

"You're sure about this, Holly? *Sports Nation* is a major player. Being published with us tends to help careers."

Holly's fingers migrated subconsciously to her lips. Lips that had just kissed the mouth of a man she cared for more deeply than she'd ever expected to. There was no choice.

"I'm sure."

STANDING OUTSIDE THE Storm's dressing room with the puck set to drop in about two hours, Holly knew she'd made the right decision.

She'd been concerned about Luke, first and foremost. She hadn't even thought about this job in the moment. That meant something. Something big. Something much too complicated to dissect right now.

But as she stood with Jay and the rest of the scrum, waiting for pregame access to the dressing room, she realized she was having fun. Sometime in the last month, she'd come to really enjoy this joke network of hers. Publishing with another company would have voided this contract, and she wasn't quite ready to do that.

The doors finally opened, and she stood back, letting the rest of the reporters head in. She had a good relationship with all the players on the team now, so she never wanted for interviews. Even the big names would carve out a little time to tell her whether they preferred dogs or cats.

She was just about to head in, when Brett Sillinger pushed through everyone in his quest to leave the dressing room in a hurry. His brow was creased and his scraggly play-off beard did little to hide his frown and the determined set of his jaw. The phone in his hand was blaring the "Charge" rally.

That damn anthem had become her nemesis. Every time she heard it—which in the course of a day's worth of interviews with twenty-three players on the active roster, was a lot—her heartbeat tripled and she went on high alert. She couldn't help herself. Even though she knew it was a clue with a lot of dead ends, it remained the most concrete lead she had.

If she could just re-create that bathroom happenstance, overhear the right conversation at the right moment, she'd have her man. She'd lost her chance for a byline on that damning article she'd written because she didn't want to hurt Luke, but the silver lining was the fact that she hadn't blown her cover with the Storm. Now she was *this* close to an on-camera exposé on a betting scandal. It was the kind of hard news story her mom would have killed for. The kind of legit sports reporting that might impress her dad.

That was why, with a quick apology to Jay and directions on a few questions he should ask should the opportunity arise, Holly hurried after the rookie. His long strides had given him a pretty good head start.

When he disappeared around a corner at the end of the hallway, Holly took a quick moment to stop and take off her pumps. Television shows that portrayed their women detectives chasing down perps while wearing high-heeled boots were such a load of crap, she decided. She resumed her chase, more sure-footed and quiet with her shoes safely in hand.

The hallway came to a T intersection, and Holly stopped for a second, debating which way to go. She decided any direction was better than no direction. She arbitrarily went left. When she got to the end of that hallway, she came to a skidding halt outside the occupied room, not at all prepared for what she found.

J.C. had his hands up to protect his face, ducking and covering as his fiancée screamed and swung her fancy designer purse like a flail.

"I can't believe you did this!"

Whack.

"I can't believe you would do this to me! To the baby! How am I supposed to show my face with the other hockey wives?" *Whack*. "Why would you sell the Porsche? Who's going to take us seriously driving some low-end four-door!"

"Come on, Tania. Quit hitting me with your purse already!"

"I'm going to be a laughingstock."

Holly tore her attention from the fighting couple, backing away slowly, trying to leave unnoticed.

She almost made it, too, but Tania gave a particularly wild swing of her bag, and J.C.'s gaze caught hers. She didn't even break stride. She just spun and ran.

Cowardly? Maybe, but she was hot on the trail of a suspect, and Tania's brand of a woman scorned was more than she cared to deal with right now.

Obviously, Sillinger had gone in the opposite direction, so she hurried back to where she'd lost him and turned the other way.

She was relieved that it did not take long to locate his nasally whine.

"What the hell, man? I thought we had a deal! I told you, I just need a little more time!"

Holly stopped short at the outburst. Her scalp prickled at the realization that this might be the break she'd been searching for. She tried to recall the harsh whisper that had echoed off the tiles in the Storm's bathroom. Had it been the rookie all along?

"Dude, you can't do this to me. I'll get you your money. Just give me a week. Two, tops. My mom'll help me out. She's in Vegas on vacation or I'd have your cash right now."

Holly frowned and leaned forward to peek around the corner.

Brett shoved a hand in his dark curls, his knuckles

white, he was clutching his hair so tightly. He pressed his back against the concrete wall, then slid down until he was sitting on the rubber floor.

"You don't understand. The Lamborghini's all I've got. My teammates think I'm a joke. This is the only thing I've ever done to impress them. Just give me a couple of weeks. I'll get you your money."

There was a long moment of silence, followed by, "Yeah. I understand you've got a business to run. Whatever."

He swore, then slammed his phone on the ground before wrapping his arms around his legs and dropping his forehead to his knees. All in all, it was quite a dramatic show.

"Brett?"

He started like she'd hit him with a cattle prod. He scrambled to his feet. The pout on his face made him seem even younger than his nineteen years, despite the pitiful beard.

"How long have you been there, Holly? What did you hear?"

Holly shook her head and started toward him slowly with her hand out, like she was approaching a skittish deer. "I just wanted to make sure you're okay."

"No, Holly. Actually, I'm not okay. I just found out they're repossessing my Lamborghini, so life pretty much sucks balls right now."

She did her best not to laugh.

After such an intensely emotional weekend with Luke, his parents, Ethan...the idea that a nineteen-year-old hockey player making a salary that most people could only dream of, herself included, was pouting like a child because he couldn't make the payments on his Lamborghini seemed the height of absurdity to her. Talk about your first-world problems.

She stared at the simpering man-child before her and mentally crossed his name off the suspect list. A man raking in extra money by betting on his team wouldn't have to ask for money from his mother. Even more damning was Brett's complete inability to deal with surprises.

Point-shaving was a delicate balance, especially in a low-scoring game like hockey. The idea that the kid before her had the chops to handle and manipulate a rink full of veteran hockey players was ridiculous. Truthfully, she was a little embarrassed she'd put him on the suspect list at all.

"You're not gonna tell the team, are you? About my Lambo getting repossessed?"

"No. I'm not going to tell them about your *Lambo*," she said dully.

"Okay, great. Maybe I can make up a story about how I totaled it or something. That would make me sound cool."

Holly let Brett disappear around the corner so she wouldn't have to walk back to the dressing room with him. Then she put her high heels on again to slow her down even further.

The dressing room was packed. She sidled up to Jay as soon as she spotted him. "What'd I miss?"

He shook his head. "No idea where J.C. is. I scored some face time with Eric and Doug, asked them the stuff you wanted for the 'How Well Do You Know Your Teammate?' segment. We're up next with Luke, after Baniuk finishes with him."

Holly watched Corey and his cameraman set up the shot and launch right into the interview.

"I'm Corey Baniuk from *Portland News Now*. Here with me is the Storm's captain, Luke Maguire. Luke, *Sports Nation* has recently published an article saying that your play, in particular, might be suffering because it's your first time in the play-offs since your brother, former Wisconsin center Ethan Maguire, took a brutal hit in the post-season three years ago. What do you have to say to those allegations?"

Shit.

Holly had hoped she'd have a chance to warn Luke before the article hit the media. John must have pressed "publish" the moment he got off the phone with her.

Why hadn't she said something to Luke after dinner? On their way home? After they'd made love? Because she was a coward, that's why. And she'd wanted to enjoy what she had with him as long as possible.

The color drained from Luke's face for a split second before it returned with a vengeance. "No comment. We're done." He pushed past the camera and headed for the exit.

Holly hurried after him, but instead of the hunt she'd endured with Brett, she found Luke pacing in the hallway right outside the dressing room door.

She couldn't keep the concern from her voice. "Are you okay?"

"I just need a minute."

"I saw what just happened with Corey Baniuk, Luke. You don't have to be fine. He coldcocked you. That was way out of line."

Luke just shrugged. "Rumor has it Baniuk's about to inherit the anchor desk. I should have expected him to go for the jugular on that interview, go out in a blaze of glory."

He took a breath. "Besides, Baniuk's not the problem. He was just the first reporter to get a crack at me. The problem is the damn *Sports Nation* article." Luke shook his head. "It's going to dredge up all the Ethan questions again. That guy really hit me where I live."

He lowered his voice, leaned toward her, and Holly could only hope he couldn't smell the culpability rolling off her in waves.

Luke continued. "The article talks about how my scoring drought started on the same day the team was mathematically guaranteed a play-off spot. This guy just laid out all my neuroses. I don't even get how he could figure out half that stuff. Much as it hurts to admit it, it's a really professional and well-written article. No cheap shots, just facts.

"It's probably for the best he didn't have the balls to sign his name to the thing. I'm not sure if I should pay him for the therapy or punch him in the face."

Luke shook out his hands. He was moving around a lot.

Holly, on the other hand, was frozen to the spot under a blizzard of remorse and shame. How had she thought taking her name off the article would ease the impact? She should have fought harder to keep it from being published in the first place. Again, coward.

Luke didn't seem to notice her anxiety. "Anyway, the article doesn't matter. What matters is that I've got a game tonight and I need to calm down and get back in the zone."

He drew in a deep breath and exhaled slowly. "We really have to win tonight. Any advice?"

She couldn't make her confession now. That would only screw with his head more. As the cause of his messed-up equilibrium, the least she could do for him now was to keep quiet.

Holly tucked her hair behind her right ear as she stepped toward him. "Montana's notoriously weak on their left side, so just keep the pressure on. Forecheck hard and whenever you get a shot on Krouse, remember to shoot stick-side. His glove has been hot in the post-season."

Luke grinned at the counsel. "Man. You weren't kidding when you said you know hockey."

"Kick the Wolfpack's ass tonight and I'll show you what else I know," she teased. It was a desperate attempt to keep the guilt from winning.

It didn't work.

12
_____

IT WAS PAST midnight by the time Luke finished doing press and they'd arrived back at his place. Still, when Luke walked out of his ensuite bathroom wearing nothing but black sweatpants, Holly's weariness dissipated at the prospect of making good on her promise. Luke had kept up his end of the bargain and the Storm had come out victorious, downing Montana 5–3.

"So, what have you got in store for me tonight?" he asked, joining her on the bed. "And bear in mind that you're going to have to pull out all the stops to impress me, since I am currently a man in possession of flavored body oils and a tin of Altoids."

"Oooh! Flavored oils? Sounds fun! Where are you stashing 'em?" Holly rolled onto her stomach and reached for the bottom drawer of the nightstand closest to her.

"No! Not that one!" Luke practically vaulted over her, pulling open the small top drawer instead.

Holly shot him a frown. "What? Is that your fetish drawer, or something? You don't want me to find your ball gag?"

Oh my God, is Luke blushing? Her curiosity bubbled to new heights.

"It's nothing, okay? You wanted sexy oil, here it is." He pulled the lube out and set it on the end table. "Ooh, look! Cherry flavored."

"Nice try." She couldn't keep the grin from her face. "What's in there, Luke?"

He shrugged but it looked painful, like his skin was too small for his body. "Remember how we were going to have sex? Remember that fun plan?"

"But how am I supposed to really concentrate on doing naughty things to your body when all I'll be able to focus on is what's in that drawer?"

"You are very bad at taking no for an answer, do you realize that?"

Holly shook her head and heaved an innocent shrug. "What can I say? Our misogynistic culture has forced me to become a fighter, to believe in my dreams and power through the glass ceiling. You're part of the patriarchy, the reason I must pursue things with such single-minded determination. Face it, Mags. You're fighting a losing battle here."

With weary defeat on his face, Luke flopped back onto the bed and slung an arm across his face. "Fine. But you cannot, upon pain of death and/or laryngitis whenever there's a camera on you, tell anyone what you've seen here today."

Holly smiled graciously in victory. "What is it? What is it?" she chanted, pulling open the drawer. "What the…?" To her utter amazement, she found a pair of knitting needles attached to what she assumed was a striped scarf. But as she began to pull, the haphazard-

ness of the striping became obvious, as did the never-
ending length. "Seriously, what is it?"

Luke heaved a long-suffering sigh. "I told you. It's
nothing."

Holly was still searching for the end of the navy,
white and teal monstrosity. It was at least twice as long
as she was tall and she still hadn't pulled it all from its
resting place yet. "It's a pretty long nothing."

"It's just knitting, okay? My mom taught me."

Holly sat on the edge of the bed, yanking foot after
foot of inconsistent stripes into her lap. "Okay, you have
got to tell me how this came about."

Luke pulled his arm away from his face and stacked
a pillow under his head. "When I was young, I used to
really dwell on stuff—especially hockey games. If we
lost, I'd go over it again and again, trying to figure out
what I did wrong, what I could do better. If we won, I'd
try to deconstruct what went right, how I could build
on it. I was a pretty intense kid, especially once my
little brother started climbing the hockey ranks. I'd get
so deep in my head that I developed some pretty bad
insomnia."

Holly ran her hand across the yarn in her lap. She
could imagine a young Luke, solemn blue eyes, a determined set to his chin as he figured out how to be
faster, stronger and better, all in the name of the sport
he adored. He was still doing it.

"So she taught me how to knit. She said knitting
would keep the chattering part of my brain occupied
so I could mull over only the most important stuff and
keep my thoughts really focused. She made the rule that
I could only go over the game until I was done knitting five inches and then I had to put the yarn away."

He smiled. "It sounds dumb, but it worked. I would replay the game for however long it took me to knit five inches, and then I was free. I didn't have to think about it anymore. I've made one of these every hockey season since."

She held up the project in her hands. "All color-coded to your team, I hope."

Luke laughed at himself. "Yep. For my Portland Storm years, navy is a loss, white is a win and teal is a tie. Every game is five inches of knitting or purling and intense contemplation."

"So it's a good thing that this is mostly white then, huh?"

"Yeah, it was a pretty good season."

"And these thin teal lines at this end? That's the start of each play-off series?"

He nodded. "No ties in the play-offs, so that's my way of keeping track of how far we make it."

"You are a very surprising man, Luke Maguire. Just when I think I've figured you out, you change the game. Although I'm pissed at you that you told me that your secret talent was speaking French. This is way cooler."

Luke rolled his eyes.

"I'm serious," she said, with a playful punch to his arm. "I just have one more question."

"Of *course* you do."

"How do you hide it from the other guys on road trips?"

Luke grinned. "Nobody ever thinks your World Junior Championship duffel bag is full of yarn."

"Hiding in plain sight." Holly laughed. "Well done."

She set the knitted record of the Storm's current season on the end table. Every piece of himself that

Luke revealed made Holly fall in love with him just a little bit more.

How could she hurt someone she loved? And she would hurt him; that seemed inevitable. But was it better to hide the truth from him and let him have his win? Or come clean and destroy everything? There were no easy answers. She only knew that she wanted him to be happy, and tonight she could make him happy.

"I gotta say, that knitting was a much sexier find than a ball gag."

"Oh yeah?"

Holly nodded. "Yep. And now that my curiosity is sated, I find myself with plenty of naughty things percolating in my brain."

"You don't say."

"I *do* say," she countered, crawling over and straddling him. She grabbed the end of his knitting project. "So here's the plan. We're about to take your knitting to a whole new level."

LUKE LAY BACK against the pillows as she tied up one of his wrists before looping the free end of the yarn monstrosity through the slatted headboard. His body was already approving where she was going with this, even before she'd finished fashioning the woolen shackle around his other wrist.

Although his restraints could easily be slipped with a few tugs, her foray into light bondage was turning him on in a big way. He loved the satisfaction in her smile as she surveyed him, all trussed up and at her disposal.

If he'd known knitting would score him this kind of action, he would have opened the damn drawer himself.

"So now what?" he asked, unable to hide the desire that was tenting his pants.

"Now," she said with a wicked grin, "we get to the naughty stuff."

"I was hoping you'd say that."

She leaned down and kissed him with a brute force he hadn't expected. But he liked this take-charge side of her, the way her tongue plunged into his mouth, the bite of her nails on his chest.

When she pulled back, the look on her face undid him. She was this incredible mix of sweetheart and vixen, and the sugar-and-spice combo was proving to be never-ending fun.

She maintained eye contact as she stood on the mattress, stripping off her jacket, then her skirt. His breath came faster at the sight of her curves, highlighted by a purple bra and matching panties.

She dropped to her knees, then crawled forward between his legs. "Your turn."

Luke couldn't help the groan that escaped as she grabbed his pants and tugged them slowly down his legs. The torturous rasp of the elastic waistband against his hard flesh culminated in a harsh gasp when his erection was finally freed of its confines.

She tossed his pants to the floor and then stretched to grab the cherry lube. He loved her body, loved watching her move. She was a real woman, not a skeleton with boobs, and when he got free from his knitted prison, he was going to do some exploring of his own.

The lid on the oil tube opened with a soft *click*, and the intent look of concentration on Holly's face as she drizzled cool liquid on his hot flesh made his hips buck.

Dropping the recapped bottle on the mattress, she

reached for his straining cock. But then she jerked her hand back. "Wait!"

"What?" The word came out harsher than he meant it to.

"Can we jump right into this, or do you need to knit first?" she asked. The fact that she would stop to tease him just then made him want her even more.

"Only if you can't come up with a better way to get my mind off the game and tire me out."

Her smile said she had some ideas that he just might enjoy.

He was not disappointed. She wrapped her hand around his cock and pumped once, twice, three times to ensure an even distribution of the oil.

Then she put her hands on the bed beside his hips and took him in her mouth. His whole world shrank to the warm, wet pressure of her lips and her magical, magical tongue.

"Mmm."

The vibration of her sound sent another level of pleasure humming through his veins, and he flexed his hips, seeking more but unsure how things could get any better.

She lifted her head, releasing him from her mouth after a hard suck of his crown. "The cherries taste good, but next time, I'd rather just taste you," she said. Then she grasped his cock firmly in her right hand and proceeded to push him farther toward oblivion.

He was dying to bury his fingers in her soft, blond curls and set her pace, but he was also loving the torture of being restrained. The soft, suctioning sounds of her mouth were his undoing.

"Holly, I need inside you. I want to make you feel as good as I do right now."

He slipped his hands free of the yarn shackles so he could reach for her, pull her up the bed, taste her lips and move her body beneath his.

She sighed as he drove into her, slow and deliberate, but it didn't take long until he gave in to the roar of his blood and sped his pace. Holly didn't seem to mind. She drew her knees up, hooking her legs around his waist. The change in position forced him even deeper, and she started chanting his name against his lips.

He gave her everything she wanted, following her whispered orders until her breath grew choppy and her fingernails dug into his back.

Then Luke redoubled his efforts, plunging harder, faster, deeper, until he felt her body clench. And then he let her cries of ecstasy pull him over the edge right along with her.

SHE WOKE UP to find the bed empty. But the curtains blowing in the warm Portland breeze solved the mystery of Luke's whereabouts before she even had a moment to be curious. With a sleepy smile, she stretched and slid out of the bed. As she was grabbing her shirt, a familiar mix of navy, white and teal caught her eye. She padded across the hardwood floor to the chair in the corner of the room.

No way was Luke getting away with this blatant show of hubris without a goodly amount of teasing. She pulled the jersey on and headed toward the balcony.

Luke stood on the balcony wearing nothing but a pair of low-slung jeans, staring contemplatively out at

the city. He looked so damn yummy that certain parts
of her anatomy perked up at just the sight of him.

Down, girl.

"Seriously, Maguire. You have your own jersey in
replica? That is so wrong."

He glanced over at the sound of her voice, and she
could tell she'd surprised him. His jaw flexed as he
took in the jersey, her thighs, calves, bare feet. His eyes
tracked every inch of her and when their gazes met,
there was an appealing cockiness to his expression.

"No, what's wrong is how much it's turning me on
that you're wearing it. I like seeing my name on you."

"How very Neanderthal," she joked, walking over
to him.

"What can I say? Me horny, you hot."

She laughed as Luke stepped behind her, placing one
hand on the railing on either side of her hips. With a
contented sigh, she leaned back against his chest. They
stared out at the city as the sun came up over Portland.

It was romantic, standing in his arms and watching
the world wake up. But after awhile, Holly couldn't silence the niggling voice in her brain, the one that said
Luke was not the type of guy to indulge in blatant self-
worship, and she turned in his arms to face him.

"So seriously, why do you have your own jersey?
And why is the number wrong? Misprint?"

Luke shook his head. "No. It's not a misprint. It was
for Ethan. I bought it for him after they gave me the *C*.
I thought maybe he'd come to a game or something."

Holly's heart went a little melty. She traced a finger
down his bare chest, hoping he'd say more.

Luke tightened his grip on the balcony railing. It
took a moment, but he finally spoke.

"He's the reason I'm the captain now. Because I have to play for both of us. It was just my way of saying thanks. But you saw him. He's been so down, I just didn't have the heart to give it to him."

Holly suddenly realized the significance of the twenty-eight on the back of the jersey. Forget melty, her heart was liquid goo, sliding down the inside of her rib cage. "Eighteen plus ten. You added both of your jersey numbers together."

Luke shrugged, as if it wasn't the sweetest thing she'd ever heard.

"Like I said, it was dumb. It's been sitting on that chair for three months now."

"I'm sorry I put it on. I didn't realize it was so significant. I was just giving you a hard time."

"You know what? Keep it. No one else is going to wear it."

Holly had plans to the contrary, but she kept those to herself. "You're sure you don't mind?"

"Why would I mind? You look sexy as hell in it."

She smiled at that. "Well, if that's what you think about me in it," she teased, ducking under his arm and heading for the door, "then you should see me out of it." Luke followed her back to bed and she proceeded to prove her point.

AFTER ANOTHER HARD-FOUGHT win at home, they'd split away games in Montana, losing the first and winning tonight. And while Luke was glad they'd managed a win, he found he owed more of his good mood to the prospect of seeing Holly again than to the game result. Luke loosened his tie and looked out the oval window at the lights of whatever city they were currently flying over.

"Mags, you okay?"

Luke glanced over as J.C. took the aisle seat beside him.

"You're staring off into nothing. I thought you'd had a stroke or something."

"How did you know Tania was the one?"

J.C. laughed. "What?"

"I'm serious, man. You two are getting married, having a baby. How did you know she was the one you wanted to do all that with?"

Normally the stymied expression on his goaltender's face would have made him laugh, but tonight he just wanted answers.

"Where is this coming from? Wait a minute, are you dating someone?"

Luke took a deep breath. He wasn't really ready to spread the news around. He certainly didn't want to put Holly's job at risk. But he was dying to tell someone, and J.C. was his best friend. He couldn't help his smile when he said her name. "Holly."

"Holly? As in, *Holly* Holly? Of Women's Hockey Network fame? The woman you don't trust because she is undermining the sanctity of the game and threatening the team? *That* Holly?"

Luke accepted the ribbing as par for the course, but when he didn't fire back, J.C. sobered a little. "You're serious? You have feelings for this girl."

Luke shrugged, which in guy talk was as good as a yes.

"Huh. Never took you for the kind of guy who'd end up with a ditz just because she's got a nice rack."

Luke's shoulders stiffened. "That's over the line, man." His voice was all steel, and J.C. held his hands up in a gesture of surrender.

"My bad, man. Just testing the waters. I wasn't expecting to come back from the can and have you start talking about your emotions and shit. Stand down."

Luke relaxed in his chair, but not until he'd stared J.C. down, let him know he meant what he said. "And for the record, she's not a ditz. She just plays one on the internet."

"Whad'ya mean?"

"The dumb blonde routine is all an act. She's actually as smart as she is beautiful." He sent his buddy a sidelong glance. "And she knows more about hockey than you ever will."

"So then what's with all the secrecy?"

Luke shrugged. "I guess the top brass doesn't think we're good enough actors to answer the questions if we thought she was only joking."

"Ha. They believe us well enough when we line up to kiss their asses at all their hoity-toity events."

Luke smiled at the dig. Everyone was aware of how much J.C. hated putting on a tux and schmoozing with the bigwigs.

"So what's Holly's deal then?" his friend asked. "She's like, a reporter or something?"

"She wants to be."

J.C. nodded. "Cool. Good for her. And good for the two of you. I'm happy for you guys. Truth is, Mags, the fact that you're asking me how you know? That probably means you already know." J.C pushed the button that made his seat recline. "I'm gonna catch twenty minutes before we land."

"'Night." The word came out distracted, though, as Luke let the words settle in.

That probably means you already know.

13

THE GAME WAS going well until the hit. The sight of Eric Jacobs lying on the ice and clutching his knee was too much.

With a feral growl, Luke dropped his stick and his gloves and launched himself at six feet, two hundred pounds worth of smug left-winger. He grabbed a fistful of Wolfpack jersey with his left hand and landed a solid hook with his right. He only had a second to relish the roar of the crowd and the sting in his knuckles before his punching bag recovered and launched a counterattack.

But Luke wasn't about to back down. He might not have gotten the chance to punish the man who put Ethan in a wheelchair, but he wasn't going to let the one who'd just sidelined Eric Jacobs get away with it unscathed.

Despite Chris Powell's attempts to wrestle him into submission, Luke managed to land a few more good blows to the jerk's face before the two of them overbalanced and fell to the ice. Luke swore when his nose made contact with Powell's helmet, his eyes welling up at the sharp sting.

He didn't have time to worry about it, as he struggled to gain the upper hand even as someone grabbed him by the shoulders and pulled him back.

"That's enough, you two. Break it up." The ref's voice managed to penetrate the angry haze that had overtaken Luke's brain, but he was too worked up to obey.

With a final jab to Powell's left cheek, he let himself be hauled off the asshole who'd just lambasted Eric Jacobs with a dirty, knee-on-knee hit.

He watched his nemesis scramble to his feet, only to be detained by the referee.

"Nice fight, Powell," he taunted, ignoring the linesman's attempts to wrestle him over to the penalty box. "I think you might have even broken a nail trying to hug me into submission."

"You should thank me for not messin' up your face there, pretty boy. Might lose your 'hottie of the month' status and then you'd have to play hockey for a living. How many games has it been since you last scored?"

The idea that he and Powell had been linemates a mere four months ago, before the other man's giant ego and philandering ways had sent the bastard to Montana, seemed ludicrous in that moment. Obviously things changed. Loyalties faded. You couldn't trust just anybody.

"Tell your boys I said good luck in the play-offs, Maguire. It's gonna be a battle without your top scorer."

Luke followed Powell's gaze toward the net, where Cubs was being helped off the ice by the trainer. Luke didn't like the way his centerman was hunched over, his left leg bearing no weight.

The ref skated up. "Shut your mouth and get moving, Powell." Then he turned to Luke and gave him a shove. "That goes for you, too."

The other linesman skated up, handing Luke his stick and gloves. The memories that came flooding back were not happy ones, and even though Eric's injury wasn't as serious as the one that was haunting him, it was cold comfort.

With a sigh, Luke headed for the penalty box. He'd gotten two minutes for instigating and five for fighting. Powell got two minors and a game misconduct.

The Storm ended up winning the game and the series with it, but Luke barely made it through the post-game press junket. By the time he and Holly got to his place, his palms were clammy and he couldn't stop shaking.

Everything with Ethan had been so close to the surface lately. To see another talented player—another centerman, for God's sake—get taken down on Luke's shift…it made his heart feel too big for his rib cage, like it might puncture any second.

"I can't do this again."

"He's going to be okay, Luke. Here, just crawl into bed, okay?"

"But what if he's not? His grandma had a heart attack a few months ago. He needs to be able to take care of her."

"He can. He got off the ice himself. He's not as badly hurt as Ethan was. And even if he had been, there's nothing you could have done to stop it. It's not your fault." Her voice was soft. Reassuring. He liked hearing it. It made him feel better.

"I'm the captain. I'm responsible for my team."

"I know you are. But you couldn't have stopped this."

She crawled in beside him, and for the first time since the fight with Powell, he began to breathe normally.

"Maybe I could have. I should have tried. I should have done something."

"Luke. Stop. You did everything you could."

Holly wrapped her arms around him. His heart slowed to its standard pace.

"Will you stay tonight?" he asked.

"Sure, of course."

Her warm fingers stroked his hair. It wasn't too long after that, that Luke surrendered to sleep.

IT WAS SIX THIRTY in the morning when the sun streaming through Luke's window woke Holly. He was slung out on the mattress beside her, and she was glad to see him resting after his post-game panic attack. He'd been through so much lately. Too much. And there was more to come.

He shifted on the mattress, sliding his hand over her hip and tugging her closer. She turned to face him. His blue eyes blinked a few times before they opened for good. "Hi."

She smiled and ran a finger down his stubbly cheek. "Hi back."

"Sorry about last night."

"There's nothing to be sorry about."

Luke sighed. "Holly, I can recognize a panic attack when one hits. I had them really bad right after, well, right after Ethan got hurt. Last night wasn't anything compared to those ones, but I really appreciate you staying here and talking me down."

"It's not a problem, because..." she trailed off.

"Because?"

I love you. She did, but she couldn't say it yet, though, so she kissed him instead.

He kissed her back and shifted closer. Before she knew it, they were naked and entwined, his body driving into hers with such an elemental force that for the first time in their relationship, there was no need for sexy words, or woolen shackles, or flavored oils. They were beyond all that. And when her climax rolled in like soft tides instead of roaring waves, it was the most exquisite thing she'd ever experienced.

They were holding hands and trading kisses and indulging in a dreamy discussion about breakfast—he was firmly in camp bacon and eggs, while she was leaning more toward French toast—when the "Charge" anthem intruded on their blissful post-coital haze.

Luke rolled away from her so he could locate his phone, and the loss of his body heat sent a chill down her spine. It took him a few moments of searching—he'd been in such rough shape last night that most of his before-bed routines, like putting his phone on its charger, had been annexed by the panic attack.

She watched as he followed the familiar music toward the chair where she'd slung his suit jacket after she'd helped him take it off. He flipped the expensive fabric around so he could access the interior breast pocket. Finally he got hold of his ringing prey.

"H'lo? Yeah, it's me."

His whole body tensed, and Holly felt the distance he put between them even before Luke pulled on a pair of jeans. He didn't miss a beat on the phone that was expertly cradled between his ear and his shoulder.

"No way. I told you, that's not an option," he said, stalking out of the bedroom. "I don't care how you do it, just get him the money. I can't have this traced back to me."

The words stopped her heart. She jumped up with some half-formed plan to follow him, but she only made it three steps from the bed before the unthinkable caught her eye.

Dazed, she walked toward his jacket, askew on the chair back, just as he'd left it. A folded piece of yellow legal paper poked out of the inside breast pocket.

She unfolded it to find a list of letters and numbers in stark black ink.

And just like that, her perfect morning crumbled.

It can't be Luke.

The man who was so sweet and thoughtful, the man who needed hockey to breathe, surely he wouldn't do something that could earn him a lifetime ban from the game he loved?

And yet there were other things—his parents' modest dwelling and pile of bills, Ethan's intense physio regime and state-of-the-art equipment, the fact that a hockey player who should have adequate funds had said things like "money's tight" and "I can't have this traced back to me." Something wasn't quite adding up there. She'd tried her best to find a more viable suspect, but something always cleared them.

Brett Sillinger had pouted when his Lamborghini got repoed.

J.C. LaCroix had done the responsible thing and downgraded to a family car because he had a baby on the way.

And Eric Jacobs, who'd been her least likely suspect in the first place, had apparently been dealing with some intense family issues that correlated with his slightly-below-average play-off showing.

Luke, on the other hand…

Holly sat on the edge of the bed, the over/under list clenched in her fist.

He'd shown up in the bathroom moments after she'd found the betting sheet, and his ringtone matched the mystery man's.

His truck was nice, but in the grand scheme of luxury vehicles, it was pretty low on the scale for a six-year veteran who was currently earning almost two million a year.

His parents must've invested huge amounts of money into making their old house fully accessible, not to mention the cost of Ethan's physio studio and medical bills. And she'd heard several sports outlets reporting that Brad Timmons had recently filed for bankruptcy, which meant the Maguires were receiving no financial help from the man responsible for their money woes.

And she'd caught Luke twice now in the midst of suspicious-sounding phone calls, the most recent one specifically about untraceable money.

She didn't want to believe it. Luke loved the game and he was fiercely protective of his teammates. It was beyond comprehension that he would jeopardize his career or his team's integrity this way.

But even as she thought it, she knew there was one thing he loved more than hockey—his family. He would do whatever it took to take care of them. Manipulating the games a little was an easy way to help pay down his family's debts, to take care of his parents and his little brother.

And maybe that straight-arrow reputation he'd built

up—the one that made her doubt he was capable of it—was the key to getting away with the crime. He had the perfect cover.

She *had* to ask him.

She was in love with Luke and she owed him the truth about her suspicions, the right to defend himself, to give his side of the story. Before she exposed it to the world.

14

"LUKE, CAN WE TALK?"

He'd barely stepped back into the bedroom after a massive fight with his brother's bank. The somber note in Holly's voice made the hair on his arms stand up. "Sure, yeah."

He took a seat on the corner of the bed opposite her. "What's going on, Holly? Is everything okay?"

"Yeah," she said, but she backtracked immediately. "No. It's not, actually." She sighed.

They made eye contact and he didn't like what he saw there.

"Luke, I'm just worried about you. I know you've had some money trouble."

"What?"

"You were obviously speaking with a bank just now. And I get it. Your family is amazing. And they needed your help, but manipulating hockey games…that's a dangerous road to start down. So if it's about money…"

His muscles tensed and his jaw hardened. This wasn't a talk. It was a cross-check after the whistle. The kind that left permanent damage.

"What are you trying to say?" His eyes dropped to the yellow paper clutched in her fingers. He shot to his feet, eyes lighting on his suit jacket, askew on the chair. "Have you been going through my things?"

"I found a list, Luke. When I was in the Storm bathroom that day that we kissed. This list. And aside from the first one, every single play-off game has ended with the same over/under as the list predicted. That's not a coincidence. Someone is manipulating the games."

"And you're accusing me?"

Her silence was all the answer he needed. Luke experienced a moment of full-body pins and needles and then…nothing. Numbness settled over him with a finality that reminded him of death. "You believe I would do that." It wasn't really a question, since she'd already said as much. More of a reckoning.

"Luke, I know how important your family is to you. You'd do anything it took to make sure they're okay."

He raked a hand through his hair. "But this? After all we've been through? I kept your secret! I introduced you to the people who mean the most to me in this world. I fell in love with you, Holly."

She looked like he'd punched her. That stricken reaction to the words he'd wanted to say for longer than he was willing to admit was the final nail in the relationship that had turned his world upside down. "And this is what you think of me."

Her brown eyes were swimming in unshed tears, and her chin trembled as she fought to hold them back. "Luke, the evidence—"

"Fuck the evidence! I would never do what you just accused me of! Not for any amount of money. I wouldn't do that to my family. I wouldn't do that to my guys.

We're a team, Holly. We trust each other. We back each other up. I can see you don't know anything about that, but that's how we operate. It's how we win games and it's how we lose games. Together."

"But the stats, and that phone call about untraceable money and Ethan's top-of-the-line rehab equipment..."

"That's your reasoning? Let me tell you something about money. Pro hockey players make around three hundred thousand dollars a year in the first three years of their contract. Unless they get paralyzed. Then they make nothing. But they still have to live, Holly. They need money to eat, to buy a wheelchair, to pay for medical bills and specialists and daily physio. Whatever it takes for the chance to walk again.

"The parents of an injured pro have to remortgage their house when they should be gearing up for retirement, because sidewalks have to be widened, ramps have to be built and garages have to be converted into rehab facilities. A paralyzed player needs a new van to accommodate a wheelchair. And when things start looking bleaker and bleaker, he has to figure out how to finance a car with hand controls so that a broken hockey player can live the fulfilling, independent life he deserves, even if he doesn't regain full use of his legs.

"So, yeah. Money's tight. My paycheck might have a few zeroes on the end of it right now, but there are millions of dollars of catching up to do. And the secrecy? The phone call you overheard? That was just for Ethan's pride. Because he's already struggling with accepting physical help, and I didn't want him to know about the financials, that the bastard who ruined his life claimed bankruptcy and that all his money is coming from me.

"He needs to focus on recovering, on himself, not

worrying about his family. And maybe I should have told him. But I'm his big brother and it's my job to protect him. I didn't do it on the ice that day, but I've damn well done whatever it takes to make up for it ever since. And that's my call. Not yours."

She was trembling now, and he hardened himself against her imploring eyes. "I'm sorry, Luke. I can see I made a mistake. I just wanted to bring my concerns to you. To be honest with you. And I realize this is hard to hear, but every prediction on the list I found has come true save one, and that is not coincidence. If it's not you, it's somebody else on the team."

His protectiveness roared up with a vengeance. "Leave my guys out of this!"

"I won't!" She came to her feet then, too, and the change in her, from meek acceptance of his lecture to formidable warrior ready for battle, was startling. "I sat here and I listened to your side. Just because you have an explanation for my evidence does not mean it was ridiculous, so don't you dare stand there and demean it. I'm an excellent reporter, Luke.

"I do my homework and I test my hypotheses. Just because my conclusion about you was proven false, doesn't let your team off the hook. This list still belongs to somebody who used the Storm bathroom that day." She held it up, and it trembled because her hand was also trembling.

"It's not mine, obviously," she said, "so by process of elimination, thanks to your ridiculous game-day superstitions, that means it's one of your teammates.

"And you want more honesty? You want to be able to trust me? You know that fair and honest article on the

Sports Nation blog? The one about how you're hurting your team? I wrote that."

Blood roared in his ears as he processed that betrayal.

"I wrote it before I ever met you and when I found out they were going to publish it against my objections, I asked them to take my name off it. Because not hurting your feelings and continuing to work for the Storm meant more to me than the byline that would have helped me reach my dream job in sports reporting.

"You think I'm out to hurt you and the team? Then why have I kept this illegal activity under the radar instead of selling the story to any number of media outlets who would pay me large sums of money and give me my pick of jobs? Your heart is not the only one that got bruised here. And while I've always admired your loyalty to your teammates, if you do not figure out who is poisoning your team right now, then you're all going to end up infected."

Luke crossed his arms, kept his voice level. "I think you've said everything there is to say. You should go."

"I agree." The tears she'd so valiantly held back spilled down her cheeks, but he refused to be moved. Holly's words were impassioned, but they didn't change anything.

All this time he'd been giving her his heart, and he meant nothing to her. Just as he'd accused her of from the start, all she'd wanted from him was a career-making story. She'd written the *Sports Nation* article. She'd been investigating them the whole time. And he'd taken her to his home. He felt sick to his stomach, like he'd just put the puck in his own net.

He'd let his heart overrule his head. Ignored the

clues—he'd caught her in her lies about not knowing hockey, listened raptly to her stories about her mother and her childhood dreams of becoming a reporter. She'd been rubbing it in his face for their entire relationship, and he was too stupid to have even noticed.

She might have kept this story secret for a couple days, but she wouldn't sit on it for long.

He should have trusted his instincts and fought harder to get her fired from the get-go. He'd had his own suspicions about the list but he'd let her distract him. And now his reputation, the reputation of his entire team, was going to be dragged through the mud in the court of public opinion. All because he couldn't keep his dick in his pants.

He was the worst kind of fool—a willing participant in his own downfall. That ended now.

"Fired?"

The word felt like ash on her tongue, chalky and bitter. The taste of lost dreams.

"I'm sorry, Ms. Evans, but it was stated very clearly in your contract that you were not to interact with players outside of your professional capacity."

"But who—?"

"I'm sorry, but we can't release that information. Suffice it to say, a reputable source came forward and we have no choice but to enforce the terms that you yourself agreed to."

Said contract sat on Hastings's formidable oak desk, mocking her. Holly raised her eyes from the blinding whiteness of the paper with binding black type marching in perfect lines that reminded her the striped prison garb in old-timey movies. She raised her eyes to the man who sat across from her.

"I don't even get to defend myself?"

"I'm afraid the informant is a rather…important member of the Storm's organization."

Hastings was one hell of a finesser, she'd give him that.

"As such, we will be terminating your contract immediately and your services will no longer be required. In return for this short notice, you will receive your full compensation, as outlined in your notice of hire. Do you agree to these terms?"

"Do I have a choice?"

"I will take that as a yes." Hastings slid another piece of paper toward her. "We do require you to sign this nondisclosure agreement, which states that you will not discuss the details of this parting of ways, or anything leading up to it, upon threat of legal action."

She grabbed the pen and with numb fingers, scrawled her signature on the designated line.

Luke had sold her out. She'd gotten too close to hurting the team and he'd turned her in.

Betrayal burned white-hot in her chest, and she had to gulp to get enough air in her lungs. The fact that he hadn't even given her a heads-up… She understood that he was angry at her, but at least *she'd* had the courtesy to bring her concerns to him first, even though it had been the last thing she'd wanted to do. She'd been honest with him. To his face. Because she loved him.

She hated herself for it, but she did. Even when she'd believed he might have been involved in illegal activity, some part of her still believed that what they'd shared was real. And now, when he'd sold her out, she was still conflicted about breaking the story.

Luke had seemed genuinely hurt by her accusation, even as he'd confirmed all the reasons that some extra money could have gone a long way. She thought of Luke's parents, of Ethan, of everything the Maguires had been through. Luke loved his family enough to do anything for them, but she hadn't considered what a betting scandal would do to them if he'd been exposed. He would never have taken that risk.

She'd interpreted the evidence, but she'd boiled it all down to numbers, to probabilities and stats. She'd been so focused on doing what it took to get the job of her dreams that she'd failed to take the man himself into account. And now she'd lost everything. Her story. Her job. And the man she loved. Unsure what to do with herself, she gathered her things and headed for her father's house. He looked up with surprise as she entered the door.

"What are you doing here in the middle of the day?" he asked.

"I got fired, Pop."

"Oh."

"Oh? That's all you have to say about this?"

All her frustration, all her anger, everything she'd kept bottled up since the night she found out her mother was never coming home again roiled up from the depths and she was powerless to hold it in.

"Everything I've ever done is to make you proud, and you just look right past me!"

"That's not true."

"It is true! I've been sitting on this couch beside you for years trying to get your attention, and all you've ever done is ignore me and watch sports! So I watched sports, too. And I learned everything there was to learn about them. Players, rules, stats, just so we could have a conversation sometime. But you wouldn't even give me that! You just act like I'm not even here!"

"Holly—"

"Don't 'Holly' me! You talked sports with Neil! Why not me? Why not me, Pop?" She was too angry to cry, too exhausted to shout anymore. She was just empty. Holly sat on the couch in her usual spot and stared at the basketball game on the television.

"When I lost Mom, I didn't think anything could ever hurt as badly as that again. But I was wrong, because Mom didn't leave me on purpose. Not like you did."

Her dad got out of his chair and joined her on the couch. In her entire life, her father had never sat on the couch. She almost jumped when he put his hand on her knee.

"You remind me of her. Especially when you're on camera. That's always been hard for me."

Holly looked at her dad, felt like she was seeing him for the first time. "What?"

"You're smart and beautiful and you're so good at everything you do. Of course I'm proud of my girl. But sometimes it hurts to look at you because I miss her so much. I didn't realize how unfair I've been to you all these years. I never meant…I never meant to push you away. I love you, Holly. I do."

The words brought tears to her eyes. She couldn't remember the last time her father had said something nice about her, or told her he loved her. Throughout the years, his sporadic comments were always externally focused: "work harder, know more, do better." And she had. She'd lived her whole life striving to be good enough for him. To actually hear that he was proud of her made her heart swell.

"They were stupid to let you go. You're an expert at that game. If they can't see that, then they don't deserve you. And you'll show them. Because when you put your mind to something, there's nothing that can stand in your way. Now don't go and cry on me. I've never been good with that."

"Well, tough beans," Holly said with a watery laugh, and she hugged him. He stiffened in her grasp, but then his arms came around her and she felt his weathered hand pat her shoulder. It was like she was six years old again. Like she had her dad back. "I miss her, too," she confessed.

"She would've been proud of you. And she would have told you to fight for what you deserve. When life knocks you down, you get up and punch it in the gut."

His arms tightened around her, and she heard an unmistakable sniff.

"You okay?"

He cleared his throat and pulled away. "S'nothin'. Just got some dirt in my eye is all. Now you gonna stop yammerin' so we can watch the game, or what?"

Holly smiled as he got up and brushed his knuckles under his eyes. "Yeah. I'll stop yammering. How about I make us some popcorn to go with that game?"

He nodded gruffly as he dropped into his beat-up old recliner. "I could go for some popcorn."

15

"PAIGE! OPEN UP! I need to talk to you."

Holly banged on the door again, this time with more force. Paige's phone had gone straight to voice mail—a regular occurrence, as her friend was notorious for forgetting to charge her phone. But Holly was desperate for counsel and she wasn't going to let a dead phone stand in her way.

"C'mon, Paige! I know you're in there. Your car's in the driveway. I really need your advice."

Finally, after what felt like a lifetime, Holly heard the snick of the lock give way. Paige's face appeared in the six-inch crack of the open door. "Holly, what are you doing here? Is everything okay?"

Holly shoved the door open all the way and barged past her friend. "*News Now* just called. They just gave me Corey Baniuk's old job. I'm the new roving sports reporter for the six and eleven o'clock news."

"Wow, Hols. That's fantastic! That's your dream job, right? Interviewing athletes on TV. That's everything you've been working toward."

Holly nodded, dropping onto Paige's couch—a sleek,

robin's-egg-blue torture device that was built for style, not comfort. "I know!" She glanced over her shoulder at her friend. "So why am I not happier about it?"

"Aw, sweetie." Paige rushed over, wrapping the lilac sheet tighter around her before she joined Holly on the couch. "What's going on?"

"I have no idea. This is everything I wanted! And since the Storm fired me, I should be doubly glad because it means I'm not unemployed, trying to scrape by on ghostwriting sports articles.

"I went for the interview this morning, and they offered me the position on the spot. But even as I was shaking hands and signing contracts, something felt... off, you know?"

Paige nodded reassuringly, readjusting her toga. All of a sudden, her new job wasn't the only thing that seemed off to Holly. "Wait a minute. Why are you wrapped in a sheet?" Holly stood. "And why did it take you so long to answer the door? Is someone here? Did I just catch you *in flagrante*?"

She walked back toward the door, cocking an eyebrow as Paige rushed after her, blocking Holly's path to the bedroom.

"Do you have a sex crush of your own? And is he, or is he not in this house right now? Do not lie to me, Paige Marie Hallett."

"What?" Paige's blush made her whole face blotchy, like she was allergic to the lie she was trying so desperately to formulate. "No, I was just... I mean I, I just..." Her eyes focused briefly on something to Holly's left before they darted back to the floor.

Holly glanced behind her. A familiar pair of worn Vans sat in the entranceway. "Those are Jay's shoes."

She whipped around to face her friend. "You're sleeping with Jay? You hate Jay! Since when are you sleeping with Jay?"

There was a long moment of silence, before a deep voice sounded from behind the door at the end of the hall. "Since she already knows, can I come out now?"

Paige sighed. "Yes. Come out."

The door to her friend's bedroom swung open, and Holly could barely process the sight of her barefooted cameraman wearing jeans and pulling his vintage Ghostbusters T-shirt over his head. His grin was sheepish as he ran a hand through his unruly brown hair. "Hey, Holly. Congrats on the new job."

The entire world had gone mad. Her dream job was making her miserable. Jay was sleeping with Paige. She was going to have to keep an eye on the sky when she left, because the odds of seeing pigs soaring over the clouds seemed pretty high right now.

"I need some water."

Holly headed into Paige's kitchen and grabbed a bottle of Evian from the fridge. She took a long swig of the cool liquid and followed it with a couple of deep breaths. "Okay, so you guys are sleeping together. I can deal with that. I'm an adult. Angry sex is a thing."

"Actually…" Jay slung an arm over Paige's shoulders. "We're kind of past the angry sex stage and on to the dating exclusively stage."

Holly knew he was telling the truth because Paige didn't slug him. Instead, her friend's bright green eyes turned imploring. "I'm sorry we kept it a secret, Hols, but we were trying to get a handle on it ourselves. I'm glad it's not a secret anymore, though, because you deserve to know. This never would have happened if not for you and the Women's Hockey Network."

"Say what now?"

Paige smiled at her. "You think the Women's Hockey Network was a joke, but the truth is you did great research and presented facts in a way that resonated with me. And with a bunch of people who aren't usually interested in sports. You gave us a foothold in a world we didn't understand. And not because we were incapable of understanding. You're not dumbing anything down. You're just coming at it from a different angle. Hockey got a whole lot more exciting for me when you snuck in a little medicine to the spoonful of sugar that is Luke Maguire's abs."

"Seriously, Paige? I'm right here," Jay lamented.

"Understanding the game made it more interesting to watch. Because of you, I suddenly understood offside, or why the whistle blew even though no one had touched the puck and why the face-off was happening somewhere other than at center ice. And that made me care more about the game."

Holly tried not to be touched, but to hear her sports-allergic best friend talking about offsides was kind of a big deal in her world. Damned if it didn't make her a bit misty-eyed.

"Basically, you made me realize what else I was missing out on. I mean, if hockey wasn't as bad as I thought, what else might be better than I gave it credit for?" Paige slipped an arm around Jay's waist. "Sometimes what you want doesn't look at all like what you thought you wanted. Nothing about Jay and I makes sense, but we just fit. And I owe it all to you because I might not have figured that out on my own."

"You think that dumb fluff is me at my most insightful? My mom is probably rolling over in her grave."

"I think she'd respect you for it as much as I do, Hols."

If she was being honest, at some point during this whole farce, the Women's Hockey Network *had* started to really matter to her. In her heart, Holly knew it was more than fluff, had known it for a long time.

It was just hard to reimagine her future, to reevaluate her priorities. She'd spent so long convinced that *real* sports reporting was her destiny. The only route to make her dad proud. The best way to honor her mother's legacy. But Paige was right, the only person who wasn't proud of her was herself.

"The thing that makes you great is that you care so much," Paige continued. "You're not supposed to be on *News Now* reading a teleprompter, you're supposed to be making real connections and improving people's lives." She remembered the little girl she'd met at the bakery. Paige was right. She *was* making a difference. Sometimes miniscule, like making people laugh, and sometimes major, like helping two people feel closer to one another. But either way, it was rewarding. It was still sports, still her passion, but it was so much more than that, too.

So she let go. All her expectations, all her goals, all her former dreams. Her chest felt light, as if her lungs were full of helium. Or freedom.

For the first time, Holly wasn't in someone else's shadow, or seeking someone else's approval. She knew exactly where her future lay and she had a phone call to make.

16

Waiting was a special kind of hell.

Every morning, Luke expected to wake up to an angry phone call from his agent and an even angrier headline in the paper. And every morning, there was nothing.

It was driving him crazy. He'd been sure it would have come by now. He'd worried about it through both of the Storm's out-of-town games, constantly monitoring the internet for any sign that Holly had broken her story. But she hadn't. Yet. The prospect loomed over his head like a guillotine.

And now they were back in Portland after two tough losses in Wyoming. They were hoping to even things out tonight with the home crowd behind them.

The tension in the dressing room was almost unbearable. His teammates were unusually quiet as they fidgeted in full equipment and waited for Coach Taggert to start his pregame speech. Instead, Taggert walked over to Luke, touched his shoulder pad. "Someone's here to see you."

Holly.

Her name popped unbidden into his heart. Was she here to apologize? Or to tell him she was going live with the story tonight? And why did the prospect of seeing her make his heart race with anticipation? He was mad at her. Furious, really.

"Now's not really the time, is it, Coach?"

The gruff, burly man motioned toward the door with a shake of his head. "You wanna stay a part of this team, you do what I say and trust me when I tell you, you wanna take this meeting."

Luke obeyed. But when he stepped out of the dressing room, it took a long moment before his brain could fully register the sight before him. "You came."

"Yeah, well. There's only so many places you can wear one of these jerseys, so..." Ethan shrugged.

Luke hadn't even noticed the damn jersey. The *C* on the front. The number twenty-eight visible on the sleeve. "Holly," he breathed.

His little brother nodded. "Yeah, it showed up in the mail the other day. Complete with a scathing letter that threatened me with bodily harm if I didn't get my ass out to one of your games. She's pretty incredible. Too good for you, really."

Luke couldn't even process the joke. "I'm glad you're here."

Ethan stared down at the ground. "I should have come before. It's been a really tough couple of years, Luke. Without hockey, I've got nothing. I've put everything into getting back on that ice, and every day it became clearer that wasn't going to happen, and I couldn't deal with that. But Holly helped me see that there are still opportunities to be part of hockey. Maybe not on the ice, but on the bench. Or in a studio. I can still talk about it, dissect it, coach it and watch my brother play it the way it's meant to be played." He looked up at that.

"You've always been in it for the love of the game. That's what makes you great, big brother. You do it for the right reasons. Not the fame or the fortune or the ladies. Because you genuinely love playing. You've got to stop giving a shit about my feelings, or what's going on with your teammates and just get out there and do what you do. And know that it's good enough, no matter what happens."

Growing up, he and Ethan had always been close, but the heartfelt words made Luke realize how much distance had crept between them since the accident. He'd been so busy trying to take care of things, he hadn't realized how much he'd missed his brother.

"Also, this is for you."

Ethan handed him a beat-up paper bag. Luke opened it and couldn't help but laugh. "No way!"

Ethan blushed as Luke held up a knitted replica of the Storm Jersey he wore, complete with "Maguire" and a big twenty-eight on the back and the coveted *C* on the front.

"You made this?"

"Yeah, well, I've had a lot of time to think lately. Had to break through some of that mental chatter. Figured if I was knitting, it might as well *be* something…not like your stupid thirty-foot lengths of nothing."

Luke shook his head. "You always gotta show me up, don't you, you prick?"

"It's not my fault I'm so much better than you at everything. Now got out there and win this game."

Ethan's words were still ringing in his ears as he stepped onto the ice. The game was going to be a battle. Down 2–0 in a series was not a great place to be, but for the first time since the play-offs began, Luke was in his element. He belonged there. Tonight, he was going to make sure everybody knew it.

A minute and twenty-seven seconds into the first period, Luke snapped his scoring drought with a beautiful wrist shot to the top-left corner.

IT WAS A hard-fought, physical game. Players from both teams spent their fair share of time in the penalty box, and despite the Storm's commanding first period, the Wyoming Stallions had battled back to a 3–3 draw with seven minutes left in the game.

Luke had thought they were destined for overtime, but with forty-six seconds left on the clock, the rookie redirected one of Kowalchuk's big booming slap shots, and the Storm had gone on to win it 4–3 in regular time. There was a tangible relief in the air as his weary teammates filed into the dressing room after the game. They'd held on, brought the series back to within one. Their dreams of the championship were still viable.

It took him a moment to notice that his goaltender was walking in front of him hunched over with the air of a man who'd just lost it all.

Luke grabbed his jersey, stopping him before he stepped into the dressing room with the rest of the team. "Hey man, you okay?"

J.C. barely looked at him as he shrugged. "Huh? Yeah, no. I'm fine. Good goal. You relaxed and played the game. Just like I told you to."

Luke frowned. "For a man who was just part of an epic, kick-ass win, you seem pretty down."

He shook his head. "It's nothing. Just tired. Play-offs are pretty grueling."

"Yeah, okay." Luke meant to drop it then, to give his goaltender—his friend—some space, but there was a niggling thought in his mind. A piece that wouldn't quite fit. J.C. wasn't acting like himself tonight. Hadn't been since... "You went down."

"What?"

"Third period. We were up 3–2. Johnson was coming in on his backhand and you went down. He scored top shelf. You never go down when Keith Johnson is on his backhand. You've been playing against him since we were fourteen."

"What are you talking about?"

"It's you." The realization vibrated in every cell in Luke's body. He stood facing his friend in the middle of the hallway, betrayal burning like lava in his veins. "Holly was right. You let that goal in on purpose. What the hell are you wrapped up in?"

For the first time, J.C. looked something other than listless. In fact, he looked downright panicked. He glanced around the hallway. "Would you keep your voice down?"

"What the fuck is going on?"

"Calm down. It's nothing." He put a comforting hand on Luke's shoulder.

Luke shook it off. "Are you betting on hockey? Are you betting on us?"

J.C. went from soothing to defensive in a split second. "What the hell's your problem, Mags? It's no big deal. It's over-under stuff. We've got a real chance this year. All I have to do is keep the score a little closer than it should be in a few games."

Luke's stomach churned with disgust. "I can't believe you! You could go to jail for this! You're about to get married. You've got a *baby* on the way."

J.C.'s face twisted with ire. "Why does everyone keep saying that like it's a good thing? Tania and I have been together for four years, and she wanted a ring or else. I didn't propose, I followed orders. And when the doubts took over, I was all set to tell her I wanted the damn ring back. But then she dropped the bombshell that I was going to be a dad."

J.C. ran a hand over his play-off beard and his voice turned beseeching. "A dad, Mags. Me. I'm too young to be a dad. I wanted to leave her, and now we're bonded together for the rest of time. And there's not a goddamn thing I can do about it. So I went to the track. A few times. Just to blow off some steam. And I got in a little over my head. But they offered me a way out—a way to clear up my debt. And we still win. Everybody wins. C'mon, man. We're the only ones left who know about this."

"What do you mean, the *only ones left*?" Realization dawned as soon as the words were out of Luke's mouth. "*You* got Holly fired? You son of a bitch! You used what I told you on the plane and you sold her out, you sold *me* out. I trusted you. I'm in love with this girl."

"She's a reporter, Mags."

"You're the one who insisted I was overreacting. That she was harmless."

"That was before I knew she was only pretending to be stupid! She heard Tania yelling about me getting rid of the Porsche. It was only a matter of time until she put it together. No one can find out about this. It wasn't personal, man. I was just covering my bases."

"J.C., what you're doing is illegal. You've put this whole team at risk. Jesus." Luke ran a hand through his hair. "What were you thinking?"

"I was thinking you had my back. Isn't that what you always say? Put the team first?"

Luke shook his head. He'd been so wrapped up in his guilt, so blinded by his insistence on protecting the team that he'd lost sight of what was important. "You think this is putting the team first? You crossed the line, man. You *deserted* your team, and as the captain, I can't let that stand."

"What, you're going to tell on me? Is that it, Luke? After all we've been through together, you're going to end our friendship and torpedo my career over a few goals that, in the grand scheme of things, don't even matter?"

Luke looked at his teammate, his friend, and saw a stranger staring back at him. "You're goddamn right I am."

17

"GOOD EVENING AND welcome to the eleven o'clock sports wrap-up. I'm Corey Baniuk and I'd like to introduce you to the newest addition to our team, Holly Evans. Usually, she'll be on the scene, covering games as they happen," he said. "But tonight we're happy to have her joining us in studio so that you, our viewers, can meet her properly. Holly, good to have you here."

"Thanks, Corey. And congratulations on your promotion." Holly smiled big and turned to the camera. "Hi, everyone. Let's start with hockey, where earlier tonight the captain of the Portland Storm, Luke Maguire, finally broke a nineteen-game scoreless streak with this beauty less than two minutes into their game against the Wyoming Stallions…"

Holly did the entire segment and it was incredible. She nailed the scores, the camera changes, every word that came out of her mouth was crisp and precise. It was a triumphant moment, but not quite as triumphant as the moment that followed it.

"Thank you, Holly. And now—"

"Actually, Corey, I'm not quite finished."

She'd never seen the golden voice of sports at a loss for words. Apparently it wasn't good for business, because the camera operators bobbled for a quick moment before every single one of them turned to focus on her.

"When I made the Women's Hockey Network video, I was being a smart-ass. I was frustrated that people would discount opinions on sports just because they came from a woman. So I created a satirical look at how women in the sports world are perceived.

"Except when my video hit YouTube, it went viral. The Portland Storm hired me for their play-off run, and everything changed. The Women's Hockey Network grew into something unstoppable, and I was just along for the ride. For a while, I thought I was making mockery of everything I loved. Then I heard from you, the people watching, and I realized that together, we had something special.

"I want to thank everyone at this station and you, the viewers, for welcoming me with open arms. This job was a childhood dream come true and I will remember this night for the rest of my life. But my priorities have changed, which is why tonight will be my only show with *News Now*. Effective immediately, I'm tendering my resignation.

"But if you liked the Women's Hockey Network, then I invite you to join me on XT Satellite Radio, where I will be hosting *The Women's Sport Network* every weekday from one to three on Sports Talk Radio. It's going to be a show where women can congregate and talk about sports. Where we can teach what we know, or learn what we need to know."

Holly could feel her smile warming as she spoke. "It's going to be real women asking real questions. If you don't understand the rules of the game, ask me. If you don't understand why the GM of your home team isn't moving on signing that free agent who lit up the field last year, we'll discuss it. And if you want to hear what cologne your favorite player wears, I'll find out for you.

"Because there are no stupid questions. I want to help every woman, every person, find the part of the game that appeals to him or her, because when it comes right down to it, sports are about having a good time. I lost sight of that for a while, but I finally found it again. And now I want to share it with you." Holly tucked her hair behind her right ear. "I'm Holly Evans, for *Portland News Now*. Thank you and good night."

Holly strode out of the studio without a single doubt that she'd made her mother proud. It was a great feeling, one she reveled in all the way to the lobby, until she glanced over at the security station and noticed a certain hockey highlight. She beelined toward the desk.

"Can you rewind that?" she asked.

The security guard grabbed a remote off the desk and turned to the monitor.

"Thanks, just run it back to the last goal that Wisconsin scored on the Storm. Yes. There."

Her skin prickled as she watched Keith Johnson walk in and score a top-shelf backhand on J.C. LaCroix, who was sprawled across the crease.

"Son of a—"

It all made sense now. The awful goal, the lackluster baby announcement, the vehicle downgrade and the purse-wielding psycho fiancée.

It had been J.C. she'd heard in the bathroom that day. He was the mole. She had to tell Luke! And if he wouldn't listen, well, she'd make him listen.

She'd just pulled out of the parking lot, formulating a plan to get Luke to let her explain herself when the radio announcer's voice penetrated her single focus.

"And we take you now live to a surprise press conference involving key members of the Portland Storm. We've confirmed that Captain Luke Maguire, Coach Randy Taggert and GM Ron Lougheed are all present, as is League Commissioner Grant McDavid. McDavid was seen during tonight's game sitting with former Blades centerman and national hero Ethan Maguire. Needless to say, the sports community is buzzing with speculation over what the big announcement is. We now go live to the Portland Dome."

Ethan had shown up?

Her grip tightened on the steering wheel, and she changed her course from Luke's apartment to the arena. But what could they possibly be talking about at a press conference? The post-game interviews had ended hours ago.

Holly shook her head. The biggest damn story of the day was unfolding while she'd been looking pretty on TV. And instead of sending her or Corey Baniuk, *Portland News Now* had probably sent some intern to cover it. Thank the hockey gods she'd quit.

"Thank you, everyone, for coming tonight. I'm afraid we're here with bad news."

Her stomach flipped at the sound of Luke's deep voice filling the airwaves.

"As the captain of this team, I would like to begin by saying the Storm organization has always prided itself on stressing the importance of sportsmanship and integrity. However, thanks to some incredible undercover work by sports reporter Holly Evans, it has recently come to my attention that there is an individual on this team who has not been living up to the code that we, the Portland Storm, have sought to play by.

"This individual has been involved in betting, and when his debt got too big, he agreed to manipulate game results during our play-off run. As the captain of a phenomenal team, I have spoken with my teammates and we have decided, after consulting with the league, to withdraw from this year's play-off run and wish the Wyoming Stallions the best of luck as they take on the winner of the Eastern Conference."

The gasps in the auditorium were audible even through the radio, and Holly sped up as she approached the turn-off that would get her closer to the Portland Dome.

"We, as a team, in conjunction with our coach and management, feel this is the best way to keep one person's actions from tainting the entire team."

He knows. Oh God. She wondered how Luke was taking the devastating betrayal of his best friend's actions. His voice sounded even, if a little somber, but she'd need to look into his eyes to be sure.

"And with the league's support, we hope to earn our way back to next year's play-offs and claim our chance to win the championship.

"I personally would like to apologize to Holly Evans and thank her for her diligent work."

The car swerved a bit at that, as Holly tried to process the shock of Luke's very public words of praise.

"I love this game with all my heart and I could not have lived with myself if I had been part of sullying its good reputation, however unwittingly. The truth has come to light, and that's exactly how it should be. And for that reason, effective immediately, Jean-Claude LaCroix is no longer a member of the Portland Storm. Thank you. Coach Taggert will now say a few words."

Questions exploded throughout the press room, and Holly could hardly breathe as she pulled into the parking lot. She was relieved the attendant at the gate recognized her and let her through without a hassle, because she was having a hard time forming words.

Luke had done the right thing even though it had cost him his dream, and she wanted to throw up for doubting his integrity for even a split second. He'd not only taken the high road and given her credit for breaking the story, he'd even thanked her publicly. And for what? For jumping to conclusions about him? She had to get in there right away.

Holly screeched to a halt and parked in an illegal zone as close to the door as she could. She turned off the car, silencing Coach Taggert's "weathering this adversity will only make us a stronger hockey club" speech.

Then she ran—in heels—for the press room. By the time she got there, the league commissioner was handing down his ruling.

A security person stopped her. "Ma'am? I'm sorry, you can't go in there. Press only."

"I am press!"

"I'll need to see some identification."

Holly dug frantically through her purse until she came upon the lanyard she'd failed to return: her Women's Hockey Network press pass. And for the first time, her wide-eyed, helmet-haired photo wasn't an embarrassment, but a badge of honor.

The security guard let her through.

"Although there will be a further investigation by the league, the fact that the Portland Storm brought this breach of ethics to our attention immediately upon learning of it will go a long way in expediting the process. Mr. LaCroix has admitted to being the sole perpetrator and has been banned from the league indefinitely. At this time, we will be taking questions."

The room was a roar of sound as the scrum exploded with queries.

"One at a time, and please use the microphone."

As she approached the front of the room, the interrogation quieted, replaced with whispers as the gathered reporters began to recognize her.

She stopped in front of the microphone and Taggert nodded at her to proceed. "Holly Evans, from the Women's Sports Network. My question is for Luke Maguire."

The way he was looking at her broke her heart, part hopeful, part wary. It took everything she had to keep herself from running up on that stage and pulling him into her arms so she could apologize.

"Luke, I was just wondering, do you think there's any chance that you can forgive me? Because if you love me even half as much as I love you, then I think we could be a great team."

There was a long, silent moment where the world went still. Seconds ticked by to the beat of the pulse echoing in her ears.

A murmur spread through the crowd.

"Teammates, huh?" he said.

She nodded.

He leaned forward to speak into his mic. "I don't know."

Dread wound its way through her stomach and into her chest, squeezing her heart like a vise. She deserved this, she reminded herself. She'd known this was a possibility.

"You think you can handle that, Evans? Because if we do this again, I'm going to need you in it for the long haul, a hundred percent commitment. Eye on the prize."

Holly bit her lip as Luke got up from the table and pushed his way past the rest of the panel members. With every step that brought him closer, hope bubbled in her chest like a lava lamp. She was nodding before he even reached her. "I believe I can manage that, yes."

"I hope so, because I love you, too." When he pulled her into his arms, his kiss was everything—an apology, a declaration, a promise. Holly wound her arms around his neck, relief and love pounding through her veins in equal measure.

The room erupted in applause and camera flashes. But all that mattered to her was the man who held her in his arms. She was never going to let him go again.

"I thought I'd lost you," she whispered.

Luke smiled and it made her heart flutter. "Not possible."

"How do you figure?" she asked.

"You ever heard people say that love is a game?"

She nodded.

"When I play, I play to win. And just for the record, I expect my teammate to do the same."

Holly grinned and grabbed him by the tie. "Aye aye, captain," she said and sealed her promise with a kiss.

* * * * *

Keep reading for an excerpt of a new title
from the Desire series,
JUST A LITTLE MARRIED by Reese Ryan

CHAPTER ONE

"Good to see you again, Chef Travis." The valet greeted Travis Holloway with a wide grin and held up a copy of Travis's latest cookbook. "Would you mind signing this for my girlfriend? She *loves* your competitive cooking show."

Travis was tired and groggy after a long night at his restaurant in Atlanta and a nearly four-hour drive to Asheville that morning. But he would always be gracious. He greeted the younger man warmly, signed the cookbook and suggested they take a selfie that would impress the man's girlfriend. Then he handed off the keys to his black Dodge Charger SRT Hellcat Widebody.

Once the valet drove away, Travis turned toward the building in front of him.

Moonlight Ridge.

Whenever he returned to the luxury resort, nestled in the Blue Ridge Mountains, he couldn't help thinking of when he'd first seen it. He was seven. A social worker escorted him here, telling him how lucky he was that this estate would be his new home. And that his new "father" and "brothers" eagerly awaited his arrival.

His stomach tightened in a knot at seeing his brothers again now, just as it had that day twenty-six years ago.

After a long absence, Travis had first returned to Moonlight Ridge a few months earlier, because his adoptive father, Jameson Holloway, the owner of Moonlight Ridge, had suffered a brain episode. He and his adoptive brothers had been forced to come together, despite years of estrangement following a car accident that had changed all of their lives—his especially.

They'd committed to working together to oversee their father's at-home care and to help restore Moonlight Ridge, which had fallen into disrepair over the past decade. Over the past few months, his brothers, Mack and Grey, had taken the lead on overseeing the updates to the resort. They'd made vast improvements, but a lot still needed to be done.

The resort's food services needed an overhaul, and that was his area of expertise.

Travis climbed the stairs and entered the rotunda. Then he made his way up the grand staircase in the lobby. The elegant space still had many of its original architectural features and decor from when it was built in the 1930s. Travis glided his hand along the banister he and his brothers slid down as boys. He grinned, recalling that winter Mack had gotten the bright idea to sled down the stairwell.

It hadn't ended well.

Travis continued to the third floor, where the offices were located. He stood in front of his father's office, the door partially ajar, and sighed.

Travis, Mack and Grey, all former foster kids, had all been a handful. Each of them was dealing with their own brand of family-induced trauma. It'd taken time, but the three of them had become brothers in every sense of the word. It was the Holloway brothers against the world.

Until it wasn't.

The night of the car accident that had changed everything would forever be burned into Travis's brain. It was the night his entire life went to shit. The night he'd lost his family and, for a time, the use of his legs. It was the night he'd lost his football scholarship, his dreams of playing in the NFL and the girl he'd believed he'd loved more than anything in the world.

It was the night he'd been reminded that there were few people he could trust implicitly. But his adoptive father, Jameson Holloway, sat atop that short list. He'd nursed him back to health, never allowing him to give up or feel sorry for himself. Always believing he would walk again, regardless of the grim initial diagnosis.

Like always, the old man was right. But it had taken him two grueling years to get there.

And though his body was whole again, he'd emerged from the entire ordeal irrevocably broken. He'd pushed his brothers away. Bitter over the loss of his dreams. Resentful that they'd come out of the accident unscathed, moving on with the lives they'd planned for themselves. Devastated over the girl whose betrayal had triggered everything that happened that horrible night. Angry with the world in general.

Through therapy, he'd worked out a lot of that anger. Since their father's illness, Travis had been forced to spend time with Mack and Grey in person and via phone and videoconferences. He'd been reestablishing a tentative relationship with his brothers. Partly out of a sense of obligation to their father. Partly out of his own guilt over how he'd handled the fallout from the accident.

He'd been wrong to blame his brothers, but he couldn't turn back time. Things would never be the same between them, so spending time with Mack and Grey in person still caused a knot in his gut. It was why he'd bailed immediately after Mack's wedding.

An emergency with the show had arisen, and Travis had taken the opportunity to delay his return. But now he was ready to get started. The sooner they got Moonlight Ridge running smoothly again, the sooner he could return to his life.

Travis entered the room and slipped into the seat beside Grey. "Sorry I'm late."

"Thought you'd changed your mind." Mack, who sat behind the desk, raised a brow. "I called. You didn't answer."

"I was on a call with a potential investor for the proposed New York restaurant." Travis imitated Mack's stern tone and cadence, causing Grey to chuckle. "But I'm here now."

Mack didn't find Travis's spot-on imitation amusing. His frown deepened. "Then let's get started. My *wife* is waiting."

"How is Molly?" Travis nodded toward the door between this adjoining office and hers.

He'd always liked Molly Haskell. Her father

had worked at the resort, and Molly and Mack had been an item as teenagers. The relationship ended when Mack left, not long after the accident.

Travis was glad his brother and Molly had found their way back to each other. They belonged together. Not that he believed in soul mates or the sunshine-and-rainbows bullshit about love. Personal experience had taught him better than to believe that.

What he did believe in was mutually beneficial alliances. That was the best anyone could hope for in a relationship. And the relationship between Mack and Molly was equally beneficial. Or maybe sixty/forty was more accurate. After all, Mack "Know It All" Holloway could be a lot for anyone to deal with.

"She's doing well." A soft grin curved Mack's mouth.

For all of his alpha male posturing, Mack was a soft, gooey-in-the-center romantic. His brother had fallen in deep. If he didn't look so damn giddy—by Mack Holloway standards—Travis would feel sorry for him.

"She's meeting with our department heads. She'll stop by and give us an update, *if* we're ever done here," Mack groused. "I know you're living the bachelor life and you've got nothing but time, but our significant others have planned a double date for us, so…"

Travis felt a twinge of envy. Mack was newly married. Grey was deeply involved with Moonlight Ridge's wedding coordinator, Autumn Kincaid. When he'd seen his brothers at Mack and Molly's wedding two weeks earlier, both men seemed settled and happy.

But before the uneasy feeling could take hold, he reminded himself *the bachelor life* he was living was a pretty damn good one. One most men would be envious of.

He enjoyed glamorous events, luxury accommodations, extravagant vacations and designer gear—most of it on someone else's dime. And there was no shortage of beautiful women clamoring to be on his arm when he walked the red carpet at the opening of one of his restaurants or some social event. He had no reason to be envious of Mack or Grey.

His life was just fine the way it was.

"Then let's get down to business." Travis opened the document Mack had handed him and scanned the index page. Then he tossed it onto the desk. "I'll read that later while you two are…more pleasantly occupied." Travis smirked.

"Let's just hit the highlights and lowlights. Have you discovered who our embezzler is?"

Since their father's illness, they'd discovered that someone on the staff had been stealing from the resort for several years. Uncovering the thief's identity was their top priority.

Mack frowned and folded his hands on the desk. "We're still working on that."

"But our forensic accountant discovered that most of the irregularities can be traced to food and beverage—the area where we need your help most," Grey added.

"So you expect me to revive the menu while working with a subpar chef who might also be the elusive embezzler neither of you nor your expensive forensic accountant could nail down? Well, that's just fucking great."

Travis walked over to the windows behind Mack that overlooked the property and provided a stunning view of the lake. He shoved his hands in his pockets.

Maybe if his brothers hadn't spent all their time pursuing romantic relationships, they would've found the thief by now.

"Let's begin with the obvious. We'll get rid of the mediocre chef and bring on someone with some real talent. Then if the current chef is the thief, we've solved both issues—the fast-food-grade menu and the embezzlement."

"We considered it," Grey acknowledged. "But Dad won't hear of it. You know how loyal he is. Hallie Gregson was Chef Fern's sous chef for years. When Fern up and left, Pops insisted on giving Hallie a shot as the executive chef. He believes she can become a world-class cook. Says she just needs a bit of—"

"Tutoring," Mack offered. "Which is what you do on those cooking shows, right?"

Mack had obviously *never* watched one of his shows.

"No, it isn't," Travis said impatiently. "I'm not a fairy godmother, Mack. I can't sprinkle pixie dust on this woman and make her a real chef. What I do is give self-taught chefs with *actual* talent the tools to achieve their destiny."

"Sounds like it came right out of the brochure." Grey chuckled.

Travis gave him the evil eye, then folded his arms. "Look, I want to help Pops and the resort, of course. But you're tying my hands and strapping a lead weight to my feet here."

"I thought you enjoyed a challenge."

Travis turned toward the sunny voice behind him and grinned.

"Molly. Good to see you." He hugged his sister-in-law. "And I do enjoy a good challenge, but I'm a chef and a mentor—*not* a miracle worker."

"*Yes*, you are," Molly countered confidently. "I've seen every episode of your shows. You've transformed self-taught chefs with raw talent and a complete lack of discipline into culinary superstars."

"That's kind of you to say, Mol." Travis realized that his sister-in-law was stroking his ego, but it was nice to hear anyway.

The chefs he'd mentored were talented but had a lot to learn, as he once had. He'd had a natural gift in the kitchen and had been cooking since he was a kid, after his biological father died and his mother went off the rails. Then at fourteen, he'd decided he could do better than Jameson's suspect cooking. So he'd honed his skills under the tutelage of Moonlight Ridge's former executive chef, French ex-pat Henri Bernard.

Each week, Chef Henri had shown him how to prepare a new meal. Cooking relaxed him. And as he became more confident, he'd enjoyed adding his own flair and turning a basic meal into something spectacular.

Travis had derived immense satisfaction from

watching his father and brothers devour the meals he'd made with such great care. But he'd never considered that being a chef was what he was meant to do with his life.

"I'm good," Travis said. "But I can't turn water into wine."

"I realize this may be your greatest challenge yet," Molly said, undeterred. "But our current staff, including the executive chef, are well aware things need to change if Moonlight Ridge is going to survive. They're all big fans and eager to work with you."

That bit of information made Travis feel the slightest bit hopeful. A self-aware chef who recognized the need for improvement was the kind of clay he could work with. Still…

"If you could turn things around here, it'd be quite the accomplishment," Molly added. "It'd make for a great book. And I'd bet one of those producer friends of yours would jump at the chance to document the process for a limited-run show. It'd mean more revenue for you and for Moonlight Ridge."

"Interesting idea, honey." Mack rubbed his chin. *Translation: he hated the idea.* "But should we really advertise that our current fare is…substandard?"

"We'd also need to invest in a serious upgrade

of our kitchen and dining areas," Grey griped. "Moonlight Ridge can barely afford the renovations of the main building we're doing now. Let alone the cottages around the lake."

A mutually beneficial alliance that could make Moonlight Ridge better than ever *and* expand his restaurant brand, Traverser. That was a proposal worth considering.

Travis already had eateries in Atlanta—where he lived—and in LA—where they filmed the cooking network shows. Then there was the gastropub in London. His sights were set on opening signature restaurants in New York and perhaps Rome. Molly's idea could garner investors for his restaurant group and for Moonlight Ridge, which would ease the financial burden on the three of them.

"Brilliant idea, Molly," Travis said.

Molly looked pleased. Mack and Grey didn't.

"Didn't you hear anything I just said?" Mack asked.

"Sure. You said, *Bad publicity, wah, wah, wah.* Then Grey said, *We don't have the money, wah, wah, wah.*" Travis imitated the trombone-created voice of the adults talking in the Charlie Brown cartoons they'd watched as kids. "But to address your concern—by the time the show airs, the property will be fully renovated. As for the money, I'll run this by a couple of producer friends of mine. If they green-light the idea, I know I'll be able to raise the capital."

"You're talking about bringing in investors?" Mack stood, and Grey looked alarmed.

"Yeah, why?" Travis shrugged.

"You know how the old man feels about this place." Mack paced the floor. "If Pops isn't willing to make changes in staff, do you really think he'll relinquish control to investors?"

"He'd maintain a controlling interest in the place. The short-term investments would give us the money for renovations and the show would give us much-needed publicity. It's a win all the way around."

Travis sank onto his chair again and crossed one ankle over his knee.

"Good luck selling Pops on the idea." Grey chuckled.

"Now, that's a challenge I'll happily accept." Travis pointed at Grey, then sighed. "As for Hallie the Food Killer… I promise to do my best with her. If I succeed, I should be nominated for the culinary equivalent of knighthood."

Even Mack couldn't help laughing at that.

"I can't help you there," he said. "But you'll

have Pops's undying gratitude and ours. Moonlight Ridge means everything to him, Travis. So I know you understand why saving this place means so much to all of us."

"Of course I do. The place means a lot to me, too." Travis's gaze drifted to the mahogany wood paneling and brass wall sconces original to the house. "I'll do everything I can to help save this place. I promise. In fact, I already have plans to meet with Chef Henri. Hopefully, he can help shorten the learning curve on some of the best local food suppliers and what diners in the area are looking for right now."

"Brilliant idea." Mack nodded.

Molly sat in on the remaining half hour of their meeting. The three of them brought him up to date on everything he needed to know to begin his monumental task of whipping the kitchen staff and catering operations into shape.

Autumn Kincaid knocked on the door as they were ending the meeting. She greeted Travis then asked if he'd be joining them for dinner.

"Wouldn't want to intrude on your double date. Besides, I need to head down to the kitchen and size up the staff. Then I'm spending the evening with Pops," Travis said.

"You wouldn't be intruding," Autumn assured him. "I made the reservation for the five of us. I assumed you'd be tagging along."

Tagging along? No thanks.

"Maybe some other time." Travis smiled.

Travis said his goodbyes, then watched as his brothers and their love interests walked toward the elevator hand in hand. He turned and headed back down the stairs.

Nope. Not even a little bit envious.

Sure, they all looked happy enough now. But relationships were constant work, and the payoff was usually disappointment, at best; betrayal, at worst.

Those weren't odds he was willing to play.

Unlike his lovestruck brothers, Travis would happily stick to his "bachelor life," get Moonlight Ridge's kitchen and catering services in shape, find the elusive embezzler then get back to his busy life in Atlanta and LA.

It was the least he could do for Jameson Holloway, who'd done so much for him.

MILLS & BOON

Book Club ♡

Have your favourite series
delivered to your door every month
with a Mills & Boon subscription.

**Use code ROMANCE2021 to
get 50% off the first month of
your chosen subscription PLUS
free delivery.**

Sign up online at
millsandboon.com.au/subscription

or call Customer Service on

AUS **1300 659 500** or NZ **0800 265 546**

**No Lock-in
Contracts**

**Free
Postage**

**Exclusive
Offers**

For full terms and conditions go to millsandboon.com.au
Offer expires June 30, 2021

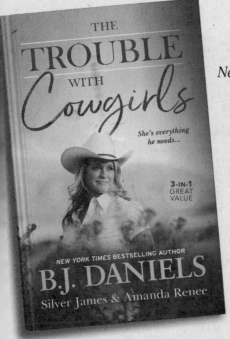

SARAH FERGUSON

Duchess of York

brings us a mesmerising novel of a young
noblewoman's coming of age that richly details
both high society and low in Victorian England.

Written with Mills & Boon novelist Marguerite Kaye,
this is a bold and thoughtful story about a rebellious
woman finding herself and her voice in an age of
astounding technological change and great social unrest.
Her Heart For A Compass is a delicious costume drama rich
in atmosphere, history, and colour.